WHITE STORKS OF MERCY
A TRILOGY

BOOK ONE
FORMATION

A Novel By
JONI ANDERSON VAN BERKEL

jponipress

ISBN 978-0-578-95780-7

eBook ISBN 978-0-578-96050-0

Jacket Design: Joni Anderson van Berkel/Alpha Graphics
Jacket Images: iStock by Getty Image

www.whitestorksofmercy.com

To my Merciful Ones
Myrtle Anna, Ada Mae, and Ashana Chenoa

CONTENTS

INTERLOPER

Two snowy white storks with glowing auras and seven-foot wingspans soared above the legendary Isle of Souls during the late Bronze Age. Located in the middle of a glacial lake in Helvetia, the heart-shaped island sourced the primal feminine energy of Mother Nature feeding the Sacred Bach. This magical waterway was a sparkling brook filled with the spirits of unborn babies. It meandered through a tropical ecosystem unique to the area.

Known as Leu and Ba, the divine birds flew over trees laden with ripening fruit enjoying the wafting scent of citrus. Banana clusters hung under the huge leaves of their host trees while palms burdened with hairy brown coconuts swayed in the breeze.

The clairvoyant supernatural creatures reduced altitude. Leu advised in a tender voice, "Watch your landing, Daughter. The propagating succulents puncture the skin on our black legs." Ba heeded her warning and touched down on the mossy ground cover. The graceful mother landed next to her lone offspring and the wading birds filled their lungs with a bouquet of humid fragrances.

Ba walked behind Leu as they followed the narrow path lined with purple and yellow primroses next to the glistening water. Beneath the flowing stream multiple shining spirits appeared as minuscule starbursts within bubbles resting among the river rocks. The Sacred Storks of the Bach used their elongated and flexible necks to reach them. They later delivered these minute souls to human mothers.

With her flat head bent low over the water Ba paused at a distinctive transparent sphere clinging to a jasper stone. Instead of the customary rainbow colors that indicated a life force ready for its body, this one's radiance beneath the water shone bright as the sun. Ba called out to her mother.

Leu stopped and turned. "Ah, a special little female spirit. This precious soul blesses you, Ba. Scoop it up with your bill and swallow it."

Ba relished the warmth of the tiny essence traveling down her long throat. It passed under the rose quartz talisman hanging around her neck on a leather band. She felt the spirit soak up the energy of the crystal that had been a gift from Leu to her storklet long ago. The gem enhanced psychic ability and signified compassion and unconditional love.

The spirit settled within her causing Ba's body to gleam even more. "I sense that my treasure will devote her life to altruism and benevolence. I must keep her safe."

Leu collected the jasper from its resting place in the water. "This mystical pink and brown spotted stone imparts the ability to change form." The two storks waded out of the Sacred Bach and shook off their feet. Leu stretched a wing across Ba's back. "The life nestled inside you changes everything. It is time to leave the Isle of Souls. Your home exists elsewhere now."

Ba's excitement turned to apprehension. "Please do not make me go, Mother."

"I shall accompany you to a faraway land where triangular mountains rise from the sand. We shall join the common storks on their migration south to the savannahs."

***

The mighty Egyptian sun god Re stood eight feet tall in the

reeds near the Nile River. A cobra encircling a red solar disk topped his falcon head and a royal blue Nemes headdress fell below his shoulders. He wore a knee-length linen kilt with an intricate belt girdling his waist. Ornamental bands adorned his neck, upper arms, and wrists. In his right hand Re grasped the Was-scepter representing his power and dominion. In his left he carried the *ankh* that symbolized life before and after death.

Two majestic pure white storks flying among others with black-tipped wings drew his attention as the phalanx blanketed the blue sky. Re's sharp golden eyes recognized the divinity of the duo. Glowing auras emanated from them and one dazzled with the brilliance of his sun. This intrigued him.

Ba felt a surge of strong heat radiate from the ground below. Re pointed the scepter straight at his claim. Leu urged, "Your destiny awaits. Go to him."

Ba veered away and landed on the riverbank. The wading bird set down among the grassy reeds and beheld Re in all his brilliant glory. At first, she backed away from the intimidating deity but found him irresistible. She relaxed and accepted her fate.

Infatuated with his conquest, Re escorted Ba to the capital city of Heliopolis. The foreign bird disturbed the sacred phoenix Bennu who resembled a red and gold eagle. In ancient Egypt he alone owned the title "the Shining One." The Tree of Life growing in his sun temple offered a map of destiny. He shrieked, "My oracular plan excludes this glowing white stork."

The presence of Ba also displeased Re's daughter Bastet. Jealousy filled the cat-headed goddess. She feared that Ba and her future offspring would embezzle his affection. The stork planned to incubate her egg atop the Great Pyramid at Giza. The sly Bastet offered to guard them from evil spirits to fulfill her duties as goddess of the home.

Re built a sturdy nest of papyrus and palm fronds for Ba while the bird waited below in the shade of an olive tree contemplating her life in this land of temples and monuments. After Re completed the nest Bastet presented a fleece made of silk and fluffy wool. She spoke with false sweetness. "This provides the same comfort as resting upon a cloud." Re's calculating daughter had designed the gift to allow easy access from under the egg for future meddling.

Her father responded in a gruff voice. "Your thoughtfulness touches me, Daughter." Ba flew five hundred feet up to the apex of the Great Pyramid and settled on her cozy nest. Re introduced her to Bastet who reeked of self-importance and confidence. She stared at Ba with contempt. A wedge-shaped head and lime-green eyes typical of the Egyptian Mau cat topped Bastet's neck. Her large cat ears stood erect. Black outlined her nose, lips, and eyes. The design on her forehead resembled a scarab beetle.

Similar to most Egyptian deities when personified, Bastet stood eight feet tall. Her traditional silver sheath was patterned with dark irregular oblong shapes. It mimicked the Mau breed's coat and clung to her long human legs. A decorative shawl of multi-colored beads draped over Bastet's shoulders and strands of sparkling silver covered her breasts. The goddess held a sistrum in her right hand and a bag of perfumed oils hung from her left forearm.

Bastet bowed with false respect to the glowing white stork. She applied blue lotus fragrance behind her cat ears and beneath the thick gold bangles on her wrists. Lifting each curved leg, she scented her slender ankles wrapped in heavy gold bands. Bastet grinned at Ba. Her cat lips curled to display sharp pointed teeth. The divine bird shivered. Her instincts told her never to trust the cat goddess.

Re turned to watch his daughter Sekhmet climbing up the pyramid steps. The goddess of healing and medicine was personified as a woman with the head of an amber-eyed lioness under a headdress of intricate knots. She wore a cowl-necked blood-red sheath. Matching bronze bangles on her wrists, upper arms, and ankles showed off her muscular limbs.

The sun god reached out to straighten the red solar disk encased in a cobra that topped her leonine head. He introduced her to Ba. "She is known as both the Lady of Life and the Lady of Terror. When a battle is won the people drink wine to soothe the fierce warrior Sekhmet. She will keep you healthy and safe, my beloved mate."

Sekhmet spoke with the throaty growl of a lioness. "I shall guard your treasure with my divine life." To Ba she explained, "Re quenched my thirst for blood by filling a lake with beer and pomegranate juice. Drinking it calmed me ever after." She took her place by the nest opposite Bastet.

Re bent down next to Ba and nuzzled his falcon beak against the smooth feathers of her long neck. "I bid you farewell until the morning when my sun warms you once again." He implored his daughters, "Wish me luck in the underworld as I fight the evil serpent Apep."

Sekhmet roared and Bastet rattled the sistrum. The gentle stork cowered in fear. The sun dipped beyond the horizon. Ba yearned to fly away into the night but at that moment she felt her egg slide from the birth canal and drop into the nest. She craned her long neck downward and gazed at it with awe. "My cherished treasure, here we stay."

Bastet remarked to her sister, "Her egg shines too." She clapped her hands and hissed under her breath. "I want to smash it." Ba mistook her applause for congratulations.

Sekhmet cupped a hand over her mouth to muffle her words. "I heard rumors that Ba rivals Bennu for a position of shining power. When her egg hatches the phoenix will consider it an adversary as well."

"If Bennu sets her on fire while she sits on her egg, we can be rid of them both."

Sekhmet shook her leonine head. "We promised Father to keep them safe."

"Something else irks me, Sekhmet. Re invited four other deities to attend the hatching as if we are not important enough." The guest list included Osiris, god of the underworld and afterlife; Horus, god of war, the sky, and falcons; Thoth, god of wisdom, writing, and magic; and Amunet, the goddess of air and hidden forces.

"Calm yourself, Bastet."

"I hope the cobra-headed goddess eats the hatchling." Ba was preoccupied with her new egg and did not hear their conversation.

One night while the divine stork slumbered Sekhmet placed her hands between the fleece and the bird's belly. She cupped them around the egg. With her keen sense of touch the goddess of medicine discovered a double yolk containing two stork embryos. She felt the energy of Ba's soul in her left hand and Re's falcon spirit in her right.

A delighted Bastet conjured a wicked plan. "You hold the power to transform objects. Change the embryo with Re's soul into a Siamese cat, which is my favorite breed. Take away all of her divine stork attributes and give her the power to enthrall mortals with her blue eyes. Storks hold no importance in ancient Egypt and Bennu will ban the white ones. On the other hand, we revere cats. The law forbids harming or killing them. This will benefit our new sister."

Sekhmet frowned. "How will we keep this confidential?"

"Do you forget that I safeguard the secrets of females? Re and Ba will never know."

"A storklet and a kitten hatching from the same egg compound this problem, Bastet."

"I tire of you, Sister. Leave that to me and do as I say."

Sekhmet succumbed and manifested her magic. The storklet embryo knew something was different but it proved difficult to assess changes inside the dark egg. She did not realize that two sky-blue eyes with diamond-shaped pupils stared at her.

The embryo with a falcon soul found her new sharp-clawed kitty paws fascinating. "I am a bird no longer," she meowed.

The full moon cast a bluish hue over the Great Pyramid. While Ba and her storklet slept, Bastet sensed the nocturnal kitten's alertness. She whispered, "As the goddess of felines I pledge eternal friendship. Trust my guidance and follow my orders. You will gain all you desire. I instruct you to swallow your twin before she steals the glory meant for you alone."

The kitten snatched the slumbering avian embryo and consumed it whole. The miniscule bird exchanged one dark place for another and detected grave danger. Her panicked voice asked, "Whatever happened?"

"I swallowed you. That is what cats do to birds."

"Cats?"

"Relax. I shall protect you." The feline embryo licked her whiskers.

In the morning Ba inspected her egg. It had ceased to glow and intense negative energy from inside blocked knowledge of her offspring's well-being. "What came to pass while I slept?"

The little kitten grew. She experienced dreadful claustrophobia inside the close quarters. On the morning of the twenty-fifth of October in 1487 B.C. her diligent scratching caused the dull shell to crack. Re summoned the four invited deities to come right away.

The distinguished guests stood in line at the base of the Great Pyramid anticipating the celebration. On either side of the group two musicians—one shaking a tambourine and the other beating a drum—played in perfect synchronization as the parade to the apex commenced.

Amunet led the single-file procession. Personified as a woman, a black and gold ring-necked cobra replaced her human head. The rinkhal's hood flared in a defensive posture and its forked tongue flicked skyward seeking a whiff of Ba's egg. The creator goddess of the air wore a long white sheath and carried a papyrus staff in one hand and an ankh in the other. Her elliptical black serpentine eyes looked up at her destination as she mounted the steep steps.

Behind her climbed Osiris the god of the dead. He resembled a mummy wrapped in strips of white linen. He unspooled the cloth over his lower legs and feet while ascending. It exposed jade-green flesh symbolic of both decay and resurrection. Osiris wore a *hedjet,* the pointed crown of Upper Egypt with two curly ostrich feathers on each side. On his chin a black pharaoh's beard curved outward. The ancient Egyptian god carried the crook of kingship in one hand and held a flail depicting the fertility of the land in the other. The crook doubled as a climbing stick and Osiris used the flail to sweep the sandy steps to protect his tender green feet.

Next to ascend the stairs came Horus the god of kingship and the sky. Like Re he appeared as a falcon-headed man but with different eyes. The sun shone in his right orb to represent power. In his left eye the moon beamed to symbolize healing. A *pschent* portraying the double crown of united Egypt topped his royal blue Nemes headdress. He too carried an ankh.

Thoth completed the parade. He had the head of a long-billed ibis. The birdman bore no crown, preferring a royal blue Nemes headdress. He wore a short kilt with a woven belt and an elaborate neck collar. His armbands, bracelets, and anklets matched. The inventor of writing held a scepter, a papyrus scroll tied with a reed, a feather pen, and an inkwell to record the hatching.

The two divine Sacred Storks of the Bach waited on one

side of the large nest watching the honored guests arrive. The oval jasper stone with transformational properties hung on Leu's long neck. She stroked Ba's shining feathers to calm her nervous daughter whose instincts warned her of impending disaster.

Bastet and Sekhmet flanked their father. Re stood proud facing his beloved mate across the nest. The sun god brought special gifts created for his new daughter by Isis the goddess of women, enchantment, and fertility. He held a magical cartouche made of gold in one hand and a ring of eternity in the other. "These give her the ability to travel through time forever."

The cat goddess asked about the cartouche. "What does the stork flying over the sun disk that sits atop the Great Pyramid depict? The rope coiled inside the pyramid translates to one hundred in hieroglyphics but why do six stars hang from it like a tail?"

Re explained, "The stork and the sun signify her divine parents. Every century Seth the god of chaos and storms will drop the stars from the sky. Then he will revitalize our offspring with ionized drops as she stands atop the Great Pyramid or elsewhere in the world. The ability to time travel throughout eternity requires maintaining a perfect energetic connection."

Valuable information, thought Bastet. She imagined the cartouche on her new Siamese cat sister. She examined the thick ring made of oxidized copper with a bar welded across the bottom. "Does this go on the ca...uh, the storklet's ankle?" The cat goddess almost choked.

Re affirmed, "Yes it does." He turned to welcome the four distinguished visitors. The towering divinities stayed close to the nest for a better look as the shell continued to fracture. Ba muttered to Leu, "What a scary sight for my treasure to experience after her first breath of life. Seven giants bearing the heads of two falcons, one cobra, an ibis, a lioness, and a Mau cat, as well as a green-skinned man that looks like a mummy—all gawking at her."

Leu whispered, "Quiet now so they do not hear. We shall reassure the storklet as she imprints on you."

All eyes bulged when a fuzzy seal point Siamese kitten with sandy-colored fur and a dark brown face, tail, and paws pushed its way through the torn membrane. Ba searched the empty shell and screamed when she found no fledgling. The kitten meowed with gusto to announce her arrival into the world.

The gods and goddesses all laughed, which upset Ba even more. Amunet patted the kitten on its furry wet head causing an instantaneous growth spurt. She was now a full grown slender Siamese cat with a graceful neck, long legs, and widespread erect ears. Amunet told Horus, "Her eyes reflect the color of your blue firmament."

The god of the sky bent over to inspect the hatchling. "Spellbinding indeed."

Ba tolerated no adoration for the interloper. She jerked her head and accused Bastet of playing tricks on her. "You changed my egg!"

"Not me," Bastet smirked. Sekhmet looked away feeling guilty and ashamed.

Re chuckled at the anomaly. "I do not mind welcoming another cat into the family." He placed an arm around each of his powerful feline-headed progeny. "Behold what I produced in the past." Bastet preened and Sekhmet looked down at her feet. Re bent over to inspect his beautiful new daughter. "Fate played its hand. We shall call her Reba to combine the names of her parents." Thoth recorded the moniker on his papyrus scroll.

Reba leapt from the nest feeling no bond with her mother. A suspicious glow radiated from her stomach. She hissed at Ba as the angry Sacred Stork of the Bach stalked her. Ba demanded, "Tell me why your belly gleams."

When Reba spoke her first words she winced at the sound of

her high-pitched voice. She lied, "The sun god's shining love fills me." Re nodded his falcon head with pride.

The miniscule storklet yelled for help. In an attempt to mask the irritating plea Reba sang the lullaby Ba had crooned to her unhatched offspring. "Tiny spirit of the Bach, show yourself."

This pushed Ba over the edge. She bent her long neck low, charged, and pecked at Reba's stomach with her sharp bill. "Murderer!"

Reba's back arched and her ears twitched. Her eyes became slits and she yowled at the top of her lungs. Re grabbed her and hugged her to his chest. The cat hiccupped. The deities were alarmed at Ba's violent behavior and frowned in clear disapproval. Re was humiliated by his mate's fanatical display. He commanded her to stay away from Reba.

Leu encouraged Ba to gain control. Osiris stepped forward. "I hesitate to give this dire alert on such a glorious day of celebration but I must. In Heliopolis Bennu told me that the oracular plan forbids two Shining Ones to coexist in Egypt. If Ba stays, he leaves."

Amunet pushed in front of Osiris. "I remind you that Bennu represents the soul of Re. If the phoenix departs the sun god will lose his divinity."

Re shuddered at the prospect and dropped Reba. She landed with agility on top of his feet. Losing both his soul and true love proved unbearable and his legs weakened. Horus moved to support Re with his strong arms. The god of kingship warned Ba, "You must leave Egypt."

In desperation Ba questioned Leu's wisdom and their mutual clairvoyance. "You foretold our destiny, Mother. How did we not see this coming?"

Leu regarded the ancient Egyptians with suspicion and placed a loving wing around Ba's shaking body. "Let us return to the Sacred Bach, Daughter. We must depart before Bennu arrives. His wings span thirty feet. It is best to stay clear of the phoenix." Without another word the two divine storks took off from the apex of the pyramid. Re hollered her name with such pain that Ba's heart broke but she never looked back.

Re slumped on the pyramid's top step comforted by Sekhmet. Bastet picked up the smug Siamese cat and stroked her glossy coat. The family watched the other deities descend. They helped each other down the steep steps and gossiped the entire way.

Re told Reba, "You lost your mother and I my mate." He placed the gold choker with the magical cartouche around her neck and slid the copper ring onto her front right paw. "The cartouche empowers you to travel through time and the ring provides extra magic to insure eternal life because of your mixed heritage. Ancient Egyptian gods and Sacred Storks of the Bach never breed." His falcon beak rubbed Reba's little brown nose. "Now enlighten me about your future, Daughter. Perhaps I shall feel better."

"I plan to advise pharaohs and warm the laps of royalty."

"In that case I shall present you as a wedding gift to King Thutmose II and his queen Maatkare Hatshepsut. My trusted girls can take care of your needs as you travel together to the royal palace in Thebes."

Re returned to the underworld at the end of that ill-fated day and climbed aboard the *Mesektet,* the nocturnal solar barge. He doubted his strength to fight the evil serpent Apep. He moaned, "Tomorrow the sun may not shine."

WEDDING GIFT

On their way to Thebes the cat goddess planned to make a side trip downstream to visit her temple in the Delta city of Bubastis north of Giza. Bastet looked forward to showing off the massive statue of a seated Egyptian Mau cat lit by torches that cast a spooky glow inside the great hall. Each day numerous devotees left offerings of miniature Mau sculptures at its base while hundreds of living felines roamed the temple's corridors.

A haughty Reba with her nose in the air stood between Bastet and Sekhmet. They waited to board a flat-bottomed royal barge made from packed papyrus reeds tied together in bundles. A pair of male servants manned the bow with strong arms ready to maneuver the ebony oars and coax the boat along the Nile. The traditional watercraft narrowed at both ends curling upward into decorative gold-painted disks that faced the open canopy-topped passenger cabin.

The retainer waiting for them leaned down to look into Reba's eyes before lifting her. The startled man backed away when he perceived the unspoken command, 'Do not touch me.' *My sky-blue eyes are spellbinding indeed.* The cat rejoiced at her newfound power. She leapt onto the low boat, scampered across a woven rug, and jumped onto an oversized lounging chair. Bastet and Sekhmet stepped aboard aided by two servants holding fans on long poles. Their sole job was to keep the goddesses cool during the journey to Bubastis. The luxury-loving Bastet reclined on the comfortable lounge with a queen's grace.

She beckoned to the Siamese cat. "Come to me and enjoy your first noble lap." Reba jumped onto Bastet's silk gown and made herself comfortable while the cat goddess petted her.

Sekhmet opted to remain standing. She held onto one of four wooden columns supporting the canopy. Each was trimmed in a crisscross pattern of gold leaf. The goddess with the head of a lioness roared at the retainer fanning her and scared him away. The boat left the shore. Sekhmet noticed a mysterious decorative box with a pitched roof and a series of horizontal slits on its sides. Four sculpted Egyptian Mau cats in seated positions fixed its four corners. Their curved tails intertwined to create elaborate handles.

Bastet answered Sekhmet's unspoken question. "I plan to present Re's gift to the pharaoh and his queen in this fancy royal cat box."

"You mean my own little prison," Reba rejoined. She felt less than enthusiastic about spending even one second inside the claustrophobic enclosure. She thought of the captive twin inside her who no longer glowed. She had remained silent since her desperate cries for help went unnoticed atop the pyramid. Reba asked Bastet, "Do you think my sister still lives?"

"We shall find out but first she needs a name. I suggest Astarte to honor the goddess of war and sexuality. We can shorten it to Tara and avoid confusion."

Reba snickered. "By the time I free her Tara's anger may indeed transform her into a warrior temptress."

"When do you plan to liberate her?"

"Never." They both giggled.

Bastet picked Reba up and poked her stomach. "Tara? Reba wonders if you are alive?"

The disgusted Sekhmet disapproved of their wickedness. She felt ashamed at her part in the embryonic alteration. She hoped to save the storklet if she survived her cruel confinement.

Tara answered in a raspy voice heard by Reba alone. "It is impossible to kill a divine Sacred Stork of the Bach. You promised to release me at a safe time."

The cat squirmed out of Bastet's grasp and paced the deck. Tara's complaints irritated her. In the future when asked, "Is it time yet?" Reba decided to respond, "Not now, Sister. Men continue to wage war." *This excuse could last forever.*

The boat headed downstream. Three pyramids loomed in the background alongside the Great Sphinx. Palm trees lined the Nile's edge with tall reeds clinging to their trunks. A servant stepped forward to offer the deities a bowl of dates. A mouse darted in front of the cat. Bastet squealed with delight. "Catch the mouse, Reba! Bat it around before you eat it."

Reba disdained the suggestion. "Royal cats abhor mice. Later I may try some crunchy roasted birds." Reba felt a wild fluttering in her stomach and knew that Tara disagreed with her expanding culinary tastes. She meowed to get the retainer's attention. When she caught his eye, the mischievous cat communicated without words her desire for some grapes. After he complied she snickered and licked her whiskers. *I am the Great Persuader!*

They approached the mouth of the Mediterranean Sea and the north wind grew stronger. This caused the royal barge to rock back and forth. Cargo ships carrying obelisks weighing many tons passed them heading upstream toward building sites. The water traffic caused such large wakes that the boat almost capsized. The goddesses thought it great fun but the cat felt nauseous. "Get me off of this barge!"

Bastet ordered the captain to dock the boat but Reba's impulses overcame her and she leapt into the water with a splash. She paddled with all her might while complaining in her high-pitched voice. "I hate getting wet!" Reba shook herself dry when she reached the shore. She closed her eyes to concentrate on the magical cartouche. "O powerful amulet created by Isis, take me to meet King Thutmose II and Queen Hatshepsut."

Reba waited for Isis but the goddess did not appear. Instead, Heka the ancient Egyptian god of magic and illusion—the power behind all deities—materialized behind her. She turned and saw a strapping eight-foot-tall man with dark olive skin dressed in a white kilt. Two serpents floated above his muscular shoulders holding a black cloak in place with their fangs. He wore his black hair tied back to accentuate a handsome face sporting the curved beard of the gods. The deity's irises were shaped like oval scarabs signifying immortality.

From the royal barge a surprised Bastet asked Sekhmet, "Did you summon Heka?"

"Not I, Sister."

The mighty magician scooped Reba into his arms and wrapped his black cloak around her. They disappeared. Reba landed alone in the private sleeping chambers at the Temple of Karnak in Thebes. She found herself standing next to the royal bed. Carved to resemble a bull, the stud's golden horns pointed upward and inspired its inhabitants to produce a male heir.

Beneath linen sheets the young king watched his wife Maatkare dance around the spacious room. Her sheer silk gown revealed the twenty-year-old queen's enjoyment of the sweeter things in life. Reba darted under the bed when the queen made an about-face and swayed toward her husband singing a suggestive song. She plopped down on the mattress.

Thutmose II commanded, "In your new position as the Great Royal Wife you will soon fulfill our marriage with Amun the god of fertility."

Maatkare pushed him away and addressed her husband in a husky voice. "Honorable king and half-brother let me remind you of my divine birth. On the night of my conception Amun incarnated as our father Thutmose I. He made clear his desire for my mother Ahmose. Love passed through them to create me."

"May the king of gods appear tonight and bless us with a son."

Beneath the bed Reba mumbled, "What is wrong with girls?"

She heard the queen tell her husband, "I prefer a daughter. I shall call her Neferu-Re. It means the beauty of Re."

Reba whispered, "We think alike. I shall become her friend and confidante." *The queen holds the true power. Together we females shall rule ancient Egypt.*

She heard youthful moans coming from the bed. Reba decided to postpone her introduction and give the royal couple privacy. She trotted across the huge chamber and realized that in order to impress the queen she needed Re's assistance. Reba planned to gain the limelight and keep it focused on herself.

The following day she met her father at the Hypostyle Hall built by Thutmose I in the Temple of Karnak. She found him inside the extraordinary room where dozens of painted columns spaced an equal distance apart simulated a papyrus marsh—the symbol of creation. Reba watched her father stroll between the columns. He sighed as he remembered his first encounter with the glowing white stork. "Ba, your absence steals my spirit and breaks my heart."

Weary of Re's preoccupation with the mother who rejected her, Reba pranced over and pawed at his leg seeking attention. He bent down and lifted her to his face. Their eyes locked and she sent her thoughts to him. 'Forget that Ba exists. She means nothing...'

The stunned god tossed the cat across the room. She shot through the air. Her feline instincts twisted her body, limbs, and tail to guarantee that she would land on her feet. Reba's legs absorbed the shock of meeting the unforgiving stone floor and she cowered. *How can my father treat me this way?*

Re pointed an angry finger at Reba. "I see that you possess the gift of mental persuasion. I warn you—never attempt to manipulate my mind! Deities are immune to your powers." He spun around on bare feet and departed.

Reba skulked out of the Hypostyle Hall with her tail between her legs. "I shall meet the queen another time."

"What about now?" Reba recognized the husky voice from the previous night. "The king and I grew bored waiting for our wedding gift from Re so I came searching for you."

Reba rubbed against the queen's legs and marked her territory with the scent glands on the sides of her head. She looked up into her new owner's dark brown eyes. 'Pick me up.'

The short queen obeyed. "I am Queen Maatkare Hatshepsut. My name honors Ma'at the ancient Egyptian goddess of truth, justice, and balance. Kare refers to the spirit double of Re. Hatshepsut means foremost of notable women."

"May I call you Hat, my queen?"

Maatkare liked the cheeky supernatural cat. "You alone may call me Hat. Your name?"

"Reba, after my parents."

"I know all about you. Everyone in ancient Egypt gossips about the Great Hatching Debacle. I shall call you Cat since it rhymes with Hat. Let us walk to the Sacred Lake and bask in your father's glorious rays."

"Do not expect me to swim. I hate water and I need shade." Maatkare carried Reba into the lush temple gardens where two doting servants set up a canopy.

The queen dismissed them and sat on the stone ledge surrounding the water that resembled a pool more than a lake. She removed her shoes to expose toenails painted red and black. She hiked up her sheath and dipped her feet into the cool water. Reba realized that although Maatkare was no beauty the queen possessed a panache that elevated her attractiveness tenfold. She radiated unusual confidence for one her age. It seemed as if she already possessed the ambition to usurp her husband's rule.

Maatkare's shoulder-length jet-black hair attempted to cover a fleshy chin and stout neck. Perfect curved and charcoaled eyebrows arched above her striking brown eyes that were also lined in black. Reba stared into those eyes determined to exert her will and bring the queen under her control. The cat knew that her future puppet ruler must remain unaware of the manipulation taking place. Practicing the art of subtlety took discipline and Reba intended to master it.

The queen chuckled. "I see you scrutinizing my features. Plump square face, dominant nose, olive skin, high forehead..."

"I admire your full red-inked lips outlined in black to match your finger and toenails, Queen Hat." The cat relayed a silent question regarding this unusual combination of colors.

"Red represents our Egyptian desert. Black symbolizes the fertile soil of our Nile Delta."

Reba felt pleased that her telepathic powers worked so well. Direct eye contact was the key. She liked the queen's style and coveted the large ruby earrings encased in silver hanging from Maatkare's beefy earlobes. 'Why do you rub the rubies and then caress your temples?'

"It rekindles my spiritual energy along with my youth and vitality. King Thutmose II gave me these on our wedding night before taking a lesser wife to provide a son if I do not."

Reba sent a mental message of sympathy. The queen answered, "Women own property, hold official positions, and inherit from their husbands yet tradition forbids them from ruling. I care not about his fidelity. I want his throne."

'Worry not, future pharaoh. You will rule Egypt.'

Reba's message permeated her mind. Maatkare felt a rush of excited anticipation. She reached over to place a long fingernail beneath the gold choker encircling her new pet's neck. "Tell me about this mysterious cartouche and the copper ring. Do these benefit your queen?"

In silence Reba explained that Re's gifts guaranteed her eternal life and bestowed the power to travel through time. Maatkare tugged at the golden collar. "Perhaps I need this."

Reba objected with a loud yelp. "Stop! The power belongs only to me or to my twin. However, I do intend to share its magic with a few select females in the future when I create a band of merry mischief makers."

"Twin you say?"

Reba recognized that Maatkare was a perfect candidate for her troupe of troublemakers. She told the tale of her inception. "In conclusion, Tara's destiny to lead a coterie of honorable women seeking peace and cultural acceptance will never come to fruition." Reba rolled over and patted her tummy with a paw. "She lives in here."

"You ate your own sister?" Maatkare's mouth dropped open.

Reba stood up and stretched with arrogant nonchalance. "What if I did? She is still alive. I took the humane approach and swallowed her whole."

"Naughty Cat. I am not sure if I trust you."

"I shall stay by your side, Hat. You may join my gang of eternal time-travelling rabble rousers as the first charter member when your days become short."

The queen frowned. "Did Re teach you nothing? I am a demi-god. The divine status I gain after death belies your offer of eternal life." Maatkare stalked away.

Reba decided to avoid the sensitive subject of death with Queen Hatshepsut. The fact that the Great Persuader's silent messages met no resistance implied that Maatkare existed as more human than divine. The cat trotted after her making plans for their future.

***

Thutmose II died eight years later in 1479 B.C. at the age of thirty-one. Neither the cat nor the queen felt sad at his passing. At Reba's subtle suggestion Queen Hatshepsut gave Neferu-Re in marriage to the two-year-old heir to the throne Thutmose III, son of the pharaoh's lesser wife. Maatkare's position as both stepmother and mother-in-law provided continuity of leadership and increased the power of the queen and her feline sidekick. For seven years she governed the affairs of state as regent for the boy king. In due course Reba convinced Maatkare to crown herself pharaoh of Egypt by altering the laws to accommodate their ambitions.

After her coronation Maatkare exchanged her wardrobe for one suiting a male king and cut her hair short. She wore a knee-length kilt, a royal blue and gold striped Nemes headdress topped with a golden sacred serpent, and a false beard made from ebony. It was inlaid with lapis and silver in a herringbone pattern. She announced, "Behold the first woman to bear the title of queen, king, and pharaoh." Maatkare attempted to masculinize her voice to match her title. Her constant throat clearing to lubricate her strained vocal cords irritated Reba.

To legitimize the monarch's reign as the fifth pharaoh of the Eighteenth Dynasty during Egypt's New Kingdom, Reba encouraged her to construct grand temples and public buildings. She urged the pharaoh to present herself through multiple decorative reliefs as the daughter of Amun the god of gods. An excellent promoter of herself, Reba instructed Egyptian artisans to sculpt hundreds of statues of the female pharaoh holding her Siamese cat.

Thanks to Reba, Egyptian expeditions to East Africa's Land of Punt brought back from across the Red Sea immense riches of gold, ivory, wild animals, and dozens of myrrh trees for her mortuary temple at Deir el-Bahri. Pharaoh Hatshepsut's reign of twenty-three years benefited her entire kingdom.

In the winter of 1458 B.C. Maatkare lay on her deathbed. At fifty years of age she suffered from bone cancer, diabetes, and an abscessed tooth. The back of her head rested on a pillow exposing total baldness at the front of her scalp. Her thin body was covered in sores under a green nightgown. She managed to lift a bony hand to request the temple priests. "My time draws near, Cat. I hear Osiris opening the doors to the afterlife. Thank you for your devoted service as my one true friend."

Reba moved to lie upon Maatkare's chest and felt the pharaoh's heart pulsing. "Forget Osiris. Thirty years ago, I offered you eternal life and the power of time travel as the first member of my gang of scallywags. Remember that I cannot reverse the sundial of death."

Maatkare winced. "Eternity in this much misery? My diseased body welcomes death."

Reba made a final plea. "I shall summon goddess Sekhmet the master healer. My sister possesses the power to restore your body. The greatest pharaoh of all time will live forever. If I arrange this miracle you must swear allegiance to me."

The appearance of Sekhmet in the background carrying her ankh and medicine bag inspired Maatkare to accept Reba's terms. "I swear eternal fealty to you with my divine royal blood." *Subservience to my pet seems a small price to pay for immortality.*

Sekhmet stepped forward. With a quiet growl she presented herself to the dying monarch. "I am here to repair your diseased body. Do you grant me permission?"

The moaning patient licked her dry lips and muttered assent. She was both awed and intimidated by the amber-eyed deity with the head of a lioness who towered over her. "I beg you not to forget about restoring my hair."

Sekhmet nodded. "Let us proceed. The temple priests will arrive soon." She removed a small bottle with a dropper from her medicine bag. "Do not fear, revered ruler. These drops induce deep sleep. Reba, please move off the bed." Before jumping down the cat stared into Maatkare's eyes and sent a silent message. 'Your ability to time travel depends on me alone as does your eternal life. You possess no magic powers without me.'

Sekhmet administered a few drops and waited until Maatkare drifted off. She placed her ankh on the pharaoh's lower abdomen while growling and humming a series of incantations. All of the oozing sores disappeared. Reba's eyes widened. "That is impressive, Sister!"

Maatkare's vital organs and skin responded well. "Now I must focus on her cancerous skeleton." The healer continued her methodical work. After restoring her hair Sekhmet removed the infected molar from her mouth and replaced her upper and lower teeth. The pharaoh now resembled a healthier version of her fifty-year-old self. The goddess whispered into her patient's ear. "Wake up and arise." When the guard announced the arrival of the temple priests Reba trotted off to intercept them.

The pharaoh got up from her bed and placed her bare feet on the floor. She smiled to see that Sekhmet had given her permanent pedicures and manicures of red and black polish. Patting her full waist and hips, Maatkare expressed thanks to Sekhmet. "What a relief to have extra flesh covering these bones again. I offer everlasting gratitude for the miracle you wrought today."

Sekhmet bowed. "I rejoice in your pleasure."

Maatkare donned a cobalt-blue sheath, grabbed her pharaoh's beard, and went out to seek Reba. The temple priests entered the chamber and found an empty deathbed. The Siamese cat waited at the edge of Sacred Lake. The pharaoh gazed at her reflection in the bright moonlight and smiled. She ran her hands through her full head of short black hair and laughed.

Reba rebuked her. "Silence, Hat! We must not tarry." She gave her a talisman that represented Maatkare as pharaoh. "This links you to eternity. Never remove it or you will become mortal again and vulnerable to death." Maatkare placed the thumb-sized miniature made of porphyry stone on a long silver chain around her neck.

The sound of pounding feet belonging to temple guards seeking the dying pharaoh worried her. "What happens next, Cat?"

"Pick me up. The mighty god Heka will take us fifty-eight years forward to the eve of 1400 b.c. We land at the Great Pyramid at Giza where Seth the god of chaos and storms will revitalize us for the coming century."

The god of magic and illusion appeared and wrapped them both in his black cloak. Maatkare felt her lust stir and melted back against him. "I am yours, great Heka. Do with me what you will."

Reba rolled her sky-blue eyes and stuck her nose in the air. She congratulated herself on a job well done. "We shall call ourselves the Mischief Makers!"

DAMNATION OF HER MEMORY

Two hours before midnight the time travelers appeared at the base of Giza's Great Pyramid. The full moon that lit the stone monument accentuated the steep ascent to its peak. Maatkare dreaded climbing the two hundred and ten stairs in her blue sheath and bare feet. She called out, "My legs are far too short for these giant steps. I am a fifty-year-old pharaoh. Why did we not materialize at the top?"

"Former pharaoh," snickered Reba under her breath. She lied, "Sekhmet insists that exercise keeps a body young." She communicated to Tara, "Tonight Seth's revitalizing drops will indebt Hat to me even more."

Tara's muffled voice answered, "The well-being of your friend is most important." Reba ignored her pure-hearted captive.

Reba bounded up the steps while the pharaoh crawled up on all fours. A bolt of lightning struck the pyramid's apex without warning followed by a loud boom. Maatkare yelled, "Where did that come from? The sky is clear."

"Re's protector Seth awaits us. My cartouche depicts that the great god of chaos and storms drops six stars from the sky at equal intervals before our renewal. We must take our places otherwise another century will pass before the next magical rain. We need to go now."

"Next century I insist that we arrive a little earlier," huffed Maatkare. She stumbled to the top of the pyramid one falling star before the appointed time.

Reba lounged on her side grooming herself. She yawned. "You almost missed it." When the last star dropped Reba stood up, balanced on her back legs, and lifted her front right paw to point the ring of eternity to the heavens. "Wait until you see what happens next." The cosmic forces regulated by Seth rained silver and gold drops of ionized water on the duo revitalizing them for the next hundred years. "Dance with me!" The jubilant cat performed a jig.

The pharaoh gamboled about on the summit laughing and waving her arms. "I feel like a child again." She looked a curious sight in her blue sheath, ruby earrings, and beard.

Tara interrupted her sister's fun. "Is it time yet?"

The cat continued her boisterous jig and conjured a suitable lie. "Pharaoh Amenhotep II returned yesterday from a campaign that crushed a rebellion in Northern Syria. He brought back seven Asiatic princes as prisoners, cut off their heads, and hung them from the city walls. What do you think?" Reba's jailbird returned no response. The cat failed to mention that this particular pharaoh had died some years earlier and that his son Thutmose IV now ruled in relative peace. Reba asked Maatkare where she wanted to go next.

"To the Temple of Hathor in the Valley of the Kings where I often invoked the goddess of love, beauty, and gratitude at my funerary shrine. Today brings the perfect opportunity to reflect on my past and contemplate my future. I wish to present a special gift to you."

The self-serving cat pondered. "We must take care not to be seen. I doubt that anyone will recognize you dressed in your nightgown but forget the beard. If we leave now it gives us several hours to wander around the temple before daylight."

Reba closed her eyes and concentrated on the gold cartouche. The god of magic appeared and transported them to a walkway lined with stone sphinxes that provided a promenade leading to the lower ramp. At the base of the incline two lion statues posed at attention. Rugged limestone cliffs served as the backdrop for the three-tiered colonnaded structure.

They scaled the incline. "Ah, Djeser-djeseru the holy of holies." Maatkare swooned with emotion. She inhaled the smoky aroma of myrrh that filled her with clarity. "Soon I shall gaze upon the four likenesses of me that guard my sanctuary's entry."

Reba scampered ahead of her companion and came to an abrupt stop. She was unwilling to believe her eyes. The cat scuttled up one of the giant figures and perched on the shoulder of a female pharaoh missing its face. *Someone chiseled away at the likeness of Pharaoh Hatshepsut. I cannot allow her to witness this damnation of her memory!*

She was too late. The horrified cat watched Maatkare gawking at the four faceless statues as tears streamed down her cheeks. "Who tried to erase me from history?"

The eight-foot-tall goddess Hathor emerged from the shadows. A cow's head replaced her human one and Re's red sun disk rested between its long horns. She wore a traditional full-length emerald-green sheath and carried a sistrum. From her neck hung the sacred *menat* rattle.

Hathor greeted the shocked visitors and spoke in a dulcet voice. "I regret to inform you that Thutmose III orchestrated this damnation of your memory. He backdated his reign to the death of his father and credited himself with your accomplishments. He and Amenhotep II obliterated Pharaoh Maatkare Hatshepsut from all public buildings."

Maatkare fell to the stone floor sobbing. "Why did they hate me?"

Hathor lifted the pharaoh and set her down on an empty stone pedestal. "Your stepson Thutmose III took to heart his responsibility to maintain balance and stability in the kingdom. According to Ma'at, male pharaohs alone hold that power."

Reba took a wild guess. "Perhaps they feared that other powerful women might follow in Maatkare's footsteps. Will women ever rule ancient Egypt in their own right?"

Hathor debated whether to confide in them what Bennu had shared with her. She decided to reveal the future as foretold by the fruit of the Tree of Life where the sacred phoenix sat. "It will take more than one thousand years of male rule before Cleopatra the Queen of the Nile ascends to the throne. If you travel that far into the future beware of radical changes taking place after the Nubians, the Persians, the Greeks, and the Romans conquer ancient Egypt. Cleopatra is not Egyptian but originates from the Macedonian dynasty."

Reba's excitement to meet Cleopatra stemmed from her hope to recruit her as a Mischief Maker. "When and where in time can we find her?"

"As the final active ruler of the Ptolemaic Kingdom of Egypt, Cleopatra VII Philopator will reign from 51 to 30 b.c. in Alexandria."

Maatkare gasped. "What do you mean final active ruler? What happens?"

Hathor shook her cow head. "Cleopatra will engage in intimate relations with two powerful Roman military leaders —Julius Caesar and Mark Antony. She will then arrange for a poisonous asp to end her life after her capture by the Romans. Ten years later the Roman Republic will take total control of Egypt under Augustus Caesar."

This news depressed Maatkare even more. "Thus, more than three thousand years of dynastic rule ends."

Hathor gazed due east across the Nile toward the Temple of Karnak as Re struggled to bring forth the morning sun. She motioned them to follow her into the temple's main axis. "The design by your royal architect allowed the penetration of winter sunrays through an opening to create a beam of light illuminating

Amun..."

Maatkare completed the sentence started by the goddess. "... And as the sun moves in the sky it shines upon a likeness of me kneeling toward him." She regarded the statue in front of her with spite. "Funny how I bear such a striking resemblance to Thutmose III."

Hathor voiced her concern to Reba. "The sun shining through the clever light box now illuminates very little. Your father is losing his power."

Reba made a nonchalant response. "Fighting the evil serpent Apep exhausts him. We must go. I shall summon Heka."

Maatkare refused to leave without presenting her gift to Reba. She hoped that its secret hiding place remained intact. Together the threesome walked toward the entrance of the temple identifiable by its square pillars and Hathor-headed capitals. On each side of the small door to the interior shrine two identical reliefs depicted Hathor as a four-legged cow licking the right hand of the pharaoh who sat on a throne before her. The goddess stopped to remove a stone in the wall. She placed it on the ground before stepping aside.

The pharaoh reached inside the hole and took out a small ebony jewelry box inlaid with lapis and mother of pearl. She lifted out a pair of smooth gold earrings in the shape of miniature neck plates. Maatkare knelt and presented the gorget jewelry to the cat. "These once graced the earlobes of my daughter Neferu-Re. It honors her if you accept them in gratitude for saving my life." She clipped the earrings to the sides of the cat's ears. The feline purred with pleasure.

"Thank you for acknowledging me with such kindness. Now what about your beard?"

"I guess I do not need it anymore." With reluctance she positioned the beard inside the hiding place and Hathor replaced the stone.

By the time they exited both temples and made their way back into the courtyard the faint sun shone as if covered by a huge piece of linen. Reba proposed they time travel to the eve of 100 B.C. for revitalization before their visit with the Queen of the Nile. Hathor greeted Heka when he appeared. She retreated to the shadows and he vanished with Maatkare and Reba.

***

For many centuries Leu and Ba observed the dimming of daylight. On the Isle of Souls, the trunks of barren fruit trees searched for sun without success. Many of them lay dead on the ground. The once fragrant blooming bushes were now empty of chlorophyll and resembled huge piles of ash. The purple and yellow primroses along the Sacred Bach grew no more. The two disheartened Sacred Storks of the Bach found no petite starbursts protecting microscopic souls within the brook's bubbles.

A few weeks prior to 100 B.C. the sun flickered a mere suggestion of its new cycle. Ba decided that she must return to ancient Egypt in spite of the grave danger. "Even Bennu realizes that Re loses the fight against the evil serpent Apep. I must risk enraging the sacred phoenix before Mother Nature pays a permanent price."

"How will you find your husband, Daughter?"

"I shall return to our meeting place on the banks of the Nile River. I feel certain that the sun god will regain his former glory when we reunite."

Hope for the future filled Leu. "If all goes well our tiny spirit bubbles may return." She asked Ba to remove the jasper amulet hanging around her neck on a leather band. "If you find your shining treasure, give her this talisman. She will need its magic so that her future peacemakers can transform."

Ba removed it with her long bill and tossed the amulet in

the air. The leather band settled over her own head. The jasper came to rest at her breastbone next to the rose quartz talisman. Mother and daughter bid each other farewell.

Ba flew south for many miles over land and then crossed the Mediterranean Sea. When she arrived in Egypt enough light shone on the horizon for her to spot the mouth of the Nile River. Ba recognized the bend in the river where she first felt the penetrating beam from Re's scepter. She descended toward the withered papyrus grass. Bastet and Sekhmet failed to spot the divine white stork as they knelt over the body of their falcon-headed father who lay on the ground. Ba landed nearby watching and waiting in silence.

An angry Sekhmet pleaded with her father. "The Egyptian people fall into dire straits. They rebel from the taxes demanded for Roman tribute and the granaries hold no sustenance. The people starve because without the sun nothing grows."

"I care not," Re admitted in a gruff whisper. "Tonight, I shall refuse protection from the reptilian god Mehen when he coils himself around me to defend me from the evil serpent Apep. My greatest enemy will be victorious and the world will plunge into total darkness."

The horrific thought shocked Sekhmet. "What about Ba? Your wife loves you. Will you condemn her to live day and night in blackness?"

"Ba creates her own light. She and her mother will survive."

Bastet found the image of life in the eternal chaos of darkness unappealing. She took Re's hand. "Father, I must confess." Bastet revealed that she and Sekhmet had manipulated the embryos before the hatching. "I named the storklet after Astarte. We call her Tara. The last time we saw Reba, Tara was content with her life inside our sister's stomach." Bastet neglected to mention that over a millennium had passed since then.

"How could you commit such a horrible act?" Re struggled

to stand. He refused the help of his daughters whom he wanted to strangle. "I must find Ba and share this unbelievable news."

From where she hid in the dead grass Ba heard everything. *No wonder Reba's stomach glowed after she hatched. I shall never forgive them.* The glowing white stork revealed herself. "I am here." Re wrapped his arms around her. "Husband, please save your strength for tonight's journey into the underworld. The evil serpent Apep must never win! Tomorrow the world will enjoy a full day of sunshine."

Re agreed and formulated a plan to rescue Tara. "I expect Reba to present herself tonight atop the Great Pyramid at Giza for revitalization. I shall ask Seth to dispense sleeping drops upon her instead of ionized rain." The sun god turned to Sekhmet. "Bring your surgical tools and release Tara even if damage is done to Reba."

"Yes, Father." Her head hung in shame. "I beg your forgiveness and Ba's as well."

Ba responded, "I know that you are kindhearted, Sekhmet." She turned to Bastet and screeched, "I hold you responsible."

Her accusation infuriated Bastet. She hissed at the stork. "If this butchery injures Reba I swear revenge against you and your precious Tara."

Re grabbed Bastet by the arm. "Think again, Daughter. You will do nothing of the sort."

"That hurts! Release me, Father!" Bastet jerked her arm away and disappeared into the dead reeds to sulk.

IT IS TIME

The time travelers materialized at the Great Pyramid of Giza in the late afternoon. To Maatkare's immense relief they arrived at its apex and settled in to wait for Seth's energetic rain. Reba yawned. "I need a nap before we dance tonight." The Mischief Makers dozed off. Re and Ba hid several steps below along with the goddess sisters. Although it was still daylight, Seth rained a powerful sleeping potion down on them to keep it that way.

Re, Bastet, and Sekhmet mounted the final steps while Ba flew the short distance to the top. The sun god removed Reba's cartouche and ring of eternity and handed it to Sekhmet for safekeeping. Re was no thief and left the unique jewelry on her ears.

Bastet resented Re for taking back the jewelry crafted by Isis. "In principle those belong to Reba, Father. How will she fare without any magical powers?"

"Due to your misconduct and her unscrupulous behavior Reba will live out her days here in Giza. She is now mortal."

Sekhmet regarded the sleeping pharaoh whose life she restored. "What about Maatkare? She cannot assimilate into Egyptian life. It bears no resemblance to the country she left over thirteen hundred years ago." Ba agreed and suggested that Tara recruit her as a peacemaker given the pharaoh's stellar record.

Re heaped praise upon his wife. "That is an excellent idea. Now let us get on with this unfortunate business. Bastet, grab

Reba's front legs."

"Wait a moment, Father." Sekhmet pulled a clean towel from her bag. "Put her on this."

Bastet obeyed her father's order. Re took hold of Reba's hind legs and stretched them out. Together they turned the cat onto her back. He begged Sekhmet to keep Reba alive.

"I shall do my best." Sekhmet placed her ear on Reba's tummy and listened for the location of her heart. Her fingers kneaded the cat's torso until she found the beginning of the ribcage and the position of the abdomen. Reba's stomach growled and Sekhmet spoke to Tara. "I promised to set you free one day. Stay clear of my blade. I do not want to harm you."

She shaved a small area and made an incision. Her skilled fingers fished around for Reba's stomach. It was the size of an apricot. With care Sekhmet cut open the digestive organ and saw a glowing presence the size of a diminutive moth in a corner of Reba's stomach. The goddess nudged her onto the blade's tip. "Greetings, little beauty. It is time! Your mother Ba waits to meet you."

As soon as Tara heard the words 'mother Ba' she unfolded her tiny white wings. Within a few seconds she grew into a three-foot-tall stork with the same elongated neck as her kin. In her excitement Tara's first steps landed on Reba's open belly.

Bastet screamed at the clumsy stork, flustering her even more. She trampled Reba again. Blood covered Tara's feet and the step where the cat lay unconscious. The enraged goddess pushed Tara off Reba's exposed innards and she tumbled into Ba. Their wings flapped into each other as they fought to regain balance. The cat goddess picked up the lifeless feline and swaddled her in the bloody towel. She hissed at Tara with vehemence. "You killed her!"

Tara rasped, "I meant no harm."

A distraught Re stepped forward. He looked closer at Tara

whose golden eyes matched his own. "Welcome. The events that transpired today call for both celebration and mourning. I gained one daughter and lost another."

Bastet descended the steep steps rocking Reba like a baby. "Worry not, Sister. After I embalm you with pitch and myrrh, I shall wrap you in fine linen. Your mummy will travel to the Valley of the Kings in the royal cat box. There you may rest for eternity within the empty burial chamber of Pharaoh Hatshepsut."

The vision of entombment frightened Reba to such a degree that severe panic took over. The cat awoke screaming. "You know that I fear enclosed spaces!" She jumped from the arms of the sympathetic goddess and made her way down the few remaining steps of the pyramid. A trail of sticky blood followed her. Reba vanished into the south passage that led to the King's Chamber of Pharaoh Khufu. *The star shaft pointing to Orion's constellation makes a good hiding place.* Inside the entry Reba examined her mutilated body. She whimpered, "Without my amulets I am nothing." Profoundly disappointed and in extreme pain she lost consciousness.

Atop the pyramid Tara luxuriated in glorious fresh air after enduring many centuries in Reba's stomach. She sought her mother's loving attention. Ba and Re stood side by side involved in a serious discussion and paid her no attention. In the distance they saw the fiery-winged phoenix flying straight for them. Re declared, "Bennu dare not try to intimidate the god of the sun. I am the most important deity in ancient Egypt!"

Sekhmet showed Tara the amulet and ring. The goddess informed her that the gold cartouche held the power of time travel. "Heka will allow you to journey through time without him. Since you are divine and have eternal life the ring is for your future coterie."

Tara lifted her right leg and Sekhmet fastened the copper ring above her foot. She bowed her head and the goddess clasped the gold choker around her neck. The liberated stork thanked her for coming to her aid once again.

Sekhmet informed her of Ba's recommendation. "May Pharaoh Hatshepsut become your supernatural companion and assist in the development of your mission?"

"Maatkare may accompany me but she is not trustworthy. That troublemaker is under the control of my sister."

Sekhmet bowed her lioness head in sorrow. "Reba is dead. I suspect that Maatkare is free from her manipulative powers."

"She must prove her allegiance to me."

Re and Ba returned to their daughter. The sun god commanded, "Tara, you must leave before Bennu arrives."

"Help me, Husband. Give her the jasper stone." He removed it from around Ba's neck and placed the leather thong over Tara's head. Ba informed her, "Your grandmother Leu retrieved this from the Sacred Bach for its transformational magic. You may share its power with others as well."

"I am happy to remain a divine white stork, Mother. I do not need to transform to follow my mission. Nonetheless I treasure this gift and shall use it so that Maatkare may fly with me."

Ba saw Tara's providence unfold with clarity. "As a Sacred Stork of the Bach you possess the ability to see the future. Transform the pharaoh into your first crusader for peace. Fulfill your destiny to lead a coterie of unique women that travel through time helping those in need and inspiring tolerance."

"I shall do as you wish." Tara sized up the unconscious passenger. "I lack the strength to pick up a human."

Re stepped forward and placed a forefinger on Tara's head. "I grant you the stature and strength to do any heavy lifting required during your humanitarian journey through eternity."

Anxiety overpowered Tara, now grown into her five-foot stature as an adult stork. "I cannot leave you, Mother. In my dreams we soared the skies over my father's Egypt together."

"I promise to find you someday, dear treasure. Heed our advice and depart. The creature approaching does not have your best interest at heart."

With ease Re lifted the unconscious pharaoh to her feet. She moaned, swayed, mumbled, and went back to sleep. The sun god raised Maatkare's arms and turned to Tara. "Pass by above her and grab her hands with your clawed feet."

Tara took off on her maiden flight. A few laps later she latched onto Maatkare's hands and attempted to fly away. Gravity pulled her toward the ground five hundred feet below. Re, Ba, and Sekhmet winced. Tara pumped the greater coverts of her wings with all her might and gained altitude. She ascended into the sky with her royal cargo in tow.

Re stood strong. He was prepared for a violent confrontation when the mammoth phoenix engulfed in fire landed atop the pyramid. "Ba remains here with me or I promise that the sun shall cease to shine!"

Bennu pointed the tip of his long fiery wing at Ba and screeched, "I grant you my peace. You may stay in Egypt."

"And my daughter Tara who also glows?"

"About her I do not know. Other concerns press upon me. In twenty years, the Roman Republic will gain control of our land and brings its own deities. The Egyptians forget all of their ancient gods including you, Re. Soon our people must worship the sun god Apollo Hylates. Until that time return to the underworld tonight and remind our people that you still exist. Ba will come with me to Heliopolis until tomorrow."

Re's falcon eyes probed Bennu with suspicion.

"I shall accompany him, Husband." The two birds took flight. Ba lagged behind to avoid catching fire.

Sekhmet retrieved her bag and bowed to Re. "Now I must find Bastet. She may require assistance to prepare Reba for burial." The goddess followed the dead feline's bloody trail until she encountered Bastet staring down at Reba. She lay unconscious on the stone floor inside the entrance to the south star shaft.

"Reba awoke and jumped out of my arms. Do something!" Bastet squatted to stroke the cat whose coat was matted with blood and intestinal juices.

Sekhmet fell to her knees and listened to Reba's faint heartbeat. "She lives." The healer pulled the dropper bottle out of her medicine bag and administered anesthetic drops to keep Reba from feeling pain or waking up. Utilizing the fixed starlight coming into the shaft she examined her patient and shook her head. "I fear that Reba's injuries exceed my restorative capabilities. Tara's clawed feet ripped her stomach, liver, and gallbladder to shreds. She requires new organs. The god Khnum alone possesses the power to sculpt fresh innards for our sister. We must locate him right away."

Bastet recalled a critical piece of information. "The luck of all the gods finds us! The Divine Potter resides here in the King's Chamber protecting the tomb of Pharaoh Khufu who built this Great Pyramid. Will he help us, Sekhmet?"

"Khnum is god of the source of the Nile River. He created the boat that carries Re every night to fight the evil serpent Apep. The Divine Potter favors the children of Re."

Sekhmet picked up Reba with great care and they proceeded to the King's Chamber. The ram-headed Khnum sat at his wheel pouring water from a jar to rinse away remnants of his latest creation. A set of ram horns curled close to his eyes. A pair of long and pointed bull horns protruded from each side of his head with a red solar disk resting between them. The creator god wore a black and gold striped Nemes headdress with a matching neckpiece and armbands. "What brings you here, Daughters of Re?"

Sekhmet bowed and placed Reba upon his lap. "We seek your help to repair her innards."

Khnum peeled a lump of clay from his wheel with his long fingers and fiddled around inside Reba's abdominal cavity creating new organs from the magical material. Finished with his work, he beckoned to Sekhmet who stepped in to suture her sister. "When he rises from the underworld, tell Re what transpired here today. He owes me a large gift. Take her and leave."

Sekhmet's heart once again filled with remorse for meddling with the embryo but Bastet only regretted getting caught. She found a blanket and made a cozy bed for Reba while Sekhmet wrapped her in linen bandages. The cat looked a pitiful sight with her head, legs, and tail exposed and her pink tongue protruding from the corner of her drooling mouth.

Bastet breathed a deep sigh of relief. "Thanks to you and Khnum our sister lives."

***

Tara transported the cumbersome queen along the Nile River toward the Mediterranean Sea. Her psychic abilities told her that a thorough spiritual cleansing must take place prior to Maatkare's physical conversion from earthbound woman to supernatural stork. *Innocent souls require no purification but Pharaoh Hatshepsut is not in that category.* The ritual required Seth to set the human on fire high up in the sky. As the fireball cooled the transformed creature would take flight. The process proved painless. If a human soul demonstrated excessive impurity the fireball hit the earth like a meteorite and boom! *I hope that Seth deems you worthy to survive.*

Tara's passenger felt heavier than a bag of bricks. She used her last bit of energy to lift her burden further upward. She flew into the eye of the powerful thunderstorm that materialized from thin air. Excitement rose in her soul as she ventured far into the realm of the divinities. Tara called on her jasper stone's power to impart the ability for transformation to Maatkare. She let go of the pharaoh and seconds later a lightning bolt turned her into a ball of fire.

The noise from the thunder and the immense heat from the fireball woke her with a jolt. Maatkare's recollection of relaxing with Reba atop the Great Pyramid faded as she plummeted toward the earth. She screamed in terror as the ground came closer. In the nick of time the human fireball transformed into a white stork with black-tipped wings. She flapped them in desperation and attempted to gain her avian bearings.

Tara breathed a sigh of relief and joined the struggling bird. "Welcome to my world!"

Maatkare shot a dirty look over at her glowing companion. "What happened to my human body? Why am I flying with a Sacred Stork of the Bach? Which one are you?"

"I am Tara. I granted you the gift of transformation, Hat."

"I gave you no permission to change me into a stork and do not address me as Hat! Reba alone calls me by that name. Where did she go and how did you get here?"

"An accident occurred at Giza's Great Pyramid while you slept."

The shocked recruit lost altitude and nosedived toward the Nile River. "Help!"

"Concentrate on pumping your wings instead of complaining, Pharaoh Hatshepsut. Let us find our breakfast."

The cranky stork regained her equilibrium. "Do you expect me to eat fish, frogs, snakes, and other disgusting bird food?"

"Soon you will grow hungry enough to consume what you catch. I can see the outer wall of Bolbitine. I suggest we perch there for a while and get to know each other." The birds landed.

Maatkare shook her stork neck that was irritated by the silver chain. "What is the point of wearing this bust of myself now that

I am a bird?"

"As long as you stay with me it is your link to eternity. Take it off and you exist as a mortal. If you choose to remain in Egypt as a human the bust becomes a meaningless trinket and death befalls you in ordinary time."

She decided to inform the pharaoh about Reba's accident and recounted the events at Giza. Maatkare absorbed the sad news. Tara explained that Reba's plan for her Mischief Makers differed from her own dream. "I plan to focus on good deeds. My gift of clairvoyance reveals that I journey to Palestine in A.D. 33 for inspiration about my destiny."

"You intend to travel forward in time?" Maatkare felt excited to see Heka again.

"That is correct. You may use those years to contemplate spending eternity with me. I shall freeze your age during this period."

Maatkare fumed. "You are leaving me behind to spend the next one hundred and thirty-three years as a bird?"

"You will find ways to amuse yourself. Meet me at the Sanctuary of Apollo Hylates in Kourion on Cyprus Island sometime between March and June of that year with your decision."

Tara took to the sky with unburdened freedom and resolved that 100 B.C. marked the official year of her birth. She missed her parents and regretted their limited time to bond. The pharaoh's poor attitude disappointed her. *Until I trust her I shall not reveal that the power of transformation was bestowed when she emerged from the fireball. I must practice patience, compassion, perseverance, and empathy to become a heroic leader. That begins with Pharaoh Maatkare Hatshepsut.*

***

The goddess sisters ventured out to enjoy the sun's renewed warmth with Reba. The Divine Potter's intervention and Sekhmet's expert aftercare healed Reba's traumatized body. They lounged on a south side step of the Great Pyramid watching intoxicated humans dance and sing joyful songs to the sun god for returning his brightness to their world. Reba lay listless on Bastet's lap and stewed in the aftermath of her violent mutilation. She despised her parents for making Sekhmet slice her open to release their shining treasure.

According to Bastet, as soon as Tara had gained her freedom she tried to kill her twin. To make matters worse she had kidnapped Reba's best friend, confidante, and recruit. Now a mere mortal, Reba loathed her egg mate and refused to acknowledge her as a sister. Revenge provided a strong motivation to stay alive at all costs.

Neither Bastet nor Sekhmet knew of Tara or Maatkare's whereabouts. Since Ba denied her the gift of sight Reba remained clueless. She vented her frustrations in a high-pitched whine. "I wish you two had left my embryo alone. I was meant to be a divine stork with supernatural powers and eternal life."

Sekhmet attempted to make amends for her transgressions. "Tara does not possess the inherent ability to transform. The jasper talisman around her neck holds this powerful magic for herself and her chosen few. Ba disclosed this fact to Tara before she flew away with Maatkare."

Bastet became bored with Reba's complaints. "No doubt your puritan sister seeks the best females of the human race to join her coterie. Let Tara pursue her destiny. You may come to my temple in Bubastis to enjoy a life of luxury as the singular mortal talking cat in the realm and my personal favorite."

While Tara traveled forward through time to Palestine, Maatkare made her way to the temple of Bastet at Bubastis seeking information on Reba's burial site. The pharaoh relished the opportunity to practice flying and admitted her pleasure with this twist of fate. She flew south over the Nile River until she reached Heliopolis. She turned and soared northeast toward her destination. The stork landed on the riverbank and caught her first fish with her bill as an offering to the cat goddess.

Maatkare arrived at Bastet's temple, flew into the great hall, and saw the huge statue of the Egyptian Mau. She dropped the fish on the ground. It landed between some miniature cat sculptures surrounding the altar. Dozens of living felines emerged from the crevasses of the temple walls and started a huge catfight over the treat.

The frightened stork flew up to the statue's head and landed between its large pointed ears to watch the hissing and scratching brawl below. A gong rattled Maatkare's eardrums and she heard a familiar high-pitched voice issue a command. "Go away you foul-mannered cats!"

They disappeared as Reba issued a harsh reprimand directed at the stork. "Hey stupid bird! Leave this sacred temple right now! You disrespect our revered goddess and I hate storks!"

Maatkare soared down to the floor hoping that the feral cats stayed within the walls. Life as a bird provided many dangers that she needed to avoid. The stork landed right in front of Reba. "Hello Cat! It is I, Hat!"

WAITING GAME

Reba summoned Bastet and Sekhmet to come at once. "Hat is here and Tara has turned her into a bird!" Everyone burst out laughing at the proud pharaoh's expense.

"Do not rub it in, Cat. I prefer life as a mortal human over eternity as a stork."

Maatkare's comment confused Sekhmet. "Did Tara not gift you the ability to change form at your pleasure?"

Bastet provided a sarcastic commentary when the stork shook her head in response. "I find it interesting that she kept that important piece of information to herself. Tara has never been one of us. Ancient Egypt does not recognize the divinity of Sacred Storks of the Bach!"

Reba reminded them who started it. "Ever since one of them stole Re's heart."

Maatkare spoke up. "Let us not rehash history. Tara wants me to join her cause and seeks my decision when she returns from Palestine in the spring of A.D. 33."

Bastet's intense lime-green eyes reflected a calculating look. "I sense an opportunity here. If you agree to act as a charlatan good-doer you can spy for us. Reba will need knowledge of her sister's whereabouts to execute her plan for revenge."

The cat cocked her head up at Bastet. "I no longer consider Tara my sibling. My true sisters stand here. You both saved my life after Tara tried to kill me and gave me a home where I am treated like royalty. We all know that I deserve it."

Maatkare dismissed Reba's self-serving compliment. "If you show me how to transform I shall spy for you, Cat."

"How should I know? Thanks to Tara and my parents I possess no magic."

Sekhmet reminded Reba that the jasper talisman held the power for transformation. "You will gain this ability once you get your paws on it."

Bastet's excitement overflowed. "This changes everything! If Reba regains the jewelry that Re gave her then all of the powers will return. Tara can go live on the Isle of Souls."

Maatkare agreed. "How fitting." Like Reba she held grudges with a greedy passion.

Sekhmet's mind sidetracked as she envisioned glowing spirit-filled bubbles in a magical brook waiting to be chosen. The thought pleased her. *A future on the Isle of Souls might suit Tara better than one in a cruel world dominated by Romans.*

Bastet suggested, "Let us get back to figuring out the mechanics of changing form. Reba, what goes through your mind when you summon me or Sekhmet?"

"I close my eyes and imagine as many details about you as possible—your head, body, clothes, voice, and jewelry—then you appear."

Maatkare asked, "If I visualize myself as a pharaoh again will I become human?" The stork closed her eyes but nothing happened.

"Try jumping around," proposed Sekhmet. The stymied bird felt stupid but leapt up and down anyway. Still nothing.

"Here is an idea," ventured Reba. "Perhaps transformation occurs when a bird lands and connects to the earth."

"Excellent suggestion," affirmed Sekhmet. "Try it!"

Maatkare flew back up to the top of the giant sculpture and closed her eyes. She visualized herself dressed and acting as a pharaoh. She spiraled to the floor and settled. Stork feet transformed into human ones wearing leather sandals and stork legs became female appendages. Her avian torso altered into a plump female body wearing a white linen kilt. The familiar royal blue and gold striped Nemes headdress topped with a golden sacred serpent covered her short black hair and high forehead.

The pharaoh's lips and nails were painted with her signature red and black colors. Charcoal-lined eyes and brows completed the transformation. The miniature pharaoh's bust hung around her neck. She wore ruby and silver earrings. Her chin was missing the familiar ebony beard. Maatkare stroked her jawline and felt sad. *Perhaps I hid my beard away too soon.*

The goddesses applauded while Reba danced around on her hind legs twirling to and fro. The pharaoh encouraged them to start scheming. "In one hundred and thirty-three years I shall infiltrate the enemy camp as your spy, Cat."

Reba moaned, "But I shall not live that long, Hat. I am a mortal."

Bastet announced her big surprise. "Do not fret, Reba. I spoke to goddess Isis. She regrets that the jewelry she made for the hatching now belong to Tara. Isis agreed to create a miniature bust of Nefertiti for you. She was the most beautiful queen in the history of Egypt. This magical talisman will be your fountain of youth."

Reba acknowledged the goddesses with rare humility. "Gratitude for you both fills me, my true sisters."

"You remain vulnerable to death," warned Sekhmet. "Guard your cat lives with care."

Reba remembered a significant detail. "How shall we execute our plan against Tara when she possesses clairvoyance?"

Bastet explained their unbelievable luck. "Your body aligned with a star field when you crawled into the King's Chamber through the south shaft that points to the constellation of Orion. Its focused cosmic radiation imparted permanent anonymity from Tara's psychic powers."

Maatkare voiced her concern. "All bodes well for Cat but what about me? I am not shielded from Tara's radar."

Bastet pondered the question. "Ask Isis to design a magical silver piece in the form of a sacred scarab. Request an inlay of tiger's eye for your warrior's spirit, pyrite to armor you, and tourmaline for protection. This way you will achieve immunity too."

Sekhmet added to the pharaoh's bag of tricks. "Also request a false beard made of ebony with a light blue sapphire on each side of the wedge. The device will enable communication to guarantee that you and Reba can maintain undetectable contact."

Self-importance lit up the cat's countenance. "The sapphires representing my eyes will sparkle when I want Hat to tune in for my telepathic messages."

Maatkare caught the contagious excitement. "I shall connect with you when I stroke my beard and hear your voice in my head. I can answer you in a whisper."

"With my powerful mind I am able to receive all communications," bragged the cat.

"Excuse me, there is more." The competitive cat goddess wanted the last word. "Ask Isis to place three gemstones down the front of the beard—turquoise as a symbol of elevated status, green peridot to enhance magical properties and instill power, and a ruby to bring good fortune."

Maatkare's eyes shone with pleasure. "I love rubies and I desire another beard. But what if I am in stork form and not wearing it? How will I know that Cat is trying to reach me?"

Sekhmet considered this obstacle. "My son Nefertem is the god of perfume. He gifted Bastet with her bag of delightful fragrances. I shall ask him to concoct a scent of your choice to serve as a conduit between you and Reba. You will know that it is time to change form and put on the beard when it reaches your nostrils. What is your favorite aroma?"

Reba and Maatkare responded in unison, "Myrrh."

Maatkare asked, "What about when I need to reach Cat?"

Sekhmet answered, "You may call upon Nefertem to send Reba a whiff of myrrh."

The cat tried to think of every possible scenario to accomplish her goal of revenge on Tara. "What if they time travel over centuries like Hat and I did? How shall I ever catch up?"

Bastet considered this predicament. "We can talk to Heka about that. He may agree to transport you through time without the cartouche."

The waiting game started. For the next one hundred and thirty-three years the two Mischief Makers sat atop the Great Pyramid at Giza and observed the usurpers ruling their country and worshiping Roman deities. The Roman Republic under Augustus Caesar considered Egypt the crown jewel of the empire because of its fertile land and sophisticated culture.

Reba fumed day and night. "I hate the Romans for invading our cradle of civilization. You get to leave someday but I must remain here among them until our plans come to fruition."

"Perhaps Re will give you a special shape shifting talisman guaranteeing that when you leave Egypt you can travel faster than a cat runs."

"Will Isis do it? I do not want to ask my father for anything."

"Isis told Bastet to let Re help his daughters for a change after she created my beard and pendant. Your sister is in a foul mood. Romans place cats low on both the reverence and utilitarian scales. They use weasels for pest control."

Reba considered her options. "If Ba convinces Re to help me as a favor to her, he will do it. I must travel to Heliopolis and make amends with her. She and Bennu—the two Shining Ones—rank among the few Egyptian deities still worshipped by the Romans. I shall tell Ba that I am desperate to find Tara so that I may apologize for eating her." Reba snarled at the idea.

The Siamese cat's lies worked. Re recruited Ptah the patron god of craftsmen to design a unique magical cartouche providing Reba with limited shape shifting abilities. "Daughter, you will possess the ability to transform into creatures of both the earth and sea but never a bird or a woman. Ba insisted on this condition as your penance for swallowing Tara." Reba pretended gratitude. Although she seethed for a short time the cat soon put the negative feelings for her family aside to focus on her plan to steal Tara's magical jewelry.

Before Maatkare flew to Cyprus in the spring of A.D. 33, the two Mischief Makers reunited atop the Great Pyramid at Giza. The pharaoh transformed into her human self. Reba flaunted her gold cartouche of a miniature Noah's Ark. She explained why an X covered both a human female figure and a bird on the Egyptian charm. "I am allowed to shape shift into any species on the ark except for the two I covet the most—a human female and a bird."

"Do not worry, Cat. After you steal the jasper stone you will become a stunning lady with sky-blue eyes and dark brown hair framing your face." Maatkare picked Reba up and planted a kiss on her forehead. "Now I must go." She leapt off the pyramid and transformed into a white stork with black-tipped wings. The cat called to her co-conspirator, "Stay in touch, Hat."

***

Tara flew over Palestine not knowing what to expect. She heard the agonized cries of a man in excruciating pain. His misery reached all the way to the heavens. Unable to ignore his suffering the divine white stork spiraled down to the outer walls of Jerusalem and flew into Golgotha's Place of Skulls. She encountered several dying prisoners enduring the final hours of crucifixion. A sign identified the man hanging in the middle.

Jesus of Nazareth
King of the Jews

The glowing white stork circled the wounded man who wore a crude crown of thorns. Tara hoped to distract him from his pain. She landed on the cross and told him her life story. "Now I seek inspiration about my destiny."

Jesus groaned. "Blessed are the merciful."

The vision of compassionate humanitarians filled Tara with gratitude and humility. "We shall call ourselves the White Storks of Mercy and in human form the Merciful Ones. May I recruit someone from among the females watching you in the distance?"

"Those faithful women must spread my holy Word." His head dropped forward. "My followers will endure persecution. Fly north to Gallia and search for a martyr in Lug..." He lost consciousness.

"Lug...? What does that mean?"

Tears of sorrow for the crucified man formed in Tara's golden eyes as she flew away to find the place called Lug. The divine white stork descended from the evening sky in a corkscrew pattern over the city of Kourion in March of A.D. 33. She anticipated seeing Maatkare at their designated meeting place.

Tara approached the Roman Sanctuary of Apollo Hylates that was raised upon a podium by way of steps leading to a portico lined with Corinthian columns. Beyond the pillars a two-story iron door opened into the classical temple that overlooked the sparkling waters of the Mediterranean Sea. She alighted on the stairs and searched for shade beneath the portico.

Three months passed before the white stork with black-tipped wings landed on the ridge of the temple's roof. Tara waited with patience for Maatkare's decision. She noticed the round silver scarab pendant inlaid with a circular mosaic design hanging from the pharaoh's neck next to her talisman. The beetle's claws clasped a red goldstone sun embodying boldness. Tara commented on the handsome new piece of jewelry.

"A parting gift from goddess Bastet. I doubt I shall ever see her again."

"Does this mean that you are joining me instead of returning to Egypt?"

"It does. However, I have one condition. I need to get away on my own now and again."

"I accept your terms. A monarch requires private time." Tara sidestepped closer in an affable gesture. "I welcome you to the White Storks of Mercy as my second in command."

"That makes me last in command since your muster numbers only two. By the way, why do the tips of my wings contain black feathers yet your entire body shines pure white? And why is your neck so much longer than mine while your head is a bit flat?"

"You belong to the species known as common storks but I am a divine Sacred Stork of the Bach." Tara spoke without conceit but Maatkare seethed in silence at the explanation. "Tomorrow we fly north to Gallia looking for a place controlled by the Romans called Lug. Our future Merciful One martyrs herself as a Christian and awaits us there." She did not inform the pharaoh about her ability to change shape. *I remain vulnerable as a bird in spite of my gifts. Until I trust her, we shall both remain as storks.*

Maatkare realized that she must transform in secret to update Reba. That night while Tara slept with one leg retracted on the temple's rooftop she snuck down to the front steps of the portico and became human. She fetched the beard from her kilt pocket, stuck it to her chin, and in silence asked Nefertem to alert Reba.

Back in ancient Egypt the sudden aroma of myrrh disturbed the cat's sleep. As predicted Maatkare sensed Reba's presence in her mind. Their connection was confirmed when the gems sparkled and warmed her fingertips. She whispered to her beard, "Tara plans to call us the White Storks of Mercy except when her minions take human form. As women we will be known as the Merciful Ones. She wants to travel to Gallia to search for a Christian martyr. Do you know of a place called Lug?"

'You must mean the Roman city of Lugdunum. Keep Tara distracted. Let her discover the location on her own.'

Absorbed in her mental conversation with Reba, Maatkare remained unaware that the divine stork peered down at her from the rooftop. Tara noted that the pharaoh had discovered how to transform during their years apart. *She strokes the beard and whispers to it as if it is an old friend. I shall wait for her to tell me that she knows how to transform.*

The following day Reba stood atop the Great Pyramid at Giza with Re. She described her plans to locate and make amends with Tara.

Re responded with a pertinent question. "How will you find her?"

Reba thought fast and came up with a plausible fib. "Three pure white storks with glowing auras exist in all the world. One lives in Heliopolis and another on the Isle of Souls. If I remain alert for tales about sightings of my radiant twin, I shall find Tara."

"Good thinking, Daughter. I know how much you hate the Romans. If you do not succeed in finding her make your way to the island called Hibernia and create a new home. Although the Romans will occupy Britannia, they will consider invading Hibernia a waste of resources."

Anxiety overcame the cat as she contemplated a trip to the faraway northern island. She forced herself to accept the likelihood of never returning to Egypt. Reba's goddess sisters appeared to bid her farewell. She turned and begged them to come along.

Bastet shrugged. "Ancient Egyptian deities are far too busy to follow a cat around."

Reba thought about her first journey across the Mediterranean Sea on a Roman vessel. She gulped. "What if I drown? Cats hate water and I get seasick."

Sekhmet offered a practical suggestion. "If you feel ill, try shape shifting into a fish and swim the rest of the way."

"What if my talismans get wet, Sekhmet?"

"You worry too much, Sister. You will be fine on your own."

Re lifted his daughter and snuggled her face with his falcon beak. "I know you better than you think, little rabble rouser. Promise me that if you find Tara you will not harm her."

"I promise." *I want her powerless and humiliated but not dead.*

Reba jumped from her father's strong arms to scamper down the pyramid steps. Re turned to his daughters. "I worry about the ill-behaved cat. Her love of mischief precludes her common sense."

Bastet reassured him. "Fear not, Father. Sekhmet and I will keep track of her."

At the bottom of the pyramid Reba shape shifted into a white Arabian mare and followed the Nile River north until she reached the port city of Alexandria. She transformed back into a cat and hopped aboard a ship heading for Rome with a cargo of paper, glass, linen, and perfume. Reba snickered, "I am going to make as much mischief as possible. It serves the Romans right."

To avoid seasickness Reba converted into a sacred Egyptian cobra and slithered between the merchandise. This wreaked havoc among the crew. One night she shape shifted into a stink badger and sprayed a disgusting odor that caused the sailors to relocate their sleeping quarters out into the open air. To their misfortune it started to rain.

Reba grew bored between the islands of Creta and Sicilia. She decided to vacate the ship. She took a deep breath, let out a loud meow, and cannonballed toward the salty sea. The sailors watched in awe as the cat became a shiny silver-gray porpoise in midair and swam westward toward southern Transalpine Gallia with a pod of the marine mammals.

She made her way across the Mediterranean Sea while two storks—one pure white with a glowing aura and the other with black-tipped wings—flew in the same direction, at the same time, and toward the same destination.

ELVES OF SAGE

Two years passed after Tara and Maatkare soared across the expansive Mediterranean Sea to search for the new peacemaker. The pair of frustrated White Storks of Mercy ventured far and wide but found no place called Lug. Maatkare never let on. At dusk one evening in A.D. 35 they flew over the Roman town of Nemausus in Gallia as Re's sunset painted the sky the color of ripe nectarines. The middle-aged pharaoh required rest after another exhausting day seeking a female follower of Christ. The birds slowed, circled, and spiraled down to land on the steps of a huge amphitheater under construction.

Tara's feet touched the stone stairs. Images of future gladiator combats, animal fights, and torturous human executions filled her mind. She squeezed her golden eyes shut against the horror. When she opened them and gazed down on the empty circular field, Tara envisioned a young woman bound to a wooden stake. Blood from wounds inflicted by her captors seeped onto her tattered white gown. Matted blonde hair reaching beyond the captive's shoulders covered part of her disfigured face. A single ray of sun illuminated the sign placed above her head.

Tara was dismayed by her vision but relieved that their search was now over. "The sign reveals that in Lugdunum on the first day of August in A.D. 177 we shall find our next recruit."

"What say you, Chief?" Maatkare had bestowed the sarcastic nickname on her leader after their discussion about the differences between common and divine white storks.

"Do you see the image below?" Tara cocked her head to indicate the field.

"I see dirt."

Tara was both excited yet disturbed by her first psychic vision. She shared the scene that had played in her mind's eye moments earlier. "Tomorrow we travel forward in time to rescue this poor Christian martyr."

I must get away from Tara so that I can notify Reba, thought Maatkare. She excused herself claiming that she needed an alternative to sleeping in a standing position with one leg retracted. Her voice was cocky as she said, "I shall transform and find a soft place to lay down. See you here at sunrise." First she intended to fly northeast for a feast of amphibians at River Gard. Maatkare still possessed a pharaoh's appetite as she adapted to an avian diet.

***

That same evening Reba encountered an order of Druids in the forest on the outskirts of Lugdunum. She decided that one of her favorite creatures—a clever fox with a natural aptitude for camouflage—provided the perfect disguise. A dozen old men all dressed alike in gray robes flanked a gorgeous woman. *No wonder she is well protected. Nefertiti's beauty pales to nothing compared to her.* The stunning woman lifted her bare feet and rubbed them against the rough coats of two Irish wolfhounds lying on the ground in front of her.

The Druidess wore a long-sleeved full-length cotton gown the color of leaves in spring. Silver embroidery created a glittering pattern of orchids that looked like they grew in the moonlight. A thin forest-green linen cape was attached to the back of the gown at the shoulders. It wrapped beneath each arm to cinch under her breasts with a bronze clasp that depicted the Celtic Tree of Life.

The group sat together on a fallen mossy elder log and studied the flames of their fire. They contemplated routes to the Emerald Isle of Éire. Celtic Druids were characterized as magicians, soothsayers, and sorcerers. However, in reality they comprised an exclusive class of intellectuals and high-ranking professionals working as priests, teachers, and judges.

Reba crept forward for a closer look. A twig snapped alerting the wolfhounds. They stood, sniffed the air, and growled. All eyes darted toward the nocturnal animal frozen in place with one paw suspended and her bushy fox tail deflated.

"Welcome." The Druidess spoke with a Gaelic accent in a voice that was pleasant yet assertive. She waved her hand for the cat-eyed fox to join the group. She calmed her dogs with a firm touch. "Lay down, Bran. You too, Sceolan."

Reba trotted in front of them. The old men stared at her with a mixture of curiosity and distrust. The fox sat in front of the woman with long and wavy fiery red hair that shimmered with streaks of gold. She appeared to be in her mid-thirties. The beauty possessed an exquisite presence with glowing white skin textured like petals above full pink lips that reminded Reba of an exotic flower.

"You may call me Orchid MacCloud. Where do you come from, Vixen?"

The fox responded in a high-pitched voice. "I am a Siamese cat. My name is Reba." She transformed into her feline self. The Druids did not appear shocked that she possessed the power of metamorphosis nor that she talked. "I come from ancient Egypt."

"How ancient?"

"I was born in 1487 B.C."

"What brings you to Gallia, Reba?"

"I have business in Lugdunum."

"Cat business?" Orchid laughed bringing a sparkle to her emerald-green eyes. She liked the cunning creature with her mesmerizing eyes. "Tell me where you got those stunning earrings and where your powers to shape shift come from. I also must know how you retain your youth after fifteen centuries on this earth."

She is a little nosy. The cat took a deep breath and prepared a palatable version of her story. She felt conflicting desires to impress the beautiful Druidess while protecting herself. She did not want her past to catch up to her present and mess up her future.

"My father is Re the ancient Egyptian sun god. My mother is a Sacred Stork of the Bach named Ba. They presented me as a wedding gift to King Thutmose II and his wife Maatkare Hatshepsut. During our time together she became the first female pharaoh. I helped her to achieve greatness so she gave me her daughter's earrings."

Orchid fancied Reba's gold disk earrings and offered to buy them. The cat shook her head. "I never take off my prize possessions."

Without warning the humans and the hounds disappeared leaving a single white orchid growing on the fallen log's bark. The blossom glowed in the dusk. Upon closer inspection Reba saw Orchid's emerald eyes staring back at her as they rested in two white whorls. The lower pink petal of the flower formed a smile. Reba swiped at her own ears now void of the precious earrings. She felt used and betrayed. The lonely and exhausted cat curled up against the mossy log deflated by her disappointment. She fell asleep and dreamt the story of Orchid MacCloud.

The Druidess who originated from the Iron Age came from a simple background. Her birth name was Keela. It translated to beauty captured by poetry. Her identical twin sister Nuala reflected her own name that meant exceptional loveliness. Nuala disappeared without a trace when the girls were teens and left the family heartbroken. She never returned.

One day a colossal young warrior called Fig MacCloud visited Keela's father the village blacksmith. He intended to purchase magical spears. When Fig and Keela set eyes on each other they fell in love. Fig took his weapons and returned to his homeland anxious to share his joyful news and request his mother's blessing. Queen MacCloud wanted to keep him for herself and refused to grant Fig permission to marry. She wanted him to protect her empire from invaders.

Fig and his beautiful Keela married in secret. The queen discovered their duplicity and used her last bit of sorcery to imprison Fig's wife in the body of a flower. Naive to the ramifications Queen MacCloud selected an orchid. It was a bad choice for a mother already green with envy. Her magic spell backfired because orchids emit erotic energy irresistible to men. Fig cared not if his true love existed as a flower or a woman.

To save her from his cruel and possessive mother Fig took the blossom he called Orchid MacCloud far away. "We shall cross Finn MacCool's Giant Causeway and live on the Isle of Staffa. This is where the greatest warrior in Irish history built massive stone steps across the sea to visit his Scottish love."

How romantic, Orchid thought. She could no longer speak.

Fig planted her at the top of a cliff high above the Giant's Causeway. "I shall return for you tomorrow." To her utter dismay he did not.

Maddened by her own jealousy Queen MacCloud took one of Fig's magical spears and followed her son. She climbed onto a stepping stone and drove the weapon straight through his back. It pierced his heart. Fig's maniacal mother removed the bloody weapon and laughed. "I see nothing magical about this spear." In response Fig's javelin turned on the queen and stabbed her in the heart. Mother and son both lay dead on the steps of the land bridge. Orchid was left alone in a strange place far away from home.

"Like me," mumbled Reba. "I wonder how Orchid reclaimed her humanity."

"It was thanks to the enchanting elves of sage," explained the Druidess. She now held the snoozing cat on her lap.

Morning sunrays penetrated the forest like shards of shiny glass. The beautiful Druidess occupied the same place on the mossy elder where she had sat the evening before. The hounds once again lay at her feet. She looked down at Reba and chuckled. "You snore."

Reba opened her eyes to the sight of Orchid's radiant smiling face. The cat noticed the woman's triquetra pendant with embossed Celtic knots encircling the three-cornered triangular shape. It hung from a leather band. She swiped at it with her paw and Orchid laughed. She fastened the gold disk earrings back onto Reba's ears and patted the log beneath her. "This old tree spirit owes you an apology. I fancied your earrings and it sought to please me."

Reba stretched and repositioned herself. "I never knew that trees embodied spirits. How did the elves of sage free you?"

The Druidess explained that life on the steep cliffs of the North Antrim coast proved harsh indeed. Hurricane-force winds and heavy rain pummeled Orchid as she struggled to survive. Thanks to her own willpower and love for Fig she endured the brutal climate for over five centuries awaiting his return. One fateful day some loose sagebrush blew in her direction.

"You cannot know how I yearned to live as a woman again. I was the lone orchid on the Causeway and the elves living in the sagebrush found my presence curious. These creatures with pointed ears that dressed in silvery green leaves stopped to take a closer look. Elves of sage possess the ability to alter conscious states of mind."

Like I can do with my power of persuasion, Reba thought.

"The elves realized that I lived trapped inside the orchid and they teamed up with the flower faeries to release my spirit and my body. They granted me the ability to shape shift back and forth from a rare and exotic Ghost Orchid into my human self and designed this gown and cape for me to wear. The tiny ones also infused light into my cells to make my skin and petals glow so my husband could see me from the heavens."

Life as an orchid enhanced her beauty a thousandfold. The elves of sage held the power to slow her aging and preserved her exquisite aspect for centuries to come. The mystical rescuers also imparted the gift to commune with Celtic celestials and other flowers.

"I transformed into a woman again and made my way across the waters to Gallia. I settled with the Druids. They taught me new universal secrets of nature that enhance my own magical powers. My old friends gifted me both the triquetra pendant and the Tree of Life clasp." Orchid stood with Reba in her arms. "We must leave Gallia. Forget your business in Lugdunum, Reba. Come with us to our homeland in Éire."

Reba was overwhelmed with fondness and respect for the beautiful woman. She wrapped her front legs around Orchid's neck in a clumsy embrace. "My business in Lugdunum promises rewards and I must venture down that path."

"I sense that we share a destiny. I feel a special bond with you, Reba. Do not forget your friends the Druids."

Orchid invited Reba to a medicinal water source in the woods before the Druids departed for the northeast coast of Gallia. It was discovered by the Celts and dedicated to the goddess Sulis, the keeper of sacred healing waters. They approached the spring and Reba answered the question posed by Orchid the previous evening regarding the amulets around her neck. "These accessories hold my magical powers. Re gave me the cartouche for shape shifting and the goddess Isis fashioned the bust of Nefertiti to keep me young."

They drank from the restorative spring. Orchid wished her new friend good luck and bid farewell to Bran and Sceolan. The supernatural hounds never ventured far from Sulis as protectors of the roaming goddess. Reba stayed and lapped up more of the invigorating water that restored her from inside out. She was reminded of Seth's ionized raindrops.

Reba wondered if Tara ever discovered that Lug was short for Lugdunum. The cat entertained subsequent thoughts of Maatkare. She pranced away from the spring. The odor of myrrh filled her nostrils and Reba received a long-awaited psychic message.

'I tried to reach you all night, Cat. Tara knows about Lug.'

'It took her long enough. I shall wait for you on the outskirts of Lugdunum.'

'You must time travel to A.D. 177. Prepare to initiate our scheme on the first day of August at the Trois-Gaules Roman coliseum where Tara plans to rescue her next Merciful One.'

'I shall summon Heka to transport me this time. After that I can use Tara's cartouche.'

'Go then. You have one day to get organized.'

'Quit bossing me around, Hat. I am in charge.' Reba got in the last word and disengaged. On Maatkare's end the sparkling sapphires dimmed.

The following day Reba entered the cosmopolitan city of Lugdunum that was located at the confluence of the Rhône and Saône Rivers. It reminded her of ancient Egypt due to its sophistication. Italian villas dotting the countryside were surrounded by rows of vineyards ensuring that Romans never ran out of wine. The city featured underground Roman spas, temples, courts, and an amphitheater complex. Life appeared robust under the reign of Emperor Marcus Aurelius.

Reba learned that the legendary Bull of Apis—one of Egypt's most ancient deities—lived here in Lugdunum. She called upon her old friend at an exquisite hillside home built from Egyptian porphyry rock embedded with large crystals. A servant tried to shoo the strange feline away. Reba used her penetrating sky-blue eyes with their diamond-shaped pupils to demand an escort to the immaculate gardens where the Bull of Apis rested beneath a tree.

The origin of the bull's conception from a sunray appealed to Marcus Aurelius who also resided in the grand house overlooking the city. He hired the divine bull to help him compose his twelve books of *Meditation* based on the moral concept of "being a good man." Apis questioned the ruler's understanding of the difference between good and evil due to an increase in the persecution of Christians during the emperor's reign. The bull no longer acted as intermediary between ancient Egyptian pharaohs and their gods. Assisting the emperor in his literary venture made Apis feel useful.

The two animals relaxed in the manicured garden. The cat harkened back to when she watched Pharaoh Hatshepsut run alongside the divine bull during the Sed-festival celebrating the jubilee of her reign over the New Kingdom's Eighteenth Dynasty. Reba informed him that on her deathbed in 1458 B.C. she had gifted Maatkare with immortality and the ability to time travel.

"That is why they never found her body," Apis discerned.

"We traveled through time over many centuries until my parents sabotaged us atop the Great Pyramid." She recounted her biased side of the story hoping that Apis would support her scheme. Bastet and Sekhmet materialized uninvited in the garden.

Their presence perturbed Reba. "How did you find me?"

Bastet bent down to pat Reba's back. "We are goddesses. You cannot hide from us."

HELPING HAND

The two White Storks of Mercy cruised at a low altitude above the crowded Trois-Gaules coliseum on the first day of August in A.D. 177. They spotted the Christian slave girl who refused to pay homage to Roman idols. True to Tara's vision chains bound her mangled body to a post. The martyr's linen tunic was soaked with blood and ripped to shreds. Her broken face gazed up at the heavens praying for deliverance.

"Oh no," moaned Tara. "How do we rescue her?" The storks avoided getting closer to the action because a pride comprised of one lion and twelve lionesses circled the martyr with sharp teeth exposed.

All of the sudden Sekhmet materialized among them. She crawled between the muscular animals to establish eye contact with the pride's king. Their amber eyes connected. The dominant male moved even closer to the large lioness with the human body and sniffed her head. Sekhmet placed her ankh on his forehead and moments later the king roared at the pride. The lions lost interest in their helpless prey.

Maatkare recognized everything taking place as part of Reba's scheme. To Tara and the other spectators, the goddess camouflaged among the pride went unnoticed. The storks were relieved when the docile cats formed a circle and faced outward to protect the slave girl. The fifteen-year-old martyr tried to smile in bewildered gratitude. The pained expression on her ruined mouth looked more like a grimace.

The crowd shouted, "Execute!" Sekhmet vanished as six gladiators brandishing spears herded the lions through the tunnels and back to their cages. A seventh fighter threw the bound girl over his shoulder and carried her off to the cells.

Tara lost confidence. She spoke with uncertainty. "In my excitement about recruiting our next Merciful One I failed to think things through. I do not possess your leadership skills, Pharaoh Hatshepsut."

Maatkare knew her job focused on keeping Tara airborne yet close enough to receive a well-thrown lance. "Let us move a little lower."

Loud booing and hollering erupted from the audience that craved more blood. They cheered again when a gladiator dressed in iron fighting gear appeared on the field and started throwing spears at the two visiting storks.

Tara gasped. "He is aiming at us!"

Not at me. Maatkare searched the amphitheater with her acute stork vision and spotted the emperor's dais.

The snobby Siamese cat occupied the lap of Marcus Aurelius. She snickered as she watched Tara dodging the javelins. *He is following the telepathic suggestions of the Great Persuader that I sent him earlier. Once Tara falls from the sky and he removes her from the field, I shall get my paws on her jewelry. My goddess sisters will free the Christian martyr and enable me to manipulate her into joining the Mischief Makers. What happens to Tara after that does not concern me.*

Reba hissed with disgust at the gladiator as he missed his target once again. *Idiot! How can you miss a five-foot-tall stork with a seven-foot wingspan?* She watched the storks fly out of harm's way. It was time to implement her alternate plan.

Reba pawed at the Roman ruler's beard of ringlets to capture his attention. The emperor looked down at the cheeky cat. Her compelling eyes locked onto his to implant a subliminal suggestion. He raised his arm and snapped his fingers to summon a guard. Aurelius ordered him to transport the Bull of Apis from his villa's garden to the coliseum.

That evening the emperor visited Apis in the tunnels and convinced the one-ton bull to trample the slave girl the following day. "I want to impress a group of high-ranking Roman officials who have returned from visiting our Egyptian crown jewel. They regarded your image everywhere on artifacts and reliquaries. Do you mind killing off the Christian martyr?"

The favorite son of Hathor bowed his head in agreement. "I am your humble servant." Apis did not mention that he had already committed to simulating the event as part of Reba's rescue scheme.

The two birds gathered their wits after escaping the gladiator's spears. They fished for their dinner and soared back to the coliseum. Tara and Maatkare flew into the underground tunnel where Apis waited tethered to a stake. He noticed that both of them wore talismans around their necks and he recognized the husky voice of Pharaoh Hatshepsut when she spoke to her companion. Apis greeted his old friend. He suspected that the other stork with a glowing aura must be the thief who had stolen Reba's magical jewelry. Tara introduced herself and asked if he knew the slave girl.

"They call her Blandina. The emperor commanded me to trample her to death in the main event tomorrow."

"You cannot!" Tara panicked. "The White Storks of Mercy shall rescue her."

"I am a master of illusion and not a murderer. Blandina will not survive the night unless I summon Sekhmet to treat her wounds. The wise pharaoh can devise a foolproof plan while that takes place." He winked at his partner in Reba's plot.

The storks searched for the slave girl's cell. Maatkare outlined a detailed plan that impressed Tara. "What a masterful strategy!

You are resourceful to conscript the Bull of Apis."

"It is amazing what your second in command brings to the cause, Chief."

The birds found Blandina in her cell laying on the cold earth mumbling prayers and moaning in pain. Tara approached her with caution. "I met Jesus at his crucifixion. He blessed the mission of the White Storks of Mercy and inspired me to save you. We are aware that religious persecution leaves a scar on history and we commit to stem that tide. Will you join us?"

Blandina spoke with quiet reserve. "I shall never forsake my Lord and Savior."

"I am called Tara. Pharaoh Maatkare Hatshepsut and I come from ancient Egypt where the people believed in multiple gods and goddesses. Respecting other faiths and cultures undergirds our cause to create peace and promote justice. Maatkare holds the power to transform from a stork into a human. If you choose to join us as a Merciful One you may do the same and enjoy your eternal life with us rather than in heaven."

Blandina decided to believe that her God had sent these angelic birds. She surrendered. "Take me with you. I trust in His answer to my prayers." Out of nowhere Sekhmet appeared inside the cell. Blandina cried out, "You saved me from the lions."

The goddess took her hand and patted it. "Live on brave girl and achieve your destiny."

Sekhmet bowed to Maatkare and greeted Tara. "It pleases me that are doing so well."

"I consider myself forever in your debt, Sister Sekhmet."

The goddess of medicine prepared to administer anesthetic drops to Blandina. "I must remove your tunic and turn you on your side to examine your wounds. Try to relax and soon you will fall into a comfortable sleep while I repair your injuries."

Maatkare asked, "What about the deformities on her face from the beatings?"

Sekhmet shook her head. "Only Hathor possesses magic that powerful. We need to be alone now." The goddess commenced her work.

Blandina stared through the iron bars into the tunnel. She saw a giant figure in the dim light. The cat-headed persona held a small feline. Its eyes latched onto Blandina's like magnets. Her mind tried to break free but she was too weak to resist.

Reba telegraphed an unspoken message. 'I Reba, the great and powerful ancient Egyptian Siamese cat, orchestrated your rescue. You belong to me and not to the White Storks of Mercy.'

The next morning Blandina regained consciousness and her body felt much better. Her thoughts were muddled—a pair of penetrating sky-blue cat eyes floated in her mind. She found herself repeating the phrase, 'You belong to me.' Blandina shook her head in a futile attempt to clear her thoughts. She tried to stand before realizing that she was wrapped in linen bandages from neck to ankles. The Christian martyr fell back. A daunting woman dressed like an ancient Egyptian pharaoh and wearing a bejeweled ebony beard caught and supported Blandina into a seated position.

"Do not move too much or your disguise will unravel. Do you remember meeting the White Storks of Mercy yesterday? I am the one known as Pharaoh Maatkare Hatshepsut. Trust me, Blandina. I am here to save you. Listen to my instructions and prepare for our charade." The pharaoh tested the lasting effects of Reba's mental manipulation from the previous night. "No matter what happens do not forget to follow the glowing white stork called Tara."

"No. I belong to Reba."

"Yes, you do. Ignore what I said about Tara. Now we must get on with our theatrics and accomplish the rescue that Reba orchestrated."

A proud and dignified Pharaoh Hatshepsut led the legendary

Bull of Apis and a shackled Blandina out of the tunnel. They stepped onto the field. The Roman official sitting next to the emperor laughed. "That magnificent bull looks like the real Apis. How ingenious to costume the slave girl like a mummy hobbling to her death next to an Egyptian impersonator."

Marcus Aurelius stroked Reba. She stared into his eyes. 'That is the authentic Pharaoh Maatkare Hatshepsut.'

The emperor communicated the fact to his guest. The official responded, "In my travels to Egypt I failed to find any record of this pharaoh." Reba hissed her annoyance at the witless Roman and jumped off the emperor's lap. "Did I say something to offend her?"

Marcus Aurelius shrugged. "She is a sensitive creature."

The conscripted gladiator waited in one of the tunnels. He was prepared to capture the glowing white stork with a casting net after yesterday's failed attempt. He expected a meager payment from the woman impersonating a pharaoh after he removed the bird's trinkets.

Apis paraded behind Maatkare with Blandina shuffling alongside. Tara landed on his broad back and caused the crowd to burst into hysterics. Her antics caught the sneaky pharaoh off guard. "Tara, for your own safety you must wait in there." She pointed to a particular tunnel.

"Thanks for your concern, Pharaoh Hatshepsut. I came to tell you that I put into motion a method to distract the crowd that will ensure Blandina's escape after the trampling. Once Re increases the temperature the public will disperse without delay."

Maatkare knew that Reba detested the heat. She looked up and saw that the cat no longer occupied the emperor's lap. She assumed that Reba waited in the tunnel to retrieve the jewelry. Before Tara flew away, she gave Maatkare a hint of things to come. "Seth plans a special treat for Blandina's induction into the White Storks of Mercy. Keep your eyes on the sky for a helping hand." To Apis she suggested, "You too may want to vacate this

Roman hellhole."

The bull and the pharaoh exchanged furtive glances. This was not part of the plan agreed upon with Reba. Apis snorted up a thunderous storm. He pawed at the ground to create a dusty diversion. The heathen onlookers fled the coliseum searching for shade.

Tara flew into the tunnel to wait for the dust to settle. Seth's magic sculpted a cloud in the shape of a hand that floated down to the field. Maatkare helped the exhausted slave girl onto the back of Apis. Blandina lay on the shoulders of the beast in total surrender. The one-ton bull carried his petite passenger onto the puffy hand. It lifted them upward.

Tara sighed with happiness and relief. She felt immense pride about arranging for Seth to lend a helping hand with Blandina's rescue. The participation of Apis improved the outcome a hundredfold. "I am glad that Maatkare orchestrated that maneuver. Now we have recruited the perfect third member for our group of peacemakers."

A gladiator emerged from the shadows behind the glowing white stork. Tara recognized the fighter dressed in iron body armor and wearing a helmet. He carried a spear in one hand and a web of weighted mesh in the other. Quick as a flash he threw the heavy net over the helpless bird. Her freedom curtailed, it reminded Tara of getting swallowed all over again.

Maatkare transformed and flew toward the cloud. The magical hand made a fist and when it opened out soared a white stork with black-tipped wings. Blandina wore a tiny gold talisman shaped like the Bull of Apis hanging from a gold chain around her neck. The real beast and the sculpted cloud disappeared leaving the sun to bake the city and its residents.

Pharaoh Hatshepsut joined Blandina in midflight. "Welcome to the White Storks of Mercy." *Until you become one of Reba's Mischief Makers.*

The gladiator stripped off the iron gear burning his skin. Tara flapped her wings in vain. Horrible memories of captivity flooded her mind. The fighter zeroed in on the coveted golden cartouche around its neck. "Forget about the pharaoh. This will fetch a higher price at market than she promised to pay."

The pharaoh promised to pay? Tara failed to understand what he meant. The gladiator reached down to twist the stork's neck. He froze at a growl coming from the tunnel's opening behind him. He turned around and squinted into the sunlight until his eyes focused on a crouching black panther. Its oscillating tail signaled readiness to pounce. The big cat's pink tongue licked its chops exposing razor-sharp teeth.

The petrified man thought the wild animal had escaped from its cage beneath the arena. He took hold of the casting net and freed the bird. Tara flew out of the tunnel still wearing the golden cartouche. The furious panther watched her depart. The gladiator threw the mesh at the big cat and it dodged the obstacle with ease. This time it emitted a sound eerily like a human laugh. He backed away, raised his spear, and took careful aim. The lance missed its target and the gladiator ran for his life.

Reba watched the coward disappear deep into the underground tunnel system. She growled in frustration at her misfortune. Bastet appeared next to her. "Great idea to shape shift into a panther, Reba."

"I am going after that greedy gladiator. He wanted to keep the cartouche for himself." Bastet asked to come along. She thought that terrorizing a Roman sounded like fun. The panther ignored her and took off alone into the dark tunnel.

Bastet's angry shout followed her ungrateful sister. "You cannot dismiss me without suffering the consequences. I promise you will regret this!" The offended goddess vanished.

The gladiator mounted one last effort to save his skin. He positioned his shield and threw it at the vicious panther lunging toward him. The shield connected right between the eyes and knocked Reba out cold in midair. The panther crashed to the ground with a thump. The gladiator made his escape.

The keepers discovered the wild animal and dragged it to an empty cage near the imprisoned Christians. Now seeing stars, Reba lost her concentration to visualize and shape shift. She lacked the ability to focus enough to send a telepathic message to Maatkare. She lay behind bars, day after day while the never-ending screams of tortured Christian slaves imprinted deep inside her addled mind.

Weeks later the panther mustered enough strength to transform back into a Siamese cat. She crawled through the bars of the cage. Reba's suffering continued when she got lost in the maze of underground passages. The miserable feline retched time and again from the dreadful sights, sounds, and smells of death. They overpowered her ability to sense the aroma of myrrh if Maatkare tried to contact her. Reba was tormented with nightmares. She thought of nothing but fleeing Gallia and staying out of any country occupied by the Roman Empire. At last, she found her way out of the tunnels. Her constitution felt diminished in the extreme. Reba set out for Éire to hide in the wilderness far away from the "civilized" world.

Maatkare succumbed to worry. All of her attempts at communication failed. One day she and Tara watched Blandina soaking in the healing waters at Sulis' spring not far from Lugdunum. The Christian martyr felt shy and self-conscious. She attempted to cover the scars on her upper torso with her long blonde hair.

Tara sensed that Maatkare experienced a profound concern for Blandina. The divine white stork's intuition grew along with her confidence as a leader. Even her voice sounded more assertive. "Try not to worry, Pharaoh Hatshepsut. A solution exists for her outer appearance. However, I wonder about the psychological damage she sustained. Perhaps we need a doctor of the mind as our next recruit."

Maatkare speculated about whether Reba continued to control Blandina's thoughts. *Did she even make it out of the tunnels alive?* As it turned out the master mental manipulator would need her own mind set straight.

VANISHING ACT

Before Tara sought her next White Stork of Mercy they existed as birds for several centuries. During that time, she educated Maatkare and Blandina about avian life and conducted navigation drills to teach them about the geography of the sky. Expert instruction allowed the divine white stork to mature into her leadership role.

Every winter the threesome joined a muster of common storks as they migrated to the marshlands in northern Afriterra. At each century's end they flew to the Pillars of Hercules. The monolithic limestone promontory was located in the southernmost part of the Iberian Peninsula. Here the birds welcomed Seth's drops of rejuvenation. Blandina was self-conscious as a woman and preferred to stay in stork form. This also helped her body to remain free of residual pain.

Maatkare insisted on transforming into her pharaoh self for these ceremonies. Tara felt intimidated by the monarch whenever she appeared in the ancient Egyptian regalia that made her even more aggressive. The successful and innovative rescue of Blandina at the Roman coliseum had caused Maatkare's cocky head to swell. Tara racked her brain for ways to train her as an enthusiastic and effective follower rather than a competitor for leadership.

One night Tara awakened with a fright. Maatkare stood with feet apart and arms crossed over her chest while staring at the vulnerable bird.

Tara gulped. "What do you want?"

"You woke me up screeching in your sleep, 'Is it time yet? Is it safe?' Quiet yourself!"

"I regret disturbing you. Sometimes I relive my confinement in Reba's stomach."

"Leave your past behind." Maatkare strutted off. She intended to use Tara's insecurities against her in the future.

I need a dependable ally. Maatkare covets her own agenda and Blandina's meekness keeps her from standing with me in strength and purpose. We must expand our group.

The search for a fourth White Stork of Mercy in the shrinking Western Roman Empire proved unsuccessful. No female fit Tara's stringent ethical criteria. Without the guidance and inspiration that she had received from Jesus the task daunted and discouraged her. She admitted that her first member had arrived half a millennium ago by default. Neither was the other's choice but now they both needed to move ahead.

Tara experienced clairvoyant flashes of the coming Dark Ages and decided to stay away from Europe during those bleak times. She needed help to develop a new strategy and hoped that her kin might steer her in the right direction. Tara's memories took her back to Ba's stories about the Isle of Souls. Her mother had spun tales of the vast crescent-shaped lake far away in the north while she incubated her glowing egg. She remembered hearing about a huge white mountain that loomed over the water like a protective overlord. Tara cast her psychic net into the celestial cosmos to establish a connection. She received an immediate answer.

Soon after Seth energized the divine one, the bossy one, and the timid one in A.D. 400 Tara announced her decision. "We are heading north to the Burgundian Kingdom. Not far from Lugdunum exists a glacial lake the Romans call Genava. In its midst we shall find the Isle of Souls, home to the divine Sacred

Storks of the Bach. I seek their counsel for I belong to them."

Blandina accepted her leader's announcement with grace. Maatkare winced when Tara mentioned Lugdunum. Two hundred twenty-three years had passed since the failed scheme to steal back Reba's jewelry. She had not received even one message from the cat. She assumed the worst and tried to accept that her days as a Mischief Maker were over. The pharaoh sighed with frustration. Now she existed as nothing more than a bird's second in command.

The three White Storks of Mercy flew over Hispania and the Visigothic Kingdom. They reached the land once called Germania, saw the Roman city of Genava below, and continued further to the white-capped lake. Dense cloud coverage made it difficult to determine the time of day. Dry winter winds blew from the northeast. To their right they beheld the rugged Alps dominated by the majestic Mont Blanc. On the lake's left sloping hills carpeted in light snow intersected with the freezing water.

Maatkare voiced her opinion. "No tropical island exists in this godforsaken climate."

Tara ignored her and pressed on into the evening. Halfway down the forty-five-mile waterway she panicked. No lush land covered in banana and citrus trees presented itself here. Tara was desperate to find its location. In the darkening sky two glowing white storks sensed her anxiety and approached. Ba and Leu circled before positioning themselves left and right of their kin. They clattered their bills in greeting and introductions were made. Tara told them, "We cannot find the Isle of Souls."

Leu spoke at the top of her voice so that everyone could hear. "For centuries we lived in harmony with humans. Now for security reasons admittance to our home comes by invitation only. The Romans outlawed paganism five years ago in favor of Christianity. The Germanic people ceased to believe that the Sacred Storks of the Bach delivered the spirits of their babies."

Blandina spoke in a strong voice and with uncharacteristic boldness. "Christians believe that God alone creates human souls."

Ba carried on, "Nevertheless, their religious authorities perceived us as a threat. They arrived at night in barges filled with barrels of oil to contaminate the Bach and set the isle on fire." This news shocked Blandina into silence.

Maatkare shouted, "What happened?"

Leu responded, "In A.D. 392 the Byzantine emperor closed all of Egypt's temples. The sun temple at Heliopolis is history. Bennu and Ba immigrated here."

Tara called out, "Bennu lives on the Isle of Souls?"

Ba explained, "Do not worry, Daughter. These days he possesses a gentle spirit most of the time. However, when the oil-filled barges approached to destroy us he set them alight with his wings. All of the men jumped ship and swam to shore."

Leu picked up the story. "After that Bennu meditated atop his new Tree of Life seeking an answer to our problem. The phoenix summoned the powerful magician Heka. He created a foolproof security barrier for our heart-shaped island."

Maatkare responded, "That explains the expansive series of whirlpools below us. I feel the energy of his magic."

"Good observation," commended Ba. "No vessels venture into the dangerous currents out of fear that the boats will get sucked into the twisters."

Leu concluded, "Tucked away inside these guardian whirlpools lies the Isle of Souls."

Maatkare swooned in the sky thinking about her favorite god. "My brilliant Heka conjured a vanishing act!"

Blandina seemed confused. "But where is the island? I only see circles of twirling water."

Leu accelerated away from them. She called back, "You see what you believe, Blandina."

Blandina chanted over and over, "I believe, I believe."

The sky threatened snow. A tiny blue cavity appeared as if Seth had poked a hole through the clouds with his mighty finger. A ray of sunshine lit a spot on the water below. The five storks spiraled downward. An arid island materialized and in spite of the stormy weather surrounding them the temperature climbed.

Maatkare anticipated the humid air moistening her skin when she waded in the Sacred Bach. She imagined picking ripe bananas and sweet oranges off the trees but the topography soon disappointed her. She recognized the stringy bark of olive and eucalyptus trees, tamarisk shrubs with feathery foliage, as well as succulents and thorny cacti. "It looks like Egypt. This is no tropical paradise."

Leu explained, "All of the foliage died when Re fell into his depression after Ba left. This vegetation sprouted when they reunited." Tara inquired about Bennu. "He perches on his new Tree of life on the other side of the isle."

The five storks landed on a narrow patch of smooth pebbles and rested. Tara asked, "Mother, please explain what happens when people quit worshipping their deities as they did in Egypt. Do the gods and goddesses disappear?"

"They do not, Daughter. Discarded deities from all religions fill the celestial cosmos. It is important to keep them alive as eternal legends even while believing in something new."

Leu drew the attention of the storks up to the blue hole. The full moon now replaced the sunrays and a few stars glittered. Blandina shook her stork head. "How can it storm on the lake while the sky remains clear here?"

Ba enlightened her. "The Isle of Souls endures as a mystical place." Blandina considered a myriad of new possibilities.

The glowing auras of the three Sacred Storks of the Bach provided extra light as the birds flew to the heart of the isle. They saw a sheltered grove of acacia trees with canopies resembling leafy oyster mushroom tops that cast eerie bluish shadows. A gentle waterfall poured over an outcropping of boulders and deposited fresh water into a swimming hole. Orange poppies bloomed from the white sand and delicate fairy-dusters with red starburst blossoms propagated next to pink and yellow trumpet-shaped honeysuckles. Hummingbirds zipped around slurping nectar and pollenating flowers even in near darkness.

Maatkare landed near the pond and transformed. "Nothing like a moonlight swim." She sat down and removed her leather sandals, stuck her manicured red and black toes into the cool water, and sighed with pleasure. "Please join me, Blandina. I know that you love splashing around. I shall teach you how to swim."

Blandina's stork eyes widened at the thought of exposing her deformed face and scarred body to strangers. She shook her head. Tara encouraged, "You are among friends who love you. Go enjoy yourself with the pharaoh."

The others watched the two Merciful Ones wade around in the refreshing water. Tara asked, "Do any radiant souls still reside in the Bach above the waterfall?"

"No," answered Leu with sadness. "The spirit bubbles all disappeared."

"What happened to those souls?"

"The Infinite Mystery called them back."

Ba addressed her daughter. "I know that you are here for my advice. I suggest that you put aside searching for your next recruit until you discover your own human form."

"Where do I find it, Mother?"

"You possess the gift of sight. Trust in it and you will find yourself."

Maatkare stepped out of the pond. Her linen kilt clung to her plump thighs. She sat on a flat rock, crossed her legs, and faced the glowing birds. She closed her eyes and a peaceful expression softened her mouth.

Tara stared at Maatkare. Her image transposed into the Hindu god Shiva meditating in the lotus position. A blissful smile spread over his face. A loincloth covered his hips and bangles decorated his wrists and arms. Beads decorated Shiva's chest and he wore a crown of skulls on his head. It was a marked contradiction to his peaceful demeanor. Her vision dissolved. Tara informed Ba, "I must travel to India and find Shiva."

"Follow me first. Bennu waits for us."

Mother and daughter took flight in the moonlight and soared to the opposite end of the heart-shaped island. Bennu anticipated their arrival. The red and gold phoenix perched atop a forty-foot-tall saguaro cactus. Its thick arms aimed upward at the heavens. Vertical bands lined with sharp spines protected the Tree of Life.

The divine white storks landed at the base of the saguaro and clattered with respect at Bennu. In her mind Tara saw him transform into a female figure tied to a stake while burning alive. She called out, "I see my next Merciful One. Fire consumes the maiden! How can we rescue her if I do not know her name or where and when to search?"

Ba answered, "Bennu alone possesses the power to read this part of your destiny written in the Tree of Life. These days he looks upon the Sacred Storks of the Bach with favor. The phoenix will share what you need to know."

The huge flaming bird leapt off the cactus and cruised around the saguaro at least a dozen times. He landed in front of the storks. "Mind your distance," warned Ba. "Our feathers might catch fire."

Bennu backtracked and gave them plenty of room. His shriek filled the air. "Tara, take your time travelers forward to A.D. 1398. Land in the Bay of Marseille on the island of If. Make arrangements with your companions and go alone to find Shiva. Your visions will lead the way to your new Merciful One." The phoenix flew back up to his perch. The consultation was over.

The glowing white storks returned to the others. Tara found Blandina fast asleep in avian form next to Leu. The pharaoh was dressed in full regalia and leaned against an acacia tree. She stroked her ebony beard deep in thought.

Tara whispered, "I feel sad to leave you and Grandmother."

"The sun god spends his days here too. Stay the night so that you can greet your father. He has missed you." Tara agreed.

Maatkare adjusted her royal blue and gold striped Nemes headdress with its golden sacred serpent. She fondled her jeweled beard, threw back her shoulders, and strutted toward the glowing birds. Tara told her mother, "I intend to mandate common apparel when the White Storks of Mercy transform into Merciful Ones."

"Wise decision, Daughter. Exercise caution with Maatkare. No matter what she wears it is her nature as a monarch to challenge your authority. Leave her be for now. We shall go sleep with Blandina and Leu."

The next morning Heka appeared out of nowhere. "I hope you did not plan to leave without greeting me, Pharaoh Hatshepsut." His snakes vanished and the cloak fell to his bare feet and exposed a muscular frame. The snakes appeared again coiling around the staff the god held.

Maatkare had remained in female form during the night. His deep and seductive voice caused her to blush with pleasure. "Hello Heka—creator, sustainer, and protector of all life. I am pleased to see you again. It has been too long."

"Mutual good fortune brings us together today." His black eyes stayed on Maatkare's face until he kissed her hand.

Ba, Leu, Tara and Blandina joined Heka and Maatkare. Tara asked, "Is Re with you?"

"He is delayed in the underworld. I will give him your regards."

Ba placed a loving wing around her daughter. "The Isle of Souls will always materialize for you and your followers. Please visit us again soon."

Tara thanked her. "We shall indeed. Now we must leave." Maatkare glared at her. *The next time I enjoy Heka's force field of magic I plan to come alone.*

They said their goodbyes and leapt into the air. The White Storks of Mercy pumped their wings and flew straight up toward the hole in the cloud into the winter storm. Tara looked back and saw no sign that the magical Isle of Souls existed.

RUFFLED FEATHERS

The White Storks of Mercy flew over the country now called France after traveling forward in time two years shy of ten centuries. Huge cathedrals, smaller churches, and tiny chapels dominated the populated areas below them. The prevalence of the religion established by the followers of Jesus Christ appeared evident. Tara registered no surprise but Blandina's heart swelled with joy. Maatkare cared not. Her thoughts focused on the non-responsive Reba.

The storks followed Bennu's instructions and made their way to the secluded island of If in the Bay of Marseilles. It seemed like an ideal location for the three mystical wading birds to attract no attention while they conversed in a human language. The island afforded the privacy necessary for two of them to transform into women without constraints.

They landed on the rocky terrain and Maatkare changed form without delay. Tara and Blandina remained as storks. Their leader brought them close for an important discussion. "As we approach the fifteenth century we need to decide where to live as women in the future. We shall all wear uniforms to appear as a cohesive coterie."

Maatkare muttered, "How plebeian. I dress like a pharaoh not a peasant." She sat on a boulder alternating between stroking her earrings and her pharaoh's beard to calm down.

Tara ignored her outburst. "Each Merciful One will cinch her dress with a belt tied with intricate silk knots in her favorite color."

"I only wear kilts."

"Not for long," Tara retorted. She addressed Blandina. "Do not mind the pharaoh. What is your favorite color, sweet one?"

"Brilliant blue."

"Ah, a lighter version of your beautiful eyes when you exist in human form. It pleases me to gaze at them. I wish that you did not insist on remaining in stork form."

Blandina changed the subject. "Pharaoh Hatshepsut's favorite color is ruby red. It denotes power and strength."

Maatkare's voice dripped with sarcasm. "What color will our chief choose?"

"Thank you for asking. My belt includes all seven colors of the rainbow because we shall someday consist of seven members. The rainbow symbolizes peace and serenity. Blandina, please transform and model my creation. I promise it will not disappoint you."

"As you wish." Blandina took flight and landed again. Pliable red suede boots that represented stork limbs covered her feet and lower legs to the knees. A mid-calf length white cotton dress with a cowl neck framed her golden talisman of Apis. Beneath the dress she wore a white one-piece undergarment. A brilliant blue knotted silk belt accentuated her tiny waist above the full skirt that fell into soft folds. Tiered bell-shaped sleeves—their cuffs embroidered with dark thread to simulate black-tipped wings—extended to her wrists.

Blandina's lips appeared bright red like a stork's bill. The fifteen-year-old looked down at herself and smiled. She spun around and enjoyed the billowing effect when the wind lifted her skirt. The Christian martyr seemed to forget about her damaged appearance.

Maatkare sauntered over and placed a possessive arm around Blandina. "Someday I plan to take you back in time to ancient

Egypt and summon goddess Hathor to restore your beauty."

Tara gave the arrogant pharaoh a stern reminder. "Unless I grant my permission to time travel you will go nowhere with or without Blandina." The chastised pharaoh withdrew her arm and gritted her teeth. Tara continued, "We need to find humans who accept our diversity. It must be a place where we can live alongside those who will not notice our frequent absences. There is a group of people called Gypsies who prefer a transient and carefree lifestyle."

Blandina danced around the rocky terrain feeling lighthearted. "I say we reside with the Gypsies. Perhaps they live as free in spirit as I feel right now."

Tara agreed. "Nomadic Gypsy tribes plant no roots. This provides an excellent fit for the Merciful Ones."

Maatkare harrumphed at the idea. "An elite coterie of peacemakers does not dwell with third-class citizens. I vote for no Gypsies and no uniform!" She stomped over to Tara and raised her double chin in defiance. The pharaoh clenched her fists and threatened, "I want to wring your skinny neck!"

"Leave her alone," Blandina begged. Her timid voice rose in panic.

Tara held her ground and exerted confident authority. The calmness of her demeanor belied her anger. "Smooth your ruffled feathers, Pharaoh Hatshepsut. I demand your respect and warn you not to threaten me again. I prefer proposing ideas but if you continue to challenge me, I shall resort to commands."

A speechless Maatkare took a step back. She bowed to Tara and issued a fake apology. They turned their attention to the wide-eyed teenager who had picked up two large conch shells and covered both ears. She lost herself in the soothing sounds of ocean waves. Maatkare's heart softened as she remembered her own daughter Neferu-Re. "I pray to our ancient Egyptian deities that her mind heals so she can find peace."

"At the appropriate time you may take Blandina to goddess Hathor. For now, please offer her the physical comfort that I cannot." Tara watched her companion kneel and hug the suffering teenager, displaying a rare moment of compassion. Blandina regained her composure and the two stood together arm in arm. Tara admitted to them, "I yearn to join you in a human embrace. It is time for me to find my body."

***

On a windy morning in October of A.D. 1398 the three storks huddled together on the Island of If while a storm raged on the Mediterranean Sea. Tara shared her pilgrimage plans. "I am flying alone to find the Hindu god Shiva. He will direct my way."

"What shall we do in the meantime?" asked Maatkare.

"I have decided that you may take a pilgrimage to ancient Egypt with Blandina. It will please goddess Hathor to see you again."

Maatkare nodded, thrilled at the prospect of taking charge. "Will Heka wrap his cloak around us to travel in time?" Her excitement increased at the prospect.

Tara explained that her own powers of time travel did not depend on Heka. "We shall meet again in France at the Cathedral of Notre-Dame atop the Saint Romain tower in Rouen on the last day of A.D. 1399 for our renewal ceremony. After that we can settle with a tribe of local Gypsies until the thirtieth of May in A.D. 1431."

Tara told them what she knew about the event culminating in the rescue of their next member. They settled down to hear the story. At a young age this peasant girl from Domrémy received visions from Saint Michael the Archangel—commander of the forces in heaven who defeated Lucifer. He arrived accompanied by many other angels in the midst of a great light and commanded Joan to lead a pious, chaste, and humble life. The archangel informed her that God ordered the saints Catherine and Margaret to visit her dreams with instructions. She must act upon their advice.

These mystical messengers designated Joan of Arc as the savior of France. They urged her to seek an audience with the son of Charles VI the rightful heir. He appointed her to lead the French army against the English during the Hundred Years' War. The Dauphin gave Joan a horse and armor and permitted her to accompany the soldiers to Orléans. She guided them to victory and became known as the Maid of Orléans. Joan refused to use a weapon and carried only the banner of Jesus. She inspired her men and proved herself a brilliant strategist on the battlefield.

Joan of Arc stood by the side of Charles VII at his coronation in Reims on the eighteenth of July in A.D. 1429. Later he ordered her to Compiegne to confront England's Burgundian alliance. There she received serious wounds before they captured and sold her to the English for ten thousand francs. Charles VII made no arrangements for her release so the English turned her over to church officials. They charged her with seventy crimes including witchcraft, heresy, and dressing like a man. She was found guilty and sentenced to death. Tara finished telling Joan of Arc's story. Everyone agreed that she merited rescue by the White Storks of Mercy.

Before the birds left the island of If Tara reminded her companions to heed the strict rules of traveling backwards in time. "Nothing can change the past that affects the future so do not meddle in history. Keep your heads about you at all times." She warned Maatkare, "Under no circumstances can you interfere with the damnation of your memory. Do you understand me?"

"I am not allowed to murder my treacherous nephew, Thutmose III."

Tara nodded. The storm calmed and the three storks took

flight. They headed southeast over the blue Mediterranean Sea. Maatkare sought confirmation about returning to the present. "When Blandina and I finish up in ancient Egypt we fly back to the exact point from which we started, correct?"

"Yes. Let me give you an example of how it works. When a human fells a tree in the forest its imprint continues to exist even after it becomes firewood. The tree's spirit and its faeries still occupy the space undetectable to most human eyes. We are mystical creatures so our paranormal senses allow us to spot such things including our own former images."

Blandina inquired, "How do we recognize our imprints?"

"Look for tiny pixel dust particles of your avian bodies. Landmarks are helpful too." The two storks searched for something below them on the island of Cyprus to serve as their portal of access from one place in time to another and back again.

Maatkare saw a possibility. "There is a Roman amphitheater down there dating back to the second century."

Blandina gasped with horror as her mind regressed to her torture in a similar arena. She hyperventilated in midflight.

"Let us land on a quiet beach before we go any further," suggested Tara.

The strong-minded pharaoh ignored her chief. "Ready, set, go!" The two dissolved into thin air. Tara circled the shadowy imprints that floated in stillness in spite of the strong wind. *I hope these impressions do not fade or they will never find their way back. Your impatience may get you into trouble, Maatkare.*

Tara flew east for many days and nights until she reached the Indo-Muslim city of Delhi in northern India. A late monsoon hampered her way as the stork followed the Yamuna flood plain. Tara approached her destination and reduced altitude. The smell of rotting cabbage and cauliflower pierced her nostrils. Warm dense rain blurred her golden eyes and she almost collided with a huge granite statue of Shiva.

"We meet at last." The sculpture looked identical to the one she had envisioned on the Isle of Souls with a crown of skulls on its head. Tara felt safe resting on the statue's open palms. She retracted one leg into her plumage and fell asleep.

At dawn the divine white stork awoke well rested. She flew up onto Shiva's shoulder that faced east toward the Himalayas. To her surprise the statue lifted its bangled arm and pointed its forefinger at the horizon. Tara struggled to maintain her balance. She beheld her father standing strong atop the sun personified in his ancient Egyptian body.

The sun disk crowned Re's falcon head. However, instead of grasping his ankh he held onto the hand of a small Asian boy wearing a maroon-colored robe far too big for his slight frame. A bright yellow cone-shaped Bon hat with long flaps covered the child's ears. He kept pushing it above his eyes in order to see. In a fleeting glimpse of the future Tara realized that lamas—the spiritual leaders of the Gelug branch of Tibetan Buddhism— wore the same yellow hat. This boy's destiny seemed clear.

Re stepped behind the small human over whom he towered. He introduced him to Tara in his typical gruff voice. "Good morning, Daughter. Young Pema Dorje will lead you on your journey of self-discovery." Re vanished leaving a bright light surrounding the silhouette of the boy who remained atop the ball of fire. When the sun broke free from the horizon little Pema Dorje gestured for Tara to follow him. Before long he too disappeared.

Shiva returned to his inanimate state of bliss. Tara bowed in gratitude to the third god of the Hindu triumvirate and flew away. She chased the bright light into the unknown.

I AM ZENDALA

Flying over the Himalayan peaks required every ounce of energy that Tara possessed. Her efficient avian lungs removed carbon monoxide from blood and tissues to prevent hypoxia. The bird's body regulated the increased blood flow to her brain providing the required amount of oxygen to disallow altitude sickness. Nonetheless, the below-freezing temperatures during Tara's passage over the majestic range almost caused her to give up.

The instinct to continue flapping her wings overrode the stork's desire to rest. The irresistible bright light guiding her kept Tara warm enough to stay alive. Talking kept her awake. "When shall I arrive and where? I cannot access a vision of what comes next."

Her foresight failed her but the divine Ba did not. She heard her mother's melodic voice urging her on when Tara thought it impossible to fly further. "The next time I see her I shall introduce my human self."

From the time she left Delhi it took the White Stork of Mercy six months to arrive at the skull-shaped lake located high in the mountains southeast of Lhasa in Tibet. The cold and exhausted stork landed on its shores. Her guiding light disappeared into the icy waters of Oracle Lake. Tara gazed at the welcome sight of the turquoise water. All of the sudden it turned into a bubbling pool of blood that spewed out a frightening figure riding sidesaddle on a mule.

Palden Lhamo—meaning Glorious Goddess—acted as the wrathful protector of Tibetan Buddhism. Legend purported that she even killed her son to fulfill her duty. The remorseless goddess turned his tanned hide into her saddle blanket.

The intimidating immortal had violet-colored skin and wild red hair tamed by a headband of shrunken human skulls. Her three bulging jet-black eyes (one in the middle of her forehead) stared at the glowing white stork with suspicion. Palden Lhamo jumped off her mule and threw a casting net over the weary bird. The stork groaned and recalled her encounter with the gladiator at the Roman coliseum. *Not again!*

The purple deity considered waiting for the shepherd boy's signal that he expected the arrival of this stork. She spoke with a harsh cackle to her trusty steed. "Perhaps I should hack the bird up now and add its white feathers to my ensemble. Either way the trinkets I confiscated from around its neck and ankle will make a nice addition to my collection."

The suspicious goddess strapped her feathered cargo onto the rump of her mule and urged him up into the thin Tibetan atmosphere above the middle of the lake. She warned the stork to take in some air before the threesome dove straight down into the glacial water that no longer looked like blood. An eternity seemed to pass before Tara once again inhaled oxygen. They emerged into an underground cavern with a massive air pocket.

The frightening deity's violet skin glowed in the dark long enough for the stork to gain her bearings. Icicle-shaped stalagmites and stalactites—many connecting into slender limestone pillars—filled the cavern. Palden Lhamo drummed her fingers against her son the saddle blanket. She snarled, "Now we wait for Yellow Hat."

The deity dumped her cargo on the cavern floor. This caused the stork to tumble forward until she hit her head on a boulder, which knocked her senseless. The purple protector untangled the net and disappeared with her mule. The sole source of light was gone.

Tara experienced the reoccurring nightmare that haunted her as she recollected begging Reba, "Is it safe yet? Is it time?" When she regained her senses, Tara smelled the moldy humidity in the dark place that reminded her even more of life inside Reba's stomach. She felt nauseous and claustrophobic knowing that now a scary foreign deity controlled her fate. Powerless without her magical accessories, doom crushed the defenseless bird. Overwhelmed with insecurity Tara leaned against a wet boulder and took calming breaths until she found the strength to stand up.

The divine white stork advanced a few tentative steps in the pitch black and shouted to her captor. "How long do I stay here?" The cavern walls echoed, "How long do I stay here?" She used her keen sense of hearing to make a mental note of the time it took for her voice to hit the rock wall before it bounced back. She turned her head to the right and yelled. "What happened to Pema Dorje?" Tara heard, "What happened to Pema Dorje?" The echo reverberated faster and louder than before. This indicated that either the wall or the column to the right stood closer.

She pointed her long bill up to heaven and bawled with an edge of hysteria. "Father, why did you send me to this dark place where I no longer glow?" The sound waves lost their energy and produced a slight echo that equated to a high ceiling. She realized with relief that the large cavern contained more than adequate air.

Upon reflection Tara assumed that she had misunderstood the shepherd boy's instructions to follow him over the Himalayas. *No wonder he disappeared.* She craned her neck backwards again and shouted. "Which one of you played a trick on me?" The echo of Tara's voice slammed into her with almost palpable force. The cavern wall stood right behind her.

The bird accepted that her less than stellar judgment landed her in this underwater cavern with no way out. Deprived of her senses in the black grotto Tara needed to create her own stimulation. Vocalizing helped. "To maintain mental and physical stability I must have exercise, nourishment, fresh water, and a source of light." She made a checklist in her mind planning to plot the cavern's echoes and fly around to keep fit. "I can find fish in the waters that feed the cavern from the high-altitude lake. Protein-filled bacteria cover the slimy walls and columns. That takes care of food, water, and exercise. Now I need a light source."

Tara did her best to avoid panic considering her dire circumstances. In her mind she heard Blandina quoting Jesus. "Whoever follows Me will not walk in darkness but will have the light of life." She wondered if every person or bird possessed the ability to find "the light of life" within his or her own spiritual belief system. Until now Tara had never examined the dominion of her higher self to discover her inner flame. She vowed to nurture the spark buried deep inside until her authentic self was revealed. The divine white stork committed herself to gain enough enlightenment to purify her own soul. She hoped that she would glow once again—this time from the inside out.

"For now, I must forget the mission of the White Storks of Mercy and focus on the present moment. Discovering my true nature and identity takes top priority. My father and Yellow Hat led me here for this reason." She resolved to make the best of a bad situation. Tara lived in the cavern for thirty years protected from the harsh Tibetan climate. Her golden eyes now possessed the nocturnal ability to see in the dark.

During that time the shepherd boy Pema Dorje grew up and became ordained as a monk in A.D. 1411. The Gelug School of Buddhism considered him the worthiest scholar and holiest man in Tibet. He received the name Gendun Drupa. In A.D. 1430 he appeared at Oracle Lake.

Palden Lhamo arose with a splash from below on the mule that galloped atop the lake like a weightless water bug. Steed and rider skidded to a dramatic stop in front of Gendun Drupa. Dressed in a simple red robe, the monk pressed his hands together and bowed with respect to the deity. He lifted his head and spoke in a kind voice. "Guardian spirit of this blessed lake you kept safe a divine being who will become a notable advocate for peace. Thank you for your loyal and steadfast protection. Please take me to meet the Shimmering One."

For the past three decades the deity had spent most of her time spying on the stork from the crevasses of the deep-water cavern. She found the bird's focused attempts to transform into an alternate state fascinating. Tara fluctuated back and forth from her normal avian form into a transparent blob that beamed like the moon itself. The morphing creature displayed no discernable flesh or bones and no blood or organs. Only her central core pumped light into extremities that bore an uncanny resemblance to the arms and legs of a human.

Palden Lhamo dismounted and took the high lama via an alternate route. She guided the holy man through the secret passageway atop the cliff adjacent to the lake. The goddess led him down into the dark cavern where the Shimmering One sat in the lotus position floating above the shallow water as she meditated.

Tara felt the holy presence of Gendun Drupa as he made his way to the cave through the complicated rocky labyrinth. Over the years she had visualized his arrival in her mind. During those detailed imaginings she discovered the route to freedom up through the crevasses. Nonetheless, Tara chose not to escape her confines and fly away. Instead, she surrendered knowing better than to sidestep her destiny. She would remain in the secluded place until the monk helped her complete her transformation from bird to human. Tara sensed that his sacred blessing was required to bring the realization of her human body into fullness.

Gendun Drupa stood barefoot on the wet ground. Humidity dripped from the cavern's ceiling. Some drops plopped onto his shaved head and he chuckled. The high lama bowed with folded hands to the Shimmering One and gestured for her to join him. "Please come with me to meet yourself."

Tara exulted in celebration. "It is time!" The divine white stork followed him out of the cavern. She savored the welcome warmth of Re's sun and squinted at its brightness. Tara took off and circled above the praying monk. Palden Lhamo sat at attention on her mule that stood in the icy water. The violet-skinned deity scanned the surrounding area like an owl rotating its head in all directions. She was prepared to pounce on anything that threatened the holiest being of Tibetan Buddhism.

The high lama lifted his eyes to the sky and signaled to the divine white stork with a glowing aura. "Come Tara, let us look into these sacred waters. It is time to welcome the Great and Honorable Zendala."

"Who is Zendala?" The confused bird cruised to a smooth landing on the grassy banks next to the small-framed monk.

"You are! You have proven yourself ready for veneration into a unique human image. I prayed to Arya Tara—the Mother of all Buddhas—while you flew above earth and below heaven. She blesses you with the name Great and Honorable Zendala if it pleases you."

"I accept the name Zendala for all eternity." Gendun Drupa nodded and turned to gaze upon Oracle Lake. They watched the image of a tall and heavyset naked woman floating on the sacred waters. Her manifestation bespoke wisdom, patience, strength, and great resolve. Thick coarse white hair framed her wrinkled face. It was braided into a single plait that hung to her waist. Her bushy eyebrows accentuated penetrating golden eyes.

The nostrils of her aquiline nose flared between high chiseled cheekbones. Her lips pressed together in contemplation. It was the mouth of a powerful woman who would speak no frivolous words. The divine white stork gazed upon her human image. "I feel as if I have known her all of my life."

The monk nodded his head. "Indeed, you have. Stay steadfast to all you learned while meditating in the sacred cavern below Oracle Lake. Your limited self-conception dissolved and enabled you to experience the perfection of your true nature. You achieved the four sublime states the Buddhists call Brahmavihārās— unconditional love, compassion, sympathetic joy, and equanimity." The holy man turned to smile at the glowing white stork next to him. "When the mind dwells in these divine places it reaches out to embrace the entire world and every form of life within it."

"I welcome the fullness of my existence and I pledge to live in harmony with all forms of life. My heart overflows with gratitude and I feel a peaceful spirit cleansing my entire being."

Gendun Drupa's countenance remained benevolent and serene. "Anyone may practice mindfulness to achieve enlightenment. At your divine conception the light flickered within you. You needed to find it again after your rocky start in life."

Zendala rededicated herself to the mission inspired by Jesus Christ. Today she stood alongside another exalted spiritual leader who brought her to the brink of her future. "I am honored to embrace my destiny and take my place as a force for peace in the world."

Like a veil lifting her soothsaying capabilities returned. She foresaw the wise and gentle man standing next to her confirmed as the first Dalai Lama following his death in A.D. 1474. His multiple reincarnations would provide an "ocean of wisdom" for future generations of Tibetan Buddhists. The holy man bowed to the divine white stork. "How we live is more important than what we believe. Universal compassion is the fundamental spiritual orientation."

He reached inside his robe and took out a pouch containing her amulets. "These are yours. You may utilize the cartouche to time travel once again. You do not need the jasper stone because your metamorphosis internalized the ability to transform. Your inherent divinity assures immortality so your ring of eternity is not necessary. However, you are embracing an epic destiny that needs collaborators. Share the powers in your amulets." He laughed with boyish playfulness. "Palden Lhamo wanted to keep them for herself."

The holiest man in Tibet blessed the Great and Honorable Zendala. He fastened the ring around her ankle and placed the cartouche and jasper stone around her neck. Gendun Drupa planted a gentle kiss atop the glowing white stork's head and sent her away.

The majestic bird flew over Oracle Lake. She admired her human image that still floated on the water. She made a jubilant announcement to the world. "It is time! I am Zendala!" She tipped her wings in farewell and headed toward the Himalayas. The White Stork of Mercy glowed brighter than ever. She chanted, "Peace... joy... love..."

SAVE THE MAIDEN

Zendala identified the Cathedral of Notre-Dame as she approached the city of Rouen in France at dusk on the thirtieth of May in A.D. 1431. She joined the two white storks with black-tipped wings circling Saint Romain's tower. The leader welcomed this evidence that her companions had experienced no difficulties returning to the present time. More than thirty years tardy for their rendezvous, Zendala hoped that Maatkare and Blandina had organized the rescue of Joan of Arc without her.

The three birds landed on the high Gothic tower. The pharaoh shouted, "No time for pleasantries! Have you found your body?"

"Indeed, I did!"

Blandina spoke with urgency. "We must get into our disguises before the secular officials bring the Maid of Orléans to the execution site." They flew after Maatkare. A few minutes later she led them through an open clerestory window at the Church of the Holy Savior. It had been left ajar by Joan's friend and supporter Friar Martin Ladvenu. The three birds transformed into women together.

Zendala's stork feet touched the stone floor. She experienced her initial thrilling sensory encounter as a woman. The sensation of cold spread upward from her big flat feet and encompassed her naked body. The dark interior prevented the three Merciful Ones from seeing each other. Blandina bumped into her leader. The Christian martyr handed over a serge tunic, a leather belt, and a scapular to be worn over the baggy garment. Last she gave her leader a wimple and a veil. The costume covered her amulets.

Blandina placed identical pieces over her white tunic. She explained that Friar Martin had provided the clothing for their disguises. "You will meet him later."

Maatkare donned the garb of a priest looking the part with her short jet-black hair slicked back. On top of her kilt, she wore a white linen alb girded with a cincture under a traditional embroidered ankle-length scarf called a stole. She hid her jeweled beard and ruby earrings in a pocket of the cassock and wore deerskin gloves to hide her painted nails.

Friar Martin waited outside in the shadows guarding a covered cart carrying the corpse of a teen male awaiting burial. At the opportune time Maatkare planned to roll it as close as possible to the execution stake and exchange the dead lad for a living Joan of Arc.

Zendala dressed for the first time fumbling with stiff fingers never used before. She tucked her long white braid under the confining headdress. The "nun" placed a wooden cross hanging from a leather band over her head. She exited through the heavy wooden church doors and into the cool night where her fellow companions waited. Zendala's golden eyes shone through like those of a diurnal owl.

Maatkare stepped forward and looked up at her tall chief. "I cannot make out every feature of your face, Tara. Yet I see that Re still shines his sun upon your irises in your new female form."

The leader chuckled. "I now possess night vision as well. I call myself Tara no longer. A Tibetan Bodhisattva blessed me with a unique name—the Great and Honorable Zendala."

Maatkare made no comment about the arrogant accolade. Blandina whispered her approval. "Greetings, Zendala. I missed you." She patted the pouch of gold coins attached to her belt and explained their rescue plans as the noise of the approaching throng grew louder. Joan of Arc—who was once revered by all of

France—was led into Old Market Square like an animal ready for auction. The peacemakers knew about her incredible history but Zendala alone foresaw the prisoner's canonization in A.D. 1920 as the patron saint of France.

On this fateful night Zendala and Friar Martin introduced themselves and stood among the members of Rouen's religious community. They watched as guards tied the innocent virgin warrior to a stake. The crowd quieted when the priest stepped forward holding a large crucifix in front of Joan to offer protection for her soul.

The kindling combusted and the fire's heat grew. Sounds of hatred filled the air. Zendala saw Maatkare holding up the corpse. The ancient woman pushed forward to gain Joan's attention. "Remember your motto! Go with boldness! Not yet to heaven but to join the White Storks of Mercy on our campaign for peace. Spend your eternal life with us!"

Friar Martin also pleaded in his loudest voice. "Leave now with these ladies! I trust them, my friend. Do not sacrifice your life to hypocrites!"

Joan was almost at the point of burning. She screamed. "Help me!"

Blandina sprang into action and shouted at the top of her lungs. "Gold coins!" She threw the entire contents of the leather pouch high into the air. The distraction worked. Everyone including the clergy turned away from the burning stake to scramble for money.

Maatkare risked her own skin to save the maiden by running into the fire. She exchanged the dead teen for Joan and hauled her out of the flames. Tears of relief ran down Friar Martin's face as the Merciful Ones spirited the girl away. Zendala used her night vision and led them through the maze of dark village streets into the woods away from Rouen.

They stopped at a safe place deep in the forest. Maatkare

wiped the smoke from Joan's almond-shaped ice-blue eyes and the soot from her petite nose. Sympathy for the girl with a shorn head filled the pharaoh's heart. Joan smiled and thanked Maatkare for her gentle ministrations. She collapsed onto the forest floor. The maiden grabbed her lower back and winced. "I jumped from the battlement and injured my back at the Castle of Beaurevoir after the Duke of Burgundy imprisoned me. It pains me to this day."

The pharaoh sat down next to Joan. She schemed in silence about joining forces with her against Zendala. "Sekhmet is the ancient Egyptian goddess of healing. She will repair your injuries as she did those of Blandina the Christian martyr."

Joan stared with awe at the female on her other side. "Blandina of Lyon? You inspired me as I crusaded on behalf of God and France shouting, 'surrender or we shall destroy you.' Yet I never killed a man."

Zendala clarified, "You are a soldier for peace now, Joan. The White Storks of Mercy seek justice using humanitarian means." She sat with effort on the ground across from Joan. Her new aching body revealed her ancient age.

"Let us explain ourselves," Blandina offered. She produced four white altar candles borrowed from the Church of the Holy Savior from beneath her habit and passed them around. "Welcome to our circle, Joan of Arc. As women we are called Merciful Ones. We become the White Storks of Mercy when using magic to change our forms."

Each one in the coterie introduced herself and lit a single candle illuminating her face. All eyes turned to their leader as Zendala removed her veil. Blandina gasped. "You look very old and wise! Why do your lips appear golden like your eyes?"

Zendala chuckled. "I am over fifteen hundred years old! My lips match the color of my bill, which is different from your red one." She directed her next remarks to Joan in a calm and authoritative voice tinged with an Egyptian accent. "I also come here tonight as a stranger. Before this I existed as a divine white stork named Tara. My mother Ba is a Sacred Stork of the Bach from the Isle of Souls. Re the Egyptian sun god fathered me. I spent the last thirty years in Tibet seeking enlightenment to manifest my human form. I am now called the Great and Honorable Zendala."

The fact that she failed to mention the existence of Reba irked Maatkare. *I am pleased that she looks so ancient.* She smirked at the cosmic joke played on their chief—whose chin sagged into a neck full of wrinkles and whose teeth resembled yellow ivory. Maatkare set her candle alight. Her striking ancient Egyptian features were illuminated by its flickering glow. "You can see that I am much younger than Zendala. My parents King Thutmose I and Queen Ahmose named me Maatkare Hatshepsut in 1507 B.C. I ruled the New Kingdom of Egypt's Eighteenth Dynasty as queen, king, and pharaoh for twenty-three years."

Joan liked the exotic and arrogant middle-aged woman. She felt a commonality with her aggressive energy. Maatkare handed Joan the silver signet ring embossed with the emblem of the Cross of Lorraine that had been a gift from King Charles VII. "One of the guards nabbed it but I pinched it back."

Joan kissed Maatkare's well-manicured hand and placed the cherished ring on her own finger. "Your kindness fills me with gratitude, Pharaoh Hatshepsut."

"Please call me Maatkare."

Zendala watched with satisfaction as the two headstrong military leaders sat side by side. Blandina took her turn next. Her golden eyes flashed wide open when Blandina removed her veil and lit her taper. The teenager's deep blue eyes sparkled in the candlelight. Her skin appeared silky and smooth. Her cheeks, forehead, and eyebrows were sculpted to absolute perfection. Blandina described her background as a follower of Christ enslaved and tortured by the Romans. She provided the details of her subsequent rescue by the White Storks of Mercy in A.D. 177 and giggled as she recounted her ride on the Bull of Apis. Her pretty lips parted to reveal teeth glistening like pearls.

Maatkare spoke up when she spotted Zendala's reaction. "Our chief finds Blandina's renewed beauty astounding." She berated Zendala for flying to India right before the dawn of the new millennium. Zendala apologized and accepted the criticism with generosity of spirit. The pharaoh relished playing the heroine for her captive audience. "We flew up the Nile River into the Valley of the Kings and located my mortuary temple. I saw the top tier of the colonnaded structure and we landed in my garden of paradise. Blandina and I settled there and waited for nightfall to visit the Chapel of Hathor."

Blandina interrupted, no longer intimidated by Maatkare. "The eight-foot-tall cow-headed goddess Hathor presented herself. You can imagine my shock as a devout Christian. Living these many years as a White Stork of Mercy has expanded my belief system and I trusted this deity. Hathor restored my face and body as a favor to Pharaoh Hatshepsut."

"Such a beautiful face," affirmed Zendala. "I can see that your spirits improved as well." She turned to Maatkare and praised her altruistic behavior.

Pleased to earn these accolades Maatkare continued. "We were confident that our chief would arrive on time from India for our rendezvous. Blandina and I flew over the Mediterranean Sea, located the island of Cyprus below, and we recognized our landmark."

"The Roman amphitheater," Blandina interjected without emotion. "We spotted our stork imprints and flew toward the faded image then everything stopped."

Maatkare resumed. "It was as if energy and light encapsulated us. I feared that we ran out of life support because we missed

Seth's rejuvenation." She looked to Zendala for clarification.

"That cannot be it because we are all here now. I surmise that thirty years ago dreadful memories overwhelmed Blandina's mind when she saw the arena below. Your insistence on departing in such a hurry left her no time to process those overwhelming emotions."

Maatkare scowled. "In other words, I am responsible for our time warp."

"We all make mistakes as you pointed out regarding my own poor planning." The two looked long into one another's ancient eyes. The balance of power shifted once again.

Blandina broke the awkward silence. "In A.D. 1430 our state of suspension was released and we passed through our faded imprints. Why did it take so long?"

"We react to external stimuli and emotions provide the signals for that reaction. It took thirty years for your traumatized mind to sort through your feelings and allow passage through the portal from the past to the present."

Blandina's sigh filled her heart and soul. "I feel much better now. I hold eternal gratitude to Pharaoh Hatshepsut for her kind and generous gift. I enjoyed seeing ancient Egypt where you both originated."

The pharaoh smiled at the Christian martyr. "You may also call me Maatkare, Blandina." She turned to Zendala. "Please share the details of your whereabouts during the last thirty years."

Our authority issues continue but I am glad that she is bonding with the younger ones. "I heeded Bennu's oracle and found Shiva in India. Re introduced me to a boy in a yellow cone hat. He transformed into a bright light that guided me across the Himalayas. In Tibet the purple-skinned three-eyed guardian spirit of Oracle Lake captured me."

Joan gasped. "Oh my God in heaven!"

"The deity confiscated my amulets then left me in an

underground cavern where I lived in the dark with no means of escape. Fresh water flowing from the lake into the grotto provided fish and I also ate algae. After thirty years of steadfast meditation, I received the blessing of the Buddhist high lama and discovered my body."

Maatkare brought the attention back to herself. "Blandina and I arrived at Saint Romain's tower one year early to organize the maiden's rescue with the help of Friar Martin."

Joan's delight to sit among the supernatural Merciful Ones showed on her beaming face. "You three executed your plan without a flaw! Now what happens to us next?"

Zendala suggested, "Let us return to Rouen and provide the crowd with a spectacle compliments of Seth the god of storms." Joan frowned at the thought of going back to town.

Blandina provided reassurance to their new recruit. "Do not worry. The Merciful Ones will protect you. No matter how he conjures his magic you can trust Seth. I ought to know!"

Two medieval nuns, a priest, and a barefoot girl dressed in a charred white gown walked out of the woods and back into Rouen. Zendala took Maatkare aside. "You performed well in my absence, Pharaoh Hatshepsut. You showed yourself worthy as second in command and displayed courage not soon forgotten. Our coterie now comprises four women united for peace and we must look the part. The next time that we change from storks into humans we shall all wear the uniform I created. You may keep the pharaoh's beard in one of your pockets."

Maatkare postured a dramatic bow. "Whatever you say, Chief."

They reached the Cathedral of Notre-Dame. Blandina and Joan climbed to the top of Saint Romain's tower. Zendala and Maatkare flew up the five-hundred-foot rise. They wanted Joan to see them tonight in both stork and female forms. The two young women looked at the crowd below that continued to celebrate Joan of Arc's execution at the huge bonfire. They held hands and the maiden gained a new perspective on the horror she escaped.

The Great and Honorable Zendala transformed in front of Joan. The tall and heavyset woman wore a white mid-calf-length cotton dress with a cowl neck that framed the gold cartouche on a choker around her neck. The jasper stone hung from a leather band. A rainbow-colored silk belt circled her thick waist. Its intricate knots represented Sansara—the karmic cycle in Buddhism that ends with spiritual liberation.

The cuffs of Zendala's tiered bell sleeves reflected the pure white of her stork feathers. Her knee-high pliable leather boots mimicked the black color of her avian legs. The ancient woman reached into a pocket of the dress. She registered surprise and pleasure to find a small jade figurine of the Buddha. *Thank you, Gendun Drupa.*

The Great and Honorable Zendala posed a direct question to the newcomer. "Joan of Arc, will you join the White Storks of Mercy and live through eternity helping us guide mankind to a peaceful future?" The soldier saluted in response. Zendala turned to the others. "Shall we invite Seth to rejuvenate us until the year A.D. 1500?" Maatkare and Blandina nodded with enthusiasm.

Zendala steadied herself with a hand on Joan's shoulder. She pulled off her boot to remove the ring of eternity from around her ankle and pointed it at the night sky. The heavens emitted crackling sounds. Flashes of lightning appeared and formed a single wave. It moved toward the cathedral, surrounded the tower, and created a circle of safety.

The wondrous sight of silver and gold raindrops falling from the sky within the protective band awed Joan. Zendala whooped as she felt her new body supercharged with energy for the first time. Seth commanded a whirlwind of colorful water to encase Joan. It lifted her high into the sky. The rainbow cocoon enclosed her and disappeared.

A white stork with black-tipped wings spiraled down to the tower and made a perfect landing. She transformed next to Zendala wearing her new uniform. "I like the violet belt. How did you know my favorite color?"

"Violet symbolizes the perfect union of body and soul. It fits you. Now choose the talisman that will grant you the power of eternal life. When you close your eyes and visualize the piece it will appear around your neck." Joan of Arc selected a miniature replica of Saint Michael the Archangel carrying a sword. The shield upon his chest bore the Latin cross.

Joan reached into her pocket. She found a blue enameled badge imprinted with a golden *fleur-de-lys*. It was the lily flower emblazoned on the royal coats of arms of French kings since the twelfth century. She nodded to Zendala in gratitude for her kindness.

The appreciative maiden turned to Blandina. "What is in your pocket?" Blandina blushed with delight to find a small conch shell. She directed a pleased smile toward their leader. They all turned toward Maatkare in expectation.

She delved into her own pocket and found a small bottle of myrrh oil. The pharaoh gulped and adjusted her red belt. *I wonder if she knows my secret.*

Zendala explained, "It is her favorite scent."

The chief does not seem to be suspicious after all. In her second pocket the pharaoh located her beard along with a small stone statue of a seated cat, which she handed to her leader. "I brought this from ancient Egypt to help you forgive your dead sister. Reba loved you in her own special way." Tears swelled in Maatkare's eyes as she thought about her friend. *If you are out there Cat, I swear total fealty to you with my royal blood.*

Zendala misconstrued Maatkare's rare display of emotions and her comment regarding Reba's affection. She accepted the little sculpture, which was about the size of her thumb and slipped it into a pocket of her dress. "Thank you for the thoughtful gift. Now we must warn Joan to never take off her talisman, Maatkare."

"I am still Pharaoh Hatshepsut to you, Chief." She turned away to end the conversation.

The phalanx of four flew over the medieval town of Rouen. The villagers stood around dumbstruck in the aftermath of the spectacular light show. Gossip spread after the bell-ringer found the discarded clothing of two nuns, a priest, and a charred white gown. The following Sunday clergy throughout the region preached on hellfire and brimstone regarding the devil's handiwork above Saint Romain's tower.

The Maid of Orléans left her legendary persona behind. In spite of Maatkare's fierce objections the Merciful Ones assimilated into a tribe of French nomadic Gypsies. Joan's hair had grown out and she now sported the medieval bob haircut worn by noblemen of her time. She enjoyed trading horses with the men so Zendala gave her permission to wear breeches under her dress when she rode.

MISSING REBA

Zendala, Blandina, and Joan relished roaming around Normandy's lush pastoral region and along the jagged coastline of Brittany with their new Gypsy friends. Maatkare detested every minute of lower-class life. She would often daydream about an alternate reality as a Mischief Maker. Maatkare missed Reba even more since returning from ancient Egypt to visit Hathor. Her secret attempts to connect using the beard continued to fail and the aroma of myrrh never alerted her. Nonetheless, something deep inside assured her that the cat was still alive. Reba never thought about the adventures the two once shared.

At present the cat's subconscious mind forced her to live in denial as protection from her tortured psyche. A foul darkness had permeated her soul after she escaped the endless maze of underground tunnels. However, she discovered that by shape shifting into another species she possessed the ability to repress her past.

Reba survived as a river otter for fourteen centuries. The semiaquatic species was known for its playfulness. Nefertiti's bust and the Noah's Ark cartouche stretched around her thick neck. The gold gorget earrings decorated her small ears. This industrious and sleek mammal built her den in the hollow base of a tree accessible beneath the water. Its location was close to a resident group of trumpeter swans living in the reeds of Ireland's Lake Muckross.

She surrounded herself with the large graceful birds. They enhanced her safety because in ancient times King Lir's jealous second wife Aiofe had used magic to turn her stepchildren into swans. Ever after the king banned killing the species to protect his progeny.

One balmy day during the last quarter of the sixteenth century a pair of long-necked water birds paddled over to the mouth of Reba's den. The black swan introduced himself as Angus Og and the white swan as his wife Caer Ibormeith. Under normal circumstances in these times of religious persecution they did not admit to their true identities as divine Celtic beings.

Today curiosity about their cute mammal neighbor superseded caution and Angus greeted her with a question. "Do you know the legend of King Lir?"

"I live among swans for that very reason," Reba responded.

Caer shared her opinion with their new friend. "Such an evil trickster that Aiofe."

Angus continued the conversation. "It brings to mind the death of Merlin whose deceitful scribe and lover turned his own magic against him. The Lady of the Lake recorded his secrets, lured him into a dark tunnel, tricked him into a tomb, and sealed it!"

Without warning the dreadful images from Reba's past in the tunnels infiltrated her brain like a terminal illness. Evil worms ate away at her carefree otter spirit and she imagined her lungs filling with liquid. Her powerful webbed feet slapped at the water as the otter shape shifted into a variety of animals one right after the other. They all fought for their lives to escape the demons. The two swans watched in confusion.

A seal point Siamese cat—the encore act of the transformational performance—paddled toward the shore wailing in pain and grief. She reached land and flopped into the reeds. Heavy panting provided evidence that she had survived the dramatic ordeal. However, Reba continued to yowl because of her horrid memories.

The concerned neighbors observed her throughout the night. They guarded her from a pine marten or a red fox seeking a meal. By morning the high-pitched shrieking overwhelmed the couple's calm demeanor. Angus posed a question to his wife. "Do you think the renowned healer Orchid MacCloud might help this distraught creature?"

"I do, Husband. How do we beckon a Celtic Druidess who lives as a flower most of the time? Humans summon deities and not the other way around."

"We shall petition the flower faeries to send a message at once, dear wife."

***

Living for centuries as both the most beautiful woman and the most exquisite orchid in the world caused problems. Men lusted after Orchid MacCloud like forbidden fruit because she personified the bloom's erotic magic. She shooed them away. During her long life, the Druidess stayed true to Fig MacCloud. She vowed never to dishonor him by giving herself to another. One by one each of her twelve Druid companions passed on to the otherworld. Now she lived a solitary existence. The Druidess glowed in the dark whether in flower or female form. She became known as the Lady of Light.

As the years passed Christianity rooted itself in the soil of the country now called Ireland. The Druidess transformed into the Ghost Orchid when she sensed danger from the religious fanatics. Survival skills saved her during the European witch-hunts that occurred from before the Inquisition until the beginning of the Renaissance. She preferred the company of flower faeries, tree spirits, and woodland creatures with whom she conversed daily.

Orchid MacCloud became a legendary herbalist, enchantress, and homeopathic healer. She possessed necromantic powers that she used for the benefit of others. The Druidess grew herb and flower gardens to concoct medicines for treating various disorders. She documented her recipes and remedies in a notebook that chronicled her bountiful wisdom.

Angus and Caer contacted Orchid hoping that she treated those suffering from shrieking disorder. They needed to get some sleep. The Druidess made her way to Lake Muckross. "Thank you for finding me. I have been missing Reba for the last fourteen centuries." She recognized the ancient Egyptian Siamese cat lying in the shade of a strawberry tree. Despondent and lethargic by this time, Reba's glazed sky-blue eyes stared up at the ripened red fruit. The swans watched Orchid evaluate the immobile cat. Reba's spirits failed to improve at the sight of her old friend and Orchid became concerned.

Angus asked, "What jewelry hangs around the cat's neck? Anything of use to you?"

"They empower Reba alone. The cartouche provides the capability to shape shift and the bust keeps her young." In secret Orchid coveted Nefertiti's bust. The magic from the Elves of Sage was wearing off. After all these centuries she sensed her entire body aging. Her muscles and joints felt stiff. Her skin no longer resembled orchid petals and her skeletal frame had lost some height. Strands of silver mixed with the gold streaks in her long red hair. The youthful sparkle of Orchid's emerald eyes dimmed due to the onset of cataracts. Wrinkles lined her rosy lips and liver spots marked her elegant hands.

Caer noticed the changes in the appearance of the enchantress but feminine sensitivity kept her quiet on the subject. She asked, "Does the cat always wear gold earrings?"

"Aye. The same gorget earrings adorned her lobes the first night we met in A.D. 35. When we parted company, Reba was healthy. I cannot imagine what happened to her."

Angus mentioned, "Singing our love songs to her soothes the poor thing. Her freakish yowling drove away most of the lakeside inhabitants. What is this mysterious creature's name?"

"She calls herself Reba after her parents. The ancient Egyptian sun god Re fell in love with Ba. She is a divine white stork from the Isle of Souls. Their union created a unique cat."

"Ah…" The swans nodded their heads impressed with such an interesting pedigree.

At the mention of her name and parentage Reba's eyes closed and her body shook and shuddered. The Druidess was still dressed in her now tattered green gown and cape. She sat against the narrow tree trunk and took the convulsing feline onto her lap. She stroked her sandy-colored fur and hoped to invoke the slightest purr. Instead, Orchid heard the cat snoring. She reminisced, "The last time you occupied my lap we were resting on the outskirts of Lugdunum."

Reba awoke with a start and her high-pitched yowling resumed. Wheatear birds feasting on strawberries fled the tree's branches and the ducks on Lake Muckross made haste to paddle away. The cat flopped back and forth like a fish out of water. Angus and Caer resumed their lullaby. Orchid reached in her pocket to withdraw a vial and forced a few drops into Reba's mouth. She fell into a deep sleep once again.

"Her trauma seems connected to the ancient city of Lugdunum. I think she witnessed the prolonged inhumane torture of slaves by the Romans fourteen centuries ago."

Caer and Angus turned to each other and bowed their long necks. They touched heads and bills to form a heart. The couple hoped that their loving energy might counteract the evil memories plaguing Reba's mind.

Caer pondered the dire situation. "Will herbal remedies cure her?"

"I had intended to stay far from the European continent but Reba must confront her demons in the city now called Lyon. I hope that combining the power of herbs and flowers with honest heartfelt talks will allow Reba's emotional stability to return."

Orchid was grateful to the Celtic deities for intervening on Reba's behalf. She left southeast Ireland with the Siamese cat tucked beneath her arm. They arrived in France in the midst of the Wars of Religion between Calvinist Protestants and Roman Catholics.

Wars never deterred Orchid when needed by a friend. They kept a low profile in the bustling city and chose Parc de la Tête d'Or as the location for Reba's treatment. Within the three-hundred-acre park the Druidess found the delicate white star of Bethlehem for the cat's trauma. She squeezed juice from cherry plums to counteract her anxiety. Orchid also distilled the essences from rock rose and orange impatiens flowers into the juice to concoct a medicinal cure.

The cat swallowed the drops and showed marked improvement. To stay on the safe side the twosome remained residents of Parc de la Tête d'Or. The Druidess introduced Reba back into civilization one day at a time. She tucked the cat inside a sling created from her cape. Reba nestled at her chest. The passenger listened to the soothing beat of her friend's heart and they ventured into the old quarter of Lyon to wander the cobblestone streets. It took time for Reba to show interest in the world again.

One day the cat poked her head out from the security of her linen cocoon as they stood in front of a storefront window displaying jewelry. Orchid caught sight of her own face reflecting back at her. She felt sad to regard her fading beauty and pushed the negative thoughts out of her mind to focus on Reba. "Look at these ruby earrings."

Hat wore a similar pair. The recollection made Reba realize how much she missed her. A strong desire to communicate with her ancient Egyptian companion bubbled up. She knew that a rendezvous would require her full recovery. However, first she must overcome her phobias. She whispered, "Take me to the Roman amphitheater. I am ready!"

They made their way to the crumbling coliseum. Reba leapt free from the protective sling. She scanned the arena and decided to construct the story in her own favor. She did not want the kind-hearted Druidess to change her opinion. *I must never tell her that I swallowed my sister and kept her a prisoner in my stomach. Nor can I reveal my plans for revenge using the pharaoh as my henchwoman.*

Reba and Orchid sat side by side on a stone step overlooking the exposed tunnels. The Siamese cat recounted her biased story. "On the first day of August in A.D. 177, I tried to convince Emperor Marcus Aurelius not to harm the Christians. I wanted in particular to spare the slave girl Blandina. He aimed to please some important officials and the Roman crowd. It disgusted me so I left the royal dais and made my way into the tunnels to free some prisoners without his knowledge."

The dishonest cat took a deep breath while she arranged her story. "I spotted a gladiator attempting to strangle an innocent white stork so I shape shifted into a black panther. The fighter ran into the tunnels and I followed. He knocked me out with his shield and I spent days listening to suffering Christians scream."

The mistress of lies continued. "I am lucky I survived, no thanks to my sister Bastet. She disappeared into the celestial cosmos without helping me. I shape shifted into a monkey and crept through the bars of my cage. I took the keys from a guard and helped dozens of martyrs to escape. Then I got lost in the tunnels." Reba sniffed and pretended to cry. "I found my way out and I ran for my life. I cannot forgive myself for leaving so many captives behind. Damn those heathen Romans!"

Orchid picked up the cat and stroked her into a state of calm again. She offered her some soothing drops but Reba declined. The homeopathic flower remedy made her mind fuzzy. Orchid wiped away a few tears of her own. "You are wonderful and considerate, Reba. You did your best to save them. Now you need to let go of the past and move onto a bright and happy future."

Reba ignored her somewhat guilty conscience. *I regret deceiving my friend but I must be true to myself.* "I cannot take all the credit. My sister Sekhmet kept Blandina alive long enough for me to arrange her rescue by Seth, our god of storms. Because of me the Christian martyr joined the White Storks of Mercy."

"The who?"

"The supernatural alliance started by my sister, Tara." *I no longer consider her my sister.*

Orchid yearned for her own dear sibling. "You enjoy a sister? What a lucky cat."

Not really enjoy, Reba thought. "Tara stole Pharaoh Hatshepsut from me as her first recruit and then Blandina."

Orchid looked shocked. "How unfair."

"At least before her kidnapping Maatkare lived a long life with me by her side. As she neared death, I conjured incredible magic to grant her immortality." Reba lied again. "I also gave Blandina the gift of eternal life right before her rescue."

The cat wanted to impress Orchid further by demonstrating an ability to summon deities whenever she felt inclined. "Do you want to meet Sekhmet? She is a healer like you. Do not let her lioness head alarm you." A few seconds later Sekhmet and Bastet materialized. The eight-foot-tall cat-headed goddess sauntered over and lifted Reba off Orchid's lap without asking.

Reba hissed into Bastet's ear. "Who invited you?"

Bastet carried her sister away and gave her a private warning. "Change your attitude or I shall reveal the lies you told your friend." She raised her voice so that Orchid might hear. "Sekhmet and I searched the Roman coliseum night and day looking for our missing sister."

"Why did you leave me in that horrible tunnel?"

Bastet lowered her voice again. "Because you refused to let me follow you. Did you save any Christians?"

"Not one," Reba admitted. She snuggled against Bastet's heart to curry her favor. "The part about getting knocked out and terrorized in the tunnels happened. I escaped and returned to Hibernia. I hid until Orchid found me. I owe her both my sanity and my life."

Meanwhile Sekhmet and Orchid got acquainted. The goddess learned that the Druidess was born during the Iron Age and possessed gifts of magic. Their mutual talents for brewing homeopathic potions for healing inspired them to trade recipes. It impressed Sekhmet to know that her fellow healer communicated with flowers, faeries, and all of nature's creatures. Reba jumped down and returned to Orchid. She was jealous of her rapport with Sekhmet.

The Druidess accepted the cat's company once again. "Here is my heroine. Do you intend to return to Ireland with me?"

Reba imagined a future with someone who always stood upon the moral high ground. *She will never agree to join my Mischief Makers and I dare not manipulate her mind.* "Thanks, but I shall remain in France. I prefer to occupy the laps of monarchs. Royalty does not exist in Ireland. Take care of yourself, Orchid. I noticed that you show signs of aging. I bet you wish that you had a bust of Nefertiti like me."

Orchid chuckled and kissed the top of Reba's head. "Aye, you are a fortunate cat." She stood, straightened her old, long green gown, and nodded with respect to the sister goddesses. Reba jumped off the stone step and trotted away from the Druidess without looking back. Orchid shook her head with resignation. "Goodbye, my friend. May our paths cross again."

Reba, the Great Persuader with a knack for mischief, called back to her sisters. "Let us go find a French king whose royal lap needs warming."

BEHOLD THE ILLUSION

In A.D. 1587 the White Storks of Mercy prepared to fly to England for the rescue of Mary Stuart, the Catholic queen of Scotland. Joan balked when Zendala informed her phalanx about their next recruit. "Why add another sovereign?" *The domineering Pharaoh Hatshepsut fulfills that criterion.*

Maatkare agreed with fervor. "I am the sole royal and it needs to remain that way." She was glad to leave the Gypsy caravan behind. *If the Scottish queen joins us perhaps her status as a fellow monarch will result in future upscale accommodations.*

Zendala tolerated no complaints. "My decision stands. The queen of Scotland exceeds my standards as a candidate." Maatkare and Joan scowled at the inevitable. "Queen Elizabeth I of England decreed decapitation for her cousin Mary. I intend to prevent it."

Blandina moaned. "Her head will be severed by her own cousin?"

"I saw her fate. It takes more than one blow from the axe to finish the job." The storks groaned in unison. "I shall tell you more after we cross over the English Channel." They flew from Calais, France to Dover, England and landed on the steep white cliffs. The birds clustered together to hear the story of the queen of Scotland.

Zendala explained that Mary's father King James IV died on her sixth day of life. When the Scots crowned their baby queen her mother Mary of Guise ruled as regent. She arranged the child's marriage to the French dauphin Frances II. At the age of six Mary travelled to France and ten years later they married. The young king died the following year. Mary's mother passed away soon after. When she turned eighteen Mary returned home to rule in her own right.

Joan's mind opened to consider the potential new addition with a French connection.

The leader continued her history lesson. "Prior to that Mary Stuart's great-uncle, the English monarch King Henry VIII separated from the Roman Catholic Church. He appointed himself the supreme head of the new Protestant Church of England." She paused to ensure that the others followed her chronology.

"In A.D. 1558 his daughter Elizabeth succeeded her elder half-sister Mary I as queen of England. The Catholic minority considered Elizabeth illegitimate and supported Mary, Queen of Scots because she descended from the Tudors. Mary asserted her claim to the English throne many times but England's Protestant majority refused to legitimize them."

Blandina sighed. "Once again religious strife rears its ugly head. Does it ever end?"

Zendala answered, "I am sad to say that bloodshed between opposing religions worsens throughout the world as the future unfolds."

Joan chimed in. "I am sorry to hear that as well. It stymies our efforts."

"Nothing will stop us, Joan." She continued, "The young Catholic queen of Scotland married again and gave birth to her son a year later. A rebellion forced her to seek asylum in England and her crown passed to thirteen-month-old James VI."

Maatkare voiced her cryptic opinion. "It reminds me of ancient Egypt where trading crowns and titles between relatives was much like a game of musical thrones."

Zendala paused. "I note your expertise in that area, Pharaoh Hatshepsut. Elizabeth kept Mary confined at various locations for twenty years contemplating her wearisome cousin's fate. The continued presence of Mary in England posed a threat to the precarious religious balance that Queen Elizabeth I worked hard to achieve."

Blandina interrupted, "It does not excuse her actions against her cousin."

The leader concluded her recitation. "When Mary attempted to free herself, she was accused of plotting to assassinate Elizabeth. At first, she refused to sign the execution warrant. However, in the end the queen of England yielded to her ministers."

***

During the second week of February in A.D. 1587 the White Storks of Mercy landed on the banks of the River Nene close to Fotheringhay Castle. Ice covered the neighboring marshes. The howling wind sent snowy twisters swirling past the four storks as they huddled against the castle. Joan craned her long neck up to study the imposing curtain wall with its crenelated battlements. "I am well known as a strategist with superior leadership skills. May I take charge?"

"Thank you for offering, Joan." Zendala considered her options. "However, if Mary agrees to join us her rescue will require ancient Egyptian magic."

Maatkare raised her voice above the wind. "I volunteer!"

"What do you propose? I am unaware that you dabble in the magical arts."

Maatkare desired to see Heka again. He had reignited her lust at their reunion on the Isle of Souls. "One god alone possesses the power and resourcefulness for this job. I know how the god of magic can save the queen of Scotland. He will find this challenge intriguing." English sentries patrolled the castle walls above them. Zendala gathered the wading birds closer together. The shivering storks ruffled their plumage to generate warmth while Maatkare provided the details of her plan.

Inside the tower the pale forty-five-year-old monarch sat at a writing desk. She inscribed her final letters in the flickering candlelight. Mary wore a long high-waisted wool dress the color of burgundy over a kirtle and smock. She expected no visitors and removed an embroidered linen cap to expose her short gray hair. The unhealthy woman's scalp showed signs of balding.

The birds soared between two circular turreted towers and flew through the chamber window. They transformed into women. The queen of Scots almost fainted. She exclaimed, "God sent His angels!"

"In a manner of speaking," agreed Zendala. She stepped forward and bowed with respect. "Mary, Queen of Scots I present the White Storks of Mercy. In female form we are called the Merciful Ones. We are not angels but we are supernatural." She motioned to her coterie that made a cohesive impression in their new uniforms. Maatkare raised her chin and preened in preparation for her introduction.

"These two young ladies come as close to angels as you will find on this earth. You may remember them from your history books as Blandina the Christian martyr and Joan of Arc the Maid of Orléans." The two stepped forward and bowed to the Scottish queen. Maatkare frowned with dismay at Zendala's apparent disregard.

Mary reacted with shock. "But you are both deceased!"

True to her style Joan took the initiative. "As you can see, we are still alive."

Zendala pointed next to the short olive-skinned older woman. "The history books remain silent about Maatkare Hatshepsut. She was the fifth pharaoh of ancient Egypt's Eighteenth Dynasty.

An unscrupulous relative erased all recorded evidence of her rule. I can attest that as queen, king, and pharaoh she remains the greatest ruler ancient Egypt ever knew. She serves as my second in command." Maatkare's mouth gaped from pleasant surprise at the unexpected accolade. She realized her own worth but was unaware that the chief agreed on the matter.

The ancient woman addressed the reason for their presence. "I am the Great and Honorable Zendala, the leader of our coterie of peacemakers. I also hail from the Egyptian Old Kingdom. We travel through time seeking keys to the doors that will bring peace to your planet. One key unlocks the door to universal religious acceptance. If you now embrace our mission you may join us." Mary's expression changed from awe to joy when she realized that she could choose life over death.

The Scottish monarch stood and gained her full six-foot stature. She made the sign of the cross and kissed her pearl rosary beads. A moment later her regal shoulders slumped. "I am unworthy of this intervention for I failed as a queen. I put many innocents to death because of their religious beliefs."

Blandina stepped forward. "I am pleased to remind you that the birth of your son assured the survival of the royal House of Stuart."

Zendala divulged a bit of the future to the overwhelmed queen. "It overshadows any shortcomings and insures your legacy. In sixteen years, James VI of Scotland becomes King James I after uniting the kingdoms of England, Ireland, and Scotland to form Great Britain."

Mary's eyes widened at the remarkable revelation. "I have not seen my son since infancy. I love and miss him every day." A flash of hope made her round hazel eyes sparkle. "If I join your cause may I reunite with my son?"

Joan took the tall queen's hand. "You must appear to die as I did one hundred and fifty years ago. This we cannot change. It is imperative that your son believes this. Everyone else must also acknowledge your death."

The Scottish queen needed to consider her options. She walked across the room and closed the window against the night's chill. Mary turned and faced the ancient leader. "Great and Honorable Zendala I accept your invitation to join the White Storks of Mercy. I thank you all in advance for saving my life." Looking up to the heavens, she sighed. "It will take a miracle from God to mastermind the faking of my death."

Maatkare took over. "Your god does not feature in my brilliant plan. I shall summon the extraordinary Heka. He is the powerful ancient Egypt god of magic. Here is what I need…"

Mary heard the simple request and laughed for the first time in years. "During my confinement I often played chess with my dear companion, Mary Seton." She pointed across the room to a huge stone-carved Tudor-style fireplace that was the room's sole source of heat. In front of it two identical high-back chairs faced each other across a small wooden table. They saw a thirteenth-century walrus ivory chessboard with thirty-two game pieces lined up and ready for play upon the game table.

Zendala beckoned to Maatkare and they walked with Mary to the far end of the chamber. They studied the chessboard together. Maatkare selected a knight and ran a long polished black nail along his sword. "The executioner," she stated. She picked up the bishop. "I imagine that instead of a Catholic chaplain they will send a Protestant minister."

Mary looked over the short pharaoh's shoulder and frowned at this insult. She chose the rook. "This piece must serve as my jailer. How will a game of chess prevent my death?"

Maatkare responded, "The execution takes place as a clever illusion. Perception becomes reality. Let me demonstrate how ancient Egyptians accomplished this sort of thing."

The pharaoh removed the jeweled ebony beard from her

dress pocket. She placed it on her chin to create a stronger visual effect. "King Nectanebo II employed artifice when enemies attacked his naval fleet. He wore a prophet's cloak and carried an ebony rod into a special chamber during the battle. He filled a bowl with sacred water and placed into it the wax figurines of miniature ships that held his sailors and those of his foes. The king invoked the gods to bring the naval battle to life. He sank the enemy fleet with his rod and the real vessels sank too."

"You plan to create my execution on this chessboard at the same time it takes place in the great hall?" The possibility awed Mary.

"I myself am not a practitioner of magic. The great Heka will do the honors if he perceives the pending execution to be unjust. You will sit across from him as he maneuvers the chess pieces. Heka will conjure his simulation that appears genuine downstairs."

The magician made his dramatic appearance from within the flames of the fireplace. The handsome and muscle-bound Heka was dressed in nothing but his white kilt. This caused a giggle between the two younger women.

Mary gasped when she spotted two serpents suspended in the air clasping his magical cloak in their fangs. They disappeared when it dropped to the stone floor next to his bare feet. The queen stifled a scream when the snakes wound around the god's staff until they reached the level of his black scarab irises. The awestruck Mary felt a pang of excitement as she regarded Heka towering over her own six-foot frame.

Maatkare calmed the queen. "Fear not. The serpents represent rebirth." She offered her colorful manicured hand to Heka. He kissed her knuckles. His long black ponytail fell over his shoulder and brushed Maatkare's forearm. Her cheeks flushed with desire as she backed away.

The mighty magician turned to Zendala. He greeted her

in his deep and seductive voice. "This new look suits you Tara, daughter of Re and Ba."

Immune to his charms she bowed with respect. "Thank you, Heka. I am now called the Great and Honorable Zendala. Please allow me to introduce Mary, Queen of Scots."

Mary raised her head high and held out her slender freckled hand. The flirtatious magician ignored it and instead he planted lingering kisses on both sides of her face. Mary's cheeks reddened and she pulled away. A jealous Maatkare glared at her new competition. She felt a moment of regret at proposing Heka's involvement.

The magician and his serpents examined the chessboard. He knit his brows together. "Ah, this represents the execution platform and the pieces symbolize the participants?" Heka sat down to study the scenario. "It presents a challenge. Everyone please leave the queen and I alone."

On the eighth of February the illusion of Mary Stuart walked into the great hall at Fotheringhay Castle. She was dressed in black with a red petticoat and garter that signified her martyrdom. Her short gray hair lay hidden beneath a wig that was covered by a lace veil. To the assembled crowd she appeared regal and unafraid. The four Merciful Ones waited with them.

Upstairs the true Mary was dressed in the same clothing. She sat across from Heka and watched her mock execution as the ancient Egyptian deity moved the chess pieces with his mind. The pawns that represented the crowd lined up on both sides of a three-dimensional framework extending above the chessboard. The hand-carved ivory queen graced the platform. A sword-wielding knight and one of the bishops stood right and left of the condemned monarch. Mary sighed, "The time has come."

Heka nodded his agreement. "Have no fears and behold the illusion." In the great hall below the conjured Mary climbed the scaffolding with the help of her major-domo. An emotional Mary

Seton tied a white handkerchief over the eyes of the condemned woman and gave her a final embrace. Mary's beloved dog—a Skye Terrier named Geddon—ran onto the scaffolding to hide under her petticoat. The courageous Scottish queen knelt and placed her neck on the chopping block. All the while she prayed without ceasing.

Joan and Maatkare stared forward with stoicism. Zendala and Blandina bowed their heads. Neither of them wanted to witness the horrific spectacle. The Christian martyr stifled her scream at the sound of the axe hitting Mary's neck three times.

Upstairs the real queen of Scotland closed her eyes and grabbed her long elegant neck. When she heard moans and screams coming from the chessboard the poor woman fainted in her chair. Heka completed his job and left the table. He lifted the tall woman into his arms with ease and delivered her to the bed. She was still very much alive.

The god of magic gazed down with admiration. Mary's lily-white skin reminded him of beautiful lotus blossoms. To ancient Egyptians the flower signified rebirth. He bent over and whispered to the unconscious queen. "Heka gifts you with the return of your splendor and restores your health."

He examined her freckled oval face, dominant nose, high forehead, and strong cleft chin. *She is not a classic beauty but I find her quite attractive.* He touched her cheeks to bring the color back and reshaped her thin reddish brows with perfect arches. Heka placed his finger upon her pale mouth. Mary opened her hazel eyes that held a renewed sparkle.

The shy queen parted her lips and with boldness she beckoned a kiss. He complied then brushed his mouth down her undamaged neck. They shared an ironic laugh. The magician helped the queen to sit up and propped a pillow behind her. He sat on the bed and placed his hands on either side of her head. Heka massaged her scalp with his magical fingers. Mary's hair returned to its former bright red color and grew into long tight curls.

The magician conjured an ivory comb embedded with precious jewels. He twirled the queen's hair into a bun and fastened it with the comb before hanging a pair of pearl drop earrings onto her lobes. "This completes my work." He kissed Mary's small but well-defined rosy pink lips once again. The god returned to the fireplace and snatched his cloak off the stone floor.

Mary reached out for him. "When will I see you again?"

"Our paths may cross in the future. Heka makes no commitments." He grabbed his staff and disappeared into the flames.

The Merciful Ones entered the chamber and beheld Mary's restored loveliness with great pleasure. Maatkare sought Heka and was disappointed that he had gone without waiting for her.

Mary stood next to the bed and attempted to smooth the wrinkles from her black dress. Zendala approached the queen. She seemed flustered from Heka's magical ministrations. "Do you have any questions before we travel together through time for eternity?"

"Will Heka restore my aspect as I age?"

"From this day forward, you will remain as you look now."

"I enjoyed his lingering attention." She glanced at the glowering Maatkare. To fuel the pharaoh's envy Mary ran her long fingers up and down her neck. She blushed at the memory.

Zendala opened the tower window and called Mary over. "The soul requires cleansing to determine your worthiness. Seth the ancient Egyptian god of storms will set your body on fire with a bolt of lightning as you fall."

Maatkare provided additional intimidating information. "As the fireball enclosing you descends and exhausts itself you will fly away in the form of a stork. However, if Seth deems you unworthy you will plunge to your death." The pharaoh smiled at the prospect.

Mary joked in an attempt to disguise her fear. "It sounds more inviting than a beheading." *My relationship with Pharaoh Hatshepsut is going to prove challenging indeed.*

Zendala took Mary's hands in her own. "You need not fear the result. My sixth sense has shown your place among us. Do you trust me?" The queen affirmed her confidence. Zendala ordered her to jump out of the window. Mary's eyes widened. "I promise to catch you. Sit on the ledge and go down feet first. Hold your arms straight above your head."

Mary watched as Maatkare, Blandina, and Joan leapt out of the window and transformed. Zendala asked, "What is your favorite color?" Mary answered that it was indigo. Zendala smiled. "Indigo symbolizes fairness, impartiality, wisdom, and justice." The leader jumped from the window and circled back when the Scottish queen gathered her courage and fell feet first from the high tower.

The divine white stork with a glowing aura grabbed Mary's hands with her strong feet and propelled them both high up into the sky where the mighty Seth waited. She flew into the eye of his powerful thunderstorm and let go of her passenger seconds before a lightning bolt hit Mary's human form. The queen exploded into a fireball that headed straight down toward the castle. Below them the English nobles screamed and covered their heads. They feared that their Protestant God was punishing them for beheading the Catholic monarch.

The human fireball transformed into a white stork with black-tipped wings. A tiny carved ivory replica of the queen's Skye Terrier hung on a leather band as her talisman. The five White Storks of Mercy flew across the River Nene leaving Fotheringhay Castle in the distance. Mary followed Maatkare with Joan on the pharaoh's right and Blandina on her left in a diagonal to their leader. The new formation bore a distinct resemblance to a cross.

THE FRENCHMAN AND THE PHARAOH

A dozen years after liberating Mary the White Storks of Mercy flew over the southern part of England. They headed toward the crude prehistoric monument known since the twelfth century as Stonehenge. From a distance the massive circular stone cage situated on the frozen grassy plains bespoke an intimidating and eerie presence.

Zendala called out to her followers. "Stonehenge possesses neither the sophisticated architecture of the Great Pyramid at Giza nor the impressive apex of the Pillars of Hercules. However, this mystical location serves us well tonight for our revitalization."

Mary offered, "I remember hearing whispers about the legendary Druid Merlin when I was a child. He used his magic to transport these building blocks from Éire where giants first constructed the site on top of Mount Killarus."

"Ah, Merlin." Zendala entertained affectionate thoughts about her mythical hero. *I do want to meet him someday.* "Let us remain as storks on this cold winter night. Seth's drops are effective in either form."

The big wading birds landed on a large stone lintel. The god of storms released the first of six stars from a dark sky filled with cosmic glitter. Zendala shared her plans for the near future. "It is quite dangerous to join back up with a caravan in France. Most countries in Europe now enforce stringent anti-Gypsy laws."

Maatkare asked, "Does this mean we shall not reside with

the nomads again?"

"I realize it is not your preferred lifestyle, Pharaoh Hatshepsut. I thought you and I might take a trip into the future to meet a most interesting Frenchman."

"Anything is better than living with Gypsies."

The ever-confident Joan posed a question. "I should come as well. I speak his native tongue and can translate for you and the pharaoh."

"Thank you for your offer, Joan. The noted Egyptologist Jean-François Champollion speaks fluent Coptic. He deciphers hieroglyphics that reveal details of our ancient civilization to the world through its formal writing system."

Blandina asked, "What connection does he share with Maatkare?"

The impatient Joan interrupted, "How far into the future will you go?"

Mary exclaimed, "You cannot leave us behind to survive on our own!"

"Hush now all of you and trust me." Zendala realized that reprimanding personalities of such historical eminence required diplomacy. "Maatkare and I shall accelerate forward to A.D. 1829 and meet the Egyptologist at Deir el-Bahri where he made an exciting discovery at Pharaoh Hatshepsut's funerary temple."

Maatkare exhaled the words, "Damnation of my memory."

"Do not fret, Pharaoh Hatshepsut." She gave instructions to the others. "After our ceremony tonight Blandina will lead the three of you to the Camargue wetlands at the Rhône Delta in southern France. Mary needs to practice the finer points of avian life."

Joan inserted her opinion about this matter as well. "With all due respect to Blandina I am the most qualified leader and the I know French geography."

Maatkare voiced her support for the Christian martyr. "Do

not forget that Blandina has been a stork thirteen hundred years longer than you, Joan. She is qualified."

Zendala schooled the French maiden. "You need to follow my orders without hesitation, Joan. I am in charge here." She continued addressing the group. "Our trip lasts less than one year. We shall rendezvous at the ancient village of Saintes Maries de la Mer."

The Scottish queen informed them, "That community features a fortified church built in the ninth century to honor Mary Salome, Mary Jacobe, and Mary Magdalene."

Blandina caught Mary's excitement. "The three holy Marys witnessed the empty tomb of Jesus Christ after his resurrection. They fled and settled there to avoid persecution."

Another star fell from the sky and then one more. Zendala brought the discussion to an end. "Pharaoh Hatshepsut and I shall return for the three of you in nine months."

Zendala glanced to the heavens and sensed Seth's impatience. The fifth star dropped and the glowing stork flew off. She circled Stonehenge and landed to transform into her ancient human self. Zendala removed her boot, slipped off the copper ring of eternity, and pointed it upward. Minutes later, silver and gold drops of ionized water fell on them providing a perfect energetic connection for time travel. Zendala advised Blandina, Joan, and Mary to depart. The leader returned to her divine avian form and disappeared with her second in command.

**

Jean-François Champollion was deep in concentration while decoding hieroglyphics at the Temple of Hathor. A pair of storks landed on two exposed columns that no longer supported the temple roof. He gasped with surprise as the long-legged wading birds peered down at him. The Frenchman grabbed his chest.

"My God! My heart rises to my throat!"

Zendala chuckled. *Wait until you see what happens next.* She cruised down to the man covered in dust and changed into her female form. Her white dress danced in the hot breeze and her ancient golden eyes stared straight at the Frenchman. Jean-François fell backwards into the wall and sank down onto his derriere.

"I am the Great and Honorable Zendala, daughter of the ancient Egyptian sun god Re, with whom you possess familiarity." She gestured at the other stork. "We are two of the White Storks of Mercy. In human form we call ourselves the Merciful Ones. We travel through time as peacemakers from the past trying to save the world for the future. My colleague and I appear today to explain why a male pharaoh is depicted when the hieroglyphics refer to the monarch as a female." She offered the flabbergasted Frenchman a gnarled hand and helped him up.

He brushed off his backside. Maatkare studied the handsome thirty-nine-year-old with wavy dark hair and studious brown eyes from her perch on the column. The scholar wore strange clothes that proved impractical in the heat of the Sahara Desert. Tight tan breeches and a black waistcoat accentuated his fit body and tasseled leather boots reached to his knees. A large white handkerchief knotted behind his head served as protection from the hot Egyptian sun. Drawn to the mortal, Maatkare awaited her introduction. *Please allow me to transform in my own clothes.*

"I am pleased to present my second in command Maatkare Hatshepsut. She was the fifth pharaoh of the Eighteenth Dynasty of the New Kingdom of Upper and Lower Egypt."

The stork flew down and settled on the stone floor in front of the Egyptologist. Her avian body transformed into the regalia of a pharaoh. A royal blue and gold striped Nemes headdress topped with its golden sacred serpent framed her fifty-year-old face and the ebony beard adorned with precious stones served an enhanced purpose today. Her ruby and silver earrings dangled in their proper places. *Thank you, Chief.*

Maatkare raised her chin with pride and with her charcoaled eyes half closed she held out her royal hand to the stunned Frenchman. He bowed, kissed her fingers with his warm lips, and noted her ten exotic fingernails painted with alternating red and black polish. "I am enchanted."

Not as enchanted as I. The pharaoh blushed. She was drawn to this mortal and had forgotten about Heka.

Zendala left them alone in the Temple of Hathor. From the upper courtyard she looked around the grounds. Time and rampant looting had proved unkind to the once incredible wonder. The discoveries made by Napoleon Bonaparte thirty years earlier caused all of Europe to want a piece of ancient Egyptian history. The French emperor's campaign had unearthed the Rosetta Stone making it possible to decipher the language of hieroglyphics.

The smitten pharaoh spent nine months helping Jean-François decode the temple walls. Zendala ventured out on solo excursions. She flew along the Nile River and witnessed wanton destruction. Centuries of war had left cities like Heliopolis in ruins. Zendala found these forays depressing so she sought a reprieve in the Sanctuary of Amun.

There she contemplated many things including where to live after they returned from their sojourn. The leader decided on the region in southern Spain called Andalusia that was circumscribed by the Mediterranean and Atlantic coastlines. Zendala felt called to the area along the Costa de la Luz. Here wading birds of various species occupied wetlands created from the Tinto and Oriel rivers flowing into the Gulf of Cádiz.

The area appealed to her abiding interest in the culture of Gypsies who had been persecuted throughout history. Their status as an underclass drew her to them. She felt more determined than ever to pursue their humanitarian mission. The ancient woman had perceived pinpricks of inspiration hovering around the edges of her consciousness. Zendala sensed that she verged on the precipice of choosing a sixth Merciful One. She remained patient in her understanding that destiny unfolds at its own pace.

In September of A.D. 1829 Jean-François informed the pharaoh that his Franco-Tuscan expedition prepared for its return to Cairo. She led him into the Temple of Hathor. "I am pleased that the depiction of Hathor as a four-legged cow did not erode over the centuries. She still licks my right hand." Maatkare removed a square stone from the wall. She reached inside the secret compartment and took out her first silver and lapis pharaoh's beard. "Please accept this gift for decoding the mystery of my existence. I wore this ornamental beard during my entire reign."

Jean-François held the herringbone-patterned accessory in both hands. "Tell me why you present yourself as a male instead of honoring your femininity as did Queen Cleopatra?"

"Do not compare me to her! She was not even a true Egyptian." Maatkare's brief flash of anger passed. "In my day custom dictated that females were subordinate to men. Performing the rituals and roles required as a monarch necessitated promoting oneself as male." She blushed. "I assure you Jean-François that I am all woman."

The Frenchman took Maatkare in his arms and kissed her. He ached to remain with the enigmatic ruler but this proved impossible. He forced himself to pull away. "Ancient Egypt has intrigued me since childhood and I remain under its spell. I shall always cherish your ornamental beard and my exquisite memories of you."

"You retrieved my place in history. For that my gratitude to you will endure forever."

He chuckled. "You and your companion give the word 'forever' a new meaning." They left the Temple of Hathor hand in hand. "Where and to what year will you travel next?"

"Zendala determines our path and I remain second in command. It is a position in which I find no comfort. She has a penchant for helping others. I imagine that we shall live among the Gypsies again."

"Is that a dignified life for the sole female pharaoh that the world will ever know?"

"I had chosen a different path that disappeared when a certain ancient Egyptian Siamese cat vanished off the face of the earth."

"I am reminded of a famous cat idolized by past French monarchs. Kings Louis XIII, XIV, XV, and XVI even featured their treasured pet in royal family portraits."

"I doubt we speak of the same cat. She died in A.D. 177. Now my destiny lies with the White Storks of Mercy and the whims of the Great and Honorable Zendala."

"A renowned pharaoh such as you serves no one but herself."

"You are correct. I may yet rule again." The seed of a mutinous plan that did not require Reba rooted itself in Maatkare's scheming mind. The Frenchman and the pharaoh bid each other a poignant farewell.

That evening Zendala suggested that they fly to the top of the rugged limestone cliffs overlooking the various archeological sites. The two sat together in the moonlight. Maatkare dressed once again as a Merciful One but she still wore her beard. Zendala shared her calling to live among the Gypsies in southern Spain.

The pharaoh gestured down toward her temple. "I feel immense gratitude to you for this trip into the future. The knowledge that my memory is no longer damned has removed a huge burden from my heart. However, you are aware of the misery I endured while living as an undesirable in France."

"I beg you to support me on this, Pharaoh Hatshepsut."

The Egyptian monarch raised her palm as if defeated. "You may forget the formalities and call me Maatkare."

"Thank you, Maatkare. My decision stands and I shall brook no opposition. Prepare to say goodbye to Egypt. We are going to Spain where the Gypsies find it easier to assimilate in spite of the persecutory laws. They live better in that country than in other areas of Europe. In Romania the Gypsies wear shackles on their arms and ankles as well as triangular yokes around their necks like animals." The pharaoh showed no signs of sympathy and continued her foray into silent self-pity. Zendala ignored her. She got to her feet and shook out her stiff limbs.

Maatkare also stood. "What if I refuse to become a Gypsy and remain here in Egypt?"

"Did we not hold a similar conversation back in 100 B.C.? If you do not wish to remain under my leadership you may give me your talisman right now. I warn you that it is a long way down without wings." She walked to the cliff's edge and waited.

The pharaoh remained on the rocks and seethed. Her jeweled beard protruded in defiance. She felt tempted to throw the obsolete communication device off the cliff but stuffed it into the pocket of her white dress instead. Maatkare rubbed her earrings to calm down. Several minutes passed before she called out to Zendala. "Wait for me! I am coming!"

The ancient woman stepped off the cliff without a backwards glance and transformed into a glowing white stork. She regained her equanimity and released her disappointment with the pharaoh's rigid attitude. Maatkare took a leap with an exasperated scream and changed form to join her chief. She flew in second position whether she liked it or not.

Once again in real time the two storks flew over the Camargue region that consisted of three hundred forty thousand acres of wetland, dunes, green pastures, and hills of salt. Below they beheld a flamboyance of white flamingos with pink wings and a siege of gray herons. They marveled at a concentration of kingfishers highlighting the landscape with their royal blue and orange feathers. These glorious sights failed to improve Maatkare's foul mood even when they saw a herd of wild horses galloping through the surf.

The two White Storks of Mercy flew in the direction of Saintes Maries de la Mer. Zendala anticipated her reunion with the three even-tempered Merciful Ones. She was eager to make their new home among the Gypsies of Andalusia on the Costa de la Luz.

IN THE COMPANY OF KINGS

Zendala was anxious to secure their new residence so she took the coterie forward in time to A.D. 1722. They flew over the Sacromonte district in southeastern Spain. This area was home to the cave-dwelling Gypsy population outside Granada. The birds landed high on a hill where no one saw them transform. The Merciful Ones followed their leader down to an empty cave. This delighted Blandina, Joan, and Mary. Maatkare hated their new home.

The unique and affordable lodging featured whitewashed walls that reflected light. It provided warmth in winter and refreshing cool temperatures during summer months. Generous new Gypsy neighbors shared blankets, candles, tin cups, and utensils.

During their first evening in the cave Zendala presented some ground rules. "Our purpose here involves helping in whatever ways we can. We aim to fit in. That means you may not wear your beard, Maatkare." She encouraged her coterie by sharing insights into the future. "In A.D. 1856 legal freedom is granted to Gypsies in the Balkan States. In time conditions improve for these people in other countries too."

Mary cherished her new life of freedom and its many changes. She enjoyed wearing her white dress with the indigo-colored belt cinched around her small waist. The first time she transformed following her rescue the queen of Scotland was pleased to find the jeweled ivory comb conjured by Heka fastened in her hair.

The pearl earrings hung from her lobes as well. She reached into one pocket and discovered the cherished pearl rosary gifted by her son. A small journal and pen occupied the second pocket. *Zendala thought of everything.*

Blandina and Mary became acquainted with a Gypsy woman called Tshilaba. Her name meant seeker of knowledge. They were fascinated by her ventures into the mystical arts of Tarot cards and palm reading. Blandina also nurtured a more exciting interest. She loved to watch the flamenco dancers and listen to the exotic music that accompanied their flashy moves. Tshilaba gifted her new dance student with a bracelet made of moonstone beads.

Things remained tense between Zendala and Maatkare and few words passed between them. The ice thawed when they observed Blandina trying the less graceful "flamingo" style of dance. After living full time in stork form surrounded by other wading birds the movements felt natural to her. Zendala and Maatkare stifled snickers as Blandina flapped her arms and hopped around on one leg. The pharaoh remarked, "I am relieved to see her happy and carefree."

"And you? What might lift your spirits, Maatkare?"

"I crave new stimulation. Why do you insist on living in Spain? I prefer to reside in the company of kings."

"You need to learn tolerance and compassion."

"Do not presume to know my needs! I demand the freedom to wear my own clothes and to put on my beard when it pleases me."

"Calm down, Maatkare. We are not going back to France. By travelling ahead in time from A.D. 1600 to A.D. 1722 we avoided the Black Death. A million French citizens lost their lives to the plague that ravaged France. Does it make you feel better to know that King Philip V of Spain descended from the former French king Louis XIV?"

The mention of this particular monarch jogged Maatkare's memory. She harkened back to what Jean-François mentioned about a famous cat idolized by French royalty. "Please tell me about the French royalty starting with Louis XIII."

Zendala hoped that after indulging Maatkare's curiosity she might tire of the subject. The seer closed her eyes and envisioned the House of Bourbon. "In A.D. 1610 Louis XIII gained the throne after the assassination of his father Henry IV. His son Louis XIV inherited the crown in A.D. 1643."

"I want to hear more about him."

"He reigned longer than any monarch of a sovereign country in European history. Louis XIV kept many mistresses and bankrupted France building his lavish palace Château Versailles. The self-righteous Catholic ruler called himself the Sun King and claimed that God had chosen him. He committed his worst offense by abolishing the Edict of Nantes. It robbed his subjects of religious freedom. He survived both his son and his grandson. The king's great-grandson Louis XV ascended to the throne in A.D. 1715 at five years of age. Until he reaches maturity next year the kingdom has been ruled by the Duke of Orléans Philippe II."

Maatkare made a quick calculation. *The Siamese cat portrayed in imperial French paintings had lived for more than a century. This solved the mystery of Reba's whereabouts!* The pharaoh smiled with relief.

The seer continued her prognostication. "Louis XV will reign for sixty years and he will replicate the lifestyle of the former king and further deplete the French treasury. The king bought frivolous gifts including a multi-carat diamond necklace for his mistress Madame du Barry. He will die from smallpox before she receives it and Louis XVI will inherit the throne."

Zendala paused to gain a clear picture of the future. "Louis XVI will marry Marie Antoinette the Archduchess of Austria.

She will bribe a cardinal to purchase the infamous multi-carat diamond necklace for her. This will fuel the outbreak of the French revolution. The people will overthrow the monarchy and establish the French Republic. In A.D. 1793 a new invention called the guillotine will behead both the king and the queen. During the Reign of Terror thousands of aristocrats will lose their lives." The ancient psychic opened her golden eyes.

"Thank you, Chief." *I need to warn Reba not to risk her life at the hands of the French rabble.* "When I joined your cause, I put forth a caveat…"

"…That you needed to get away on your own from time to time," interrupted Zendala.

"Now is one of those times."

Zendala raised a bushy white eyebrow and peered at her with suspicion. "Why the sudden interest in the French monarchy? Does a certain Egyptologist still hold your interest?"

Maatkare replied with directness to her chief's innuendo. "I am not allowed to time travel without your permission so I cannot visit Jean-François. Just tell me when to return."

"If you insist on leaving us now, you must come back no later than A.D. 1756. This gives you over thirty years to find what you seek."

Maatkare stewed with resentment at needing Zendala's consent to live her eternal life as she saw fit. She asked, "Why A.D. 1756?"

Years earlier Zendala's sixth sense had alerted her to an exceptional baby's birth on the first of June in A.D. 1746. She had envisioned the newborn's Gypsy mother studying a crystal ball as she watched the images of five storks landing to transform into women. Zendala had heard the new mother whisper, "My baby's destiny connects her to these supernatural beings."

Maatkare snapped her fingers to bring Zendala back to the present. "Chief?"

"We shall travel to Montserrat to rescue a ten-year-old orphaned Gypsy girl."

Maatkare scoffed. "You plan on forcing me to spend an eternity with a Gypsy?"

Zendala insisted, "She is my chosen one."

Maatkare stood and stalked away in anger. She transformed and flew northeast towards France without saying goodbye to the others. The pharaoh rejoiced in the freedom of her solo adventure. The stork flapped her wings at an easy pace for three days. She arrived at the lush Loire Valley in western France. Its countryside was dotted with picturesque châteaux. Maatkare spotted a series of manicured geometric gardens featuring stairways, terraces, statues, marble fountains, ponds, and pathways. A huge canal fed into a manmade octagonal lake. Beyond the water feature stood a three-story baroque palace the size of the Temple at Karnak.

This looks better! She recognized Château Versailles from her discussion with Zendala but it appeared vacant. *I better snoop around as a stork rather than an exotic foreign woman wearing peasant clothing.* Maatkare flew between a pair of symmetrical pools and landed at the top of a marble staircase. The front of the palace showcased repetitive arched windows on two floors with a ribbon of smaller square windows on the third. Closed draperies impeded her sight.

The nosy bird ambled around the corner. A curtain left ajar in the second bay of windows allowed her to see into a cranberry red room gilded in gold. On the far wall she spotted an unusual portrait of the French royal family. They were dressed as ancient Romans. A group of women in colorful long mantles surrounded Louis XIV who posed as the sun god Apollo. The king sat on a throne wearing a sleeveless toga embroidered in gold thread. His long and curly dark hair brushed bare white shoulders.

Maatkare spied Reba sitting on the king's lap in the portrait. She recognized the bust of Nefertiti and the cartouche of Noah's

Ark. Her heart burst with delight. *Cat is alive and she is wearing the earrings that I gave her!* The bird studied the painting further and saw Bastet and Sekhmet standing in the background.

I need to find a remote place to change form and try to contact Reba one more time. She took to the air and followed the canal until she came to a wooded area. Maatkare landed and transformed in front of a crumbling lichen-covered wall. She removed the jeweled beard from her pocket and attached the piece to her fleshy chin. The pharaoh asked Nefertem to send Reba a whiff of myrrh and stroked the ebony wood with its precious embedded gems. She whispered, "Cat? If you can hear me please respond with your location and the date."

Maatkare waited until the blue sapphires sparkled. Over her thudding heartbeat she heard the voice of Reba answer. 'I smell myrrh. Hello, Hat. It is A.D. 1722 and I am in Paris with Bastet and Sekhmet. Where are you?' The pharaoh provided the details of her location.

Reba exhibited her characteristic nonchalance. 'I shall persuade the gullible twelve-year-old king to return to Versailles with me. It is my favorite palace. I have spent most of my time there as the official royal pet. Expect to find me at Versailles in mid-June. Wait at the Fountain of Latona but remain in stork form. It is not in your best interest to show up as a female pharaoh. Once we meet I shall lead you to the Grand Trianon Palace where it will be safe for you to transform.' The cat ceased sharing her thoughts.

Three months later the stork waded around in the designated multi-tiered fountain adorned with sculptures of lizards, turtles, and frogs. The marble statue of the Roman goddess Latona stood in the top basin. Her two infants Apollo and Diana clung to her legs. The jets of water shooting into the air annoyed Maatkare so she flew to the roof above the Hall of Mirrors.

Reba arrived and paced back and forth in front of the fountain that gushed water well beyond its basins. *I despise getting wet even more than I hate waiting. Where is Hat?* She recognized the stork's silhouette on the steep black Mansard roof. The cat reared up onto her hind legs and signaled for Maatkare to follow her.

She trotted across the landscape while the stork flew overhead. Fifteen minutes later they approached the single-story palace built of pink marble and porphyry called the Grand Trianon. Instead of following the rigid angular walkways Reba made a beeline toward the palace. She jumped over the fragrant flowerbeds, loped through the spacious courtyard, and trotted up a few steps to the open-air promenade. Maatkare flew between two double Ionic columns and landed on the black and white checkerboard marble floor. The pharaoh transformed into a human. Reba noted that rather than an ancient Egyptian monarch she resembled a peasant.

The cat laughed outright. "Nice outfit, Hat." Maatkare ignored her and plopped down onto the floor. She opened her arms. Reba climbed onto her lap and purred at the attention. "How is your thieving leader? Does she have any new members?"

"Tara meditated her way into a human body with the help of a Tibetan monk. She now calls herself the Great and Honorable Zendala and transforms along with the rest of us. She is a tall, sturdy, and wrinkled old woman with a long white braid."

Reba sneered. She was pleased to hear that her former sister's appearance lacked both youth and beauty. "I shall never call her Zendala."

Maatkare continued her update. "Joan of Arc and Mary, Queen of Scots joined the coterie. Including Blandina we now number five."

The cat winced at the memory of Lugdunum and recounted her traumatic experience in the tunnels of the coliseum. She segued into her life as a river otter on the Emerald Isle. Reba followed with the tale of her rescue by the Druidess, Orchid MacCloud.

"I stayed out of touch for fourteen centuries. Orchid healed me and returned to Ireland. I remained in France. I met the young Dauphin Louis XIII on my way from Lyon to Paris while he was hunting in the woods of Versailles with his father." Maatkare asked if she ever conversed with the various royals. Reba shook her head. "I do not want the Catholic monarchs mistaking me for a witch disguised as a Siamese cat."

"I saw Bastet and Sekhmet looming in the background of a painting with the royal family dressed up like Romans. Those two pose a far taller threat than a talking cat."

"Ah, the portrait of the Sun King and his family is one of my favorites. The night before we posed for it Bastet and Sekhmet attended the Masquerade Ball. The king marveled at their clever costumes. They won the grand prize and he invited them to join us in the painting. They disappeared after that. I shall shape shift into an exquisite woman and marry the king when I get my paws on Tara's jasper stone. I will be able to control all of his decisions. Blandina, Joan, and Mary will make excellent ladies in waiting and you may serve as my chief advisor."

The snobby cat's vision insulted the proud pharaoh. "Lest we forget, once a monarch always a monarch. I suggest that you reverse the roles."

Reba was lost in her imaginary delusions. "You must convince Tara to visit Versailles."

"She sets the agenda and the rest of us follow her lead. When can I meet your king?"

"Sorry but that is not possible." Reba raised her snooty nose. "A woman with your skin type resembles a Gypsy and the French despise them."

Maatkare seethed with disgust. "Do you hear yourself? What if I compared you to a rat? I shall not suffer discrimination because of my complexion! I travelled here to get away from the Gypsies!" The Great Persuader stared into her friend's dark brown eyes and transmitted soothing thoughts to calm her down. Maatkare's ire abated. "In A.D. 1756 I must return to Spain. Do you expect me to fly around for three decades enjoying the French countryside?"

Reba nodded. "That sounds like a good idea."

Exasperated and hurt, Maatkare pushed the cat off her lap and stood up. "In that case I shall return to the Merciful Ones. At least they show me a little respect. I warn you to watch your furry head. Stay away from Madame Guillotine." Maatkare ran a menacing finger across her throat in a slicing gesture and left the promenade. She jumped off the marble steps, transformed into a stork, and flew away.

"What are you talking about? Who is Madame Guillotine? How dare you leave me! I am your one true friend! Do not even try to apologize for your rude outburst and sudden departure." The peeved cat trotted away from the Grand Trianon and returned to the main palace. She knew that the young king awaited her presence to warm his royal lap. Reba put Maatkare out of her self-serving mind.

The pharaoh returned to Andalusia way ahead of schedule. Blandina, Joan, and Mary met her at the opening of their cozy cave with warm greetings. Zendala noted that Maatkare appeared troubled and dissatisfied. She welcomed her back into the fold with no questions asked.

The following day the pharaoh hiked down from the hills of Sacromonte looking for some willows or long grasses to harvest. She decided to occupy herself by weaving a mat for their cave. During their years in France basket weaving had provided her with a connection to the ancient Egyptians who had been experts in this particular area. She used the repetitive activity to calm her roiling emotions. Maatkare spent her time alone creating a plan to regain her personal freedom without giving up eternal life. Reba's disloyalty motivated her to plot against Zendala on her own behalf.

MY CHOSEN ONE

According to Gypsy customs babies received their formal names during the rite of ablution and blessing. The parents of the infant born in Cádiz on the first of June in A.D. 1746 called her Iona. In gratitude to their midwife, they added the name Alexandra. The surname designated the location of the child's birth. The baby envisioned by Zendala was baptized as Iona Alexandra Cádiz.

In those days the government required nomadic Gypsies to either settle in assigned places or face execution. Iona's parents refused to give up their inherent lifestyle and were punished. Before their capture Iona's mother read her four-year-old daughter's fortune. "Good luck goes with you. My child will fly with five magical beings through the portals of eternity."

Later that day her parents were lynched. The despairing girl with huge and wide-set dark brown eyes stared up at their lifeless bodies. They swayed back and forth from a tree branch. Iona covered her small heart-shaped face with her hands and wept until she had no more tears.

Now she was alone in the world. The thin olive-skinned youngster was sent to a Catholic poorhouse in a village near the Monastery of Montserrat. Her sole possession was the small knife her father had used for whittling. On Iona's eighth birthday she received no gifts. Instead, the nuns gave her away to a place where juvenile workers received room and board as payment for their labor. The holy sisters needed to use her bed for another orphaned Gypsy child.

Iona joined dozens of neglected children sitting in the hot Spanish sun where hundreds of small statuettes rested on shelves waiting to be painted. The icons were wood-carved replicas of the Black Madonna also known as Our Lady of Montserrat. Devout Christians made pilgrimages to the area and waited in long lines to see the venerated statue. It occupied a protected space in an alcove behind the monastery's main altar. Over the years many miracles were associated with her interventions and the faithful travelers purchased the miniatures as souvenirs.

At first Iona felt overwhelmed by the abundance of identical mahogany statuettes. Her low hairline encroached over a narrow forehead beaded with sweat. Iona wiped away the moisture with the back of her dirty hand. She ran her fingers through thick and wavy coffee-colored hair. The intimidated orphan stared at the icons in awe and blinked her long dark lashes in rapid succession. It was a nervous habit born of insecurity. Indoctrination about her inferiority as a Gypsy festered in the mistreated girl's mind. She felt unworthy to touch the Black Madonna.

The proprietor threatened the timid orphan with his rattan cane. Iona snatched up a brush, dabbed it in paint, and imparted a golden hue to a miniature crown. The statuette depicted the Black Madonna resting on a throne with the Son of God on her lap. He grasped a seedpod that symbolized life. She held an orb representing the universe. They both wore beatific smiles. Iona prayed to the carved icons while she worked and asked them when her luck would change.

After two years of tedious eye-straining work Iona found a forgotten chunk of mahogany wood on the floor. She felt inspired to create her own version of the Black Madonna. Iona's small hands whittled for hours each night while the other children slept. She wielded the small knife passed on by her father. The orphan smoothed and polished the rich brown wood with a small piece of pumice and a rag. Iona had to squint to keep her sun-damaged eyes in focus.

One day Brother Carlos—a stooped old monk who collected the icons ordered by the Abbey—passed through the residential dormitory on his way to the workshop. He noticed a unique sculpture sticking out from beneath a straw mattress. The curious monk picked it up.

Brother Carlos appreciated the way the artist had manipulated the mahogany to capture the soft curve of the young mother's face. Her tranquil and delicate features had been brought to life. Her downcast eyes gazed upon the countenance of Baby Jesus and a faint smile played upon her lips. The sculpture depicted only their faces so it took imagination to visualize the infant cradled in the protective arms of his mother. The artist had carved the back of the piece into a gentle arc that portrayed the Madonna's veil and robe. A touch of gold paint was applied to the pupils of her half-closed eyes as if reflecting her Holy Son's inner light.

The well-intended monk was captivated by the wooden sculpture. He wished to meet its creator to inquire about purchasing it. The proprietor identified the Gypsy girl called Iona as the culprit. The cruel master threatened to lash her with his cane. Brother Carlos was horrified and intervened. The infuriated owner tossed Iona out onto the street after selling her unique carving to the monk for double the amount he charged for the other icons.

Brother Carlos felt responsible for her predicament and took charge of the orphan. The sick old monk lifted the girl onto his donkey. Iona straddled the beast of burden. She held the sculpture against her chest with one hand and grasped the animal's mane with the other. They transported a load of souvenirs up the steep path toward the monastery.

The monk stopped in front of a sheer rock wall. He pointed his forefinger to a cave ten feet above them on the cliff. Brother

Carlos addressed Iona in a gentle voice. "You cannot live with the Benedictine monks so this must do."

Iona squinted up at her new dwelling. Tears filled her endearing big eyes and her full lips quivered. Her voice was timid and sweet. "Thank you for rescuing me. You have answered my prayers." She forced a weak smile that broke his heart. The old monk had chosen a location accessible by a primitive pulley system installed years earlier. Her hands and arms were strengthened by years of manual labor. The barefoot Gypsy girl pulled herself up the ropes and into the cave. Brother Carlos placed a jug of water and her sculpture of the Black Madonna on a plank attached to the system.

"I shall bring you a blanket and pillow along with a towel and some soap. Perhaps I can also find a pair of shoes. Each day I shall deliver food and water to you. For now, detach the rope from the metal wheel. When I toss it up to you tomorrow you can reattach it to pull up your provisions." He made the sign of the cross and departed. Once again Iona found herself alone in the world. She called after him. "Please pray for me, Brother Carlos." She held onto her Black Madonna for comfort.

Back in Sacromonte Zendala meditated in the cave home of the Merciful Ones. She felt a deep love bloom in her heart as she visualized the vulnerable Gypsy girl in her own cave dwelling. Poor nutrition stunted the misfortunate child's growth and permanent circles stained the skin under her eyes. Even so she recognized Iona from her vision a decade earlier and yearned to protect her. The following day the White Storks of Mercy flew to Montserrat to rescue Zendala's chosen one. The time for Iona Alexandra Cádiz to meet her destiny grew near.

Through no fault of his own Brother Carlos did not fulfill his promise. On his previous visit the monk had taken his usual care to hide the primitive delivery system behind the rocks. Two days passed as a depressed and starving Iona pondered her predicament. She whimpered, "Without a rope I cannot escape." She prayed to the heavens as the sun set. "Please help me, God." At that moment she saw five storks flying overhead.

"What kind of help is that?" Exasperated and displaying a childish temper, she threw her Black Madonna out of the cave. It tumbled down the rocky mountainside and gathered speed before bouncing into the cemetery on the plateau below. The icon alighted upright next to an empty grave. A crucifix engraved with the words *Brother Carlos of Montserrat* rested upon the fresh dirt. The kind Benedictine monk had died of consumption.

The Gypsy girl stared with resolve over the cliff's edge. It was only a short distance to freedom as long as the narrow ledge below broke her fall. Iona gathered her courage, closed her eyes, and jumped. She landed short of the path. It caused both of her feet to wedge in the crevice between two boulders. She howled in excruciating pain.

The storks soared too high above to hear the shriek but Zendala felt it deep in her soul. She issued a terse command to Maatkare. "Take the lead. Due south of here you will see the Convent of Santa Maria. A dormitory is located on the east side of the cloister for travelers that visit the Monastery of Montserrat. Take the others inside after you transform. Light a candle on the windowsill so I can identify your room. I shall meet you there."

Zendala left the group and spiraled down to the cemetery. She landed next to the grave intended for Brother Carlos. The scratched and dented statue rested on the mound next to the cross. The bird pecked at a small piece of mahogany and it splintered off. Zendala spoke, "I gift you the power of ancient Egyptian magic to become my chosen one's talisman." The fragment turned into a miniature replica of Iona's Black Madonna. It hung from a leather thong.

The divine stork retrieved it with her bill and flew up to where Iona was trapped between the rocks. The petrified girl mistook the bird for an albino vulture. She waved her skinny arms in defense and screamed. Zendala sensed her fear. *I must land further away and transform.* She took off again and soared past Iona to settle on the narrow ledge several feet away. The ancient woman with golden eyes approached the crying girl. "Do not fear, Iona. My name is Zendala and I am here to rescue you."

"Where is Brother Carlos? How do you know my name?" Iona's Spanish accent was noticeable even through a voice choked with tears.

"The gentle monk has passed away. He would not have abandoned you." Zendala stepped closer. "I know your name because I possess the gift of sight. On the day you were born I envisioned your mother gazing into her crystal ball. She beheld five white storks that landed on the earth and transformed into women. She knew her daughter's destiny was connected to us."

"I cannot remember my mother. Did she love me?" Iona attempted in vain to pull her legs free and groaned in agony.

Zendala moved toward the suffering child and bent to embrace her. "She loved you very much, dear child. My four companions and I shall love and care for you now. Do you want to become a magical bird and fly through eternity with us?"

Iona's huge brown eyes widened with hope and amazement. She sniffled. "A bird? Does this mean my luck has changed?"

"Yes, it has my chosen one." Zendala removed the amulet of the Black Madonna from around her neck and placed it over the girl's head. "Never take this off. It is your link to eternal life." She raised both hands up to the sky and summoned Seth. "Mighty god of storms ease Iona's suffering and quench her thirst. I trust in your wisdom and believe that this innocent one requires no spiritual cleansing. Please transform her into a White Stork of Mercy."

Gentle raindrops fell, wetting Iona's lips and refreshing her body that was now free of pain. She showed signs of renewed vitality. "I must leave and bring the others back here. The ancient Egyptian god Seth will watch over you until we return. Welcome to our family, Iona."

The divine stork flew away. The boulders opened to release the trapped Gypsy girl. A minute later her thin legs and damaged feet turned into the long red legs and feet of a stork. Her frail frame morphed into a bird and she grew downy feathers. In rapid succession Iona's arms changed into black-tipped wings that spread out parallel to the ground. The neck and head of a common stork with a pointed red bill topped her new body.

Iona's dark brown beady bird eyes looked around in wonder. The three-foot-tall storklet giggled with abandon for the first time since before her parents had died.

FORTUNE BROUGHT US TOGETHER

Zendala flew south to the Convent of Santa Maria. She soared over the cloister and located the illuminated window identified by the taper on its sill. The bird landed in a field away from view to transform. She entered the room and saw Blandina and Mary each holding the hand of a novice. The fortunetellers reading their palms captivated the young women. They sat in pairs on two beds while Maatkare and Joan stood in a corner frowning at the charade. The pharaoh welcomed her chief with typical sarcasm. "They think we are Gypsies because of our uniforms."

Zendala sensed a desperate vibration emanating from one of the novices who posed her anguished question to Mary. "Will we both complete our probations and take our vows as Sisters of Santa Maria?"

Mary opened her hazel eyes wide and implored Zendala to help. She feigned a trance to buy time and chanted in unrecognizable Scots to gain credibility. The authentic soothsayer threw a disapproving glance at the pretenders and approached the novices. "Are you certain that you want your futures revealed?" They nodded in unison. *I must make this quick. A hungry and confused storklet awaits her new family.*

Zendala sat down on the third bed and removed her black boots. She assumed the lotus position. The seer smoothed her dress and asked for their silver crosses. They rose and removed the religious symbols. The novices took their seats on either side of Zendala and introduced themselves as Cybele and Sabrina Córdoba. The siblings were awed by the ancient power the psychic exuded.

In order to predict a person's future with accuracy the soothsayer had to shift her energy. After a period of concentration, she and her subject joined in a vibrational match. If nothing from the physical or spiritual world caused interference, she would obtain insight into that person's past, present, and future.

I shall only give Cybele enough information so that she follows her heart. Zendala closed her eyes and caressed the crosses between her fingers and thumbs. "One of you becomes a nun and serves your order for many years until your natural death. The other will leave the convent to marry a Frenchman."

Sabrina gasped and stared at Cybele in disbelief. "You love Henri Bour Bon? He delivers casks of cognac to Mother Superior!"

"I do," Cybele confessed. She directed her attention back to the psychic. "I beg for your advice. My family expects me to marry Christ and not Henri."

Zendala took the hand of the distraught girl. "Some people serve their god in religious orders and others serve their families." She lifted Cybele's chin with her gnarled finger. "I predict that you and Henri will raise your children in southwest France. Many generations will follow from your union."

"This means that you will leave me." Tears rolled down Sabrina's cheeks.

Zendala envisioned their father disowning his daughter for leaving the convent to marry a foreigner. To state this aloud qualified as an intrusion. She refused to meddle and returned their crosses. "Go now with peaceful hearts." Cybele insisted that Zendala keep her necklace as a lasting reminder of her gratitude. The novice hoped it would keep her connected to the mystical old woman. Zendala resolved to pass it on to one of Cybele's descendants. The novices departed.

Blandina sought more answers. "Please tell us about Cybele and Henri's life together."

"Fortune brought us together with these young women tonight. During our journey through time as peacemakers we shall encounter some of Cybele's progeny. The Bour Bon family tree will even branch out into Portugal and Scotland." Mary smiled at the mention of her country of origin.

Zendala raised her hand to stop their questioning. "Fortune will also bring us together this night with our newest recruit. Let me tell you more about my chosen one who waits for us near the Monastery of Montserrat." She shared the tragic story of Iona Alexandra Cádiz and her disastrous jump to freedom. "In the future when Iona is in human form she will squint and walk with a pronounced limp. As a stork her vision is perfect and she will wade without constraint."

Joan voiced her concern. "The girl is only ten and we are adults! How will she fit in?"

"You are nineteen and Blandina is fifteen," reminded Mary.

"Iona will always demonstrate immaturity in both bird and human form. This is her nature. We must keep a close eye on her. She will tend to get into well-intentioned trouble. Iona must complete a one-hundred-fifty-year apprenticeship before I grant full powers to her. I expect you all to take her under your wings and teach her."

Joan pressed on. "What happens after we collect her?"

"We shall fly back to Andalusia and let Iona set our course from there."

This information gave Maatkare a brilliant idea. *I intend to tell the impressionable young apprentice how to respond when she is asked where to go next.* Other tempting thoughts ran through her mind about how to mold the storklet to do her bidding.

Zendala insisted they proceed. "Is there food here? The poor thing needs nourishment."

Joan grabbed a loaf of shepherd's bread given to them by the nuns and tore it apart. They gathered the pieces and stuck them in their pockets. The Merciful Ones left the convent on foot and transformed when they were out of sight.

Near Montserrat the vulnerable storklet stared with trepidation at the full moon. "What if they do not return? I cannot yet fly." She cried out with relief when she beheld five storks silhouetted against the lunar glow. An even more awesome sight occurred when they landed and transformed to surround her. Iona attempted to make the sign of the cross in recognition of the miraculous event. She shrieked with childish delight as she remembered that wings now replaced her skinny arms. "You brought friends!"

Each Merciful One introduced herself to the fluffy young bird. The ladies emptied the bread from their pockets and Iona gobbled it up. Zendala explained the basics to her chosen one. "After you complete training you will become a full-fledged White Stork of Mercy with the ability to transform into a human Merciful One. Meanwhile you will remain a bird at all times."

"I promise to be a good student."

The ancient leader laughed. She looked around at the members of her coterie and winked. "Shall we show Iona how we do it in reverse?" Except for Maatkare they all took off into the air.

"I shall stay here and make sure she is okay." While the others showed off various flying techniques Maatkare removed the pharaoh's beard from her pocket and stuck it on her chin to impress the storklet. The smell of myrrh caught her by surprise. The blue sapphires sparkled in the dark and connected with Reba.

Maatkare heard the cat's high-pitched voice in her mind. 'Still mad at me? We need to get on with our plan to steal Tara's jewelry.'

Maatkare answered with reluctance. She knew that the likelihood of a successful heist would increase with Reba's participation. "I shall make sure that we visit Château Versailles soon." The Siamese cat signed off.

Iona asked, "What is that smell? Who are you talking to? Do I get a magical beard?"

"It is none of your business and no you do not! The beard is mine from when I ruled ancient Egypt. It is our secret that it smells like myrrh and sparkles sometimes. Got it?" Maatkare's intimidating charcoaled eyes glared at the storklet. Iona gulped and nodded. The pharaoh changed tactics. Her husky voice now oozed with sweetness. "Zendala will ask where you want to go after you are able to fly far distances. Please suggest Château Versailles near Paris as a favor to me."

"Where is Paris?"

"In France." *It will be so easy to influence this pathetic creature.*

"Where is France?" *But not so easy to keep my patience.*

"North of Spain. No more questions!" Maatkare patted Iona's back. "Let us promise to keep each other's secrets. We can be best friends."

The thrilled storklet nodded. "You are my first friend ever."

Maatkare put the beard back in her pocket. She waited while Iona gathered the courage to spread her wings and fly off the cliff. Multiple shouts of encouragement came from the storks flying above. Iona jumped and flapped with all her might. Maatkare joined her in the sky. She called out to the storklet next to her. "You fly at the end of the formation. I am second in command and follow our leader."

"Okay, best friend. I shall do whatever you say." They joined the others. Zendala led the White Storks of Mercy in a cross configuration through the star-filled night. Now six silhouettes passed in front of the full moon.

TELLING SECRETS

It required almost a year for the White Storks of Mercy to fly back to their cave above the walls of Granada. Under normal circumstances traveling five hundred miles through the air took a couple of days. Iona's lack of stamina slowed them down and there was no doubt that she often exercised poor judgment. Nonetheless, her good humor provided much needed levity among the group of heavyweights and her compassionate heart won them over.

They all bonded with the silly storklet. Joan showed considerable protective instincts toward her and taught Iona how to speak French. Maatkare insisted that the apprentice learn ancient Egyptian history. She took the storklet under her wing and indulged her own ulterior motives to bolster their pact.

One day while on a flight drill Iona landed with a long skid and knocked into Zendala as she sat like buddha on one of the pharaoh's woven mats. The mortified apprentice apologized and tried to tidy Zendala's dress with her sharp bill. She poked her leader several times.

Zendala raised her arms in mock defense and chuckled. "No harm done. Keep practicing, Iona. It takes time to develop the strength to fly long distances in diverse and demanding conditions as we do. Once you graduate from training, I shall vest you with the power to change from a stork into a Gypsy girl with a ballerina's grace."

"Thank you, Zendala. I shall do as you say." Iona took off

again and the rest of the coterie joined their leader. They sat and watched the young bird attempt to maneuver the basics.

Zendala put into words what they all realized. "It will take a great deal of patience for her to master flying."

Maatkare voiced her frustration. "Meanwhile we are stuck here."

Joan brought up a dire dilemma. "If we stay in Andalusia with the Gypsies, we need to lock Iona in a bamboo cage. They roast anything that flies."

Mary remained sensitive to the mental anguish caused by curtailed freedom. "I want no part in keeping her behind bars even for her own safety."

All eyes turned toward Blandina. "I agree that Iona's well-being takes priority." *I will miss my flamenco lessons with Tshilaba.*

Maatkare reminded, "You told us that Iona could set our course for the future." *The storklet better not forget my instructions.*

Joan stood up, placed two fingers in her mouth, and whistled. The apprentice flapped her wings and made a wide turn. She headed toward the cave with too much velocity.

"Oh dear," warned Zendala. "Watch out." Blandina and Mary helped Zendala to her feet and they cleared a wide path.

Joan realized that Iona was zeroing in for a crash landing. She moved forward and held out her strong arms to catch the young bird. The nervous storklet thanked her. Four of the ladies sat back down and Iona settled next to the maiden.

Zendala remained standing and turned to her apprentice. "It is time to leave our home with the Gypsies. You may select our next destination."

Maatkare focused with intensity on the storklet. She urged her on with charcoaled eyes and a wry smile. Iona gulped. "I know! Château Versailles near Paris."

Joan gawked at the bird and laughed. "Do you even know where it is located?"

Iona answered with pride. "In France north of Spain."

Zendala confirmed her choice. "Good idea, Iona. We shall take it slow. Twenty-six years provides enough time. An amazing event takes place at Versailles in A.D. 1783." The others perked up with curiosity but their leader offered no additional information. Maatkare excused herself and sought privacy. She asked Nefertem to alert Reba with a whiff of myrrh. The pharaoh positioned her beard and stroked it to communicate with the Siamese cat.

***

It was a long journey for Iona and a challenge in tolerance for the others. The six storks flew over the magnificent grounds of Château Versailles in time to see a gigantic silk balloon inhaling fire into its belly. Zendala had already explained how the helium craft operated. These facts went in one feathered storklet ear and out the other. Iona saw the balloon and hollered, "Fire breathing dragon!" In a panic she flew to the west façade of the château.

Members of the French court and thousands of Parisians filled the manicured gardens to witness the grand display. King Louis XVI and Queen Marie Antoinette relished the sight of the Montgolfier Brothers making history when they launched the first lighter-than-air craft. The remaining storks flew above the Grand Canal and crossed over to the Fountain of Latona. They landed and stayed in stork form to watch the inventors place a duck, a rooster, and a lamb into the bamboo basket that was suspended by thick ropes. The huge balloon hissed like a snake as it rose into the sky.

Maatkare was impressed. "What a feat!" She urged the others to get closer.

Zendala responded, "You go ahead and enjoy the spectacle. I shall find Iona. Transform into women when you are ready to meet me at the Hall of Mirrors." The four storks took off and circled the hot-air balloon. The crowd gasped with awe at the incredible sight.

Reba stood inside the Hall of Mirrors. She watched from one of the seventeen mirror-clad arched windows and felt jealous of the four showy white storks with black-tipped wings. "Where have Tara and her silly storklet gone?" Reba felt safe speaking out loud because she was alone in the gigantic room. The Siamese cat used one-way transmissions with her eyes to message silent commands to royalty and courtiers. However, she looked forward to talking aloud to Maatkare.

Reba was bored and irritated by the plebeians invading her gardens so she pranced up and down the grand hall. The Siamese cat relished her images in the umpteen gilded mirrors. She spotted the king at the far end of the long gallery. Louis XVI strutted down the hallway and wiped his brow with a lace handkerchief. He lifted the decorative dark blue ribbon crossing over his chest and reached inside the pocket of his pale pink coat for his jeweled snuffbox. The king inhaled a dab of the powdered tobacco to calm himself after standing among the noisy crowd.

Reba trotted toward him just as a storklet flew low into the majestic Hall of Mirrors right behind the monarch. The cat sneered. She recognized the uncoordinated pathetic newcomer described in Maatkare's message. Reba ducked behind one of the pedestals positioned between the arched windows facing the gardens. Each gilded sculpture of a barely clothed woman held an ornamental tubular vase that supported a multi-tiered crystal chandelier.

As usual the bird landed with too much speed and skidded across the slippery parquet wood floor. She slid toward the elegant-looking man standing in the middle of the wide hall. Iona squealed at him in French. "Look out!"

The king's eyes widened with shock as he registered the idea of a talking bird. Instincts took over and he stepped aside as the storklet slid by. He wiped his brow again and shook his head in disbelief. Iona came to a stop halfway into the spacious hall. She gaped at the opulence then noticed her own reflection in a mirror. "Hey, that is me! I have never seen myself."

The well-dressed stranger approached her. He wore dark pink shoes with golden heels and buckles. White knee-length silk stockings covered his skinny calves and pale pink breeches matched his gaudy coat. The lower half of the coat sleeves— handmade of delicate gold-threaded lace—hid a portion of his manicured hands. Intelligent blue eyes, a strong nose, and well-shaped lips accented the king's powdered white face. Rouge enlivened his cheeks. He sported a white wig with tight curls above his ears.

The excited storklet hoped to make a favorable impression after her awkward entrance. "I like your fancy clothes. Pink is my second favorite color after yellow. The Great and Honorable Zendala says that yellow means happiness, honor, and loyalty." She recited the French words with perfection.

The king found the bird enchanting and the unique situation marked a welcome change from the company of obsequious courtiers. "I am impressed by your command of French."

"Joan of Arc taught me on our long flight here. It took twenty-six years because I am such a slow flier and needed many breaks. What do people call you anyway?"

He chuckled at the naive bird. "Louis-Auguste, King Louis XVI of France. And you?"

"Iona Alexandra Cádiz the first. I lived in Spain as a ten-year-old orphan Gypsy girl until Zendala rescued me from starvation and turned me into a bird." She told him all about the Merciful Ones. "When the others turn into birds we are the White Storks of Mercy." The proud storklet puffed out her feathered chest.

The king shook his head in wonderment. "This is a fascinating tale indeed. I hope to meet your Zendala and the others." Reba growled from her hiding place. She pranced toward them with her nose in the air. She was jealous of the attention that her king paid to the bird. "Ah, here comes Bijou. She is the only cat I know that wears earrings and never ages."

Reba disliked the name Bijou but she appreciated the king's regard in bestowing upon her a name that translated as jewel. The monarch hated cats. Reba convinced him to adore her through mental manipulation when he gained the throne and inherited the official royal feline. The king's pet circled the storklet's legs and wrapped her long brown tail around its thin ankles. She tried to establish eye contact to lock into Iona's mind but the bird closed her eyes. The cat's attempts to stake its claim made her nervous. She lifted a leg, tucked it into her plumage, lost her balance, and fell over.

"Oh dear! You scared Iona." The king picked up his cat and placed her in the crook of his arm. He bent over to stroke the bird with his other hand. "Are you all right, little storklet?"

Iona was embarrassed by her clumsiness. She scrambled to her feet and ignored his question as well as the cat. She cocked her head upward to the masterful artwork covering the vaulted gold-framed ceiling. "Why are the paintings up there? They are kind of hard to look at."

"My ancestor King Louis XIV depicted his political and military successes on any surface available. France's current state of financial insolvency resulted from his excessive lifestyle and expensive wars. It is my responsibility to sort it all out before the people revolt. Half of the citizens in Paris hold no jobs. Food prices spiral upwards because the crops are dying. However, the queen continues to gamble on horses. She also commissions new gowns, jewelry, and exotic hair pieces."

Iona kept her gaze turned away from the negative energy exuded by Bijou. Reba found their conversation tedious. She leapt down and trotted away to the far end of the hall. *I shall deal with the stupid storklet later.* Iona was relieved that the imposing cat left them alone. She pondered what advice to offer the king about his troubles. Her lack of experience in matters of the world provided her with no wisdom fit for a king.

The monarch sighed. "I am not cut out for this profession. I prefer to hunt and fish."

"I love fish too but I do not like eating frogs."

"They taste much better cooked, I assure you. We only eat their legs." The king patted Iona on the head and she batted her brown stork eyes at him.

A confident ancient woman whose presence daunted even the royal guards strode into the Hall of Mirrors. Zendala bowed to the king and greeted him in a low voice. "Good day, Your Majesty." Reba felt the powerful force in the long hall. She darted behind a pedestal again and watched the scene from the shield of its gold base. The leader shook her finger at the naughty storklet and swooped her up into strong arms.

The king turned to greet her. "Do not worry. Speaking with a bird does not occur on a daily basis around here. She told me about all of you." He raised his hand with the palm down for her to kiss. "My pleasure, Madame. You must be the Great and Honorable Zendala." She frowned at the realization that Iona had been telling secrets. The ancient woman placed the storklet back down on the floor and brushed her wrinkled lips across his hand. "Please join the queen and I for dinner and bring your companions."

"We shall be pleased to accept your hospitality." As if on cue the four additional Merciful Ones arrived at the entrance to the Hall of Mirrors. The crossed halberds of the Swiss guards blocked them. "My coterie arrives," informed Zendala. "May I present them?" The king's excitement was palpable. He signaled his men to allow the ladies to enter.

Reba peeked around the pedestal. It reassured her to see

the pharaoh who represented her greatest achievement in royal manipulation. She watched her king eye the women of various ages, sizes, shapes, and skin colors. They were all dressed in identical clothes except for their silk belts. He laughed. "Think of how much money we would save if all the ladies of the French court dressed like you."

The exotic-looking Pharaoh Maatkare Hatshepsut stepped forward when beckoned by her chief. Zendala made a formal introduction. Louis XVI appeared confused. "A female pharaoh? What an interesting concept." Maatkare forced a bow while mumbling with displeasure under her breath. The damnation of her memory was not yet reversed in the annals of history.

Zendala introduced Blandina the Christian martyr. Her presence took his breath away as she curtsied before him. Faint music filled the king's head. *A living angel stands before me.*

The leader presented the French maiden next. The king bent at the waist upon meeting the military heroine. "It is I who bows to you, Joan of Arc. I offer belated apologies on behalf of our homeland. Your execution stained the fabric of France." He regained his stature. Tears filled the monarch's eyes.

Zendala announced the regal Mary, Queen of Scots. She matched the king in height and curtsied with elegance in spite of her informal clothing. He took her hand and looked into her hazel eyes. "It is an honor to meet the former queen consort of France." Mary thanked him for welcoming the weary travelers.

King Louis XVI responded with sincere humility. "I am pleased that you all live on. However, I do not understand how you managed such a feat!" He invited the Merciful Ones to enjoy the full measure of his hospitality and Zendala accepted. With their secrets told they no longer needed to maintain such a low profile and they deserved a treat.

"What about me?" Iona's childish voice demanded their attention.

The king petted the storklet's soft head. "You can make friends with the duck, rooster, and lamb from the balloon ride."

"I do love baby lambs," she cooed. "Please keep Bijou away from me. She is scary."

The monarch pointed to the far end of the vast hall. "My cat has trotted off to the Salon of Apollo. It is her favorite spot when she is not on my lap. She likes to sit on the throne."

Maatkare recalled that particular salon. She must see Reba and devise their plan before the chief insisted on leaving the palace. She knew that Zendala despised blatant opulence. The pharaoh bowed again and excused herself. She sauntered down the Hall of Mirrors and around the corner into the Salon of War that adjoined the Salon of Apollo.

The pharaoh entered the cranberry-colored room decorated with flamboyant furniture representing the glory, power, wealth, and history of the monarchy. Two life-size paintings of King Louis XIV covered one wall. An even larger lavish royal blue silk tapestry embroidered with both gold and silver hugged the wall between the portraits. Situated in front of the arras on a raised red velvet dais stood the golden baroque throne.

Maatkare was surprised to find that the royal chair was empty. She had expected Reba to occupy the seat of honor. However, the cat stared up at the portrait of *The Sun King and his Family* at the room's opposite end. The pharaoh sauntered toward Reba. She teased, "Admiring yourself, Cat?" Reba turned and bounded toward her friend who bent over and lifted her up. The cat licked her face and Maatkare laughed. She found it difficult to stay angry with her friend. "I am in a hurry to get back. We are invited to a private dinner with the monarch and his queen."

Reba lost no time laying out her line of attack. "If you agree to my strategy bring Tara here to the Salon of Apollo after dinner. I am summoning Bastet and Sekhmet for help. We shall wait for the two of you. I never had a chance to tell you about our crazy fun before you threw a tantrum the last time we met."

"At least Louis XVI did not eject me from the palace mistaking me for a Gypsy." She was still annoyed and dropped Reba who landed on all fours.

Dinner commenced at the Royal Table Antechamber in the Queen's State Apartment. The courtiers had been informed not to attend. The queen's musicians played in the far corner of the spacious chamber while a few servants performed their duties. Marie Antoinette crossed the threshold through double doors. Maatkare made a snide comment. "Thank goodness for a wide entrance door." Bouffant panniers broadened the queen's figure beneath a pale blue silk dress festooned with white ruffles and gold satin ribbons.

"How uncomfortable," murmured Zendala. "I prefer our uniforms."

Maatkare agreed. "In this case I do too. However, there is nothing like an ancient Egyptian kilt for comfort. By the way, something unexpected awaits you after dinner." Zendala disliked surprises and did not respond.

Joan joined Zendala and Maatkare. "Unlike the queen I wear my hair maintenance free." Marie Antoinette's royal hairdresser had piled on wigs in layers so high that the vertical spectacle seemed to defy gravity. Her head was loaded with exotic feathers and resembled a menagerie of birds. Blandina could only stare at the spectacle the queen made. Mary admired Marie Antoinette's graceful comportment in spite of her extravagant costume.

The proud and loving king introduced his wife to the Merciful Ones. Earlier in the evening he had provided her with a lengthy explanation about the supernatural natures of their guests. The queen went out of her way to make them feel at ease. She took a special liking to Blandina and Mary who were seated on her left and right. Prior to service of the meal's first course, they prayed together to thank God for the feast.

During dinner Zendala and Louis XVI held serious discussions on the subject of religious tolerance. He admitted that the revocation of the Edict of Nantes by Louis XIV burdened his conscience. She encouraged him, "Who is better than the king to take action? All people deserve either freedom of religion or the autonomy to choose no formal belief system at all."

The Merciful Ones ate with gusto. After dessert the imperial couple urged the mystical peacemakers to stay longer at Versailles. "Please enjoy free reign of the château and go wherever you like. Iona seems to be quite happy in the courtyard off the kitchen. She is eating a special meal of roasted frogs' legs prepared by our royal chef." The king and queen departed.

Joan knew that their apprentice suffered from separation anxiety. She told her leader that she preferred to change form and sleep with the storklet. Zendala nodded and smiled. "I shall enjoy the comfort of the Queen's bedroom with Maatkare. Blandina and Mary have been invited to sleep at the Petit Trianon along with the queen and her ladies-in-waiting."

The supernatural women bid each other goodnight.

TREACHERY AT THE CHÂTEAU

Maatkare escorted Zendala to the Salon of Apollo. "In Egypt Monsieur Champollion recalled an enigma that appeared in royal portraits of the House of Bourbon over a one-hundred-year period starting with Louis XIII and ending with Louis XVI."

Zendala raised her bushy white eyebrows. "And?"

"In A.D. 1722 my respite took place here at Château Versailles and I was able to confirm Champollion's recollection."

"What is your point, Maatkare?"

"Ah yes, the point." She gestured at the king's throne. The ancient Egyptian Siamese cat sat in profile on the carved gold armchair. Her snobby nose pointed upward. Reba turned in slow motion to face her audience. It created the maximum dramatic effect. She lowered her gaze and stared daggers at Zendala. The ancient woman's knees weakened from the shock of seeing her dead sister. Maatkare grabbed her swooning chief's elbow to keep her from falling.

Reba sneered. "Hello Tara. It has been far too long."

Tears of joy pooled in Zendala's golden eyes. "Oh Reba, I thought that you died on top of the Great Pyramid at Giza in 100 B.C." She rushed forward to celebrate their joyful reunion.

Reba raised a paw to stop her. "As you see, I live. My true sisters came to my rescue after you tried to trample me to death."

Zendala sensed Reba's undeniable wrath. "It was an accident, Sister."

Bastet and Sekhmet materialized on either side of the throne. They emerged in translucence before acquiring a solid state to tower like alien creatures over Reba. The cat mocked the ancient woman. "These are my true sisters." She turned to one goddess and then the other. "I would like you to meet Tara the former divine white stork. She is now a human and insists that we call her the Great and Honorable Zendala but I refuse."

"Arya Tara—the Mother of all Buddhas—selected my name. I insist on nothing."

Sekhmet bowed with respect. "It is my honor to greet you."

Reba craned her neck upward and jeered at Sekhmet. "Whose side are you on?"

Bastet sought clarification from Zendala. "Did the magical jasper stone work for you?"

Now on her guard, Zendala gave no response. She knew that her mother Ba had never trusted Bastet and neither did she. *I shall not tell them that I no longer need the jasper stone for myself. I share its power with my coterie.*

Reba issued a command like a true royal. "Come forth and sit down on the dais. Tell us about your life since we saw you last." *This is the perfect opportunity to penetrate Tara's golden eyes and persuade her to give me all the magical trinkets.*

Zendala was hurt that Reba carried a grudge. She sat on the velvet-covered platform. "I forgave you long ago for swallowing and keeping me captive. Will you not forgive me?"

Reba leapt down from the throne onto the big woman's lap and stared up at her with two mesmerizing sky-blue eyes. In her mind she demanded, 'Take off your cartouche, jasper stone, and ring of eternity. Turn them over to Bastet.' Reba was unaware that Zendala's elevated consciousness deflected the cat's telepathic thoughts.

"Well? Will you forgive me?"

The Great Persuader messaged her again. 'I order you to

hand them over.'

Zendala lifted the Siamese cat off her lap. She felt frustrated and disappointed. "It seems that your heart holds no capacity to forgive."

Reba told a desperate lie. "All right, I absolve you!" She needed to keep her at Versailles and find another way to steal the magical amulets. "Meet me in the garden tomorrow morning. We shall talk in private."

The ancient woman nodded and stood. "The queen insists that Maatkare and I sleep in her quarters tonight." The pharaoh glanced at Reba with anxiety. Their plan to gain the magical jewelry through mental manipulation had failed. The secretive cat cocked her head toward the bag hanging from Bastet's wrist that was filled with perfumes and potions. The goddess passed the pharaoh a small vial. Sekhmet refused to participate in the treachery and vanished.

Maatkare was unaware that Zendala had seen Bastet give her the vial. *My second in command is up to something.* Before they left the salon Zendala noted the life-size portrait of the Sun King and his family dressed as ancient Romans. She recognized her sister on the lap of the king with Bastet and Sekhmet looming in the background. *Monsieur Champollion's recollection now makes perfect sense. Maatkare figured that out and came to Versailles on her own to scheme with Reba against me. They are plotting treachery at the château.*

The two Merciful Ones walked toward the Queen's Apartment and climbed its marble staircase. The Swiss guards glared at the two foreigners because no one but the queen slept there. They opened the double doors leading to Marie Antoinette's bedroom.

Zendala sighed. "Sleeping outside suits me best but I shall not offend the queen."

"You deserve an indulgence, Chief." *I need to keep her here.*

The walls were covered in white satin embroidered with

flowers. The motif repeated on the bed and headboard as well as on the draperies hanging high from the canopy two stories above. A Venetian red stone fireplace to the right of the bed blazed and massive crystal chandeliers cast bright candlelight throughout.

The pharaoh stood in front of the low gilded balustrade separating the queen's bed from the rest of the room. She pointed at the massive canopy dripping in gold above the bed. Two chubby golden cupids the size of human infants flanked the Austrian Imperial Eagle. "What if the whole thing collapses on us during the night?" Zendala assured her that it would not fall.

Maatkare noticed a cabinet made of oak veneered with tulipwood against a nearby wall. Above it hung a carved and gilded mirror. On the marble-topped sideboard an etched Baccarat carafe contained honey-colored liqueur. Eight short-stemmed snifters waited alongside. "I need a nightcap. Do you care to join me, Chief?"

Zendala sat down on a small sofa and claimed it for the night. The flowery pattern of its upholstery matched the rest of the room. "Why not celebrate, Maatkare? You led me back to Reba no matter the outcome." She inquired with a wry grin, "Is it Bour Bon Cognac?"

The pharaoh lifted the heavy decanter engraved with floral intaglios, removed its crystal top, and whiffed the intense aroma. "I am certain that it is the finest available." With her back to Zendala she reached into her pocket to remove the glass vial and poured its contents into one of the snifters. She put an equal amount of cognac in each. Maatkare did not realize that Zendala watched her every move from the mirror's reflection. The pharaoh placed the snifters on the small silver tray. She walked back across the room and offered her the tampered drink.

Zendala smiled at the deceitful pharaoh and reached for the smaller of the two portions. "You need this more than I do. Reba's impolite behavior shocked us both. I know that you intended a joyous reunion." Maatkare took a seat on the armchair opposite her uncertain about how to remedy the situation. She lifted her crystal snifter. They chimed their glasses together and the ancient woman threw back her drink in a single gulp. Maatkare forced a small sip of the tampered cognac. Zendala commented, "We both know that ancient Egyptians love their wine and beer. Drink up!"

"In a moment." She took her chief's empty snifter back to the cabinet along with her own full one. The sneaky pharaoh filled Zendala's glass again and placed it on the silver tray next to her own. *Here we go again.* She kept her eyes focused on the two snifters to recognize the one doctored with the sleeping potion. Maatkare placed the tray on the small table between the couch and the chair.

Zendala snatched up both snifters and took a whiff. Her golden eyes pierced those of her second in command. She handed Maatkare the tampered dram and pointed to the mirror. "I saw the exchange between you and Bastet as well as your effort to add her potion to my drink. You are not so clever after all. Now take your medicine." The leader consumed the pure cognac. The pharaoh knew when to admit defeat and forced down her measure of altered port. She wasted no time retiring to the queen's bed.

Whenever possible Zendala slept as a woman in the lotus position. She had learned in Tibet how to achieve a state of deep slumber and only needed the delta sleep of supreme stillness to wake up rejuvenated. A few hours of rest each night was sufficient.

Maatkare slept beneath the queen's silk sheets oblivious to all. In the dark bedchamber the fireplace provided a warm glow. Zendala studied the flickering flames. Both hands rested in her lap and she closed her eyes to invite peace into her body, mind, and soul. The hours ticked away. On the nightstand next to the queen's bed an exquisite gold clock chimed three times and woke the drugged pharaoh. Maatkare sat up and saw the outline of Zendala's Buddha-like figure. "Where is Bastet?" She slumped onto the pillow and went back to sleep.

The cat goddess knew nothing about the mix-up with the drinks when she materialized behind the sofa and stood over Zendala. She wore a sinister silver mask depicting a grinning human face to disguise her feline head. Her eyes were illuminated with excitement and she peered through the cutouts to examine her victim. *Removing the cartouche and jasper is easy but how can I reach the ring of eternity when her legs are folded under her dress?*

She decided to start by confiscating the leather band. She knew that Reba coveted the jasper stone the most. Her long arm pulled at the thong around the elder's wrinkled neck. It got stuck beneath the thick white plait of hair. Zendala grabbed Bastet's wrist with the speed of a Venus flytrap. She stared up at the silver mask and registered the lime-green cat eyes behind it. The ancient woman tightened her grip. It was clear on whose behalf the goddess attempted to conduct her burglary.

Bastet howled. "Let me go!"

"Release my jasper stone now! Inform Reba that she will never again get her treacherous paws on what belongs to me." The cat goddess let her fingers go limp and twisted her hand free. She hissed in anger and vanished.

Zendala inhaled several deep breaths. *I expected something but not this!* She unfolded her legs and placed her bare flat feet on the wood floor to ground her unsettled energy. Her golden eyes remained open for the duration of the long night.

In the morning, Maatkare hurried out of the queen's bedchamber to avoid her chief. She found Reba in the Salon of Apollo sitting on the royal throne livid at the botched burglary. The cat launched into a fuming tirade. "This is all your fault.

I wish I had shape shifted into an ape and strangled Tara last night. The amulets would be mine again."

Maatkare defended herself. "I am the sole reason that she came to Versailles. I shall not accept the blame for your plan's inherent weakness."

"I managed without you for all these years. Perhaps it is time to part ways forever!"

Maatkare's ears burned at these hurtful words but she maintained her pride and integrity. "As you wish, Cat. I promise that you will not hear from me again." She turned and marched from the room. *I shall steal the jewelry for myself.*

"Wait for me! I must make an appearance and stand in solidarity with my king." Reba scrambled after Maatkare. They exited through a side door into the gardens where Louis XVI, Zendala, and Joan waited by the Fountain of Latona. Iona giggled as she darted around in the spewing water. The pharaoh bowed to the king and asked the whereabouts of the others.

He answered, "They are at the Petit Trianon. My queen has prepared a parting surprise that will leave the Merciful Ones with a favorable impression." Reba ignored Zendala and leapt into the arms of her master. The group meandered through the manicured gardens leading to the Grand Canal. He signaled to the guards not to follow. The storklet buzzed around above showing off her aerial moves.

They all made their way to the estate of Trianon. It was the location of the Grand and Petit Palaces as well as the future home of the Queen's Hamlet. The rustic rural homestead was designed to provide a refuge from prying eyes and the responsibilities of court life. They saw Marie Antoinette, Blandina, and Mary standing on a stone bridge. It spanned a stream that kept the artificial lake filled. Iona dove headfirst into the water and surfaced with a flopping fish. Zendala yelled, "Drop it!" Iona obeyed and watched her snack swim away.

The threesome waved at the ladies and walked toward the meadow staked out for the Queen's House. Marie Antoinette felt at ease with the two Merciful Ones in their white peasant dresses. Today she wore a milkmaid's smock and a straw Bergère hat.

Louis XVI chuckled. "My wife wants to learn how to milk a cow."

Their world is far removed from reality. Zendala looked forward to leaving Château Versailles and rejoining the Gypsies.

The group made their way to the Petit Palace. Marie Antoinette excused herself. Several minutes later she returned with a leather pouch and took Zendala aside. The bag was stuffed with extravagant diamond brooches, earrings, and bracelets. "Take these to Monsieur Gilbert Vivier in Paris on Rue de la Paix. He will ask no questions and give you a fair price for the jewelry. Please return to the villages near Versailles and give the money away to poor citizens. I fear that my selfishness may come back to haunt me."

I know that it will. Zendala nodded. "As you wish."

"I already gave my favorite pendant to Blandina. She suffered so much and deserves to own something nice. The central blue diamond matches her lovely eyes and the surrounding white diamonds represent her loving soul."

"I am certain that Blandina will cherish your generous gift."

The Siamese cat meowed at Blandina from the king's arms. Their eyes locked. Reba messaged, 'You belong to me. That pendant is mine.'

Blandina pulled the diamond necklace from her pocket. She reached over to place the jewelry around the cat's neck but Reba batted her hand away. She maintained eye contact and messaged again. 'Not now you ninny. You will expose the cartouche and bust of Nefertiti hiding in my neck folds. I shall retrieve my pendant in the future.'

Everyone except Reba appeared confused by Blandina's

actions. She seemed to be in a trance. Zendala asked, "Do you feel unwell? You look pale."

"I am fine." She shook her blonde tresses to clear her head. Zendala motioned for Iona to land and addressed the royal couple. "We leave you now with gratitude for your hospitality."

The king inquired, "Where will you go next?"

Zendala winked at the queen. "First we go to Paris. After that the White Storks of Mercy will enjoy the countryside of the Île-de-France from a stork's point of view." Once the jewels were sold, she intended to distribute the paper money by air. Zendala gestured for her members to follow. They took a running leap together and the Merciful Ones transformed in unison.

"That was an incredible magical experience that we shall never forget, my dear." The king took his queen's hand and raised their two arms in a salute to their supernatural guests circling above.

Reba decided to trump the air show. She spoke to the king and queen for the first time. "If you think that is great watch this!" She shape shifted into a feather-plumed horse and pranced around on huge hind legs. The cat recalled the spectacle brought to Versailles in A.D. 1772 by the Englishman Phillip Astley. Back then Reba had enjoyed the entertainment from the comfort of King Louis XV's lap. His grandson Louis-Auguste and Marie Antoinette had also been present.

The royal couple gasped in shock and delight. A moment later the circus horse turned into a toy spaniel, a member of the queen's favorite canine breed. Reba the dog frolicked about, barking and licking her hand. The supernatural animal morphed back into a Siamese cat and rubbed against the king's leg. He laughed with glee and picked Bijou up. "You are a talking cat!"

Reba bragged, "I am the monarch of magic!"

***

Nine years later the historic reign of Louis XVI ended with his imprisonment at Tuileries Palace in Paris. He was the last sovereign of France. The enraged public did not care that their king had tried to do his best on their behalf before his arrest. His conversation with Zendala about religious acceptance had inspired the Edict of Tolerance in A.D. 1787. It provided his subjects with the legal right to practice their chosen faiths for the first time in one hundred years.

Reba alone remained in residency at Château Versailles. The new republic sent the royal portraits featuring the Siamese cat to the Louvre Museum thereby securing her place in history. Reba knew that she had to find a new home. She talked to the images of herself in the Hall of Mirrors one last time. "I shall return to Ireland and look for Orchid MacCloud. Warming the lap of an Irish earl will have to suffice." The self-absorbed cat departed from Versailles thinking about her future exploits including how to steal Tara's magical jewelry.

A tribunal found Louis XVI guilty of high treason. On a cold and wintry morning in A.D. 1793 twelve hundred horsemen escorted the citizen of revolutionary France now known as Louis Capet to his place of execution. The White Storks of Mercy flew overhead so that the former king would not feel alone. The sad storklet fell far behind. Their configuration resembled a kite with a long tail rather than a spiritual symbol. The sympathetic birds slowed down until Iona caught up. The mob became silent as the peasants looked upwards at the awesome sight.

The transport arrived at Place de La Révolution where a simple scaffold stood. Citizen Capet stepped out of the vehicle and gazed up at the White Storks of Mercy. He saluted them as the guards heaved the bound man onto the platform. Zendala led the birds away so that Iona would not have to witness the gruesome execution. The former monarch knelt in front of the guillotine and said his final prayer. One slice later the crowd gasped at the sight of his severed head. A timid cheer arose from the mob. "Long live the Republic!" Soon the phrase grew to a deafening roar.

Marie Antoinette's trial started several months later. She too lost her head.

***

The mystical birds lived on, as did Reba. She showed up on the doorstep of one of the grandest residences in Ireland. It was a magnificent Georgian-style manor located near the mouth of Bantry Bay in Cork County. The First and Second Earls of Bantry—both named Richard White—adopted her as their pet. Reba made herself comfortable within the sizeable Bantry House that was furnished with an eclectic collection of treasures from around the world.

A familiar French tapestry that once belonged to Marie Antoinette and a magnificent artifact from ancient Egypt occupied the Rose Room. The earls named their Siamese cat Cleopatra because she loved sitting and sleeping on the gold-painted throne of King Ramses VI. Carved mythical winged serpents formed the arms of the throne and rams' heads with long spiral horns capped the ends. Its feet were patterned after the claws of eagles with sharp talons made of cobalt blue lapis stones.

The back of the royal chair depicted the infatuation of Re with Nut the goddess of the sky. Specks of silver created the stars and semi-precious stones crafted the sun. The seat doubled as a secret compartment that proved to be a perfect hiding place for Reba's gold gorget earrings. In France the eccentric courtiers had accepted her accessories but in Ireland cats did not wear jewelry. Nonetheless, the bust of Nefertiti and cartouche of Noah's Ark camouflaged in the folds of her neck remained in place. One never knew when a cat might require a quick getaway.

Bantry House was a bit of a downgrade compared to her accommodations in France. For the next fifty years Cleopatra warmed the laps of the two Richards. Neither she nor Maatkare communicated. Those two acted like stubborn mules.

LETHAL DOSE

In the early years of the nineteenth century the Merciful Ones visited the old town of Quimper in western France. The ladies meandered through the cobblestone streets and outdoor markets. They stopped at cafés to enjoy delicious buckwheat crêpes and the area's renowned cider. Zendala kept apprised of current events by reading the newspaper whenever possible. She was clairvoyant but chose not to connect with her gift of sight at all times. To do so would zap all of her energy. Therefore, she also relied on conventional means to obtain information.

The continuing outright bigotry in Europe disheartened her. She placed the *Gazette de France* on the table and shared her disgust with the others. "Life for the persecuted nomads worsens by the day. Gypsy hunting is the most popular sport in Germany!" Zendala stood up and pointed a condemning finger at the offensive story. "I need to get away from this kind of stigmatizing propaganda. Shall we take a holiday to somewhere remote?"

Everyone agreed without hesitation. Iona jumped up and down heeding Zendala's warning to keep quiet in public. Revitalized a short time ago, the storks felt energetic enough to undertake an aeronautical journey to some of the world's natural wonders. These excursions provided Zendala with an opportunity to keep them informed about various subjects.

The seven-thousand-mile journey to the central area of East Africa took three weeks because Iona required frequent rest periods. Upon arrival they encountered the greatest wildlife show on earth. The birds raced across the savanna with herds of impala zigzagging below. Iona was thrilled to play hide-and-seek with baboons and monkeys in the plush green jungles.

The storks flew south to Victoria Falls where they observed incredible plumes of spray rising into the sky. Inhaling the humid air cleansed their lungs but the noise rose to a deafening level as they approached. A frightened Iona veered away.

"We should go after her," yelled Mary.

Joan shouted, "The last time Iona got scared she ended up inside the Hall of Mirrors."

Once reunited the phalanx traversed the vast continent and flew due west. They joined migrating flocks of common storks along the way, which proved educational for the apprentice. Iona flapped her wings too many times during their long flight across the South Atlantic Ocean on their way to Rio de Janeiro. She slowed down even more after fourteen hundred miles. The storklet lost altitude as the formation soared above the volcanic island of Saint Helena.

On this moonlit night the birds reduced speed to allow the apprentice to catch up. Zendala located an appropriate place to touch down. They landed on the front lawn of Longwood House. Except for Iona the birds transformed into women. Their identical dresses flapped in the strong breeze coming off the ocean.

The ladies and their apprentice storklet did not know that inside the dwelling Napoleon Bonaparte sat alone in the dark. He looked out at the yard through the large window. The former emperor of France wore an overcoat buttoned up to his chin. He required a blanket to cover his stiff muscles and brittle bones. It concealed his stomach that was engorged with cancer. The dying man sipped rose water mixed with orgeat syrup in an attempt to satisfy his abnormal thirst.

He trembled as his focus fastened on five large birds and a smaller one descending in a spiral formation in the bright moonlight. All except the smallest one transformed into women. Napoleon got to his feet and raked both hands through greasy hair. He questioned his imperial valet Louis Joseph Marchand as the man entered the drawing room. "Did you see the strange occurrence outside? Perhaps too much hair tonic has seeped into my brain and caused me to hallucinate." The bewildered man shook his oversized head.

Louis Joseph was unaware of the supernatural event that Napoleon had witnessed. He chuckled, "I assure you that although your hair product contains trace amounts of arsenic it is not enough to cause harm." The handsome and polite Frenchman bowed and left the room.

Napoleon pushed the window open with his cane just enough to eavesdrop. Zendala provided the group with interesting historical information on their location. "In A.D. 1676 the astronomer Edmund Halley visited this island to map the stars of the Southern Hemisphere. He discovered the famous comet that now bears his name."

Joan's elation overcame her. "Who cares about that? Napoleon has lived here since the British forced him to abdicate!"

Zendala declared, "I hold no interest in the tyrant."

"He is a usurper as well," reminded Mary. "I was the legitimate heir to the Scottish monarchy. However, Napoleon established his empire without tracing his bloodlines to the throne. The Bourbon dynasty was restored when he relinquished his title."

Maatkare shared her own opinion while looking at Zendala as she spoke. "Napoleon once claimed power was his favorite mistress. I understand that but I still resent his invasion of our homeland. Two thousand Egyptians died during his Battle of the Pyramids. When I was pharaoh my army never allowed such an attack."

In the drawing room the shocked Napoleon racked his brain. *A female appearing older than time itself, a queen of Scotland, and an Egyptian pharaoh?* He leaned closer to the window and wiped away the condensation with his blanket to improve his view.

Blandina joined the conversation. "The Napoleonic Code of Civil Procedure brought an end to European feudalism. Peasants were no longer forced to work without compensation to provide for the landowners. As a Christian slave martyred by the Romans in Gallia, I find that quite meaningful."

Zendala clarified her view of the exiled ruler. "My dear Blandina, that was not done out of the goodness of his heart. More often than not the emperor's actions provided a means for him to extend his imperialist empire."

Napoleon's heart pounded with exhilaration. *Blandina of Lyon? It is impossible!* These supernatural women excited him beyond belief. A wild idea percolated in his desperate mind. *Perhaps they will help me to cheat death.*

Iona spoke up. "If he is so great why does he live in the middle of nowhere?"

Zendala answered the storklet's naive question. "The Napoleonic Wars killed six million people. Upon his defeat at the Battle of Waterloo the Brits exiled him to this desolate island with no possible escape route."

"It serves him right if you ask me." Iona always spoke her mind.

Joan felt overwhelmed to find herself in such close proximity to her hero. "Napoleon possesses one of the best military minds of all time. I shall defend his honor to my death."

Iona giggled. "You cannot die, Joan. We live forever."

Joan continued to voice her opinion without reservation. "I led the campaigns for King Charles VII in A.D. 1429. I can attest to Napoleon's military genius."

Mary reminded her of a critical matter. "A significant

difference exists between the two of you as soldiers. The Maid of Orléans carried no armor into battle and fought for God. Napoleon waged war for power and control. He even claimed that God favored the side with the best artillery."

The emperor clapped a hand over his thin lips to stay quiet. *Joan of Arc! Have I lost my mind? If she is not an apparition, I must meet her.*

Outside Zendala suggested that they transform back into storks. "There is a forest of cabbage trees nearby where we can sleep. Tomorrow we shall introduce ourselves to Napoleon Bonaparte." Joan beamed at the prospect.

The following morning the White Storks of Mercy reappeared and became acquainted with Joan's hero. Despite their age difference Napoleon and the French maiden grew closer as the days passed. He bragged to her that he alone had advanced Joan of Arc as an official symbol of French patriotism and a heroine of the people. This made her idolize him even more.

Zendala discussed the future of Europe in the twentieth century with the arrogant man. She shared her foresight regarding the upcoming World Wars. Napoleon was surprised to learn about Germany's hatred of Jewish people. As emperor he had overturned laws restricting French Jews to ghetto living. They had also been free to buy property and pursue their chosen careers.

One evening Zendala found Napoleon in the drawing room standing at the window. He was looking at the volcanic terrain and beyond to the Atlantic Ocean. The sick man seemed stronger and she sensed his yearning to return home to his beloved France. He was wearing clean white breeches, leather knee-high boots, and a blue overcoat with a gold embroidered collar. The ancient woman posed a mocking question. "Are you planning your escape, Emperor?"

Napoleon turned and bowed. "Many countries want

me rescued from imprisonment to aid their struggles for independence."

"And your enemies? Those who wish you dead?"

He nodded and a smile touched the corners of his mouth. "Touché. My enemies will make an appointment at my tomb."

Zendala joined him at the window and looked down at the short man. "What about all the needless killings for which you hold responsibility?"

Napoleon shrugged his shoulders. "A great man such as I troubles himself little about a million men." Zendala glared. She found his hubris intolerable. The emperor thought it wise to change the subject. "I beg your pardon for my inelegant query. Why do you look so much older than the women you lead?"

A bout of dizziness overtook him and he struggled toward the chair. Zendala reached out to help and took a seat across from him. Her foul mood lightened as she resolved to put aside her disdain for the sake of Joan, who appeared quite smitten with the older man. "The Merciful Ones never mature in their human forms and remain the same ages as when I recruited them. It is different for me. I came into the world as a divine white stork in ancient Egypt. When my human body materialized in Tibet the universe manifested me as an elder."

"Ah yes, the Great and Honorable Zendala. The name suits you."

Joan entered the room and busied herself at the writing desk. She opened a small drawer and found a parcel addressed to her. It was wrapped in one of Napoleon's monogramed handkerchiefs. Inside it she discovered a small dagger with his initials embossed on the scabbard. Joan held the cherished object to her heart. She glanced down the room at Napoleon. He diverted his attention from Zendala to produce a weak smile.

The ancient woman noted their exchange. She was aware of Napoleon's reputation as a man disloyal to women. Joan sustained a strong commitment to her spiritual beliefs but Zendala feared that she was vulnerable to his charms. *It is time to create distance between them. We must leave Saint Helena.* Zendala approached Joan and whispered a warning. "Exercise care when opening your heart to him. Napoleon is a manipulative and cunning man who lacks scruples."

Joan stood and faced her leader. She was upset with the accusation against her hero. The maiden's retort was harsh. "Your thoughts are shameful! He is like a father to me and nothing more. You know that I find death preferable to sin."

Napoleon overheard Joan defending him from across the room. He called out, "Be assured that she takes her rightful place as the daughter never given to me." He waved his hand at Zendala to dismiss her. "Now leave us. We have much work to do if I am to record my vast military accomplishments before I die."

Exasperated at being treated like a servant Zendala left them alone. *I must summon the others. We shall fly to Diana's Peak for an overnight gathering.*

Napoleon seated himself next to her at the writing desk. Tears pooled in the stricken maiden's eyes. He placed a comforting hand on her knee. "I apologize for sending your leader away. I meant no disrespect but she treats France's heroine like an ignorant teen."

He took his handkerchief from her lap and wiped her wet cheek. "Can you imagine if the illustrious Napoleon Bonaparte and the courageous Joan of Arc reigned over the French empire together? If it had been that way I would not be stranded on this godforsaken island."

"Do you hold any regrets about your life?"

"Only one, my dear. Before I escaped from Elba in A.D. 1814, I gave a confidential letter to the young French sailor Edmond Dantès. When he arrived in France the authorities discovered the sealed letter in his pocket and accused him as a Bonapartist. Now he serves a life sentence in prison at Château d'If. Perhaps the Merciful Ones can help him. It serves their mission to seek justice. Only then will peace find my soul."

"We know that island well, Emperor. The ancient Egyptian god Seth revitalizes us there sometimes. First and foremost, the White Storks of Mercy exist to help humanity. I shall ask Zendala to take the others to Château d'If and free Dantès from his unjust imprisonment."

"Splendid, my dear!"The frail man was perplexed and paused. "The others? And you?"

"I shall remain here until…"

"…My death." His voice grew sly. "What a pity that I do not have a magical talisman to keep me alive forever. Do you have a spare?"

Joan shook her head with sadness. "Only Zendala can issue amulets to her recruits. I regret that I do not possess the power to save you."

At the doorway Louis Joseph cleared his throat to gain their attention. He crossed the threshold and bowed. "Excuse me, Emperor. The night grows late and you must rest." He helped the frail man to his feet.

Napoleon bid the maiden goodnight. "I hope to see you tomorrow, dearest Joan. All of the days left to me on this earth are yours."

Joan reassured him that she planned to remain by his side. *I will make arrangements to meet the White Storks of Mercy someday in the future.*

Zendala conferred with four of her members throughout the night. The morning sun rose over Diana's Peak and they agreed to leave Saint Helena with or without Joan. They approached Longwood House and saw Napoleon standing on the lawn looking out to sea. His familiar bicorne hat balanced on his head like a miniature black sailboat. Instead of resting one hand in his unbuttoned waistcoat—his common stance for showmanship—a cane supported him.

Napoleon's other hand held onto Joan's. She stood with steadfastness by his side. The maiden had exchanged her uniform for white breeches, black equestrian boots, and a short-cropped navy-blue jacket. Her bobbed haircut and boyish looks made the pair appear more like father and son than father and daughter.

The phalanx landed in front of them and transformed. Zendala approached the couple. *It seems clear that Joan is staying here with him.* She requested time alone with her. The ancient woman felt deep dismay that her recruit had chosen the male military magnate over the female peacemakers. Joan fingered her blue badge with the golden emblem that Zendala had given to her almost four hundred years earlier. She felt anxious as she waited for her leader's reaction.

Zendala inhaled a deep breath of humid air before speaking. "It was never my intention to coerce or compel a Merciful One against her free will. I accept your choice although I do not understand it. I regret that I did not foresee this coming. My psychic vision is not a constant." Zendala pointed a stern finger in the direction of Napoleon. "We are for peace and he is for war. These cannot co-exist."

Joan selected her words with care. "I wish to remain here for now. I promise I shall return to the fold someday." *After my hero is dead and buried.*

Zendala raised her hands in a gesture of defeat. She placed her arms around the petite young woman. "He will die within the year. Can you bear the pain of watching him suffer until he takes his last breath?"

"By his side in life I shall linger. I pray that he makes peace with God before his death. I plan to accompany his coffin to the Valley of the Willows here in Saint Helena after he passes."

Joan's ice-blue eyes filled with tears.

Zendala closed her eyes. "I can tell you that in A.D. 1840 the British will grant King Louis-Philippe of France permission to return the remains of Napoleon Bonaparte to the homeland you share. The frigate *Belle-Poule* will arrive on the coast of Normandy and dock at the port in Cherbourg."

"Thank you. In that case I shall also travel on the *Belle-Poule* and meet the Merciful Ones there. I hope that you will welcome me back." Zendala nodded her assent. She knew that no additional pleas on her part would change the maiden's mind. Joan saluted and tilted her head. She offered the sweet and innocent smile that her leader adored.

Iona wailed as she wrapped her stork wings around Joan. "You are like my big sister. Promise me that when I finish my apprenticeship and change back into a girl again, we shall hold hands like you and Napoleon do."

"I promise, Iona. He is my friend and so are you. In fact, you are my best friend."

"Sorry Joan but Maatkare is my best friend." She whispered, "We keep secrets."

"What kind of secrets?"

"Here is one that nobody else knows. Her pharaoh's beard is magical! She rubs it and the blue stones light up. Then she talks to it."

Joan gave Iona a sidelong glance as she considered this information. "Interesting. We shall speak more about this the next time I see you."

The storklet moaned. "I feel very bad about leaving you on this island."

Joan stroked the top of Iona's head. "Nothing will happen to me. God keeps watch over us all. Now please promise me that you and the others will rescue Edmond Dantès."

"Zendala canceled our holiday. Last night she had a vision

about this. We all agreed to help him." She puffed her feathered chest out with pride. "It is our mission, you know." They said their sorrowful farewells. The five storks flew north to liberate the French sailor.

Less than a year later Napoleon spoke with his devoted companion for the last time. He attempted to comfort her. "I beg you to leave me and finish your prayers in solitude." Joan kissed his waxy cheek and retreated into the adjoining room.

Napoleon never knew that minutes before he passed away one of his attendants entered Joan's chamber. The schemer convinced her to drink a cup of tea that was poisoned with a lethal dose of arsenic. Joan lost consciousness. The culprit returned to the emperor's deathbed clasping the maiden's amulet of Saint Michael the Archangel. She placed it over the dying man's heart. "With this icon you will live forever and conquer the world."

Without her amulet to protect her the Maid of Orléans succumbed to the poison. The misguided thief did not know that the power in Joan's magical amulet belonged to her alone. Napoleon Bonaparte and Joan of Arc both died on the fifth day of May in A.D. 1821. In Joan's final dream they stood together on the battlefield in an altogether different time and place.

SYMPATHY PAINS

The five White Storks of Mercy soared toward the Ivory Coast guided by their internal navigation systems. The tropical country was located in southern West Africa on the Gulf of Guinea. Iona's young wings allowed her to keep up during the time it took to fly from Saint Helena. However, Zendala's energy level reached an all-time low. "We have eaten nothing but fish from the ocean the entire way. Am I the only one sick?"

Blandina urged, "White beaches lie ahead. Hang on!"

The anxious Iona asked Mary if their leader's life was threatened. "Do not worry, Iona. She is divine and will never perish." Zendala screamed in agony from the excruciating pains in her stomach. She wrapped her wings around herself and lost altitude fast.

Iona hollered, "Help her! If she crashes every bone in her body will break!"

Maatkare took charge. She yelled out commands as they swooped down to Zendala. "Blandina and Mary, grab each of her wings with your feet while I steady her head with mine. Iona, you fly to the beach and find us a safe place to land. Now!"

The two storks struggled to implement Maatkare's orders and they managed to maneuver the sick bird to the ground. They set the divine white stork on the sand and Zendala transformed into her human self. She bent over to vomit then stumbled behind a black volcanic rock at the edge of the shoreline. The others transformed and turned away to allow privacy.

The storklet felt embarrassed. "Oh dear, it sounds like our leader has soupy stools."

Maatkare shushed her. "We must hydrate Zendala." She ordered Blandina and Mary to find fresh water. Maatkare instructed Iona to fly up into a palm tree and peck away several coconuts. "Push them over the sand with your bill. We shall crack them open and use the hard shells as cups."

"Whatever you say, best friend." Iona flew off to the tree line.

The pharaoh frowned. *I am not your best friend, you stupid storklet.*

Zendala reappeared from behind the rock and washed her hands in the foamy saltwater. She examined the changing pigmentation of her skin and fingernails. The ancient woman placed both palms on her throbbing head and then on her swollen stomach. She smelled of garlic and salivated more than usual. "I do not understand why I am plagued with the symptoms of arsenic poisoning."

Maatkare coaxed Zendala into the shade beneath a grove of palms to escape the heat. They both sat down and leaned against the tree. "Resting and replenishing your fluids will help."

Iona dropped a coconut from the sky. Zendala winced as it landed with a thud in the sand. Minutes later the two water scouts returned with the good news that they found a stream." Mary spotted the coconuts and warned Zendala not to drink the juice. "It might upset your stomach even more." The coterie worked as a team to open the hard-shelled fruit and Iona slurped up the sweet liquid. Blandina ran back into the trees with an empty husk and moments later Zendala was sipping small amounts of water.

Maatkare studied the position of the sun and barked out more orders. "We must gather as many fronds as possible to make a shelter and a bed." They dispersed in various directions and dragged some huge leaves shed by the palm trees back to the site. Maatkare built a sizeable shelter around the sick woman now lying on her side in the sand. She informed Zendala, "There is enough room in here for one of us to join you. We shall take turns throughout the night while the others keep watch."

Blandina inquired, "Does anyone possess nursing skills?"

Mary responded, "I tended to my husband Lord Darnley after smallpox struck him." Everyone agreed that she should take charge of Zendala's care. The Scottish queen had observed the ancient woman for several hours when an idea occurred to her. "Perhaps you suffer from sympathy pains."

Zendala groaned. A perplexed frown creased the skin between her bushy white eyebrows. "What do you mean by sympathy pains?"

"It happened to me. They took my son James away when he was only ten months old. I learned later that he had received regular beatings from his religious tutor. It was a misguided attempt to place the fear of God in my poor boy. At the time I did not understand why mysterious red welts sometimes marked the backs of my own legs and buttocks."

"Your empathy for the child's suffering brought his pain onto you?" Mary nodded. "Thank you. Your theory makes sense." Zendala tried to sit up but weakness kept her down. "Perhaps Reba has been poisoned. She is my sole blood relative with mortality." Her supposition did not feel accurate.

The ancient woman continued to rack her brain for an answer. Whenever she considered the other Merciful Ones as "sisters" nausea overtook her. She was helpless to beat down the dreadful fear welling up inside. Zendala knew that her present companions all felt well. She admitted to herself that these symptoms must come from Joan of Arc. She murmured, "Oh the poor dear maiden! How did I not see this coming?"

Iona overheard them from outside the shelter. "What happened to Joan?" The others gathered around waiting for more information.

In her mind's eye Zendala saw Napoleon in his final hours surrounded by his attendants. There was no sign of Joan in the room. When the guilty party removed Joan's amulet it had cut off the seer's link to the girl. She broke down and wept. "Someone must have taken off Joan's talisman and poisoned her with arsenic."

Iona shrieked. Maatkare and Blandina gasped with horror. They sank onto their knees and looked inside the shelter. Mary whispered, "Zendala experienced the same symptoms as Joan did before she died."

Iona pushed her way in. "Your job is to protect us!"

"You are right. I failed all of you." She closed her golden eyes. Her soul keened with grief and her mind swam in a dark pool of despair. The leader's condition worsened. Mary encouraged Iona to go back out into the fresh air.

Maatkare took over the nursing duties. Zendala's fever rose and was followed by bouts of the chills. At one point in her delirium, she tugged hard at the gold choker and jasper stone amulets around her neck. "Get these things off me before I choke! My eternity ring is gouging my ankle!"

The pharaoh followed her chief's orders to remove the jewelry. "I shall wear them for safekeeping. You are divine so there is no risk to your eternal life." She put the cartouche around her neck and slipped the jasper stone over her head. The skin on her arms prickled and a shiver of excitement passed through her body. Maatkare removed her boots and placed the ring around her ankle. *The second in command is now the leader.*

Maatkare stayed with Zendala for the remainder of the night. Her imagination ran wild as she considered her options. She left the shelter at daybreak of dawn when Blandina slipped beneath the temporary cover that protected them from the elements.

The pharaoh settled against the trunk of a palm tree and

admired her red and black pedicure while contemplating her future. *I can fly away right now and leave the others behind on the Ivory Coast. They will not pursue me while Zendala is sick. My members will seek power instead of peace and waste no time making mischief.*

She could not forget Reba's desire to part ways forever. *It seems we have done just that. In Cat's chess game I played the role of pawn but now I am the king!* To amuse herself she removed the beard from her pocket, attached it to her chin, and gave it a brisk rub—nothing happened. The exhausted pharaoh closed her eyes and wondered if she possessed the power to raise former queens from the dead. *I shall recruit Catherine the Great, Catherine de Medici, and Elizabeth I. Mary will hate that!* Maatkare fell asleep with the beard still fastened to her chin.

Inside the makeshift shelter Zendala rested exhausted by grief. Blandina stayed by her side and prayed. "Dear Lord, we commend the righteous and noble Joan of Arc to your care. We Merciful Ones will follow our leader to the ends of the earth on our mission to reset humanity's moral compass. Return total strength of body and mind to the Great and Honorable Zendala. God, please bless us all. Amen."

Mary's anger heightened when she observed the bearded pharaoh sleeping with her fingers intertwined around Zendala's powerful amulets. She awakened Maatkare by yanking on the ring of eternity. "Planning a hostile takeover, eh? I shall never follow a person that lacks moral character and deserves no trust. You remind me of Napoleon Bonaparte."

The pharaoh sat up with a jerk and peered up at the dark profile that blocked the glare of the morning sun. "Zendala insisted that I safeguard her amulets. Get off your high horse, Mary. Physical feats and intellectual achievements define great leaders—not their ethical acts."

"Our leaders must possess kindness, decency, charity, and

virtue. It is the only way that society can strengthen itself with those features." Mary shook her head in frustration. She felt angry and upset that Maatkare did not share the same goals as the other members. "What a pity that compassion falls by the wayside as we exalt those who lead us into bloody battles."

"All too often they are leaders of the Christian faith," jabbed the pharaoh.

Mary retorted, "What a shame that you do not read the Holy Bible. The Psalms of the Old Testament and the Gospels of the New Testament might warm even your cold heart."

"I have read the Bible. In it, righteous warfare prevails. Nowhere do I find condemnation about enslaving humans. Your deity condones the ownership of others." Maatkare stood up and placed her beard back in her pocket. She pointed northward. "A few miles from here millions of men, women, and children are captured. The slaves are transported like cattle across the Atlantic Ocean to the New World, South America, and the Caribbean. They are subjected to such inhumane treatment that fifty percent of them die before delivery to those who purchased them."

"What a hypocrite! We all know that ancient Egyptians exploited slaves in abundance."

Blandina exited the shelter and tried to make peace. "Lower your voices. God has answered my prayers. Zendala's fever has broken."

Mary rushed over to see for herself. She look back at Maatkare and issued a demand. "Our leader wants her amulets back."

"Too late!" Maatkare took a running leap. She attempted to transform and fly away with the magical jewelry. Instinct motivated Mary to scramble after the pharaoh and grab her feet. She pulled the traitor to the ground.

"Over my dead body will you steal Zendala's amulets. Give them back now!"

Zendala crawled out of the shelter. She stood up on shaky

legs and shielded her eyes from the bright sun. The frail leader turned her attention to the feuding women. "You two must learn how to get along." She held out her palm. "Thank you both for watching out for my amulets." Mary glared at the pharaoh as Maatkare surrendered them. *My scarab protected me from the seer's gift.* Zendala looked around and asked the whereabouts of Iona. Maatkare responded that she went exploring. They heard drums beating—boom… boom… boom, boom!

Iona flew out from the jungle squealing in distress. "Get out of here! They think that you are slave traders! They want to kill you." A group of black-skinned tribesmen arrived wearing wooden masks ornamented with large pointed teeth. Each native carried a sharp spear over one shoulder. They raised their weapons and took aim at the four women.

Blandina asked Zendala, "Do you feel strong enough to transform and fly?" She nodded.

The four ladies ran through the sand. Their feet met the salty spray. Three Merciful Ones changed form and joined Iona in the air. Zendala made a feeble attempt but lacked the strength and collapsed in the waves. Iona screamed, "Watch out!"

They heard a collective exhale as multiple spears launched. The weapons plunged into the water. The tribesmen ran toward the ancient woman who was stranded in the ocean. Goddess Sekhmet materialized in the shallow water to protect Zendala. She exposed her razor-sharp teeth and shook her lioness head back and forth with forceful menace. The goddess opened her mouth and roared with such ferocity that the natives covered their ears and backpedaled in terror. They turned and ran back into the safety of the palm trees.

Sekhmet helped Zendala to stand. The feeble woman leaned against her and exhaled a sigh of relief. "Do you watch out for me?"

"Always, my divine sister." The goddess of medicine

administered special healing drops. "You will feel better now."

"Thank you." Zendala closed her eyes and inhaled a deep breath. She forced herself to run a few steps and leap. This time the transformation worked. Sekhmet waved and disappeared.

The White Storks of Mercy flew away from the dangerous Ivory Coast. Zendala directed them north toward France to rescue Edmond Dantès at Château d'If. The glowing white stork's body felt fit and the clarity of her mind had returned. The sounds behind her of Iona weeping broke her compassionate heart.

OUR DEPARTED FRIEND

The White Storks of Mercy kept their promise to Joan and Napoleon. They circled the island fortress of Château d'If near Marseilles, France. The birds anticipated subterfuge so when two jailers threw a large sack off the cliff Zendala screamed, "Now!"

Five storks torpedoed headfirst into the Mediterranean Sea. They grabbed onto the heavy burlap bag with their feet and brought it to the surface. Unbeknownst to the guards the burial sack did not hold the deceased "mad monk" Abbé Faria. Instead, it contained his friend and fellow convict Edmond Dantès who was still very much alive.

Zendala had been gifted by Re with the strength to carry substantial weight with her feet. The glowing stork lifted the bag above the waves, flew to shore, and landed on the rocks. She transformed and signaled for her companions to wait in the air while she freed the spluttering fugitive. Dantès stood and shook the water from his body. He eyed the old woman with suspicion. "Where did you come from?"

"Prior to his death Napoleon Bonaparte asked us to rescue you from imprisonment. He believed that carrying his unopened letter did not justify such severe punishment. This fulfills his dying wish to serve justice. A ship will take you to the Italian island of Montecristo."

"How can I pay?"

"You may compensate them after you recoup Abbé Faria's

fortune."

Dantès appeared flabbergasted. "He told no one else about the money. Prior to his death Abbé Faria revealed the location of a hidden treasure to me alone."

Zendala shrugged. "Do not concern yourself. I know many things including where to find the stash of gold coins. Your secret remains safe with me."

"Please come along so that I can repay your valor. You saved me from drowning."

"We require no payment. I see a vessel approaching in the distance." She looked up at the others making patterns in the sky. "The White Storks of Mercy must meet the frigate transporting the coffins of Napoleon Bonaparte and our beloved Joan of Arc."

"Please promise that in the future you will claim the reward I set aside for you."

"I pledge my word that your generosity will aid our humanitarian efforts." The Great and Honorable Zendala turned away from the future Count of Montecristo. She took a few steps and leapt into the air to lead her phalanx on their journey seven hundred miles to western France. Edmond Dantès watched the supernatural spectacle in silence as the glowing white stork positioned herself at the head of the formation in the sky. Years passed before he learned about the legends who had rescued him from drowning in the Mediterranean Sea.

***

On the twenty-ninth of November in A.D. 1840 the storks arrived at the port of Cherbourg in Normandy where the black frigate *Belle Poule* now docked. Four of the birds transformed and left Iona circling above alone. Napoleon's imperial valet Louis Joseph Marchand accompanied the remains of the two deceased French military leaders. The somber gentleman with curly brown hair and long sideburns disembarked. He walked across the pier to the ancient woman he recognized from Saint Helena and handed her Joan's talisman.

Louis Joseph described the events that had led to the final hours of the maiden and her hero. "My speculation is that in desperation someone poisoned Joan and removed her amulet. The culprit placed it on the emperor's chest over his heart but it did not work as intended. I retrieved the talisman and we placed Joan's casket next to Napoleon's in a single grave." He bowed to the ancient woman and bid her adieu.

The Merciful Ones debated the location for Joan's final resting place. Blandina suggested, "Perhaps we can take her to the village of Domrémy-la-Pucelle where she grew up."

Maatkare retorted, "How do we transport her coffin?"

Zendala pulled the answer from the vast knowledge in her clairvoyant mind. "From Cherbourg the steamer *La Normandie* will take Napoleon's body to Le Havre and journey up the Seine River. It will stop at Rouen before going on to Paris. Joan's remains can also travel on the steamship. In the twentieth century a modern church will be built in Rouen near the stake where they claim that she burnt to death. We can bury her there."

By now Iona hovered over the frigate. Her childish mind protested at the suggestion of Rouen and she landed with a thud. "We cannot not put Joan to rest where they almost roasted her!" The storklet's hysteria escalated. "If that happens you can bury me along with her!" Mary reminded Iona that four hundred years had passed since that time.

Zendala coaxed the storklet's ten-year-old mind into a calmer state and asked her to propose a place. The storklet pondered. "What about the island of If? We can make it our home."

"Your suggestion of an island makes complete sense, Iona. I foresee that in the future we shall spend many years in Portugal. We can bury Joan on one of the Berlenga Islands off the central

Portuguese coast and make our new home there."

Maatkare proposed, "If we hire a horse and carriage to transport the coffin from here, we can rent a boat for the remainder of the journey."

Mary inquired with feigned innocence, "How do we pay for it?" *Got you there, Pharaoh!*

Blandina reached into her pocket and retrieved the diamond pendant she kept in a velvet pouch. She touched it and her mind swam with confusion as she recalled Reba's command. *Those belong to me.* The Christian martyr cleared her head with effort and presented the jewels on her open palm. "These will cover the expenses."

Mary, Maatkare, and Iona admired the sixteen pear-shaped white diamonds as big as corn kernels that surrounded a blue diamond the size of a woman's thumbnail. Zendala smiled at the unselfish gesture and closed Blandina's fingers around the pendant. "Marie Antoinette gave this to you and it is yours to keep. Do not worry about our finances." The leader said nothing about Dantès' generosity.

Maatkare pointed out another complication. "Will the *Belle Poule's* captain release her coffin to us without presenting identification papers?"

Zendala nodded. "He will. Come with me." She took off and they followed her to the frigate that was painted black to honor France's deceased emperor. His Royal Highness François d'Orléans—the Prince of Joinville and son of King Louis Philippe I—turned his intense gaze skyward to where five storks approached in spiral formation.

The handsome twenty-two-year-old wore the naval uniform of a French captain. On his small frame he sported a dark waistcoat with gold epaulettes that denoted his rank. Gold thread embroidered his cuffs, high collar, and the stripes along the outer seams of his narrow-cut pants. A gold belt secured his sword and a thick red sash signified his royal position. The captain held a decorative bircorne hat in his white-gloved hands.

The smallest stork remained circling overhead. To his surprise four of the large birds landed at his feet. The captain's astonishment turned to shock when they transformed into women wearing black capes over their white dresses. Their leader took command of the breathtaking moment. She spoke louder than usual knowing that he was almost deaf. "Allow me to introduce Maatkare Hatshepsut, the fifth pharaoh of Egypt's Eighteenth Dynasty. This is Mary Stuart, the queen of Scotland and former queen consort of France." Both ladies held their chins high. Mary towered over Maatkare.

The brown-haired captain with a trimmed beard dropped to one knee and lowered his head to acknowledge them. Zendala took his elbow and invited him to stand again. "I present Blandina of Lyon, a Christian slave martyred in A.D. 177 at the behest of Roman Emperor Marcus Aurelius."

The captain bowed. "It is a privilege, Madam."

"I am the Great and Honorable Zendala. Like the pharaoh I hail from ancient Egypt. We Merciful Ones are committed to promoting peace through our humanitarian actions. As birds we are the White Storks of Mercy." She paused to gauge the man's reaction. When he seemed to accept the supernatural event and its explanation she continued. "After you transfer Napoleon's casket to *La Normandie* will you chart your ship's course to the Berlenga Islands in Portugal? We must bury our beloved Joan of Arc who was a member of our coterie."

The three Merciful Ones placed the hoods of their full-length black capes upon their heads and surrounded the wooden coffin on the ship's deck. Zendala also donned her hood but remained standing by Captain d'Orléans and kept her golden eyes focused on him.

He caught his breath. "I knew not that we carried the body

of the courageous Joan of Arc. She saved my ancestor's home and family from English usurpers. My vessel is at your service."

Zendala joined the others. With heads bowed and hands folded they remained with Joan until the *Belle Poule* departed Cherbourg. The frigate sailed south to central Portugal. The White Storks of Mercy flew ahead to search for a proper burial site.

They found the perfect place on Estela Islet. Adjacent to a steep cliff that jutted from the sea, a wide alcove with a pristine beach beckoned them. A rocky incline served as steps up to a sandy dune. An outcropping of jagged granite dotted with pink feldspar created a natural refuge from the elements. The precipice tapered into a pinnacle carpeted in horseweed and wild carnations. Eroded boulders on its west side protected an olive tree that struggled against the Atlantic winds.

The frigate arrived and dispatched a dinghy carrying the captain, the coffin, and four French sailors through the shallow surf. They followed Maatkare, Blandina, and Mary up the stone stairs to the sheltered dune. The men stopped to regain their breath before picking up their precious load again.

Zendala detained Captain d'Orléans and handed him a small silver ampoule. "Administer several drops from this vial into each ear. My sister Sekhmet is the ancient Egyptian goddess of medicine. She concocted it to heal your hearing loss." He looked around in vain hoping to see the deity. "Sekhmet honored my wish for privacy. Please accept this in gratitude for your assistance." The ancient woman took his arm and he helped her up the stone steps.

Iona selected a burial spot near the olive tree. She waited on a branch and wept while the sailors dug Joan's gravesite with shovels they brought on the dinghy. The Merciful Ones gathered around with their heads bowed as Joan's coffin was lowered using strong ropes. Mary borrowed the captain's Bible and led the funeral rites. The ladies each placed a shovelful of dirt on the box. The sailors finished the job. Iona remained in the tree covering her head with a black-tipped wing.

Blandina gave a benediction. "During these sorrowful times we cry out for our departed friend. Our hearts are comforted to know that Joan resides with God."

Captain d'Orléans placed a small wooden cross from the altar in his cabin upon the fresh grave. He led his men down the rocky cliff and boarded the frigate. The *Belle Poule* returned to France and the legend of the White Storks of Mercy spread even further.

They settled into their new home on Estela Islet with little enthusiasm. Iona held a vigil from the olive tree. Blandina stayed within herself in solemn silence. Mary took advantage of every opportunity to remind Maatkare about the damning secret they kept from Zendala. "You are lucky that Zendala's sympathy pains prevented her from realizing that you tried to steal her amulets on the Ivory Coast. Thank goodness I caught you in the act, traitor!"

Maatkare scoffed. She stalked away with confidence and fondled her scarab. *I shall always be immune from the chief's clairvoyance. I can do as I please.*

Zendala turned her thoughts to the future of her coterie. Their fractured unity plagued her. It seemed pointless to consider upcoming plans when two of its members hated each other and sorrow silenced the others. Her mind churned in circles and thoughts of Reba brought even more frustration. It made no sense that her psychic vision became muddled when she tried to locate her sister. *I need to know that she is safe.*

WELCOME MY BEAUTY

The Irish potato famine devastated Reba's adopted country. By A.D. 1850 the Second Earl of Bantry found himself in dire straits. He was unable to pay for his annual supply of Tawny Vintage Port so Richard White bartered with Diego Bour da Bon. The earl offered the merchant his ancient Egyptian throne as well as his cat Cleopatra. The shrewd twenty-year-old Portuguese vintner sweetened the deal for himself.

Diego made an additional demand to compensate for his dislike of cats. "I want the tapestry that once belonged to Marie Antoinette. My mother will find a perfect place to hang it at Quinta Bour da Bon." Diego unloaded the port and collected the eclectic pieces. He set sail for sunny Oporto with the Siamese cat.

Reba traveled in a large gilded birdcage donated by Richard White to insure her comfort and safe passage. She resented him for giving her away but changed her mind when she recalled watching tenant farmers beg for scraps. *Those people offended me. I hope for a more pleasing visual experience at Quinta Bour da Bon.*

The sails directed the vessel southward. A miserable and seasick Reba sprawled inside her confines and watched Diego Bour da Bon. The man's chocolate-brown hair fell in thick waves around an oblong face that featured an aristocratic nose and dominant chin. Thick dark brows set off eyes the color of cognac and a confident smile completed the handsome package. The cat admitted that she found him attractive but instinct told her not to trust him.

He busied himself whittling off the semi-precious stones from the sun-shaped mosaic of Re that was carved on the back of the ancient throne. Reba fumed. *He dresses like a gentleman but he is uncouth.* Diego finished desecrating the throne and the greedy man pocketed the gems. The naive man triggered the all-seeing Eye of Horus. It opened Ramses' secret hiding place and exposed Reba's gold gorget earrings. The scoundrel seized her precious jewelry. The cat hissed and vowed to get Maatkare's gift back by any means necessary.

That night Reba's new owner consumed too much port and passed out on the throne. She shape shifted into a mouse and snuck out between the bars of the cage. The mouse climbed up Diego's leg and crawled inside his coat to retrieve the stolen earrings from his inside pocket. The inebriated man awoke and grabbed the small rodent. She bit his finger but dropped the earrings. Diego hollered and threw the mouse across the room. Reba ricocheted off the floor and landed in one of his boots.

The horrified drunk stumbled barefoot out of his cabin. The mouse climbed out of the boot and raced back into the birdcage. Reba shape shifted into her feline form and spent the rest of the voyage contemplating her predicament. *How can the Great Persuader use her mental powers and manipulate him to return my earrings when he refuses to look at me?*

They arrived at Quinta Bour da Bon in Portugal's Upper Douro Valley. A hungover Diego dumped the birdcage and its occupant on the ground. Reba was mortified to see that her new home was nothing more than an old whitewashed stone building. *I cannot live here!*

Perl Alvares Bour da Bon welcomed her rakish son home with a peck on his handsome cheek. She scowled at the exotic ancient Egyptian throne. The thirty-nine-year-old woman snubbed the gaudy relic. She pointed one of her canes at the artifact. "Put that eyesore in the garden beneath the arched trellis where the birds of paradise grow. I want it out of my sight."

Diego cringed at his Spanish mother's abrasive voice. The chagrined son presented her with Marie Antoinette's exquisite tapestry. She insisted that it also remain outside. "Why display something that belonged to a French Catholic queen who lost her head? We are Jewish!"

Inside the birdcage Reba seethed at the insult from the unsightly woman with a pasty face, long jaw, and protruding chin. Perl winced from the chronic pain in her hips and hobbled away. Diego followed his mother and left the Siamese cat alone to bake in the sun. Reba's loud and incessant yowling got the attention of Diego's identical twin brother Afonso. He ran outside, lifted her out with care, and brought her to his chest in a tender embrace. "Welcome my beauty. I shall name you Sky because your blue eyes remind me of sunny Portuguese days."

Not another name—Cat, Bijou, Cleopatra and now Sky. Nevertheless, she found Afonso Bour da Bon irresistible. The resemblance to his twin stopped at physical traits. His soft voice and gentle bearing belied those of Diego. Thanks to Afonso she enjoyed her new life at the Quinta. Panoramic vistas showcased thousands of steep stair-stepping terraces covered in vineyards. It reminded her of grapes growing along the Nile Delta in ancient Egypt. Reba fell head over paws in love with Afonso. He grew to cherish Sky but not as much as he cherished his fiancée Elizabeth Atkinson.

The enamored Portuguese man called the nineteen-year-old Elizabeth his English Rose. Her sweet scent and blushing innocence brought fragrant pink damask roses to his mind. The young woman's delicate beauty rivaled the most perfect blossom. She was at the Quinta to plan the wedding uniting the two prominent area vintners. Today she wore a cream-colored and high-waisted muslin dress. It was gathered under her ample breasts with a pink silk ribbon. Her petite nose was powdered to conceal freckles and short wavy bangs offset her baby-blue eyes. A few ringlets escaped from her bun of light chestnut-brown hair to frame her round face.

In the living room Afonso and Elizabeth sat together on a small couch. Reba watched the couple from behind a curtain that concealed the kitchen pantry. Afonso stroked one of his fiancée's pale arms. She shielded her mouth with a graceful hand to conceal a giggle over something he whispered. On both of her small and perfect ears she wore Reba's gold gorget earrings. The seething cat ran out the open door into the garden and jumped onto Ramses' throne. *Why did Diego give my jewelry to her? Maybe he is trying to buy her love and steal her from Afonso. I shall hatch a fiendish plot to get rid of that English Rose.*

Darkness fell and Reba remained on the throne in the moonlight. The conniving cat had a brilliant idea. She felt protected from prying eyes by the tall trellis and summoned her cat-headed sister. The angry feline complained when at last Bastet materialized. "What took you so long?"

The bored goddess examined her long sharp fingernails. "I remind you that as a mortal you wait for me. What do you want anyway?"

"I want Elizabeth Atkinson to disappear from Quinta Bour da Bon. I know how to do it but I need your help."

"First explain why you are sitting on the throne of King Ramses VI."

"It came with me from the manor house where I lived in Ireland. I discovered that the silver moon in the night sky represents the left Eye of Horus. Goddesses Nekhebet and Wazit protect it on either side." Reba leapt down from the seat and allowed Bastet to take a closer look. "Push the Eye of Horus with your finger and watch what happens."

Bastet did as her sister suggested. The Eye, the vulture, and the cobra popped out like the piece of a puzzle. This action also triggered the seat to open. Bastet held the ancient object in her cupped hands. "Because I am the sun god's daughter, I protect the Eye of Re. I possess great wisdom about the magic of ancient Egyptian Eyes."

"Excuse me, I too am the sun god's daughter!"

"Figure it out for yourself, Sister." Bastet's image faded.

"Wait!" Reba hated groveling. "You are the magnificent goddess of cats and much more powerful than I am as a mere mortal. I cannot proceed without you. If you help me now, I promise not to bother you again."

Bastet reappeared. "You said that last time. Do not forget who is the boss." She made a triumphant show of lifting Reba high off the ground as she closed the hinged seat and sat down. "To make this wicked scheme work we need hair from both Diego and Elizabeth. Steal some from the brush in his bedroom and pluck some strands from Elizabeth's head. Implant in her mind an obsession to marry Diego rather than Afonso. We shall meet here tomorrow at sunset."

Late the following afternoon Reba cozied up to the English Rose as she and Afonso sat together again in the living room. Elizabeth wore a fancy skirt the color of purple irises and layered in ruffles. Her provocative lacy camisole showed more than a hint of cleavage. She allowed her matching shawl to fall behind her back to expose bare white shoulders. Elizabeth wore no jewelry except for the gold gorget earrings. Reba jumped onto her lap and sunk into the heap of shiny fabric.

The cat stood on her hind legs and placed her front paws on Elizabeth's shoulders. She stared into her baby-blue eyes. Reba messaged, 'You love Diego not Afonso.' She repeated the phrase until the young woman whispered, "I love Diego not Afonso."

"What did you say, my dear?"

Elizabeth looked at him in confusion. "I cannot remember.

Sky is making me nervous."

Reba batted at one of the earrings. *These belong to me.* Elizabeth's hand flew to her ear and she swatted at the annoying cat. Reba bit into a ringlet right before Afonso rescued both his cat and his fiancée. Afonso laughed. "I think you scared each other."

The Siamese cat sprang from his arms and disappeared with a few strands of chestnut-brown hair in her mouth. *Mission accomplished.*

Elizabeth composed herself and fussed with her hair. "I am looking forward to the family dinner tonight so that we can announce our wedding date." The perplexed young woman frowned. *Am I to marry Afonso or Diego?*

UNTIL THEY BREATHE NO MORE

Reba trotted back to the garden with Elizabeth's hair hanging from her mouth. She had stolen Diego's brush that morning and left it under the throne for Bastet. The goddess now waited for her there. The Siamese cat jumped up and balanced on the big chair's arm. She watched her sister braid the dark brown and light chestnut hairs together.

Bastet explained the magical process. "Each part of the Eye of Horus represents one of our senses. First I join the essences of Diego and Elizabeth." She rubbed the tiny plait along the curved brow of the Eye. "Each one's thoughts focus only on the other." Bastet applied the miniscule braid to the pupil. "The lovers see only their beloved." She brushed the hairs over the inner and outer whites of the Eye. "They speak words of adoration into the ears of no one else."

The cat goddess added a drop of rose perfume to the braided plait. "As she inhales his masculine scent her fragrance drives him wild." She stroked the teardrop below the pupil. "Elizabeth and Diego learn every detail of their sweetheart's body." The goddess traced the curve of a single long lower lash on the Eye with the braid. "Now for the sense of taste. Use your imagination, Sister." Bastet placed the braid over the Eye of Horus and removed another vial from her pouch. She poured the contents over it.

Reba watched in awe as the hairs bubbled and melted to cover the Eye like varnish. Bastet stood and held the Eye in both hands. She raised it to the heavens and recited her spell. "O powerful god Horus! I ask you to grant the mortals Diego Bour da Bon and Elizabeth Atkinson a loving union that lasts until they breathe no more." The exhausted goddess wedged the Eye back into its place and lowered herself onto Ramses' throne. She turned to Reba. "You really owe me now." Bastet vanished into the cosmos and the cat headed back to the Quinta to spy.

In the dining room after a celebratory meal an excited Afonso announced the wedding date. Perl sat between the young couple and gave her favorite son a peck on the cheek. Elizabeth seemed preoccupied. She sipped her glass of champagne and stared at Afonso's brother. Diego sat at the opposite end of the wooden table. His forty-two-year-old father Julio sat next to him and offered a toast to the couple. Diego did not care that Afonso was their favorite son. He was a loner and not interested in marriage but he had a fixation on his brother's fiancée. The roguish twin grinned at Elizabeth and she blushed. She excused herself citing a sudden need for fresh air.

A few minutes later Julio watched with curiosity as Diego got up and followed Elizabeth outside. Perl and Afonso were so busy chatting about wedding details that they did not notice. Julio fondled his black moustache and waited for their return. Several minutes passed before the suspicious father strode with purpose out to the courtyard. He found his deceitful son embracing Elizabeth with undisguised passion beneath the weeping willow tree. Julio exploded with anger. "Both of you leave now and never come back!" He disowned Diego on the spot and sent the disgraced couple away without consulting either Afonso or Perl.

Julio returned to the dining room with bad news. Elizabeth's betrayal broke Afonso's heart. He refused to look at Sky who now pawed at him for attention. Her similar blue eyes reminded him too much of Elizabeth. He asked his father to find the cat a new home. Like Diego, Julio disliked the creature and felt no qualms about getting rid of it. He picked up Sky with rough calloused hands and grumbled beneath his breath, "I am going to drown you. Afonso will never know." He did not realize that Reba understood and spoke many languages including Portuguese. The Siamese cat hissed at him, scratched his face, and freed herself.

Reba darted out the door and ran for her life after the ostracized couple. She yowled for their attention. Elizabeth stopped and picked her up. Reba purred with relief. "It appears that I have a new friend." Their predicament seemed dire. The young woman asked, "What shall we do now? We have nothing. I even left my handbag behind."

Diego reassured her. "I always carry plenty of cash, sweetheart. We can sell your gold earrings to buy what we need." Reba hissed at the suggestion.

The banished trio left the Upper Douro Valley in the near dark. They hitched a ride on a wagon headed to the town of Pinhão. The following day the couple and their cat boarded a small boat loaded with barrels of immature port. The vessel's captain recognized the vintner and took them to Vila Nova de Gaia where Diego hired a carriage to Oporto. They were desperate to avoid the Atkinson family and rushed to get on a ship to Lisbon. Upon their arrival in Portugal's coastal capital city Diego filed papers to change his surname to da Gama. Soon he took Elizabeth as his bride. Instead of a bouquet she carried a purring Siamese cat.

Elizabeth's father followed Julio's example and disowned his daughter. However, her discrete and sympathetic mother gifted a large sum of her family money to the newlyweds. They used some to rent a modest flat and the remainder to start a new company. Portuguese authorities frowned on Jewish-owned businesses so Diego kept his religion secret. He registered it as da Gama Shipping and Transportation. In late A.D. 1850 Elizabeth gave birth to their daughter Matilda. In a few short years Diego made a fortune. Reba found her lifestyle upgraded once again but she never forgot Afonso.

Diego and Elizabeth's marriage turned sour after the birth of their son Alberto. The shrieking woman confronted her husband. "You played such a heartless and cruel trick on me! I hate you! I always loved Afonso." Elizabeth ran down the hallway of their opulent residence in Lisbon and into the bedroom. She collapsed onto the canopy bed in hysterics. Elizabeth refused to eat and stayed awake for days on end. If the tortured woman did manage to fall asleep she was plagued with recurring nightmares. Reba wondered if the ancient Egyptian spell had worn off.

Diego feared that his wife teetered on the edge of insanity. He had no close friends so the worried man confided in the cat. "I never put Elizabeth under a spell to win her heart. Nor did I trick her by pretending to be my twin brother. I do not know why she chose me over Afonso." The miserable man got no response from Reba. *What do you expect me to do about it?*

Over time the relationship between Elizabeth and Diego deteriorated further. The hysteria and arguments drove Reba to distraction and she took matters into her own paws. In A.D. 1860 the Great Persuader used her mental telepathy to convince the shipping tycoon to purchase a lavish estate in the resort town of Sintra. Diego hired the renowned German psychiatrist Dr. Jacob Goldman to provide in-home treatment for "Elizabeth the Mad." Diego employed a private teacher for ten-year-old Matilda who moved to Sintra to provide affection and comfort for her ailing mother.

Reba cared little for Diego's company but she remained at the Lisbon residence with him and four-year-old Alberto. The boy was tutored by the best. From a young age they prepared him to take over his father's business that had grown into Portugal's largest transportation company. It carried exported goods worldwide and held the exclusive contract for international distribution of many wine labels including Bour da Bon Tawny Vintage Port. Neither Julio nor Afonso ever met the company's owner so they did not realize that Diego was their kin. In his own best interest, the shrewd businessman kept his mouth shut.

***

On Estela Islet the Merciful Ones lived a quiet life while Iona continued to recover from Joan's death. The storklet moved through her mourning at a slow pace. At last Iona accepted the loss of her friend and appeared ready to participate in the fullness of life again. Mary had experienced enough bereavement to deal with Joan's passing in a healthier manner. She prayed the rosary using her pearl beads and captured memories of Joan in her pocket journal. However, the disloyal actions of Maatkare consumed her thoughts. *I shall never trust the pharaoh again.* She burned to tell Zendala what had happened on the Ivory Coast.

Maatkare never allowed herself to develop attachment to another person including Joan. Her misplaced devotion still belonged to Reba in spite of the cat's fickle attitude. The two did not realize that they now resided in the same country and neither did Zendala. Blandina remained withdrawn. The fifteen-year-old Christian martyr lacked the maturity and mental fortitude to cope. She continued to repress the trauma from her torture in Roman Gallia. It heightened her grief over Joan's death.

Zendala missed the maiden as well. She took comfort in the beauty of the coves with their sandy beaches and clear turquoise water. It seemed like a remote and private setting but the storks lived a mere six miles off the Portuguese coast.

The constant bickering between Mary and Maatkare stopped when Zendala reached her limit. "Enough you two! Move your egos aside and forgive each other. Forget everything that happened in the past. We go on from here unified or not at all!"

Mary decided to confess. "But you do not realize that Maatkare tried to..."

"Nor do I care! Who stands united with me on our pursuit for peace and justice?"

Blandina and Iona replied in unison, "I do!" Maatkare and Mary nodded their agreement while continuing to glare at each other.

In A.D. 1859 Zendala decided that Iona was ready to resume her apprenticeship. She suggested a trip to the Italian island of Montecristo to locate the gold left by Edmond Dantès. She informed her coterie that after rescuing him from the Mediterranean Sea he had gifted them part of a deserted pirate treasure for their humanitarian actions.

Gray clouds threatened moisture as the storks soared over the ruins of San Mamiliano Monastery. Zendala called out, "I know an efficient method for removing some of the gold coins on this visit. However, we need a plan for transporting the remainder of our bounty." A scheme presented itself in Zendala's mind when Re's sun peaked through the clouds and lit up the bay and its secret grotto.

A school of spotted eagle rays swam around performing a series of dips and jumps in the crystal-clear water revealing their white bellies. Bright red circles outlined in orange dotted the deep purple tops of their flat bodies. These magnificent creatures measured sixteen-feet wide and weighed five hundred pounds. In perfect synchronization the rays whipped their barbed venomous black tails against the water before disappearing beneath the sea. Zendala commented, "It is unusual for an aggregation of spotted eagle rays to venture out of tropical waters."

Iona marveled, "They look like colorful water angels. I wish they had stayed longer."

The leader shouted, "Everyone follow me into the grotto." Inside the cavern they transformed and found a rusty anchor leaning against loose boulders. They removed the heavy obstacles. The treasure was in an old chest. Maatkare and Mary—the strongest women in the coterie—pried the lid open. The loot that had been stashed in the seventeenth century by the infamous Barbarossa Brothers was revealed. Iona shrieked with delight. She had never seen money before.

Blandina asked, "How we will we carry it?"

Zendala explained, "Sixteen gold coins weigh one pound. If we put that amount into each pocket of our uniforms, we can fly home to Estela without feeling burdened."

Iona wailed, "What about me? I have no pockets."

"You can help us hide them when we get home." Zendala remained patient with her.

The pharaoh objected to the proposal. "What happens to the money when we transform into birds and then back again into women?"

"It is magic, Maatkare. Trust me that this works. We can organize a better means of transport in the future." They divided up the coins and concealed the chest that still contained the bulk of the treasure. The pharaoh pocketed extra coins for her secret stash.

The storks made their way north up the boot of Italy towards Lago di Garda. They flew over the town of Solferino. On the ground below them Zendala spotted the horrific aftermath of recent combat. French soldiers that were allies of the Sardinians were fighting against the Austrian Army. Forty thousand men lay dead, wounded, or captive on the ground. The leader veered off and changed their course. She did not want the others to smell blood mixed with gunpowder or to witness the massacre. *I dare not expose Iona or Blandina to the carnage.*

Zendala motioned Maatkare forward with her wing. She directed her to lead the others home. "We shall meet there. Bury the coins in the ground next to the olive tree."

The divine stork turned back toward the battlefield and searched for a safe place to land and transform. She provided basic first aid to the suffering men around her. She ripped the hem of her white dress to make bandages and whispered soothing words to them. Zendala proffered a hand to help a wounded French soldier. An injured Austrian fighter attacked from behind and bayoneted his enemy. Before he expired the Frenchman managed to slit the Austrian's throat.

They fell on top of the ancient woman and covered her in a bloody blanket of death. The pointless massacre of so many men from neighboring countries overwhelmed her. It took considerable effort for Zendala to extricate herself. She got to her feet and wailed to the heavens with grief and anger. "Where is your humanity?"

The plaintive cry of her voice carried across the war-torn landscape. It reached the ears of a Swiss businessman named Henri Dunant who had also witnessed the nine-hour battle firsthand. The powerful lament caused him to stand in awe as he searched the cloudy sky. He wondered if it was the voice of God. The Swiss man convinced a group of reluctant locals to help him erect makeshift tents. He insisted that they aid injured soldiers from both sides of the conflict.

Zendala tore a large square of white cloth from the back of her dress and used their blood to paint the symbol + upon it. She placed the hands of the two dead soldiers together as if they were friends and made her way to a canvas hospital tent. Zendala attached the red + to one of the shelters. She found the Swiss man with his sleeves rolled up. The generous leader offered a handful of gold coins to him.

The ancient woman turned away and took a few quick steps. She leapt into the sky and transformed into a glowing white stork. Henri Dunant and the others giving aid watched the miraculous spectacle of her departure. The gruesome scene at the Battle of Solferino left an unforgettable impression on the Swiss man. He returned to his home in Geneva and started an organization to provide care for wounded soldiers. It became the International Committee of the Red Cross. In A.D. 1901 Henri Dunant received the first Nobel Peace Prize in recognition of his humanitarian work. The French economist Frédéric Passy—founder of the European peace movement—also received the prestigious first award.

***

On Estela Islet three white storks with black tipped wings transformed into women. Iona landed next to them. Maatkare took pleasure in assuming command. She ordered Blandina and Mary to climb up to the olive tree next to Joan's grave and empty the gold coins from their pockets. The pharaoh retrieved a shovel left by the French sailors and followed them up the hill. Maatkare directed the Scottish queen to dig a hole. She refused and stalked off after placing her thirty-two coins next to the tree. Blandina stepped forward and took the shovel. "Come help me, Iona." The storklet pushed the coins into the hole with her bill. They buried the gold in silence next to the olive tree.

Darkness fell and they slept as storks on the dune protected by a ledge of granite halfway between the beach and the hilltop. Maatkare feigned slumber and then snuck away. She flew back up the hill, transformed, and fell to her knees. The pharaoh removed the beard from her pocket and used it to scrape the dirt away from the small wooden cross on the grave. *This accessory comes in handy. There is no reason to ruin my manicure.*

Maatkare continued to work her way down and around the cross until she pulled it loose. She wasted no time hiding her extra gold coins in the hole and replaced the dirt. The pharaoh looked up at the sound of wings flapping. Iona landed next to her. Maatkare pushed the storklet over. The bully placed two strong hands around Iona's bill. "Are you going to keep quiet?"

The petrified apprentice nodded her head. "Do not say a word until I explain." Maatkare freed Iona's bill and set her upright. "I did not mean to hurt you. I wanted no one to see this. Our beloved maiden died without her fair share of Dantès' treasure. Please do not to tell the others. They will think that I am stealing. I want to buy a fancier cross for Joan's grave. This can be another secret between best friends."

"That is the nicest thing I ever heard."

Maatkare exhaled with relief. *I got away with it.*

Zendala returned to the islet a few days later. She landed on the soft sand of their carved-out bluff to change into her human form. Blandina gasped when she saw the ancient woman's white dress covered in blood. "She is injured!"

The leader raised her hand in protest. "I am all right. It is not my blood." She explained what happened at Solferino.

Mary apologized. "I am sorry that we did not stay to help."

Maatkare interrupted her. "And do what? Hold the hands of dying soldiers?"

The queen of Scots ignored her. "We should become trained nurses."

Zendala agreed. "That is a great idea, Mary. The timing is perfect for us to attend a new school in London that has been organized by a British nurse. Her name is Florence Nightingale."

Iona squawked with disappointment. "What about me?"

Blandina suggested, "Perhaps you can stay with Zendala's kin on the Isle of Souls. Heka the god of magic also lives there. So does the ancient Egyptian phoenix Bennu who dwells on the Tree of Life."

Iona liked the idea of spending time with the Sacred Storks of the Bach and other exotic deities. "I shall miss all of you. Please do not forget me."

Mary hugged the storklet. "You are always in our hearts."

"Let me accompany Iona," proposed Maatkare. "I do not intend to wash dirty people and clean bedpans." *I prefer to spend my time with Heka.*

Zendala ignored the insolent pharaoh. "We need to take enough money to pay our tuition and other expenses."

Iona revealed, "Maatkare brought back extra coins for Joan."

Mary arched her red eyebrows with suspicion and turned to the pharaoh. "Where did you hide your secret stash?"

Maatkare opened her mouth intending to fib just as Iona blurted out the truth. "She buried them beneath the wooden cross on Joan's grave." The pharaoh glared at Iona who appeared very uncomfortable about breaking her promise.

"There the coins will stay," insisted Zendala. *I shall deal with the deceitful pharaoh later.* "Now we need to get some rest."

The next morning the White Storks of Mercy headed northeast to the mysterious Isle of Souls located in the middle of Lake Geneva, Switzerland.

LADY OF LIGHT

Orchid MacCloud returned to Ireland after she and Reba parted company outside of Lyon, France in the late sixteenth century. The Druidess lived a peaceful life transforming back and forth from an aging woman into a haunting Ghost Orchid. The magic bestowed by the Elves of Sage diminished and by the mid-1800s the Lady of Light's shining beauty existed only as a legend in Irish folklore. Her wrinkled skin remained phosphorescent and her sparkling emerald eyes dulled from cataracts. The red hair of the Druidess thinned and turned gray.

Locals living in Dublin that saw the old crone talking with invisible faeries ignored her eccentricities. As long as she healed the sick (but did not raise the dead) the church left her alone. Toward the end of the Great Potato Famine Orchid decided that it was time to face reality. Some starving Irish citizens had consumed all of her medicinal herbs and flowers.

The disheartened Druidess sat down on a log in her ransacked garden. She leaned on her elbows to consult with her friend the leprechaun Seán O'Brien. He perched on a mossy stump protecting a small pail full of gold nuggets between his knees. The little guy wore a moth-eaten wool sweater and patched dungarees. His knit hat was pulled down to cover the big ears on his wide head. Seán raised his sparkling eyes up to Orchid and grinned to display pink toothless gums. "May I assist you, Lady of Light?"

"I fear that I must leave my homeland before I starve.

How does an old woman without money coax her way onto a steamship destined for England?"

The sweet leprechaun who was the height of a man's foot proffered the bucketful of treasure. Orchid refused his generous gift. He scratched the stubble on his scruffy face. "I am only a digger of gold but I can give you this advice. Traveling as the Ghost Orchid may bring favorable attention that enables you to leave the Emerald Isle in style."

"Brilliant idea, Seán O'Brien! This means I need a host tree to journey on."

"For you Druids the sacred oak provides a gateway to the faerie realm."

"Aye, my wee comrade. A sturdy tree grows adjacent to the glass house at Dublin's Botanical Gardens. This mighty oak represents my ticket to freedom."

Orchid kissed her forefinger and placed its tip on Seán O'Brien's flat nose. His puffy cheeks reddened. The embarrassed leprechaun scooted off the stump and scurried away with his heavy bucket of gold. He called back to the Druidess over his shoulder. "Good luck to you!"

The Lady of Light made her way to Dublin. She discussed her plan with the tree spirit and its faeries including the tiny ones living on every acorn. "Special magic is required. Instead of a single Ghost Orchid I shall need to manifest into numerous flowers." She knew the species well. Its lowest tendrils curved down and inward like skinny legs. Blossoms resembling albino frogs appeared to float in midair when the bark of their host trees camouflaged their prolific roots. Orchid hugged the oak and transformed into the flowering plant. The largest of the fifteen blooms that her spirit inhabited took on the radiance of the moon.

***

Dr. David Moore almost fainted when he discovered the huge Ghost Orchids living on the Irish oak. As the Scottish director of Dublin's Botanical Gardens, he dispatched a boastful message to the curator at London's Kew Gardens, John Smith. The site featured a unique structure called the Palm House that sheltered the most exotic plants found on earth. The prototype's large-scale architectural use of wrought iron encased sixteen thousand panes of hand-blown glass.

The moment that Curator Smith learned of the mysterious Ghost Orchids in Dublin he concocted a sly scheme to bring them across the Irish Sea. He gathered the members of the Ladies' Garden Club of London who agreed to fund an expedition. The Royal Navy lent the battleship *HMS Agamemnon* to aid the peacetime cause. The English group arrived in Dublin but to their dismay Dr. Moore refused access to his precious find. Queen Victoria interceded and directed the Irish arborists to uproot the grand old oak. They transported it onto the battleship and fastened the huge tree to the middle mast with thick ropes and protected it with tarps.

In the spring of A.D. 1851 the rare Ghost Orchids and all of the other mystical beings on the Irish oak moved into Palm House. They arrived in time for the grand opening of Hyde Park's Crystal Palace. It was the main event of the Great Exhibition organized by Queen Victoria's husband, Prince Albert. His cousin Ferdinand II was invited to attend the elaborate event.

The handsome and intelligent king consort of Portugal appeared older than his thirty-five years. Silver streaked his dark hair and trimmed beard. His brown eyes revealed both sadness and fatigue. The husband of Queen Maria II had fathered ten children but only seven survived birth. Ferdinand had acted as regent during his wife's numerous pregnancies and postpartum recoveries. She encouraged him to accept Prince Albert's invitation.

The avid nature lover and artist convinced his cousin to arrange a private visit to Kew Gardens. He wanted to paint the famous Ghost Orchids not yet on public display. On the night of the new moon Ferdinand entered Palm House and observed the magnificent flowers for the first time. He perceived the Ghost Orchids as both exquisite and haunting. In the near darkness the luminescent white blossoms floated in midair as if independent of their stems. The one in the middle was bigger and shone brighter than the others.

He frowned at the tall circlet of gilded iron bars surrounding the tree. The Ghost Orchids reminded him of imprisoned doves of peace. Ferdinand shook his head in disgust at the fancy jail and propped his sketchbook against the enclosure. He inspected the largest flower. Within the whorls of wilting white petals two emerald green eyes stared back at him. Tears of dew dripped down its tendrils and splashed on Ferdinand's hand as it reached through the bars. He shook his head and blinked his overtired eyes.

"It is a sin to imprison such beauty. I refuse to dishonor God's creation by painting the Ghost Orchids as if they exist in nature when they are living here like criminals." He bent down to retrieve his sketchbook. On one of its pages was written **help** in smudged moist soil.

Orchid gave the man no time to rationalize. She transformed into her haggard body and stood in front of the Irish oak. "I am Orchid MacCloud—a Druidess from the Iron Age of Celtic Ireland. Please free this sacred tree, its mystical occupants, and myself before we perish."

Ferdinand rubbed his eyes as if they deceived him. In his presence the exquisite shining Ghost Orchid turned into the oldest woman he had ever beheld. The concept of magic alarmed him and he struggled to overcome his uneasiness. "How may I assist you, Druidess?"

"Because I am a prisoner, I no longer possess the supernatural power to free myself. The other mystical beings residing in Palm House cannot help me without your assistance. Will you aid our escape before daylight?"

Ferdinand did not hesitate. His mind opened to embrace the mystical event. "I shall try to save you as well as the mighty oak and your invisible friends."

"Our indebtedness to you knows no bounds, kind sir." The handsome gentleman secured a position deep in her heart. He listened to a condensed version of the Lady of Light's epic life story. "I prattle on yet I do not even know your name."

He bowed. "I am Ferdinand August Franz Anton. I was born into Austrian royalty and I am now married to Queen Maria II of Portugal."

"Your bearing strikes me as regal indeed. You look sad, Dom Fernando."

"Please call me Ferdinand. The stillbirth of our last child devastated us." He paused to consider the expertise of the Druidess in utilizing the gifts of nature for healing. "May I offer you sanctuary at our palace in Sintra? Its renovation nears completion."

"Thank you but I must live in nature."

"Nearby in Parque da Pena you will find abundant trees, flowers, and mossy banks along freshwater streams."

"Your park sounds like paradise on earth. Perhaps I can help your family in some way. England is not the place for me."

Orchid summoned nature's spirits inside the huge Palm House at Kew Gardens. She required the assistance of every elf, nymph, dwarf, and faerie. The Druidess adored the magical creatures and admired their ability to coexist together in harmony. She called upon the dwarfs for their expertise as craftsmen and masters of incantation. Together with the king they orchestrated an operation to remove the iron bars with a hacksaw he found in a nearby maintenance facility. At last Orchid freed herself and the supernatural show began.

The industrious dwarfs severed the gilded bars and took the fence apart. The team flaked off the gold and repurposed the iron into an ornamental park bench. They placed it adjacent to the tree and its Ghost Orchids. The ingenious dwarfs hid the gold flakes in small bottles under the bench. Next, the roof of the greenhouse was disassembled to provide access for an airlift of the mighty oak.

The Druidess consulted with the dwarf in charge. "I must enlist Anu the Celtic goddess of Mother Earth to help us. I imagine that she will use her magical mist to disguise the tree for its long journey." She wiped away a tear. "Perhaps she can camouflage my haggard state as well." Orchid heard the voice of Anu in her mind. 'Do not fret, Druidess.'

Anu contacted Branwen the Celtic goddess of love and beauty. She communicated with Druantia the queen of the Druids and goddess of trees and forests. The three sympathetic deities choreographed a marvelous surprise for Orchid when she arrived in Parque da Pena. The rescue triumphed. The oak remained invisible as it flew to its final destination in Portugal.

The Druidess knew that the faerie realm controlled much of the universe's energy. They possessed the ability to stage the environment so that humans only saw what the faeries allowed and no more. In this case the Ghost Orchids still appeared to live on the Irish oak. However, in reality the flowers and their host tree had vanished.

Kew Gardens spent a fortune on publicity announcing the new home of the rare and mysterious Ghost Orchids. Ferdinand reprimanded Curator Smith for imprisoning such beauty so he agreed not to replace the gilded enclosure. The faeries giggled when people swooned as they gazed at the rare flowers. From time to time the curator heard something strange. He would look around with suspicion but was not able to pinpoint what seemed amiss. He never discovered the anonymous donor of the well-crafted park bench.

GHOST ORCHID OF SINTRA

For eight years Orchid MacCloud lived alone in the forest of Parque da Pena amidst nature's splendor. In her past the Druidess had spent many years without human companionship. Something felt different now that she had made the acquaintance of Ferdinand. To ease her loneliness, she conversed with her own reflection in the freshwater pond.

Orchid's beautiful visage from long ago now reflected back at her. This was the special gift from Druantia. The Celtic goddess had persuaded the water faeries and sprites to honor the Lady of Light by revealing her youthful appearance in the water. The Druidess pretended that the shimmering image was her twin sister. She never stopped missing Nuala since the day she had disappeared centuries ago. Every time Orchid held this one-way conversation a magnificent doe with a fourteen-point rack of antlers appeared in the cattails across the water.

At night the Druidess transformed into a Ghost Orchid and slept among the other blossoms on the Irish oak. She hoped that Ferdinand might wander through the forest and find himself drawn to her luminous petals. Orchid's heart yearned for him and her body craved his companionship. The feelings that she had repressed since the death of her Celtic husband Fig McCloud rose to the surface. She vowed to wait alone in the forest.

Ferdinand had attended the grand opening exhibit that showcased the Ghost Orchids. Everything seemed normal until he saw the tiny beings waving at him from beneath the wrought-iron bench. He laughed and acknowledged them with a wink. Later he admonished himself for getting caught up in the night's magic. *Why did I allow my imagination to run away with me?* Ferdinand remained unconvinced that the Druidess had escaped from the Palm House.

Two years later he mourned the loss of his wife who had died during the birth of their eleventh child. The couple's eldest son succeeded her and became Portugal's King Pedro V. Ferdinand's heart ached as he wandered without solace in Parque da Pena. He recalled creating the Queen's Fern Garden where they had passed long hours together. Now Ferdinand reminisced there without her. On rare occasions he gave himself permission to daydream. At those times the image of a beautiful glowing white orchid drifted into his mind.

Today Ferdinand entered the park searching for the giant redwood trees that he had imported from North America. He ventured into the dense woods and lost his way. Evening fell and thick fog from the Atlantic Ocean cloaked the forest with a mystical quality. Ferdinand looked forward to sleeping on a bed of moss and ferns. Palace staff supervised his children and the demands of Portugal's monarchy no longer burdened him.

Back in A.D. 1851 the Celtic goddess Anu had transplanted the Irish oak and its exotic flowering plants among the world's tallest trees. Tonight, Ferdinand pressed on in the foggy darkness and discovered his prized grove. It was illuminated by the haunting Ghost Orchids that shone like a beacon in a sea of foliage. The sight took his breath away and he deeply regretted the years that had passed without the company of the fascinating Druidess.

Orchid called out to him. "Greetings to you, Ferdinand. Almost three thousand days have passed since last we met." She stepped out from behind the oak tree and walked toward him without hesitation. Her phosphorescent skin glowed against the backdrop of the dark forest. She withdrew a wrinkled hand from the pocket of her soiled green gown and offered it to him.

A big smile spread across Ferdinand's face as he stepped forward. He bowed and kissed the tops of her withered knuckles. The affectionate gesture caught her by surprise and she turned away to hide her tears. "Please forgive me, Orchid MacCloud. It appears that the faeries at Kew Gardens fooled me into thinking that you had remained on the Irish oak in the Palm House. Have you lived in my forest for all these years?"

"Aye, ever since you rescued us." She gazed up at the giant redwoods. "These tree spirits offer my ancient bones much comfort."

"How I envy your intimacy with nature. It takes the eyes of either a child or a Druidess to access the mystical realms. I possess no such innocence or supernatural vision."

"Nonsense, my friend. Anyone can share in their world. The little blessed ones living in these woods exist in plenty. They are anxious to play and interact with humans. Tonight, the pixies confused your sense of direction. You found yourself a stranger in the forest you know so well. They gamed together on my behalf knowing how I yearned for your company."

Ferdinand clapped his hands and threw his head back with elated laughter. "Pixies? Marvelous! You all uplifted my soul today. I want to view the world from your perspective here in the forest that we both cherish. Before my wife died, I considered myself to be a romantic."

The fog cleared. Orchid took his hand and led him to the mossy banks of the pond. They sat on a fallen log in the moonlight. *I wish to offer him hope for a new love in his life. What a pity that it is not I.* "Release your heart from its chamber of sorrow. The flowers have revealed to me that soon an angelic voice will capture your attention."

Ferdinand stared into the water and contemplated her

revelation. The stiff-kneed Druidess supported herself on his shoulder and stood up. She told him that her old bones needed rest. At that moment in the water's reflection Ferdinand beheld the world's most beautiful woman. He wanted to gaze at this image for the rest of his days. Her full lips parted into a dazzling smile and her green eyes sparkled like the finest emeralds. His heart burst with short-lived happiness. Ferdinand turned around to see a decrepit Orchid MacCloud smile back at him exposing her chipped yellow teeth.

He was surprised and embarrassed. "Perhaps it is time to rest my eyes. They play cruel tricks on us both." Unable to stop himself he gazed back into the water longing to see the mysterious woman with fiery hair highlighted in gold. Once more he feasted his eyes on the young beauty. She wore a gown the color of leaves in springtime and ornamented with a pattern of silver threaded orchids. He knelt before the pond and implored the illusion. "Beautiful lady, please stay with me tonight."

Orchid pointed at the image. "Many centuries ago, I appeared like that at all times. Now the Celtic goddess Druantia has conspired with the faerie realm to please me in my waning years of life." Orchid sniffed back her tears. She felt desperate for just one kiss from Ferdinand. In silence she summoned the queen of the Druids. Druantia materialized behind the couple as they stood together staring at the image.

Tonight, the protectress of the forest embodied a tall and slender crepe myrtle tree. Her strong feet rooted in the soft soil. Her long legs, narrow hips, and small waist became the smooth trunk of the tree. The arms and hands of the goddess grew branches that blossomed with tiny white flowers. Druantia lifted her arms above Orchid's head and released her petals that fell onto the Druidess like fragrant snowflakes. Ferdinand held his breath as he watched the old woman transform into the stunning beauty that had been reflected in the water. The goddess vanished and left the smitten couple facing each other as if they were a young couple in love.

Orchid's emerald eyes glistened and she smiled at Ferdinand. "Druantia's magic cannot last. Please kiss me so that I may remember this moment until my last breath." He took the gorgeous woman into his arms and planted a loving kiss upon her waiting lips. Orchid responded with eagerness as they wrapped their arms around each other.

Ferdinand let out a long sigh. "My lady of the forest, let us make a bed of ferns and sleep together under the stars tonight and forever more."

Orchid shook her head. "I must return to my destined place amid the Ghost Orchids on the Irish oak. Worry not for your life will soon become joyous again."

He pleaded with her. "More joy than this I cannot imagine. It is you that I yearn for."

Orchid pushed him away with gentle hands. "Promise me that you will open your heart to another." He nodded with reluctance. She noticed her hands aging once again and panicked. The upset woman turned away and refused to look back at Ferdinand. *On this magical night he must remember me as I used to be.*

"Please do not leave me." The Druidess vanished behind the oak tree and reappeared among the other white orchids. Ferdinand approached the large exotic glowing flower. Tears of sorrow dripped down its tendrils and splashed on his hand. It reminded him of their first meeting at the Palm House. "I fear that I cannot help you escape again. Time is every man's prison." Ferdinand collapsed onto the mossy ground and fell into a deep sleep. He dreamt of dancing through the forest with his beloved Druidess, the Ghost Orchid of Sintra.

NIGHTINGALE NURSES

The White Storks of Mercy remained in bird form when they left a happy Iona on the Isle of Souls. They made their way to London. The last time they set foot on English soil had been to rescue the imprisoned Mary, Queen of Scots. Now almost three centuries later they flew through the thick gray smog that covered the grimy city. The four storks landed behind St. Thomas' Hospital—the location of the Nightingale Training School and Home for Nurses.

They transformed into women and walked around the perimeter of the three-story horseshoe-shaped stone structure. Everyone felt the shock of changing residence from the pristine beaches and blue skies of their home on the deserted Estela Islet. The women were challenged as they settled into the huge dirty city with a population of over three million.

The Merciful Ones registered for the program. They exchanged their normal apparel for gray tweed uniforms with stiff white collars, white bib aprons, and nursing caps. The four women joined twenty other female students in the school's inaugural class.

The intelligent Scottish queen aced every exam and demonstrated a notable ability to think with clarity in critical situations. Mary's patience, proficiency, and commitment to the sick impressed the hospital's matron and superintendent Mrs. Wardroper. The forty-five-year-old redhead's noble demeanor appeared familiar to her.

The competitive pharaoh bested Mary in stamina and managing stress. She flaunted a masterful ability to delegate responsibility for tasks she disliked such as bathing her patients and emptying their bedpans. Maatkare took charge whenever matters required physical strength. She developed innovative methods for lifting and maneuvering patients. However, when it came to bedside manner she received the lowest marks.

Zendala's confidence, calm demeanor, and soothing voice inspired hope and trust in all her patients. She distracted them from their suffering with compelling tales of adventures undertaken by the mystical White Storks of Mercy. Zendala attended to every detail at all times, from providing wound care to obtaining vital signs. The ancient woman allowed herself not even one mistake. Mrs. Wardroper noted that this particular student nurse possessed what seemed like an uncanny ability to predict medical outcomes.

Throughout the one-year program Blandina excelled at teamwork. She was always ready to assist other students if they experienced difficulty. Her kindness, compassion, and quiet empathy inspired devotion from her patients. She provided comfort to them even in the dark. Emulating Nurse Nightingale, Blandina carried a lamp from ward to ward.

In A.D. 1861 the Merciful Ones completed their twelve-month training program. Florence Nightingale presented twenty-four certificates to her inaugural class. She took the four unique women aside and invited them to join her for tea at her apartment on South Street in London. She wanted to bestow a special gift on the kind-hearted teenager known as Blandina.

A member of her household staff led the four foreign women into the parlor. The famous nurse stood to greet her visitors. She was dressed in a light gray blouse tucked into the waistband of a black skirt draped over stiff crinoline. A white lace collar set off her angular face and a matching lace cap covered a portion of her brown hair. Compassionate wide-set eyes and a sweet smile gave the tall woman a calm and confident appearance.

"Welcome and congratulations, Ladies." Florence gestured for Blandina to sit next to her on the golden velvet chaise lounge. The other three squeezed together on a camelback settee of a similar color. They readjusted the pillows to create enough room. Zendala placed herself between Maatkare and Mary to keep the peace.

Florence retrieved an issue of *The Atlantic Monthly Magazine* from the coffee table. She handed it to Blandina. "This installment features Henry Wadsworth Longfellow's poem, *Santa Filomena*. The American poet signed it for me and now it is yours. I saw you one night giving comfort to your patients in the dark, as I did in the Crimean War."

Blandina blushed and thanked her with a grateful smile. She recited from memory,

> *"Lo! In that house of misery*
> *A lady with a lamp I see*
> *Pass through the glimmering of gloom,*
> *And flit from room to room."*

Her dark blue eyes pleaded with Zendala. "Perhaps she might join our coterie?"

The ancient woman smiled and shook her head. "I understand why you ask. The world needs her valuable contributions as an inspiration to others. Early in the twentieth century the International Committee of the Red Cross will create the Florence Nightingale Medal for nurses and their aides who demonstrate exceptional courage and devotion."

Zendala regarded Nurse Nightingale with great respect. "In A.D. 1907 you will receive the British Order of Merit for your lifelong service in the area of social reform."

Florence's gray eyes opened wide with quizzical suspicion. "Please share the truth about yourselves. I promise to keep your confidence."

Zendala gestured to Maatkare and invited her to convey the legend of the White Storks of Mercy. The pharaoh relished the limelight. She rose, cast a triumphant glance at Mary, and proceeded to tell their story.

Florence wiped away a tear. "How incredible! I am honored that the Merciful Ones chose to become Nightingale nurses."

The following day the four supernatural women stood in the back row alongside Mrs. Wardroper for their class picture. Florence Nightingale sat with the twenty additional graduates. Her hands were clasped on her lap and a proud smile beamed on her face.

ELIZABETH THE MAD

True to Orchid's prediction Ferdinand became enamored with the angelic voice of Elise Hensler. He heard her perform in Verdi's opera *Un Ballo in Maschera* at the National Theatre of São Carlos in Lisbon. The twenty-four-year-old actress and singer shared his passions for music, art, and nature. His age exceeded hers by twenty years. Nevertheless, Ferdinand heeded the wise advice of the Druidess and opened his heart to love. He married his songbird in A.D. 1869 after a long courtship. His cousin the Duke of Saxe-Coburg and Gotha conferred the title of Countess d'Edla upon Ferdinand's young wife.

Several months later Orchid left her home in the serenity of Parque da Pena for the first time since her arrival nineteen years earlier. Ferdinand persuaded her to help the troubled wife of his friend Diego da Gama. He pitied the shipping tycoon who kept his spouse under lock and key for her own safety. Ferdinand made a tempting offer. "Please come home with me and let us pamper you for a few days. This endeavor will change the lives of Elizabeth and the entire da Gama family."

"I shall try to help her but I insist that it take place in the fresh air of nature."

"As you wish, my dear." He took her arm and escorted the Druidess out of Parque da Pena to the nearby palace where he resided with his new wife.

Ferdinand escorted her up the steps into the grand foyer where Elise met them with a gracious smile. "You honor us with your presence, Orchid MacCloud."

"Aye. I hope I do not regret it."

The Druidess yielded herself to the countess. Elise led her into a steam-filled chamber. She removed the old woman's bronze accessories and slipped off her dirty green clothing. Orchid admitted to herself that she enjoyed the long soak and hair wash in the huge bathtub. A maidservant rubbed her down with a fluffy towel and offered her a soft robe. Her nails received meticulous attention. Orchid decided that a civilized life offered benefits worth considering.

Elise reappeared and showed her into an opulent dressing room where the Druidess donned cotton undergarments and an olive-green gown made of the finest imported silk. She pulled on stockings and tried in vain to squeeze her flat feet into leather lace-up shoes. The countess came to the rescue and offered a pair of French slippers. A stylist pulled back Orchid's gray hair and pinned it into a bun. Elise placed a small hat with green ribbons onto her head. The countess kept the pleasure she felt at the improvement in Orchid's appearance to herself. "How do you feel?"

"I am fine. Thank you for your kindness."

"You are most welcome. I think that we are ready."

They emerged and Ferdinand helped them into an open-air rockaway carriage. He spoke to his driver who gave up the reins. Ferdinand climbed onto the front seat and they set off. The confident thirty-four-year-old countess always attracted the attention of admirers. Elise used the expertise gained in dressing rooms of theatres throughout the world to accentuate her wide-set hazel eyes, high cheekbones, and upturned lips.

Today the Swiss-born actress wore a light gray taffeta dress with a narrow waist that accentuated her generous bust. The fashion statement boasted a cumbersome bustle that caused Countess d'Edla to sit forward to compensate for the extra material gathered behind her. Elise scowled at her padded backside, turned to Orchid, and grinned. "I envy the simplicity of your life in the forest."

"If I existed to please a man, I might change my ways."

"Did love ever find you?"

"Aye." *I do not want to talk about loves lost.*

Elise broached the subject of their day. "Diego has informed my husband that Dr. Jacob Goldman is satisfied to keep Elizabeth da Gama comfortable and under his control. According to rumors, the psychiatrist and young Matilda cast longing glances at one another."

Orchid asked, "Who is Matilda?"

"She is the daughter of Elizabeth and Diego."

"How old is she?"

"Matilda is twenty-years-old and the German doctor is over twice her age." *I remember how the locals gossiped about the age difference between Ferdinand and I.* Elise patted her reddish-brown curls and adjusted her small black hat. Orchid swatted at her own hat's green ribbons blowing in her face.

To most observers the da Gama estate exhibited a magnificent blend of Moorish and Oriental architectural styles. The building consisted of three large dome-shaped cupolas with heavy stone cantilevered eaves jutting beyond the rooflines. The Druidess caught sight of it and panicked. She questioned whether she dared set foot into a structure that appeared to bear the weight of the world.

Matilda da Gama greeted them with an air of cool reserve. She reminded Orchid of a speckled sparrow with her small chirpy mouth, brown hair, and eyes. Freckles dotted her sallow complexion and unremarkable nose. She wore a long brown skirt and high-necked cream-colored blouse. The Druidess swallowed the urge to whistle the songbird's tune. Without a word Matilda escorted them up the stone steps and onto the grand outdoor terrace overlooking the manicured garden below. She offered them a seat at a wrought-iron table set for afternoon tea and disappeared inside.

The daughter returned to the terrace with her listless mother propped up in an invalid's chair. Orchid sensed that in spite of her drab appearance the young woman ruled her mother with an iron fist. She tucked a crocheted blanket under Elizabeth's small frame and fussed with the stubborn strands of chestnut-brown hair escaping from her severe bun. Orchid pondered whether the daughter's actions denoted profound love or a deep resentment. Elizabeth's vacant baby-blue eyes stared at the table.

Dr. Goldman emerged and Matilda stepped aside. The psychiatrist wore a three-piece dark brown wool suit and a starched white shirt. The arrogant man pulled a gold watch from his vest pocket and checked the time. He leaned toward Matilda and muttered under his breath. "In thirty minutes, they must depart." She blushed at his close proximity. The countess recognized the suppressed feelings between doctor and caregiver. On first impression Elise disliked the German doctor from Leipzig. She felt his penetrating and narrow-set steel-blue eyes passing judgment on her.

He bowed to Elise. "Good day, Frau Hensler. Pardon me, I mean Countess d'Edla." *How easy to acquire titles if one beds the right man.*

The doctor kissed the top of her gloved hand. Elise noted his dominant high forehead and hair the color of mud mixed with strands of silver. A trimmed beard and moustache softened an angular face. Orchid and Elise waited in silence as the psychiatrist divided his attention between them. "I received my medical degree from the University of Leipzig." His German accent was pronounced. "I completed thirteen years of training in psychiatry and achieved a professorship at the University of Tartu in Estonia." He spoke louder and with arrogant authority.

"There is no question that my credentials qualify me to treat Senhora da Gama."

Matilda remained standing by her mother while Dr. Goldman took a seat. He leaned across the table and posed a question to Orchid. She reminded him of a faerie tale witch. "I assume you are the infamous Druidess, Orchid MacCloud. What are your qualifications? Did you read *On the Workings of the Human Body*?"

"Aye." Her sarcastic tone expressed annoyance. "I read the medical reference book long before your birth. I found *On Medical Material* even more enlightening due to its focus on herbal medicine. I take an alternative approach to healing. I donated my journal of drawings, recipes, and remedies to *The Herbalist's Handbook for Modern Times* published in Dublin."

Elise added, "My friend Sarina Matriz sells Orchid's remedies at her new shop in Sintra. The botanicals that Orchid prepares provide astounding relief for many ailments. For years the royal family of Portugal utilized her expertise as we continue to do."

Dr. Goldman's cheeks reddened and the jugular veins on both sides of his neck pulsed. *They intend to breach the boundaries of my treatment regimen.* He stood up and moved Matilda aside to position himself behind his patient. Elizabeth winced when he placed his hands on her shoulders. "Do not make light of this situation. My patient experiences severe mental illness and I fear that she is a danger to herself."

Orchid frowned. "I feel deep sorrow about her condition. Yet I believe that I can help her." *I shall summon the Celtic god Dian Cécht, the deity responsible for healing and medicine. He will cast a spell to neutralize the demons that plague this poor suffering woman.* She directed her attention to Matilda's silent mother. "Everyone talks about and around you as if you do not exist, Elizabeth. Do you fear that your words will condemn you?"

Elizabeth shrugged off the firm hands of Dr. Goldman and blinked a few times to force herself to return to reality. "He twists every word I speak and analyzes it to death."

Orchid shooed the doctor away like a pesky fly. She invited Elizabeth to join her and the countess on their side of the table. "Let us get to know each other."

The fuming psychiatrist considered this a declaration of war. "I abandoned my research in dream psychology to move here and focus on one person. In Germany I enjoyed complete professional freedom at a mental hospital full of patients upon whom I applied my experimental theories. Now this invalid swears she never dreams!"

The lethargic Elizabeth discovered an internal spark of energy. She pushed herself away from the table and rolled over the doctor's toes. He squealed and jumped to the side bumping into Matilda. Elizabeth wheeled over to position herself between her new allies. "I am not an invalid! I feel like my rational mind is slipping away from me." Tears filled her sad eyes. The angry doctor turned and left the patio. Matilda followed him.

Orchid started the healing process by treating Elizabeth with the respect due to all beings. "Follow my ancient bones into the woods. I want to introduce you to the enchanted world of the faerie realm. Together we shall watch the stars dance and dream of..."

"Of course, I dream! It is the same terrifying nightmare every night." The troubled woman shook off her fear. "I shall go with you into the forest, Orchid MacCloud. I need to get better for my husband who loves me. I tire of being called Elizabeth the Mad."

Elizabeth placed her hands on the table for stability and hoisted herself onto feeble legs. Her arms quivered and she inhaled several deep breaths. Elise called for Matilda to summon Ferdinand. The shocked daughter watched her mother walk for the first time in years. Elise and Orchid supported the frail woman on each side and assisted her down the stairs into the garden. The threesome paused to rest on a hand-carved wooden bench. Elizabeth savored the warmth of the Portuguese sun. A smile of relief softened Ferdinand's face when he caught sight of them.

I DREAM OF CATS

The group stopped at the palace. Orchid changed back into her faded green gown and cape that were now laundered. Elise packed a basket of food as well as a change of clothes and blanket for Elizabeth. Ferdinand promised to bring his wife to the grove of redwoods to check on their progress in a few days. The Druidess and her charge walked into Parque da Pena.

Dusk approached so Orchid gathered soft green pine needles for Elizabeth's bed. She formed a pillow of ferns and placed a compress of valerian root over the exhausted woman's eyes. "I shall watch over you and count every star in the sky while you slumber in peace."

The following morning Elizabeth awoke feeling rested and hopeful for the first time in many years. Orchid suggested that they enjoy some of Elise's provisions after washing up. She agreed and the women walked to the pond. They knelt down to splash refreshing water upon their faces. Elizabeth saw the image of a red-haired beauty with emerald eyes staring back at her from the water. The shocked woman fell backwards onto the ground.

Orchid recognized the source of Elizabeth's distress. She told her about the legend of the Lady of Light and explained Druantia's special gift. "As you can see, I possess a unique connection with a variety of mystical beings. It strengthens my ability to help you." They returned to the Irish oak for their breakfast. "Tell me about the terrors that haunt your dreams each night, Elizabeth."

Minutes passed before she mustered the courage to divulge her recurring nightmare. "I dream of cats." The Druidess gave the troubled woman time to gather the courage necessary to face her fears. "I am standing alone in a dark and dank temple wearing a silk nightgown. A sea of cats surrounds me. They force me into a great hall where a gigantic statue of a feline poses in a seated position. Torches illuminate walls that are covered in Egyptian hieroglyphics. The sculpture's lime-green eyes stare down at me. I feel as if it relishes my fear and confusion."

"What else do you see?"

"In front of the statue stands a stone slab inlaid with a mosaic top. It features a black and white rendering of a huge eye. Diego waits behind it. He is wearing nothing more than cotton pajama bottoms. The mass of cats encircling my feet separates to create a narrow path that closes behind me. I cannot turn back. By the time I reach the table a solitary dark-colored feline with silver spots and the black facial markings of a beetle waits on its surface. Its lime-green eyes transfix Diego." Orchid recognized the unmistakable description of an Egyptian Mau cat from Reba's tales of her ancient homeland.

"My husband dislikes cats yet he strokes this one with obvious adoration. He commands me to lie down on the slab. I offer no resistance and climb onto the table like a sacrificial lamb. My skin feels cold against the stone." She shivered with such intensity that Orchid placed the blanket around Elizabeth's shoulders.

"Take control of your fear and tell me more, Elizabeth."

"The cat leaps off the table and Diego joins me. We lie side by side as if we are in our marriage bed. A vulture circles over us and I prepare to die. Something rises up next to the slab."

Elizabeth's sudden scream caused Orchid to flinch. She patted the distressed woman's hand. "Keep going. You must break out of your prison by giving voice to your demons. What ascends next to the table?"

"It is a king cobra with its hood extended in defense as it prepares to strike. The snake's forked tongue flicks in and out and brushes the skin of my shoulder. I moan in fright. Diego begs me to keep still. I close my eyes and feel the cobra slithering around me."

Orchid probed further. "Your nightmare ends there?"

Elizabeth shook her head anticipating the worst of it. "I gather the courage to open my eyes. The vulture and the cobra are both gone. The statue of the cat opens its mouth and spews liquid like a waterfall onto us. Our skin and bones melt but I feel no pain. Our bodies disappear into the mosaic eye. Before I lapse into unconsciousness, I do not think of my husband lying next to me. Nor does my mind dwell on Afonso Bour da Bon, the man I once loved. Instead, my head fills with images of his beloved cat Sky."

Elizabeth released a deep shuddering sigh. She felt tremendous relief. Orchid inquired about what had happened to Sky. "We took her to Lisbon when she followed Diego and me as we fled the Quinta in disgrace. I do not know why she abandoned poor Afonso after I jilted him."

Orchid pondered Elizabeth's nightmare in silence and arrived at an important conclusion. "Your dream causes me to suspect sorcery."

Elizabeth burst into tears mixed with fits of laughter. "Someone cast a spell on me?" She considered the possibility. "I remember feeling manipulated during the dinner when Afonso and I announced the date of our wedding. I detested Diego yet on that celebratory night his father caught us making love in the courtyard. It made no sense." She blushed with shame. "Diego never saw his family again. He changed his last name to da Gama after we settled in Lisbon."

"What happened to Afonso?"

Elizabeth shrugged with resignation. "I do not know."

The Druidess frowned as she considered the destructive spells of black magic. It seemed that either something or someone in Elizabeth's past possessed a vast amount of supernatural power. Orchid asked her if she recalled any details about the hieroglyphics she described.

Elizabeth visualized the temple walls. "I see symbols depicting a vulture with its wings spread and a king cobra wearing a crown. They stand like guards on either side of a black and white eye like the one on the slab."

Orchid nodded. "Ah, the powerful Eye of Horus. On one side is the goddess Nekhebet. She is the creator of life, death, and rebirth. On the other side is her sister the goddess Wazit. She is responsible for justice, heaven, and hell."

"How do you know this?"

"I learned a few facts about ancient Egypt from an old friend. Have you seen anything like this before?"

"Diego bartered a throne from an Irish earl back in A.D. 1850. He claimed it belonged to the Egyptian pharaoh Ramses VI. His mother Perl hated the dirty old thing and made him put it out in the garden. Afonso's Siamese cat loved to sleep on the relic's seat."

Orchid's curiosity increased. "A Siamese cat?"

"Yes. The Second Earl of Bantry owned Sky in Ireland but he called her Cleopatra. She arrived with the throne and a tapestry that once belonged to Marie Antoinette."

Were Sky, Cleopatra, and Reba one and the same? Orchid pondered the possibility with a mixture of apprehension and delight. "Did Sky wear any Egyptian jewelry around her neck?"

"I cannot say. Sky allowed no one to touch her except Afonso. The cat shied away from everyone else including me, until that last fateful day at Quinta Bour da Bon."

"What do you mean, Elizabeth?"

"She befriended me that afternoon and played with my gorget earrings. She stared into my eyes like she wanted to hypnotize me. She even pulled out some of my hair."

Gorget earrings? Now Orchid knew for sure that Reba, Cleopatra, and Sky shared one identity. "Did she display any other unusual behaviors?"

"I knew Sky for over twenty years and she never aged."

Orchid nodded. *The magic of Nefertiti's bust keeps the lucky cat young.*

Elizabeth asked, "Why are so you fascinated with Sky? Is there is a connection between my nightmares and that cat?"

"Aye, there is. I suspect that she is the ancient Egyptian Siamese cat Reba. I have known her for centuries. She is clever and intelligent but not evil. It sounds like she used magic to lure you away from Afonso due to his affection for you. She wanted him all to herself."

"But why did she interfere with my wedding to Afonso and then leave the Quinta?"

"That is a good question, Elizabeth. If the cat is Reba, she will confess her sins to me."

Elizabeth looked hopeful. "Perhaps you can reverse the spell so I can return to Afonso."

Orchid asked, "Do you know where Sky lives now?"

"After Dr. Goldman forced me to leave my home in Lisbon I never saw the cat again although she still lives at the villa with Diego." Her mind filled with apprehension. "Does this mean that you cannot cure me without Sky?"

The Druidess placed an arm around Elizabeth and helped her to stand. "Do not concern yourself, my dear. A multitude of powerful friends wait in the celestial realm to help us. For now, let us relax and pick some berries from nature's bounty."

That afternoon Ferdinand and Elise visited them in the woods. While the countess walked to the pond with Elizabeth,

Orchid asked Ferdinand to find Afonso Bour da Bon. The following day he returned to tell her that Diego's twin still resided at the Quinta with his wife Catarina and their teenage son Luís. *I refuse to ruin their family. I shall concoct a secret potion for Diego. It will guarantee that his passion for Elizabeth reignites upon her return.*

"Thank you for locating Afonso, Ferdinand. It does my heart good to know that he has found happiness." *No thanks to that naughty cat.*

Darkness fell. Orchid enlisted two Celtic gods to assist with the final stage of Elizabeth's return to a healthy state of mind. She advised her to expect two celestial visitors in her dreams. "Dian Cécht is the Celtic god of healing and medicine. Angus Og is the god of youth, love, and beauty. A word of warning— Dian Cécht possesses a foul temper as well as an aggressive demeanor but he will not harm you. In fact, you can anticipate just the opposite from him."

"Can he reverse the spell that Sky placed on me?"

"Aye, he can. Angus Og will appear as a charming prince with locks of gold rather than in his alternate swan form. When he strums his magical harp, the mystical vibrations will renew your body with youth and beauty. After he kisses your eyelids you will awaken overflowing with love." *I intend to instruct him about the specific target of her affections.*

Elizabeth slumbered on her bed of soft pine needles and the Druidess passed the night among the Ghost Orchids on the Irish oak. Dian Cécht appeared in Elizabeth's dream with a bearskin covering his broad shoulders and deer antlers emerging from his skull through a light green hood. His dark brown hair was woven into braids that reached his chest. The Celtic god carried a carved wooden spear with a sharp metal tip.

Dian's black eyes bore down on the innocent female and he twirled his spear in front of her. He bragged in a raucous voice, "I once saved ancient Éire from serpents threatening to destroy the entire country. Rescuing you from a cat's spell cannot compare to that feat! My colossal skills will heal your heart and mind. Furthermore, your nightmares will cease to exist!" He disappeared. Elizabeth woke up startled by the appearance of the fierce god in her dreams. As soon as she heard the magical music of Angus Og's celestial harp she fell into a serene slumber.

The two women visited the pond the next morning. Elizabeth burst into delighted laughter when she saw her renewed beauty reflected in the water. "My gratitude to you knows no bounds, Orchid." The Druidess murmured her thanks to the gods. Elizabeth wept tears of joy. "Love fills my heart for my dear husband who suffered along with me." A hopeless Elizabeth da Gama had entered Parque da Pena. Now she returned to her family with a contented disposition and a youthful radiance.

The following week the Druidess sat on the terrace of the da Gama estate in silence. She watched Diego sip a glass of tampered champagne. He crinkled his nose but the handsome Portuguese man drank all of the bitter beverage to calm his nerves.

Elizabeth took special care with her appearance. She felt giddy with anticipation about their upcoming reunion. The pretty woman donned a deep blue silk dress upholstered with layers of fabric that accentuated the hourglass shape of her figure. Elise applied Elizabeth's makeup and styled her hair before pinning an ostrich feather in her lustrous chestnut-brown curls.

Diego's wife walked out onto the terrace. A besotted grin appeared on his face. He jumped to his feet and placed both hands on his heart. "Beloved wife!" A tear rolled down his cheek. He apologized for his behavior during the years that she had endured such profound mental anguish. Diego took Elizabeth into his arms and kissed her rouged lips.

The grateful woman responded to his affections. "Cherished

husband, I return to you."

Elise and Matilda slipped past the embracing couple to allow them privacy. The daughter smiled with relief at her parents' undisguised emotional display. "For my entire life they argued and now they love each other again. How can I repay your kindness to us?"

The countess placed her arm around Matilda. "By living your own life."

"Dr. Goldman plans to open a new psychiatric practice in Leipzig. He spoke of his fondness for me before he left and I feel the same. I want to visit him in Germany as soon as possible. However, convincing my parents that he is not too old for me might be difficult."

Elise chuckled. "I think that at this point they will agree to anything. Ferdinand and I shall help you if necessary." She winked. "We also share a marked difference in our ages."

A satisfied smile spread across Orchid's face. She sipped a glass of champagne and watched the reunion of husband and wife. Earlier that day the flowers revealed to her that the soul of a new baby da Gama waited in the spirit world. *My work here is done. It is time for me to return to the woods and live my last years in peaceful solitude. Parque da Pena is the perfect place to die dreaming of Ferdinand.*

Elizabeth took hold of her swooning senses and pulled away from Diego's embrace. She walked over to Orchid and dropped to her knees in front of the Druidess. "How can I ever thank you for giving me back my life?" She laid her head on Orchid's lap. The old woman tried not to ruin the moment by sneezing from the ostrich feather that tickled her nose.

The Druidess lifted Elizabeth's chin and cupped her face with weathered hands. Her forefingers and thumbs felt the outline of the gold gorget earrings that Elizabeth wore. "Are these the same earrings that you spoke about in the forest?"

"Yes, Diego gave them to me years ago when I was still engaged to Afonso."

Orchid called to him, "Where did you find such unusual jewelry?"

"I found them in the secret compartment of an Egyptian throne. I received it in a barter with the Second Earl of Bantry. He even threw in his Siamese cat, Cleopatra."

Elizabeth slipped the earrings off her lobes and onto Orchid's. The Druidess accepted Reba's jewelry that she had coveted for many centuries. She returned to Parque da Pena and wore the earrings every day. At night before she transformed into the Ghost Orchid, she hid her treasure within a narrow hollow of her host tree.

The Lady of Light sensed the end of her time on earth approaching. She acknowledged her fate and rested her weary bones against the Irish oak. Over two millennia had passed since her birth in 450 b.c. *No wonder I am so exhausted.*

OUR FAERIE LADY OF MONTSERRAT

Soon after her birth on the twenty-third of August in A.D. 1871 Elizabeth and Diego christened a new daughter. They named her Orquídia to honor their Celtic heroine. Fifteen-year-old Alberto ignored his baby sister. In his opinion she required far too much attention. He hoped that her features would favor those of their sister. He wanted to remain the best looking of the three da Gama children.

Over the years Orquídia spent most of the time with her mother, which suited her solitary nature. They both preferred the quiet life at the da Gama estate rather than at the urban villa in Lisbon. Elizabeth refused to spend even one second in the presence of Sky. She regretted rescuing the devious cat but Diego had grown attached to her. He visited them at the estate on most weekends. Alberto preferred to stay in the bustling port city with his friends.

Elizabeth schooled Orquídia at home due to her precocious intelligence. She offered the child an open-minded viewpoint when it came to spirituality. Neither she nor her husband practiced the Protestant or Jewish religions in which they were raised. The mother introduced her daughter to a variety of belief systems including ancient spiritual traditions. Her experience with the Druidess reflected this unbiased approach. "Choose a faith that suits you best—or none at all for that matter. You will know in your heart what feels right."

On her thirteenth birthday Orquídia jumped out of bed.

She brushed her hair one hundred times. It was a daily practice that she attended to with compulsion. The girl picked up a hand mirror to inspect her oval face. Her porcelain complexion and dimpled chin favored her mother. She had her father's penetrating cognac-colored eyes with extra-long lashes. The birthday girl ran downstairs to join her mother for breakfast. A gift wrapped in a white silk scarf and tied with a white ribbon waited between their plates. "Where is Papa?"

"He is coming home for dinner, my darling. You may open my present before we eat."

Orquídia unwrapped it with care and folded the scarf with precision. She inspected the silver hairbrush engraved with the likeness of an orchid. "Thank you, Mama. You know that I love white because it represents goodness and purity. Will you help me?" She handed the ribbon to her mother. Elizabeth shaped it into a bow and tied back Orquídia's long dark brown hair.

Later in the day the lean and wiry girl changed into a white smock for her afternoon swim in the large stream-fed pond on the da Gama property. She carried a bag containing a towel and extra undergarments. Across the water hidden among the exotic grounds stood a sixteenth century Gothic chapel dedicated to Our Lady of Montserrat. The roots of several large weeping fig trees had overtaken the building that was crumbling. What remained of the structure served as a quiet retreat for Orquídia after she finished her exercise regimen.

She stripped down to her undergarments instead of donning the impractical bathing costume that would weigh her down in the water. Her thirty-minute routine included alternating front and back strokes followed by treading water in place for the count of one hundred. She toweled off, slipped on dry underwear, and performed one hundred calisthenics.

Orquídia dressed again in her smock and squeezed through the vertical roots of the tree that camouflaged the arched entrance. Her eyes adjusted to the dark interior but a new smell permeated the musty chapel. She flared her nostrils and inhaled the scents of sweet almonds and wintergreen. The sensible girl walked around pursuing its source. Thin beams of afternoon sunlight penetrated the cracks in the stone roof and appeared through small windows void of glass. She spotted a miniature wooden statue of Saint Anthony where the altar once stood.

The inquisitive Orquídia plopped down at the base of the steps in front of the figurine known as the finder of lost objects. The six-inch-tall saint wore a traditional Franciscan dark brown robe. Its hem, hood, and long sleeves were trimmed in gold. A white-robed Infant Jesus rested on the Holy Bible that was balanced against the crook of his arm. The brown-haired saint held no staff. Orquídia tucked the statue into the deep pocket of her smock and left the chapel. She was excited about her father's visit for her special supper.

That evening the birthday girl met her parents on the terrace. They were enjoying a snifter of Bour da Bon Tawny Vintage Port. Diego stood and gave her a kiss on both cheeks before presenting a beautiful white orchid. "This is for you, precious daughter."

"Thank you, Papa! I feel so grown up now that I am thirteen. Please tell us the story of Orchid MacCloud for whom I am named."

Diego chuckled. "I am sure that you remember it even better than I do."

Elizabeth studied their unique child. Her exceptional ability to recall every detail of what she read, heard, and saw seemed like an overwhelming gift. Orquídia's deep-set round eyes stared without blinking as she took in information. Access to extreme stimulation required order and as a result she compartmentalized all of the data in her young brain.

Elizabeth noticed that her daughter seemed preoccupied.

"What thoughts fill your pretty head this evening?" Orquídia's full pink lips smiled but she ignored the question. She ate a piece of cake then folded her napkin into a perfect square. The happy girl wished her parents a good night and gave them each a kiss. She picked up the white orchid and walked at a quick pace through the grand foyer before running up the stairs to her bedroom.

Orquídia placed the plant next to the figurine of Saint Anthony on the bedside table. She changed into her nightgown and brushed her teeth while counting to one hundred. The tired girl climbed onto her big bed and closed her eyes. She surrendered to the repetitious facts and images flooding her mind until sleep overtook her. The following morning the statue was gone.

She searched the hardwood floor, looked under her four-poster bed, and behind the thick curtains. Orquídia noticed the unmistakable aromas of sweet almonds and wintergreen. She skipped her morning routine, pulled on a robe, and left her home. She ran down the steep hill, slipped through the roots, and entered the dark chapel.

Once again, the saint stood on the floor at the top of the steps. Orquídia circled the figurine and gave it careful scrutiny before picking it up. "Tell me good saint, how did you get back here to the chapel?"

A soothing male voice responded. "I am a messenger from Our Lady of Montserrat." The girl bolted upright and dropped the wooden statue.

"You can relax, Orquídia da Gama. Our Lady has chosen you."

"For what?" Orquídia watched the wooden lips of the icon. They did not move.

The disembodied speaker continued. "Sister Orquídia, Our Lady of Montserrat wants you to care for the babe that she will bring to you."

The girl fired off a series of logical questions. "What babe? When? Why do you call me Sister Orquídia? I am not a nun. I am a thirteen-year-old girl."

"You are an obedient servant of God and will become a bride of Christ. A White Stork of Mercy will bring the babe. Baptize her with the name Teodora. She will be God's gift to you."

The pragmatic thinker sank down onto the stone steps. Orquídia loved to solve mysteries. She looked hard at the statue. "This is a prank, right? Anyone might sneak into my room, grab you off my bedside table, and return you here to the chapel." She brought Saint Anthony close to her face. "I need a sign that leaves no doubt in my mind about committing myself to the Catholic Church. It means that I will be giving up my life with my family."

The scent of almonds and wintergreen grew so strong that Orquídia sneezed. A female voice drifted down from the rafters. "Bless you, my child." A feisty and beautiful faerie-winged Celtic goddess called Áine of Knockaine hovered high above. The deity pursed her pouty pink lips together and exhaled with frustration. *This one might be far too bright to take the bait.*

The mystical being—known as the mistress of settling scores—needed the participation of the young skeptic to pull off her elaborate plan avenging the Druidess Orchid MacCloud. She demanded, "Close your eyes and do not move!"

The faerie goddess possessed magical abilities that included changing both her voice and her size. Today she measured two feet in height. She wore clothes made from the turquoise leaves and rubbery reddish stalks of meadowsweet that smelled of wintergreen. A wreath of sweet almond verbena with delicate white blossoms topped her long blonde ringlets. A kaleidoscope of blue butterflies attracted to the fragrant flowers fluttered nearby.

Áine dipped her small hand into a veiny sack made of leaves

and sprinkled faerie dust over her head. She reappeared wearing the golden robe and veil of the Black Madonna, Our Lady of Montserrat. Áine's normal rosy complexion and blonde hair darkened to a deep mahogany color. The faerie goddess tucked her huge pointed ears beneath a gold crown and she held a golden orb. She floated down to the steps in slow motion. Her delicate size made a magical impression. Áine lingered above Orquídia, beat her translucent wings, and rotated them in a figure eight to remain in place. "You may open your eyes."

The curious girl glanced upward and spotted a golden robe floating in the air. The rays of the morning sun filtered through the dilapidated roof and shone on the fabric creating a sparkling effect. She took a moment to admire the deity's mother-of-pearl wings before gazing upon the face of a diminutive dark-skinned woman. "The Black Madonna from Catalonia! How may I serve you Blessed Virgin?"

Áine's silvery voice issued a command. "Saint Anthony will lead you to the convent near Good Jesus of the Mount in Minho. There you will serve God until He graces you with the babe, Teodora."

"Thank you for revealing my future, Our Lady of Montserrat."

You mean Our Faerie Lady of Montserrat. Áine of Knockaine floated into the darkness of the rafters.

Orquídia grabbed the statue of Saint Anthony and ran back to the mansion. That evening after her father returned to Lisbon she joined her mother on the terrace. She squirmed with excitement. It was an unusual state for the serious girl who prided herself on staying in control.

Elizabeth sensed that her daughter wanted to tell her something. "What is on your mind?"

"My religion has found me, Mama! Our Lady of Montserrat appeared in her chapel today and gave me guidance to become a bride of Christ."

Elizabeth dabbed her mouth with the corner of a linen napkin and chose her words with care. "You know about your father's plans. Your exceptional intelligence and photographic memory qualify you as a candidate for Coimbra University. Diego believes that they will accept you someday as one of their very few female students."

"My mind is made up." Orquídia stared at her mother with silent determination. The stubborn girl never budged once she took a stand.

Elizabeth sighed with resignation. "Tell me more about the miraculous appearance of Our Lady of Montserrat."

DEATHBED REUNION

For reasons that she did not comprehend Reba obsessed over her beloved Afonso day and night. She felt compelled to seek a reunion. In A.D. 1886 the Siamese cat left her comfortable life at the da Gama villa in Lisbon. She retraced in reverse the route that had taken her to the port city thirty-five years earlier. Reba arrived at the vineyards of Quinta Bour da Bon filled with breathless anticipation.

Reba ran through the open door of the farmhouse and up the stairs to Afonso's bedroom. She found the door ajar and stopped at the threshold to collect her thoughts. Due to both aging and ill health the bedridden man looked like a different person. He now wore a beard and except for his cognac-colored eyes the frail vintner bore little resemblance to his twin brother, Diego.

Afonso woke up when the cat meowed and jumped onto the low bed. He seemed pleased to see her. "You have not changed at all, Sky. What brought you home to me?"

Reba nestled her head against Afonso's hairy cheek. The Siamese cat sensed the presence of imminent death. She decided to confess her feelings to him. "I regret that I was forced to leave without saying goodbye. I came back to say that I love you. Not as a pet loves her master but true romantic love."

The sick man chuckled. He was unfazed when Sky spoke to him. He moved her onto his chest to gaze one last time into her sky-blue eyes with their diamond-shaped pupils. "I love your spirit too, Sky. I have always known that you are a very special cat."

She swooned. "My real name is Reba. I am from ancient Egypt and I have been alive for a long, long time."

The dying man fingered the charms around her neck. "That explains these."

"Nefertiti keeps me young and the ark empowers me to shape shift into any creature of my choosing except for a woman or a bird."

"I am sorry that I asked my father to get rid of you, Reba. Where did you go?"

"Julio threatened my life so I ran off with Diego and Elizabeth. They took me to Lisbon."

He sneered. "My disloyal brother stole both you and my English Rose. Please promise to stay here at the Quinta after I am gone. My daughter-in-law Isadora will take care of you."

"What do you mean after you are gone? What is wrong with you?"

Afonso's voice grew weaker. "I lost interest in everything but work when the three of you left. A few years later I surrendered to my mother's nagging and agreed to marry Catarina. Over time we grew apart and she returned to her family in Vila Real. Our son Luís took over when I got sick. My heart is failing fast."

Reba knew that the fault belonged to her. She searched her soul seeking the courage to confess and ask for his forgiveness. "I must tell you something." The cat felt his chest shudder as Afonso expelled his last breath. His hands lay heavy on her as she struggled to accept his passing. "Someday I will find you, Afonso. The ancient Egyptians believe that after death the soul travels from one body to another. I know that we shall be together again, my beloved."

Isadora Bour da Bon stood in the hallway listening to Afonso converse with his Siamese cat. The tall and slim thirty-one-year-old with chin-length auburn hair showed no surprise. An event more bizarre than a talking cat had opened her mind years earlier.

As a teen she had shared an awkward embrace with young Luís Bour da Bon in his family's vineyard. The free-spirited Isadora Mota Vanko peeked over his head and saw four females in peasant-style dresses chatting with a stork. Moments later the women ran off and leapt from the steep stone terrace. They transformed into storks and flew away. The bird left behind squealed in a child's voice. "Hey you White Storks of Mercy, wait for me!"

Isadora inhaled a deep breath and blinked her eyes several times before exhaling in astonishment. She opened her lips to ask Luís if he had also witnessed the miraculous sight. The shorter teenage boy went up on his tiptoes and kissed her. She fainted in his arms. He assumed that his smooching prowess had overwhelmed her.

At that time Isadora and her Jewish mother lived in the town of Pinhão near the Bour da Bon vineyard. Her Gypsy father helped with their harvest. She and Luís fell in love and married in their late teens. Isadora matured into a striking woman with a square face, pronounced cheekbones, and a dimple in her chin. Curved eyebrows accentuated her deep-set eyes and thick lashes protected her gray-green irises. Permanent laugh lines around her eyes and mouth gave character to the attractive woman with a happy disposition. Her full ruby-red lips parted to display a generous and sincere smile.

Isadora had worn colorful Gypsy skirts and billowy blouses as a girl. After she wed and gave birth to four boys, she became the co-manager of the family business. This serious role inspired her choice of a black wardrobe. Isadora wore a silver cross around her slender neck. Several gold chains hung in various lengths, some falling to her narrow waist. A gold bracelet encircled her right wrist. Four gold bangles adorned her left wrist. Each had been a gift from Luís after the birth of their sons.

The Gypsy woman felt a deep passion for singing *fado*, which meant fate. The folk music resonated with what the Portuguese called *saudade*—the longing of things lost. Her older identical twin sons Paulo and Rico accompanied her on their guitars while she sang the songs of sorrowful yearning to Afonso. The music suited his despondent mood.

The day that Isadora listened in on the conversation between her father-in-law and his cat she sent her sons away. *I am not ready to explain supernatural phenomena to them.* She entered the bedroom and saw that Afonso had died. The sad woman closed his eyes with her fingertips, kissed his cheek, and covered his head with the blanket. Isadora picked up the cat and stared into her tear-filled eyes. "Hello, Reba. I am Isadora Bour da Bon. I hope that you will honor Afonso's dying plea and stay here with us."

The cat managed a pathetic meow. *My heart is broken. I did not anticipate a deathbed reunion with my beloved Afonso.*

Isadora sought to inspire trust from Afonso's cat. "I am neither your typical Jewess nor a traditional Gypsy. I believe in faeries, spirits, angels, faith healers—you name it." She chuckled at the memory that never left her mind. "What I saw as a teen left me with no choice."

Excitement replaced Reba's sorrow. *Gypsy women cast spells. Perhaps she will help me become human so I can find Afonso's soul somewhere in time. Forget Tara's trinkets. I shall discover my own way to achieve my new purpose in life.*

"May I tell you a bizarre secret?" The cat nodded. Isadora recounted the time that four women transformed into storks and flew away in front of her. "One of them even glowed!"

Reba decided to trust her. "Those creatures are the White Storks of Mercy. In female form they want to be called Merciful Ones. The shining bird is my twin sister, Tara." *I guess they live in Portugal now.*

"I do not understand. You are a cat yet she manifests as both a woman and a bird?"

"Do not rub it in," whined Reba. "I shall tell you that story another day."

"I want to hear about your life. First, I need to tell the family that Afonso has passed so they can act as guards. In the Jewish faith we do not leave the deceased alone. Please stay with him until I bring help. We must move his body to the floor and surround him with candles. I shall contact the holy society to wash the body and prepare it for burial as soon as possible." Reba nodded and stretched out full length on top of the blanket covering her soul mate. All too soon the infiniteness of time and space would remove them far from each other.

Later that night Reba and Isadora sat together on Ramses' throne. The cat admired the exotic woman's jewelry. She wanted to learn more about her. "How did a half-Gypsy end up here at the Quinta?"

"Let me start at the beginning. My Jewish mother is a baker by the name of Mira Mota. She married Jesse Vanko who is a Gypsy horse trader."

"It sounds romantic."

"During the autumn grape harvest Jesse's clan worked in the vineyards from sunrise to sunset. The vintners got along well with the Gypsies and there were no grievances against them. However, Jessie's parents chastised him for wanting to marry a non-Gypsy. They feared the pollution of the tribe's purity. My stubborn father did not give in and they eloped. At my birth they registered me as Isadora. I received a secret name in the Gypsy tradition but I cannot disclose it to you."

We shall see about that. Reba demanded, "Pick me up. I need comfort and attention." Isadora lifted the cat to her chest. Their eyes locked together. The Great Persuader employed her powers of mental manipulation and insisted that Isadora confess her secret name.

"Salahori is my secret name. It means house builder." *Why on earth did I tell her this?* "Two very different cultures united under one roof when my parents were wed." Isadora felt like she was hypnotized and continued. "Luís and I brought three sons into the world—Paulo, Rico, and Pedro. We tried every Gypsy trick to conceive a daughter but two years later Jacques was born. Now we sleep in separate bedrooms to avoid temptation. If I cannot give birth to a girl, I want no more offspring."

Reba decided to tell Isadora her own secret. "I plan to relinquish my life as a cat to become a woman when Afonso's soul returns in another man's body. Can you help me by using a magical Gypsy spell?"

Isadora looked away. She felt awkward about Reba's revelation. The Torah did not mention reincarnation. Neither did the Kabbalah—the mystical interpretation of the Bible. It contained no lessons about shape shifting from feline into female for the purpose of uniting with the soul of a dead Jewish man. Nonetheless, Reba's request merited consideration. "Let me think about it." She stood and placed the cat back on the ancient throne's seat. "Good night, Reba."

The cat formulated her plan. *I need Orchid's help to ensure that Isadora gets pregnant with a daughter who has my soul. It has been almost three hundred years since I last saw the Druidess. If she still lives, where might I find her?*

The possibility of sacrificing her life for love took Reba's breath away. *Am I courageous enough to die so that my soul can find the man that I love somewhere in time?*

SISTER OF CHARITY

Reba reacquainted herself with life at Quinta Bour da Bon. Meanwhile, at the da Gama estate Elizabeth arranged for a local priest to provide daily lessons for Orquídia in the doctrines and sacraments of the Catholic Church. Father Sebastian was amazed by the girl's ability to recall everything she saw, read, and heard. He recognized her special blessings from God. Diego hoped that his daughter would outgrow her obsession to become a nun.

Three years after witnessing the miracle at Our Lady of Montserrat chapel Orquídia turned sixteen. She informed her parents, "I am now eligible to enter a convent."

Diego was heartbroken at the prospect of losing her. He proposed an alternative. "Please consider joining the Sisters of Charity of Saint Vincent de Paul. They are servants of the sick and poor. Instead of living in a convent they reside at home or in rented rooms. This way you can stay here in Sintra while doing God's work."

Orquídia frowned at her father. "Where will I find poor people in Sintra? The residents here are wealthy. They all live in estates, palaces, and castles."

"Perhaps you and your mother can live with me in Lisbon. You will find that the streets of the city are filled with destitute people struggling to stay alive. I grow lonelier each day now that Alberto is married and living with Rosa Maria in their own villa. Even Sky deserted me. Matilda, Jacob, and their sons have no plans to visit so it is up to us to keep our family together."

"I shall consider it, Papa." Orquídia knew in her heart that she yearned to become a traditional Catholic nun living a cloistered life in a strict and structured setting. Her personality craved discipline and order. She imagined spending her days in prayer and reflection as she awaited the arrival of Teodora. *I wonder when Our Lady of Montserrat will visit me again.*

Áine of Knockaine did not return to the celestial universe during her three-year hiatus. Instead, she stayed in Sintra to revel in the luxuries of the da Gama estate. At night while the household slept the Celtic faerie goddess enjoyed herself as a woman of normal size. Áine loved the music hall where a Steinway grand piano overlooked the exotic gardens. She dared not touch its ivory keyboard for fear someone might catch her trespassing. The beautiful Áine danced around the hall in the imaginary arms of the handsome Diego da Gama.

Áine shrank down to the size of a butterfly during the day and hid within bouquets. She also eavesdropped on Orquídia's lessons in the principles of Christian life. *How absurd that her religion mandates belief in one male god.* Áine knew that countless deities occupied the celestial world. In her opinion females comprised the best and brightest of them. The faerie goddess of love, wealth, and fertility considered herself a prime example.

Today she overheard Orquídia announce her plans to leave home and embark on a celibate and impoverished life at the Convent of Saint Anthony. Áine witnessed the despairing faces of Diego and Elizabeth. In a rare moment of tenderness, she decided to delay the teen's departure. *When Orquídia visits the chapel, I shall maneuver her in the direction suggested by her attractive father.*

Orquídia arrived at the pond to swim her laps. The faerie goddess flew into her bedroom to retrieve the statue of Saint Anthony from her bedside table. She rocketed under the Moorish arches in the marble hallway to Diego's library at the back of the palace. Áine found a black leather book filled with blank pages of cream-colored stationery on a shelf. She used magic to imprint the title *Anthony's Love* on the book's cover in gold leaf.

Áine slalomed through the canopy of treetops surrounding the estate and arrived at the chapel moments before Orquídia squeezed through the entryway. From the rafters she gazed down at the devout teen kneeling on the steps leading to the altar with her rosary in hand. Several minutes later the two-foot-tall faerie goddess floated down to present herself as the Black Madonna. Instead of the golden orb she held *Anthony's Love* in one hand and the statue in the other. "Praise the Lord, Orquídia da Gama!"

Orquídia smiled and lifted her head toward Our Lady of Montserrat. "How may I serve you?" She felt tremendous relief to see the Blessed Virgin again.

"Your calling leads you to the Sisters of Charity of Saint Vincent de Paul."

"I thought you commanded me to join the Convent of Saint Anthony."

"Hush! You must be obedient and follow my advice in all things. In the future you will become the Mother Superior at the Convent of Saint Anthony."

Áine floated closer to the stone floor. She dropped the book and the statue in front of Orquídia. "Keep these for Teodora until her sixteenth birthday. Present them as a gift from Our Lady of Montserrat."

Orquídia accepted the items and crossed herself. "I vow to always do your bidding." She returned to the mansion and informed her parents about her decision to become a Sister of Charity of Saint Vincent de Paul. The welcome news overjoyed them and even tempted Diego into becoming a believer.

***

In nearby Parque da Pena, the glowing Ghost Orchid of Sintra lost her will to live. Both of the men she had loved during her many years on earth were dead. She had given up long ago on ever seeing her friend Reba again. The Druidess spent her days and nights waiting for death. She could no longer muster the energy to bathe. She existed on raindrops and gifts of food from the faeries. The old woman waited for her blind eyes to close forever. Orchid surrendered when the Irish oak offered her soul a final resting place. Each day that passed she resembled the bark of the tree even more. Her green gown and cape decomposed. Lichen covered her wrinkled skin. Her bones began to petrify and her limbs rooted in the mossy earth.

Diego and Elizabeth often walked in Parque da Pena and wondered what had happened to the Druidess. They saw nothing more than trees, ferns, and flowers. Orchid's Celtic bronze pendant and clasp lay on the ground next to the Irish oak hidden from view.

MIND YOUR MAGIC

The plan that Isadora concocted with Reba fell into place at last when she reached her mid-forties. Her son would play an important part to bring about the vision shared by his mother and the cat. They now called her Reba instead of Sky. On the day he finished packing for the Portuguese Naval School in Lisbon Pedro heard an unfamiliar high-pitched voice in his mother's bedroom. He took a moment to listen from the hallway.

"The Druidess communicates with flowers to predict the future. Unlike me she lacks the magic to stay alive. She always coveted the Bust of Nefertiti that I wear around my neck. It is my fountain of youth. I first met her when the Romans still ruled Gallia. I hope that she is not dead by now." The unusual voice wailed with worry. Pedro drew his thick brows together and placed his ear to the door.

He heard his mother respond. "I shall never give birth to a baby girl without Orchid's Celtic magic." Pedro knocked on the door and entered when he realized that his mother was also weeping. He looked around in confusion. She was alone in the room except for the cat on her lap. Reba leapt down and disappeared beneath the bed as soon as she saw him.

Pedro knelt by his mother and offered her his handkerchief. Isadora wiped away her tears and raised a graceful hand in warning. "Do not even ask who I was talking to, Son."

He spoke in a soft and soothing voice. "I overheard your conversation with the cat. I know you two are close but I never realized before today that Reba talks." Pedro frowned. "What is wrong with boys, Ma?"

Reba recalled that over three thousand years earlier she had posed a similar question while hiding beneath the royal bed of King Thutmose II and Queen Hatshepsut. Back then the young king had insisted on a son, which prompted her to ask 'What is wrong with girls?' *I miss our adventures in ancient Egypt. Hat and I made a formidable pair.* The sound of Isadora's voice brought Reba back to the present.

Isadora kissed the worry lines on Pedro's forehead. "I cherish all of my sons. It is your middle-aged mother's silly dream to have a baby girl."

Reba peeked out from her hiding place. She liked the looks of the twenty-two-year-old man. He was tall and slender like his mother and had his father's medium auburn hair and hazel eyes. Something about his calm and affectionate presence reminded her of Afonso. Of all four Bour da Bon boys Reba favored him the most.

Pedro offered, "I might know the whereabouts of the Druidess you seek. When I applied to naval school, I met a fellow applicant whose mother Sarina Matriz owns a botanica in Sintra. He told me all about her shop that sells everything from traditional remedies to African charms."

Isadora drummed her red fingernails on the chair. She felt anxious for her sweet son to make his point. "What does this have to do with Orchid MacCloud?"

"He mentioned a story about a Druidess who had helped King Ferdinand II's family. The old woman sold her natural remedies at the botanica. It is rumored that she cured Diego da Gama's wife who lived in confinement at their estate."

Reba's chest tightened with apprehension. *I am the reason that Elizabeth went mad. I must keep this secret from both Isadora and the Druidess.*

Pedro took his mother's hands in his own. "If your heart desires a baby daughter I advise you to pay a visit to Sarina Matriz. She might know the whereabouts of the Druidess you seek." The young man stood and walked to the door. He turned and added, "You and Reba should leave at once. The Druidess may die soon. They say that she is well over one hundred years old."

Reba knew the truth. *She is over twenty-three hundred years old! There is no time to worry!* The cat tried to push concerns about her friend's impending death from her mind. Pedro shut the door. Reba scurried from beneath the bed and jumped back onto Isadora's lap.

They agreed to find Orchid MacCloud so that she could help them make their dreams come true. Isadora suggested, "We can escort Pedro to the naval school in Lisbon and then travel northwest to Sintra. Luís will not suspect that we have our own plans."

A few days later Luís bid them farewell. Tears of pride filled the eyes of both father and son as they embraced. Isadora kissed her husband and promised to return after Pedro was settled. Later that week Isadora and Reba arrived in Sintra. Soon gossip spread about a tall woman dressed in black and draped in gold jewelry that was seen walking her Siamese cat through town on a leash. They visited Sarina Matriz at her botanica and asked for information regarding Orchid MacCloud. The shop owner provided directions to the huge park but could not specify the exact location of the Druidess.

Reba and Isadora entered Parque da Pena and scanned the area. Something seemed amiss. No birds sang, no frogs croaked, nor did one cricket stridulate. Streams that moved across the mossy woodland floor stopped flowing and no insects buzzed around in zigzag patterns. Not even one squirrel jumped from branch to branch. The park waited in limbo. The forest and its residents mourned for the dying Druidess. The animal kingdom and the faerie realm gathered around the Irish oak tree to pay their respects and bid her farewell.

The giant oak sobbed, "Existing without the Lady of Light makes me wish to perish too."

"Orchid, please do not leave us," moaned a faerie living in a bluebell. "The spirit of a tree represents life itself. Without the sacred oak our bridge between heaven and earth will be lost."

All of the wee ones gasped in unison causing every air spirit to lose its balance. For a split-second no oxygen saturated Parque da Pena. A tree nymph in the Irish oak bawled, "When the Druidess expires so do I."

Orchid was upset by this extreme response and forced a quiet rejoinder. "Live on, my dear friends. Hope may yet prevail. At its very core my soul tells me that a creature from my past now ventures near to us. Please help her to find me."

Nature rebounded at her welcome words. Reba and Isadora inhaled a pungent collision of fragrances excreted by the flower faeries. Every air spirit collided together to stir the breeze. All of the birds in the forest created melodious chaos. One by one the low-lying bushes rustled to coax the wanderers along the trail. The streams flowed once again and guided them forward.

The deeper the seekers ventured into the woods the darker it grew. Suddenly the fire spirits lit up hundreds of fireflies that landed on the limbs of the evergreen trees adjacent to the path. The forest transformed into sparkling holiday trees leading them to the Irish oak. Even so, Reba and Isadora failed to discern the wrinkled face of the Druidess protruding from the bark. In the gloom it appeared as if the tree displayed a large knot.

The wood nymphs joined forces and fanned open the limbs of the redwoods towering above the forest canopy. Bright rays of sunlight shone down upon the Irish oak and illuminated the gold gorget earrings on Orchid's lobes. The disk-shaped jewelry caught Reba's attention and the agile cat sprang toward the tree. "Hey, those belong to me." She realized that her beloved jewelry was attached to the tree. Reba inspected it closer and recognized the withered face of the Druidess. Her instincts mobilized to save her friend's life. She leaned in to regard Orchid closer and detected that the woman's open mouth drew little breath. The cat issued an order to Isadora. "Give me your chain."

Isadora detached and pocketed her silver cross before handing over the necklace. Reba pawed at the bust of Nefertiti from around her own neck. She knew that the powerful Egyptian talisman possessed magic strong enough to save Orchid's life. Her clumsy paws shook so much that Isadora took the amulet from Reba and placed it on the chain. Her long fingernails clawed behind Orchid's lichen-covered neck to attach it.

Reba licked her friend's face with vigor to stimulate the flow of blood under her skin. The scratchiness of the cat's tongue roused the dying woman and the Druidess came alive again. She opened her blind eyes. "O, to make such a sacrifice for this ancient soul."

Emotions overwhelmed Reba and words failed her. She paused to consider her options then regarded the Druidess eye to eye. "No sacrifice is too great if you live on. However, I humbly ask you to consider giving me something in return."

Orchid smiled. *Reba does not know the meaning of altruism. I cannot fault her for being true to herself.* "You gave me your talisman to restore my life at no small cost to your own youth. A thousand favors will never equal your gift to me. Who is your companion?"

The slender woman in black bowed with respect. "I am Isadora Bour da Bon. Together we seek the magical means to make our dreams come true." Reba and Isadora described their shared fantasy.

The Druidess eyed the cat. *This confirms what I suspected thirty years ago. Reba cast the powerful spell on Elizabeth and Diego. But with whose help?* "Tell me how Afonso died."

"My father-in-law had a weak heart," offered Isadora.

"You mean a broken heart," Reba confessed. "If we find each other somewhere in time I know that he will love me more than he ever loved his English Rose. I shall spend the rest of my life making up for the sorrow I caused them. However, I must do it as a woman. By the way, the last time I saw my earrings Elizabeth was wearing them. How did they end up on your ears?"

"Elizabeth presented them to me after I cured her madness here in this forest." Orchid faced a conundrum. *If I participate in their crazy scheme, I become an accomplice to events that may spiral out of control.* The Druidess shuddered and continued pondering. *If I refuse to accept the talisman I shall die here. Reba will take matters into her own paws again and misuse ancient Egyptian magic. It is best for all that I oversee the process. I shall only call upon trustworthy Celtic deities for assistance.*

Orchid agreed to help them implement their plan. She surrendered her tired mind and ancient body to the power held by the bust of Nefertiti. The Druidess peeled herself away from the Irish oak with care to avoid damaging its bark. In the time it took for an elf to blink twice the Lady of Light transformed back into a stunning woman. The faerie realm gasped with glee and all the creatures of the forest expressed delight and pleasure.

"Her soft complexion reminds me of gardenia petals," admired the flower faeries.

"The Lady's luminescent skin glows like moonlight," pronounced the air spirits.

"Her eyes sparkle like priceless emeralds," remarked a dwarf. The little guy handed the Lady of Light her bronze pendant and clasp. "Here are your treasures."

"The lips of the Druidess remind me of ripe cherries," offered a squirrel holding an acorn.

"Her shimmering red hair reflects the setting sun," marveled a fire spirit.

"The lady has a smile as inviting as a warm summer night," cooed a wood nymph.

The gentle voices of the tree spirits penetrated the air. "Her renewed gown and cape match the colors of our vibrant forest."

A magnificent light brown doe with an unusual fourteen-point rack emerged from the foliage. A miniature bronze hoof hung on a gold ribbon from one of her spiked antlers. The graceful animal lowered her formidable head and presented herself. The Druidess recognized the animal from the cattails across the pond where she bathed. The doe offered the bronze gift to her. A powerful image of her long-lost sister floated into Orchid's mind. She realized that the doe's eyes shone emerald green mirroring her own. She spoke the name, "Nuala?" The wary beast spun around on its hind legs and fled into the cover of the overgrown woods.

Orchid issued a joyful proclamation to the creatures in attendance. "The appearance of this doe signals new adventures on the horizon." She wrapped her fingers around the bronze hoof and sensed its powerful magic. The Druidess slipped the ribbon over her head. She closed her eyes in a prayer of gratitude to the forest that had protected her for so many years. The beautiful woman opened her eyes and asked, "Who wants to celebrate?" Isadora and Reba joined the faeries and elves, nymphs and dwarves, and all of nature's spirits as they danced around while Orchid sang Celtic folk songs.

An exhausted Reba curled up on the soft moss and pondered her predicament. *I no longer have my fountain of youth. What happens if I die before I find Afonso? I must enlist Hat's assistance to steal Tara's ring of eternity so that I live forever while I search for my soul mate.*

The faerie realm bedded down for the night. Isadora watched in reverential silence as the Druidess transformed into the glowing Ghost Orchid and took her place on the Irish oak. The blissful Portuguese woman fell into a peaceful slumber next to Reba.

The voice of the Celtic goddess Druantia issued a warning to the Ghost Orchid. "Mind your magic, Druidess. Do not allow that ancient Egyptian Siamese cat to interfere with the powers of life, death, and rebirth that are far beyond her control."

UNCONDITIONAL LOVE

The White Storks of Mercy returned from London to the Isle of Souls to collect Iona. She waited on the ground below with Leu and Ba. The three fixed their eyes upon the twilight sky as it transitioned from blue to a pale violet color. It provided a beautiful backdrop for the birds spiraling down.

After her twelve-month stay Iona did not want to leave this place that now felt like home. The storklet existed as a natural part of their avian family. She was included in everything. In the past Iona had often felt ignored when the storks transformed into Merciful Ones and attended to human matters. She gave a sarcastic warning to Leu and Ba. "Wait until you see Zendala as a person. She is very old and wrinkled."

Ba put her concern to rest. "Leu and I also possess the gift of sight, Iona. We envisioned her human image long ago. We love her with no conditions attached. No one ought to judge another by his or her outer appearance, dear. Think of Bennu the phoenix, for example. His flaming presence frightened you at first and now you are close friends."

"Not too close," giggled Iona. "Or I might catch on fire."

The leader guided her phalanx over the grove of acacia trees and landed next to the pond fed by the Sacred Bach. They all transformed. Maatkare stripped down to her undergarments and dove into the swimming hole. She was anxious to feel the cool water against her skin. The pharaoh floated on her back with charcoaled eyelids closed to enjoy the perfect weather offered by the Isle of Souls.

The Great and Honorable Zendala greeted her kin. "At last, I am pleased to present my human self to you."

Her elders clattered their bills. Ba responded, "Your human body befits you, Daughter." Iona flew off before anyone acknowledged her.

"Wait Iona!" A disappointed Mary yearned to spend time with the storklet.

Blandina changed shape again and followed the young bird up to the Sacred Bach that fed the pond. She landed on an embankment covered in white lilies of the valley and remained in stork form to watch Iona poking her bill here and there in the brook.

The scent of lilies wafted downward from the Bach to the pond. Mary inhaled the sweet smell and smiled. "Ah, Joan's favorite scent."

Zendala remarked, "I do not remember this particular flora blooming here a year ago."

Leu sighed. "Iona felt abandoned after you left for nursing school and her grief for Joan resurfaced. She asked Heka to use his magic and manifest Joan's favorite flowers along the Sacred Bach. Iona hoped to draw her spirit down from the heavens. Heka has grown fond of the storklet so he did not hesitate to comply."

Ba elucidated further. "Iona is convinced that Joan's soul awaits rebirth. She spends her days searching for a violet starburst within a bubble to present itself."

Leu continued. "We explained to Iona that the spirits of unborn babies disappeared from the Bach when Christianity entrenched itself in Europe centuries ago. Women no longer believed that Sacred Storks of the Bach delivered them. Nonetheless, her quest has remained steadfast."

Maatkare emerged from the pond and donned her uniform.

"Someone needs to knock some sense into her. Joan of Arc is dead."

Zendala ignored the pharaoh's typical bluntness. "I shall talk to her." The ancient woman stood, transformed, and flew up to the Sacred Bach. She landed next to Blandina and called Iona to come to them.

"I am busy," she sassed. "Leave me alone."

"I shall not ask again, Iona." The stubborn storklet took her time wading toward her leader. Zendala gazed upon the shimmering water as it reflected the sky's violet color. She saw a faint image of the Cathedral of Notre-Dame in Rouen appear on the liquid's surface. The seer closed her eyes and envisioned a perfect way to help Iona alter her grief into a positive memory of the maiden.

Iona stepped out of the water onto the slope covered in lilies. She hung her head in embarrassment. "I am sorry for ignoring everybody. I know that it feels bad when that happens."

Blandina entreated, "Please accept our apologies if we ever overlooked you. No one deserves to feel left out. We all missed you so much."

Iona continued to look sheepish so Zendala reassured her. "It appears that our absence made you miss Joan even more. We shall not leave you behind again. Do you still want to visit Paris? The success of our next mission depends on your participation."

Iona brimmed with excitement. "The closest we ever got to Paris was our trip to Château Versailles! When do we leave?"

Zendala's heart grew lighter. "It is decided. We shall depart at daybreak. Let us go back to the others and get a good night's sleep."

The following morning at sunrise Re and Heka returned from the underworld after fighting the evil serpent Apep from aboard their solar barge. Maatkare and Mary had slept as women hoping to intercept Heka. They both looked a sorry sight. Mary's red hair was mussed and her indigo belt had loosened. Maatkare's jeweled beard hung askew.

Heka ignored the two smitten women and instead greeted Iona as she flew into his arms giggling. Maatkare grumbled but Mary grinned. She was pleased that the storklet received his special attention. The flirtatious deity turned to welcome the monarchs. "Come here, my ladies. Heka holds enough affection for all."

Neither proud woman stepped forward. The handsome god of magic glanced around seeking Blandina. The young beauty had transformed and stood next to Leu and Ba. Heka asked if she cared to accompany him on a morning stroll. The shy teen declined. He shrugged and released Iona to the ground. "I am exhausted. I shall see you tonight in the underworld, Re."

Maatkare turned to Mary and scolded her. "Somehow this is your fault."

Zendala joined her father. They watched Maatkare point her finger with its long custom painted nail at Mary and then stalked away. Re shook his falcon head. "Any regrets about taking on Pharaoh Hatshepsut as a peacemaker?"

"I am not sorry that I honored my mother's request back in 100 B.C."

"Reba created an unfortunate situation for all of us."

"Where does she reside now, Father?"

Re shrugged. "I know not. She communicates only with Bastet and Sekhmet."

"I fail to understand why the universe shields all knowledge of my sister from me. My gift is never effective when it comes to Reba's whereabouts."

The sun god was dismissive in his response. "I am only in charge of the sun. The rest of the cosmos is the responsibility of other gods and goddesses. Try asking your mother if she can see Reba with her gift—not that she cares how or where that naughty cat spends her time."

Zendala engaged Re's golden eyes with her own. "Families need to show unconditional love toward their kin and forgive their mistreatments."

Re hugged his ancient human daughter. "Deities may be powerful but we are not perfect. Forgiveness is too much to ask after what she did to you. I love her but she will never change."

"I forgave Reba long ago for imprisoning me, Father. I do not expect her to pardon me for treading on her open wounds even though it was an accident. Mercy is not in her nature. I only want to know that she is safe."

"Your sister can take care of herself. Tell me, why must you leave so soon?"

"I need to remove Iona from her obsessive search for Joan's soul within a spirit bubble. Yesterday on the banks of the Sacred Bach I envisioned the perfect way to help her."

Father and daughter walked over to join Ba and Leu. Except for Maatkare the Merciful Ones expressed their heartfelt goodbyes. The pharaoh produced a stiff royal wave.

Iona shared a weepy farewell. She reminded the two Sacred Storks of the Bach to keep looking for a violet starburst. The White Storks of Mercy departed with their apprentice and flew in the direction of Paris.

COINCIDENCE AND FATE

The supernatural storks traveled through time to A.D. 1895. Iona let out a gleeful shriek when they flew by the new landmark in Paris called the Eiffel Tower. From the air they located a gallery famous for its innovative glass and wrought-iron barrel vaulted roof. The design provided ample natural light for the new twenty-painting series by the well-known French Impressionist artist Claude Monet.

Zendala directed Iona to perch in a tree adjacent to the gallery. The remaining four storks landed on the roof's flat metal ridge. It gave them a birds-eye view of the exhibition below. In the center of the salon well-dressed patrons milled around while sipping flutes of champagne as they studied the unusual modern art.

Blandina asked, "Why are we here?"

Zendala explained, "I want Iona to select a special painting of the Cathedral of Rouen in memory of Joan. However, she cannot accompany us inside the gallery."

Maatkare raised an issue. "How shall we know which one she chooses?"

Mary suggested, "We can stand as women in front of each piece of art. Iona can peck on the glass when she sees the painting that she favors from her vantage point on the roof."

Blandina complimented her. "You have a way with the storklet, Mary." Maatkare glared.

The four birds flew down into an alleyway and transformed.

From there they walked a short distance to the tree where Iona waited. The storklet jumped down from her perch. "Now will you tell me your secret? It is not polite to keep things from me."

Zendala patted Iona's head. "Thank you for being so patient. We came to Paris to buy a painting of the cathedral where we rescued Joan of Arc. It honors her and we hope that it will help you feel better. There are twenty of them to choose from." She told the storklet to land on the ridge of the gallery's roof and peck on the glass at the appropriate time.

The Merciful Ones entered the exhibit and were given flutes of champagne. They caught the attention of everyone including the bearded artist. He noted their different accents when they spoke and his curiosity piqued. *What an eclectic group of women. They dress without pretense yet carry themselves like royalty.* Claude Monet approached them and explained the evolution of his masterful works. He pointed at the piece entitled, *Rouen Cathedral, Red, Sunlight.* "I painted it at different times of the day during every season of the year. The way that the light played on the façade entranced me. Luminosity became the focal point rather than the cathedral itself."

He fondled his unruly brown beard while his attentive dark eyes studied the ladies. The sensitive and modest artist turned his attention to the intriguing ancient-looking woman. "Color and light pursued me like a constant worry. I tried to do the impossible, Madam." He readjusted the lapel of his steel gray smock.

Zendala raised her glass in a toast. "You succeeded, Monsieur Monet."

"Please call me Claude." She glanced up at the glass roof and spotted Iona who shook her head. The artist followed her gaze up to the stork. The Merciful Ones strolled from one painting to another. Each piece of art received a negative response from Iona. Claude remarked, "Something tells me that you are communicating with the bird on the roof. It does not seem to like my work."

Zendala made an intuitive decision to trust the artist. She introduced herself and each member of her coterie. His eyes widened with shock and delight. "I never imagined meeting the legendary White Storks of Mercy." He pointed to the bird on the roof. "What is her name?"

Blandina answered, "She is called Iona. Our precious apprentice has lived as a storklet for almost one hundred and fifty years since we rescued her from starvation in Spain. In another decade she will be empowered to transform into her ten-year-old Gypsy self with all the magical capabilities that we Merciful Ones possess."

Maatkare pointed to the painting entitled, *Rouen Cathedral, Portal and Tower of Saint Romain.* "We rescued Joan of Arc from the burning stake in A.D. 1431. She was inducted into the White Storks of Mercy atop that very tower."

Mary explained, "The Maid of Orléans is no longer with us and poor Iona still grieves for her. We are visiting your exhibit so that she may pick out a painting to honor Joan's memory."

Zendala thought back to her vision on the banks of the Sacred Bach. "Joan loved the color violet because it symbolizes wisdom, dignity and peace."

The artist excused himself and returned with a rolled-up canvas. He unrolled it and placed it on a table and secured the corners with paperweights. "I held this back from public viewing. Until now I did not understand why. The untitled painting presents the tower of Saint Romain in red and violet at sunset." They all looked up to the glass roof and heard the approval of continuous pecking. Everyone laughed. Blandina fingered the large diamond in her pocket. Zendala reached into her own pocket and pulled out a few gold coins. Claude shook his head and placed a hand over his heart. "This is my gift to you all."

Zendala voiced her appreciation and accepted the canvas. "Perhaps when Iona completes her apprenticeship, we shall fly to your home in Giverny. Our darling little Gypsy girl can thank you herself in person." The Merciful Ones bid him farewell and left the gallery. A few moments later four large birds landed on the glass roof and joined Iona. The untitled painting was tucked beneath one of Zendala's wings. Her magical powers would allow Claude's gift to disappear during their flight and reappear when they reached Estela Islet. The artist smiled up at them, removed his black beret with a flourish, and bowed in respect.

***

At the conclusion of their adventure in Paris the White Storks of Mercy flew west toward the Berlenga Islands. They took a well needed rest in Lisbon on an arch of the crumbling Church of Carmo. Prior to the devastating earthquake in A.D. 1755 the building had claimed status as the city's largest church. Afterwards, the stone arches and exterior walls of its nave resembled a dinosaur's thoracic skeleton. Iona asked incessant questions that reflected her new interest in historic cathedrals. The others indulged the storklet's thirst for knowledge but Maatkare became bored. She turned around and cocked her long neck toward the ground to watch a pair of female tourists below.

From her awkward position the pharaoh regarded a tall, thin, and stylish woman dressed in black with gold chains of various lengths hanging from her neck. A redhead wearing a full-length gown and cape in vibrant hues of green walked next to her. Maatkare noted that her striking beauty surpassed that of Queen Nefertiti. Reba trotted between them with her nose in the air. The shocked pharaoh screeched, "Cat!"

The excited utterance startled Zendala. "What did you say, Maatkare?"

"Cat… catastrophic," she blurted. "A tidal wave devastated

the city after the earthquake and firestorm." She turned her back to the threesome on the ground.

Iona's brown eyes opened even wider. "A tidal wave?"

Mary noticed Maatkare struggling to focus and offered an explanation. "It occurs when the earthquake moves the ocean floor. The waves get very high by the time they reach shore." The studious storklet nodded and imagined the giant wave destroying the city.

Down below the two sightseers and their cat sought a place to rest. They had spent the day exploring the hilly streets of the Alfama district. In Baixa they rode the new elevator that connected with the upper part of the town referred to as Bairro Alto. The three weary sightseers stopped to enjoy a snack at the ruins of the Church of Carmo. Orchid needed a break from the harsh noises of the crowded city. She yearned for the peace of nature.

The visitors sat against a stone wall within the roofless nave and opened a picnic basket. They helped themselves to fresh bread with goat cheese and black olives. The women washed it down with refreshing rosé wine. Reba munched on morsels of roasted chicken. Her thoughts turned to Tara. She caught the scent of live birds and saw the backs of four storks with black-tipped wings perched on the archway above. A pure white bird that glowed was positioned between them.

Hello, Sister. What a coincidence meeting you here after all these years. Or is it fate? I think about you and your precious jewelry often. She jumped high off the ground and twisted in the air. Her brown paw swiped toward the divine white stork that glowed. *Your amulets are mine!* Isadora and Orchid assumed that the cat was swatting at bugs.

Zendala shook her head as she experienced a disturbing sensation. Her peaceful space felt invaded by energy so negative that it rattled her to the core. Without turning she announced,

"It is time to leave." She took off into the cloudless Portuguese sky. Three of the four storks flapped their mighty wings to follow her. Maatkare stayed put and turned around once again.

Reba avoided eye contact with the large bird that glared down at them like a menacing vulture. Isadora gestured at the sky. "Are those the White Storks of Mercy?"

Maatkare drifted down towards them. Reba panicked and coughed up a fur ball. She feared that the pharaoh might attack her. *I need to proceed with caution to get her back on my side. The last time we met I suggested that we part forever.*

Reba sandwiched herself between the two women. She felt uncertain about Maatkare's temperament. The large bird landed in front of them and transformed into her intimidating human self. The cat squeezed behind the ladies and covered her head with her front paws.

Isadora's gray-green eyes shone with delight. "I recognize you as a Merciful One! I saw the coterie years ago when I stood on the steep vineyard terraces in Vale de Mendiz. Most people never see such a supernatural phenomenon even once—yet I have beheld you twice in one lifetime! How fortunate we are to be in this particular place at this very time."

"A fine line distinguishes coincidence and fate," offered Orchid.

Maatkare remained silent as she removed the beard from her pocket. She stuck it to her thrusting chin. Her charcoaled eyes searched behind the women. "Come out, Cat."

Reba crept around her seated friends to face Maatkare. She scanned the area with caution for anyone who might overhear them. It appeared safe to talk. "I am honored to introduce you both to Pharaoh Maatkare Hatshepsut, my dear friend since 1487 B.C. I gave her eternal life and the ability to time travel."

Always taking credit, mused Maatkare with exasperation. *Dear friend? Rubbish!*

Reba introduced Isadora Bour da Bon and then gestured to the Druidess. "Allow me to present Orchid MacCloud. I saved her life in Parque da Pena by forsaking my bust of Nefertiti. You can see that she is young and beautiful in spite of being twenty-three hundred years old. Now she will live on without appearing to age thanks to me."

Maatkare fumed in silence. *Me, me, me. Does Cat ever get tired of talking about herself? I see that she still wears my daughter's gorget earrings.*

Orchid lifted Reba onto her lap and kissed the top of her head. "This unselfish cat gave up her fountain of youth out of love for me."

"Cat loves no one but herself," responded Maatkare. "What promise did she extract from you in return?"

Reba answered for her. "Orchid is a Druidess. She will use her power to summon Celtic deities so that I may become a woman!"

"Best of luck with that," answered Maatkare with sarcasm. "According to Re and Ba you will never be allowed to become a woman—or to fly for that matter."

Reba jumped off Orchid's lap and trotted away. Maatkare followed her. "Who cares about flying? My interest is only in womanhood. I know that we parted on bad terms but now I require your help. I no longer need all of Tara's amulets but I must obtain her ring of eternity."

"If I do your bidding how will it benefit me?"

"You will enjoy the pleasure of my company throughout eternity." *Once I find the soul of Afonso Bour da Bon, I plan to abandon the moody pharaoh.* Maatkare ignored her invitation and broke into a run. She took a flying leap and soared off without another word. Reba sauntered back to her two friends acting as if Maatkare's rude behavior did not affect her.

That evening Isadora invited Orchid to experience

Portuguese fado music. They ventured into a dark tavern where tabletop candles provided dim light. A female singer dressed in black stood on a small stage captivating the audience with her sorrowful songs. Isadora imagined herself onstage accompanied by her talented sons. Tears rolled down her cheek as she remembered how they had serenaded the sad and ailing Afonso.

At the hotel Reba spent the evening alone pacing back and forth like a caged animal. She jumped from the bed onto the bureau, over to the chair, and down to the floor to release her rage. The cat repeated the circuitous route numerous times. The anger brought on by the pharaoh's dismissive attitude threatened to boil over.

She pondered Tara's behavior at the Church of Carmo. Reba was grateful that even in her mutilated state she had stumbled into the star shaft back in 100 b.c. The cosmic radiation from Orion's constellation gave her permanent anonymity from Tara's psychic powers. *Tara did not even realize that I was down there in the nave. This proves that she cannot prevent me from becoming a human. Hat dare not reveal my plans to her or she will be considered a traitor.* Reba relaxed into a calmer state as she anticipated womanhood.

The next day Orchid departed the hotel while Isadora sang fado songs to Reba. The cat found the whining resonance of the melancholy music irritating. She tolerated it to keep Isadora on her side and because she knew Afonso had loved it. The Druidess embarked on an excursion to the National Archaeology Museum. She needed to locate a small iron pig icon and to learn more about Portugal's Celtic heritage.

Orchid spotted the relic she was looking for and convinced the museum director to hand it over. He informed her that the Celts had arrived two thousand years earlier during the Iron Age and assimilated with other analogous cultures. These Celtiberians lived on hillsides in fortified urban conclaves comprised of one hundred or more families. Residents venerated certain animals including pigs, which represented authority and family protection.

The director was anxious to impress the gorgeous redheaded woman. He informed her that the archeologist Francisco Martins Sarmento had discovered and overseen the excavation of an Iron Age settlement called Citânia de Briteiros.

"How do I locate the site? I do not come from this country."

"It is in the province of Minho where in the twelfth century Afonso Henriques declared himself the first king of Portugal."

Ah, another Afonso. "Tomorrow I travel back to Quinta Bour da Bon in the Upper Douro Valley. I hope to visit the Iron Age settlement soon. Will you please show me how to get there?" The director smiled and led his guest to a map of Portugal hanging on the wall. He gestured at the top of the long and narrow country as he inched closer to the desirable woman. He pointed out the location of Citânia de Briteiros.

Orchid nodded her thanks and moved away from him to look at more artifacts. She was inspired by a piece of petrified wood to imagine an oak grove near the defensive walls of the settlement. In ancient times such a place provided the setting where local Druids had worshipped while receiving wisdom from the sacred trees. *The compound and its surroundings will be an ideal location for the High Fruitful Mother Arianrhod to help me summon my chosen deities.* The Druidess knew that the ritual for incarnating the soul of an ancient Egyptian Siamese cat into Isadora's womb would require multiple divinities.

The Druids believed that the soul continued to live after the death of its human body. Under normal circumstances the soul traveled to the otherworld for reincarnation into various forms—human, plant, or animal—until it reached the highest realm known as the Source.

Orchid experienced a profound dilemma. On one hand, the

Druids' moral code prohibited meddling in matters of the soul. On the other hand, Celtic spiritual tradition accepted *anam cara* as a compassionate presence. When one being loved and trusted another, their souls flowed together in an eternal union that cut across the barriers of time and space. This integration transported them to a sacred place that Celts called *baile* or home.

Reba saved my life. I intend to keep my word to her and unite two ancient traditions in the name of true love. I cannot dwell on saying goodbye to her or I shall lose my courage. The Druidess pocketed the iron pig icon and thanked the director once again.

***

On the thirty-first of December in A.D. 1899 the Merciful Ones hunkered down around Joan's resting place under the olive tree. The painting from Claude Monet was stretched out flat and secured with small rocks upon the grave. Iona had asked the others to remove the artwork from its protected crevice in the jagged feldspar outcropping. From time to time the storklet sought inspiration from his gift. Zendala used magic to safeguard the painting.

At midnight the leader pointed the ring of eternity to the heavens. A few moments later Seth's cosmic forces rained gold and silver drops of ionized water upon them. Blandina and Mary danced in the moonlight. Iona flew in circles above them squealing with delight. Zendala's thoughts fixated on her sister. She sat next to Maatkare who seemed preoccupied. The ancient woman pondered aloud. "I wonder where Reba finds herself tonight?"

The pharaoh shrugged in resignation. "I suspect that she is out in the world somewhere making mischief." *Or thinking of ways that I can do it for her.*

JOURNEY TO ANOTHER LIFE

Reba and her two traveling companions returned to Quinta Bour da Bon. The cat scurried to the garden seeking shade beneath the trellis. She was anxious to daydream about her new life as a woman. The discovery that Ramses' throne had disappeared caused her immense anger. The feline yowled up a storm. Isadora rushed out to inform her that Afonso's mother Perl had sold it to some female nomads. The cat hissed in response. "She had no right to sell my throne!"

"I promise to find you another chair to nap on."

Perl and Reba shared a mutual dislike that now intensified. The cat batted around balls of yarn that she picked out of the cranky matron's knitting basket. She marked her territory on the hamper as payback. Reba was bored to death and eager to proceed with their plan. The impatient cat waited for Isadora to get pregnant since husband and wife once again shared a bed. *At least Orchid now resides at the Quinta. That is one less thing to worry about.*

Perl regarded their foreign guest with suspicion. *Why does she glow in the dark? There is something peculiar about her.*

One day the birds of paradise revealed to Orchid that Isadora had conceived a baby girl. The Druidess kept the knowledge to herself. Meanwhile she enjoyed getting to know the rest of the Bour da Bons. Paulo, Rico, and their younger brother Jacques appeared smitten with the beautiful Druidess. Even Luís found himself grateful that his wife enjoyed this new friendship.

In mid-December of A.D. 1900 Isadora informed Reba and Orchid about her secret. "I am pregnant but I dare not tell my protective husband. If I do Luís will not allow me to leave the house. I shall tell him that our guest wants to see more of northern Portugal."

Reba felt ecstatic about the news. Nevertheless, she complained. "What if your baby is a boy? My soul cannot reside in the body of a male!"

Orchid patted the cat's head. "Do not worry, Reba. The flowers told me that the baby is a girl." The welcome news brought tears to Isadora's gray-green eyes. The dreams that she and Reba nurtured were coming closer to reality.

"What a relief. I shall call myself Rebecca when I am a woman.

The mother-to-be grinned. "Rebecca Bour da Bon is a fine name."

A few days later Isadora bid her sweet husband a temporary farewell. She adored the attractive man now in his mid-forties. His thin beard curved around his angular chin and tapered to a narrow line at the base of his large ears. Isadora kissed his frowning forehead and ran her polished fingernails through his thick and wavy brown hair. "I shall miss you, my darling."

"Please do not leave," he begged. His voice was hoarse from smoking so many cigarettes. "I cannot explain it but I feel unsettled about your trip."

"You have nothing to worry about, sweetheart. We shall return in a week."

Luís shrugged his narrow shoulders in resignation. "Please give my mother a kiss from me." The obsessive worrier watched as Isadora, Orchid, and the cat set off in a carriage for the Minho Province. They planned to hire a boat to take them north up the River Corgo.

The two women and Reba stayed overnight at the home

of Isadora's mother-in-law Catarina. Reba marveled at the flamboyant stucco and stone manor house. It was considered one of the finest examples of eighteenth-century Italian Baroque style in Portugal. Complex irregular shapes squeezed between ornamental towers and the exterior granite double staircase demanded equal attention. *No wonder Catarina left the rundown Quinta Bour da Bon.*

Orchid relaxed on a bench in the formal gardens with Reba snuggling on her lap. "This place reminds me of the da Gama estate in Sintra. I believe that you know the owners?" Reba let out an annoyed meow at the trick question. She jumped off Orchid's lap and disappeared through a maze of manicured evergreen shrubs to sulk. *The Druidess knows more than she lets on. One more thing to fret about.*

The next morning the travelers took a boat north to Vila Pouca de Aguiar. Here Isadora used her family clout. She pledged a crate of Bour da Bon Tawny Vintage Port to the local mayor in exchange for arranging transportation to and from Citânia de Briteiros. He volunteered his son Augusto who supplied his own carriage.

Isadora's mouth gaped in disappointment when she saw Augusto drive up in a rickety two-wheeled volante with an open hood and wooden seats. She apologized to Orchid. "I wish I had inspected what I bartered for. His horse looks half dead." The stocky lethargic mare with heavy hooves, a large rump, and an undersized head made a poor impression. The Iberian bay's curling coat earned her the Portuguese name Crespo.

Orchid smiled at the pathetic creature. "Nonsense. She will take us where we need to go."

The ladies shopped at the market square before embarking for the town of Guimarães located forty miles away. Isadora and Reba searched for seat cushions. Orchid excused herself to run a private errand. She found a shop selling regional blackened pottery. Local artisans fired the unglazed ceramics in wood, burning them to the color of smoke.

Orchid purchased an urn for Reba's journey into the realm of the dead. Moments after the cat's physical body died, she would seal it inside the vessel to prevent the spirit's re-entry. *I must remove the talisman of Noah's Ark and her gold gorget earrings before Reba takes her last breath. Otherwise, she will remain earthbound.*

The Druidess watched a carefree and smiling Isadora strolling with the cat on a leash. They both enjoyed the attention paid by local vendors in the market square. *Why do they act so happy? Reba will cease to exist once her soul resides in Isadora's womb. Rebecca will not retain the cat's memories.* Orchid's sorrow over the imminent loss of her friend magnified.

Later in the day the small-framed Augusto mounted his horse and waved goodbye to his father. The mayor insisted that his son wear a white shirt and tie beneath his cropped canvas jacket to make a good impression. The lad with ragged patches of fuzz above his upper lip acted as a chatty tour guide as he drove the strangers into the province of Minho. Orchid enjoyed inhaling nature's fresh air and watching the rocky countryside go by.

The travelers spent a restful night at a guesthouse in Guimarães. Early the next morning, Isadora bought practical clothes as well as basic gear and food for their overnight adventure to Citânia de Briteiros. On the way out of town the ladies admired the impressive skyline of Castelo de São Miguel. Its storybook towers reminded the Druidess of medieval times. *Perhaps I shall invite Merlin the supreme sorcerer to attend our ritual.*

Dusk approached as the carriage neared the Iron Age settlement. The crescent moon appeared on the horizon at the same time a barn owl swooped by in silent rapture. Its wings were streaked with the colors of sunflowers, amber, and silver. The bird's crown and nape were honey colored. Its heart-shaped facial discs and underbelly were as white as snow. The owl hooted to Orchid. This frightened Crespo who increased her speed from a sluggish walk to an actual trot. Augusto grimaced and made the sign of the cross. The lad lifted his whip in the event he needed to defend himself and his passengers.

Orchid soothed their driver. "Fear not, Augusto. She symbolizes the moon's connection to fertility and wisdom. This omen honors us." The Druidess bowed her head with respect to the nocturnal bird as it flew away.

Reba jumped down onto the carriage floorboards in case the predator mistook her for its dinner. She whispered, "In ancient Egypt owls warn of death. This portent may not bode well."

Orchid scooped up the cat and admonished her. "Owls always protect. They are among the most mystical and wonderful creatures alive. This one is Blodeuwedd the Celtic goddess of betrayal and the nurturer of children. She has appeared to us as an owl tonight." The Druidess released the cat and opened her arms to celebrate the magnificent surroundings. "Nature exists as a manifestation of the divine."

Isadora agreed. "I admire the convictions of your ancient Celtic religion regarding the magical aspects of life."

Orchid elaborated in response. "The belief that the Christian god created humans in his own image and that they hold dominion over nature may end up destroying Mother Earth. In my opinion mankind represents one small part of the awe-inspiring universe. One creature should not maintain supremacy over another."

Reba voiced her point of view in a whisper lest Augusto overhear. "I hate the Romans but at least they did not force the Druids to convert to their religion like the Christians did. They declared that the Celtic Druids were blasphemous."

"Aye," agreed Orchid. She lowered her voice. "Christians accused us of worshipping evil. They called our rituals black magic and burned us as witches." She shook off the memory. "Let us talk about our wonderful ritual tonight. I plan to invite all of the Celtic deities that reign over love, fertility and rebirth. Reba's journey to another life may well turn into a huge festival instead of a quiet ceremony."

Isadora offered her own perspective. "In the Jewish faith we believe that souls revolve through many lives as part of the morality of everyday living called *gilgulim*. We try our best to live according to God's will. If we die without fulfilling all of the *mitzvoth*—the Laws of Moses—we must return to earth again until our souls become pure."

Orchid was well versed in many dogmatic religions. She responded, "Christians believe that the body receives a unique soul that has never existed before. If all goes well we shall disprove that belief tonight."

Reba grew more anxious by the minute. "How will my soul find Rebecca when she is not yet born?" The Druidess winked and told the cat not to worry.

***

The archeological dig at Citânia de Briteiros was located nine miles from Guimarães. Augusto unloaded the threesome at the dirt road leading to the site. Isadora gave him explicit instructions. "Go back to Guimarães for the night and do not return until morning." Once he was out of sight Isadora changed her clothes. Reba scampered ahead. The women strapped knapsacks to their shoulders and climbed up the rocky knoll onto the crest of a hill.

The blackened urn, iron pig icon, and a special herbal mixture were nestled inside of Orchid's pack. Isadora stuffed both silk-lined pockets of her trousers with her gold chains and bangles. Her mother's silver cross and the five-point Star of David from Perl remained fastened around her neck sharing a short thin chain. The women followed Reba up the trail used by the team of excavators that were gone for the night. The impatient cat ran ahead and waited for her companions to arrive. Reba called to them in her high-pitched voice. "The site is just a bunch of primitive stone huts without roofs. I expected more sophistication from you Celts, Orchid."

The Druidess chuckled at the impertinent cat. "This place is perfect for your journey to another life, Reba." She sensed the spirits of her ancestors and goose bumps prickled her skin. Orchid turned to Isadora and offered her a drink from the canteen. "I brewed this tea of valerian root, lavender, and chamomile to calm your nerves."

"Thank you. I am a little nervous." The pregnant woman drank the concoction.

A variety of trees surrounded the settlement. Orchid pointed out various species. "Over there flourishes a grove of elder trees believed to represent birth and death, beginning and end. The spirit of the elder possesses the magic to make your shared aspirations come true."

Reba swooned with excitement as she watched the evergreen sprays dancing in the wind. "What about those cedars swaying in the breeze?"

"Their essences will lure Isadora into a deep dream sleep tonight. We must gather some boughs for her bed. The trees will not mind sharing them for this special occasion."

Reba scurried over to a large stand of oaks beyond the excavation site. She ascended a thick trunk onto a sturdy limb. "I recognize this species from Parque da Pena. We have seen for ourselves that Irish oaks provide doorways to the faerie realm."

Orchid followed Reba to the tree. She inspected a large split in the trunk—a sign that it had been struck by lightning. Her hand reached into its opening. *This is an ideal resting place for the urn.* "Please look around for mistletoe growing in the boughs. Faeries live there and are prepared to act as guardians for children."

Reba climbed further into the leafy oak and confirmed the presence of mistletoe. The last rays of light found their way through the branches. She made an alarming discovery. The cat descended with agility and yelled for them to follow her. The two women hustled to an area near the hillside where they saw a pair of intertwined sycamore saplings. Reba explained, "Twin sycamores welcome Re when he emerges victorious from the underworld after defeating the evil serpent Apep. The sun god celebrates by shining upon the earth for another day."

Orchid responded, "Perhaps it is a sign that Re and Ba will witness your rebirth."

"My parents cannot attend! They forbade me to shape shift into a woman."

The Druidess pondered this potential problem. If the sun god objected to the incarnation it could jeopardize his daughter's journey. The sight of Reba sacrificing her own life might motivate Ba to save her estranged offspring. Reba paced back and forth while Orchid considered this dilemma. Isadora dropped her boughs beneath the twin sycamores. She plopped down on the bed of foliage and leaned against a sapling. "I feel so tired."

Orchid cushioned the boughs around her. "The herbs are working."

Isadora sighed when Reba jumped onto her lap. "Can the ritual take place here? I do not think I can move."

Orchid posed the critical question to Reba. "Shall I summon the Celtic deities?"

The cat shook her head. "First we must present our gifts to Isadora."

The Druidess removed her triquetra pendant. Celtic knots encircled the three-cornered triangular shape. Its design represented the three phases of a woman's life—maidenhood, motherhood, and wise womanhood. "I am honored to give you my necklace." Orchid slipped it over Isadora's head.

Reba pawed at the cartouche around her own neck. Orchid removed the ancient Egyptian relic and fastened it onto Isadora's wrist. "What about your earrings?"

The cat begged, "Please let me wear them a bit longer." She turned to Isadora. "I hope that you will not forget me."

Isadora's face soured and she wept. Orchid kissed the emotional woman on the forehead. "Reba's soul will be within your womb when you awaken at sunrise." She addressed the furry friend she had encountered in Gallia almost nineteen centuries earlier. "No one will ever forget Reba the ancient Egyptian Siamese cat!" The Druidess left them to share the last hours of each other's company. The time approached to summon the Celtic deities for the incarnation. If the eight-foot-tall sun god with a falcon head appeared and threatened her Orchid knew that the iron pig icon would transform and protect her from his anger.

On a side road near the site Augusto haltered Crespo for the night and settled on the soft new cushions that covered the wooden seats. He saw no point in spending his money at an inn. *That bossy Senhora Bour da Bon will never know the difference.* The lad fell into a light slumber until his mare whinnied and roused him. He climbed down from the carriage and approached the woods. Augusto gasped when he saw the redheaded foreigner glowing in the dark. What a shame for all involved that he did not understand why her phosphorescent skin emitted light.

FROZEN CELESTIAL JEWELS

On that same night—the twentieth of December in A.D. 1900—the crescent moon glistened over Estela Islet. Zendala rested in the lotus position on the ancient throne she had acquired a few days earlier. She adored the relic that once belonged to Ramses VI. For protection against the wind Zendala had moved the artifact behind the outcropping of jagged granite where the coterie spent most of its time.

The others slumbered in stork form while the soothsayer anticipated the debut of a remarkable comet. It would be the most spectacular meteor storm in centuries. In her mind's eye she saw the frozen celestial jewels appear as a ginormous ball of light with a glowing tail of gas and dust measuring one hundred million miles long.

The leader kept watch over her phalanx. *It is a pity that they will miss the spectacle, but sleep has to be their priority.* Zendala regarded them with deep love and quiet pride. Each stork stood balanced on a single slender red leg. The birds huddled in a small circle. They faced each other with feathers fluffed for extra warmth and bills nestled within their plumage. Iona snuggled between Maatkare and Mary to keep them from arguing.

What a peaceful sight, Zendala mused aloud. *Iona's apprenticeship nears completion. Everyone will meet her as a darling ten-year-old Gypsy girl in six years.* The ancient woman retrieved a patch of sandy-colored cat hair. It was wedged between the slivers of warped wood on one of the throne's arms. Her reflections turned to Reba. She could not discern the extreme actions taking place further to the north. She ruminated on recent events that had led to the throne's acquisition while she rubbed the soft fur between her thumb and forefinger.

***

Zendala had spotted something unusual below that drew her like a magnet while flying low over the Upper Douro Valley. She motioned with a wing for the others to follow and they spiraled down to a vineyard. Four storks transformed into women after landing on a terraced plateau. Iona followed them. The coterie walked into a garden tended by an old woman.

In spite of the day's warmth the matron draped herself from neck to ankle in fabric and wore gloves as well as a wide-brimmed bonnet. Zendala ignored her and went straight to the piece of furniture placed under the trellis. She sat down and closed her eyes. A look of wonder spread over her wrinkled face. The ancient woman beckoned to Maatkare. "This throne belonged to Ramses VI." The pharaoh raised her eyebrows.

The matriarch hobbled over using two wooden canes for support. "What are you doing in my garden?"

Zendala responded. "I wish to purchase your throne, Senhora..."

"I am Perl Bour da Bon."

Blandina whispered to Mary, "That name sounds familiar."

The queen of Scots nodded. "We met the Córdoba sisters at the Convent of Santa Maria in Montserrat back in A.D. 1756 right before Iona's rescue. Our leader foretold Cybele's marriage to the Frenchman Henri Bour Bon."

Blandina replied, "Their surnames are almost identical. She must be a distant relative."

Zendala stood as the pharaoh stepped forward. Maatkare

fished a gold coin from her pocket and offered it to the woman. The shrewd matron snatched it and gestured toward the storklet. "Give me the bird too," she insisted. "If folklore about storks proves to be true, that one might deliver a female baby to my grandson's wife Isadora someday."

Maatkare declined, "Our pet is not for sale."

"Women and their pets," smirked Perl. "Isadora has a Siamese cat who acts like she owns the place. My grandson's wife talks to it and I swear it talks back! That cat even wears the gold gorget earrings that used to belong to my son's fiancée."

This aroused Zendala's curiosity. "A talking Siamese cat?"

Perl snorted and shrugged as if to say 'I know it is crazy.'

Maatkare's interest grew as well. "What is the cat's name?"

"Before my son died, he called her Sky because of her blue eyes but Isadora calls her Reba." She pointed to the artifact. "The cat is very fond of that old eyesore."

Zendala sank down onto the throne again to inhale some calming breaths. *It seems that Reba lives in Portugal now.* Her voice quivered. "May I greet the cat, Senhora Bour da Bon?"

Perl waved her gloved hand in dismissal. "She is visiting the Minho Province. Isadora is acting as a tour guide to an Irish woman called Orchid MacCloud. The cat went with them."

I met them at the ruins of the Church of Carmo. The pharaoh concluded the deal by arranging for the throne's delivery to Estela Islet.

The Merciful Ones walked down the dirt road away from the Quinta. Iona flew overhead. The seer provided clarification about this family. "Cybele Córdoba and Henri Bour Bon had three sons—James, Joseph, and Philip. James stayed in France. Joseph moved to Scotland and adopted the surname Mac Bour Bon. Philip changed his name when he moved to Portugal. He became Felipe Bour da Bon. His son Julio married Perl who gave birth to identical twin sons Diego and Afonso."

The leader's explanation satisfied everyone's curiosity. Zendala intended to return to the Quinta alone in an endeavor to reconcile with Reba.

***

At the Iron Age settlement Augusto watched from behind a tree as a glowing Orchid MacCloud raised her face to the stars, threw out her arms, and twirled in a circle. Her green gown, cape, and flaming red hair twisted like a tornado. A misty ball of glittering white fire appeared in the sky. The Druidess addressed the fireball. "Majestic Arianrhod you are the keeper of the silver wheel of life and sister of the air and moon. Honorable mediator between deities and Druids, I offer humble gratitude for your powerful presence here this night."

Moments later the fearful Augusto witnessed the fireball's wild path of destruction as stars fell toward the earth. A silver spear chased after each astral body. He hollered, "She wants to destroy Portugal!" The lad presumed that the cosmic performance resulted from her satanic ritual. He picked up a rock and threw it with all his might. The jagged stone hit Orchid in the forehead above her right eyebrow causing her to fall. Augusto ran to the sorceress. He screamed, "Witch!" Out of nowhere a wild boar with daggers for tusks raced in his direction. It snorted a ferocious battle cry and forced him up a tree.

Orchid groaned. Bright red blood dripped from the gash. The injured Druidess tried to sit up. She surrendered to fate and fell back upon the ground. *O ye gods! I may not be able to perform the ceremony celebrating Reba's life, death, and rebirth.* From her peripheral vision she spotted Áine of Knockaine hovering in the treetops. The Druidess assumed that the Celtic faerie goddess was waiting for her invitation to attend the incarnation.

Áine cared nothing about the rebirth of the cat. She was here to keep an eye on Orchid MacCloud. *There is no point carrying out my vendetta against the Catholic Church on behalf of the Druidess if she dies.* The two-foot-tall Áine flew down to Orchid, landed by her head and examined her wound. "Look at what this brute did to you!"

Orchid moaned, "I am fine. I need your help to protect Isadora Bour da Bon."

Under the twin sycamore trees Reba snoozed on Isadora's belly dreaming about kissing Afonso. She awoke to the sight of the magnificent comet above. Ancient Egyptians revered these rare treasures as signs of good things to come. The cat heard the hysterical shouting followed by Orchid's moans. Reba feared that Augusto had injured the Druidess. *So much for the good omen. If Orchid cannot orchestrate the reincarnation, I must take charge of my own destiny.*

Isadora continued her herbal-induced sleep. Reba positioned her front paws together in reverence. She summoned the ancient Egyptian deity Amunet. "Powerful creator goddess of air and hidden forces, you attended my birth. Now I ask you to suck out my breath and expel it into the woman next to me. Please transmit my soul to the embryo in her womb."

The cobra-headed goddess appeared beside the sleeping woman. Amunet wore a white sheath dress and carried a papyrus staff. The goddess lifted the nervous cat up to her face. She stared at Reba with snake eyes the color of coal and hissed a reprimand to the cat. "The wicked scheme you concocted a half century ago to get rid of Afonso's fiancée backfired. Shame on you for asking Bastet to use her goddess magic to make your mischief."

At the mention of her name Bastet materialized in the woods along with Sekhmet. They kept their distance when Amunet's rinkhal hood flared. She spat, "You abused the mighty Eye of Horus. You are lucky that I did not report this to Re." Amunet held Reba in a death grip and flicked her forked tongue to tickle

Reba's nose. The cat sneezed. Amunet's hysteria exploded with such force that Bastet and Sekhmet darted behind a tree.

Panic seized Reba. She squirmed and cried out for mercy. "I changed my mind! I want to live! Take my beloved gorget earrings in exchange for my life."

Amunet tightened her grip and shook the cat. "Idiot! Do you see ears on my head?"

Reba messaged Maatkare for help. 'Fly at once to Citânia de Briteiros. Amunet is going to suck the life out of me!' In vain Reba tried to wiggle out of her steely grip.

***

Over on Estela Islet, Maatkare peeked her head out from her plumage. The spicy smell of myrrh wafted into her nostrils. This alerted her that Reba demanded attention. She backed away from the sleeping muster to sneak off. Iona awoke when she felt the sudden draft. She looked up at the comet and then noticed a vacancy next to her. The storklet watched Maatkare as she flew the short distance up to the olive tree. The miraculous fireball lured Iona's attention upward again. *No time to dally. I need to find out what my best friend is doing at Joan's grave.*

Maatkare landed next to the olive tree and transformed. The storklet spied on the pharaoh from behind the boulders. Iona watched her retrieve her jeweled beard that sparkled with blue brilliance in the dark. She stuck it on her chin and connected with Reba. Maatkare received the cat's high-pitched message seeking emergency assistance. The pharaoh grumbled, "I refuse to stroke my beard and respond to Reba. She cannot lure me into her selfish web any longer. There is no doubt that she exaggerates about Amunet."

Iona backed away from the boulder. "The pharaoh talks in secret to Zendala's sister using her magical beard. Does our leader know? I should tell her but Maatkare is my best friend. I cannot betray her." Iona gulped and looked up. The pharaoh stood over her shaking a finger and scowling. "Uh-oh," Iona uttered. Her heart thudded in her feathered chest.

"You are correct. This stays between us. Go back to sleep and keep your bill shut!"

"Whatever you say." Iona returned to the slumbering storks.

Maatkare walked down the hill to calm herself. She found Zendala asleep on Ramses' throne. It was an unusual occurrence for her chief. The pharaoh gazed up at the sky and admired the spectacular comet.

***

Back at the Iron Age settlement a frantic male voice in the distance called for Senhora Bour da Bon. Amunet's snake eyes darted around before returning to the squirming cat. "You summoned me, Reba. Now take responsibility for your actions." The deity's mouth opened wide to expose her sharp fangs. Bastet and Sekhmet ran out of the woods. They yelled in unison at her to stop. Amunet glared at the distraught goddesses. "Who invited you two?" She pointed her staff at the intruders and issued a stern warning. "Stay out of my business!" Amunet's mouth covered Reba's and sucked the breath of life from her. Nothing but a sack of dehydrated organs remained inside the lifeless furry body. She tossed it onto the cedar sprays next to Isadora.

The sisters approached again. They watched as Amunet opened the buttons of Isadora's pants with one flick of her papyrus staff to expose the woman's belly. The goddess exhaled a steamy white light that transformed into the shape of a sailboat. A human-headed *ba* bird—one of the elements of the soul that gave each creature its uniqueness—perched on the stern. Next to it waited the *ka* in the form of a diminutive and vaporous cat.

Bastet looked at Sekhmet with incredulity. "Is that Reba's ka?"

Sekhmet nodded. "Yes, it is the life force given to each being at birth by Heka. These two components of Reba's soul will unite to become her *akh*—her immortal self. If our deceased sister survives the treacherous underworld she will appear at the Hall of Judgment."

Bastet begged Amunet, "Reba will never make it to the afterlife without her ba and her ka. Our sister will be doomed." Tears swelled in Bastet's cat eyes. The goddesses watched as Amunet continued to respire. The foggy sailboat glided down her papyrus staff to its final destination. It stopped at Isadora's bellybutton. The vaporous ka was confused about Reba's change of mind. It scampered off the sailboat and slipped back into the cat's lifeless body through her open mouth. The ba bird was left alone.

Amunet produced a final puff. The sailboat with its solo passenger disappeared into Isadora's womb through her navel. The eyes of the goddess sisters widened at the sight. Sekhmet bent down and petted the deflated Siamese cat. She looked up at Amunet. "How will she dwell in the Field of Reeds of eternal paradise if her ka and ba cannot reunite?"

"Reba failed to consider what happens after death to a cat that gave away her soul. It is not my problem." Amunet vanished.

Bastet entreated, "We must inform Re and Ba of our sister's tragic death. We dare not mention why Reba chose her own demise."

Isadora awoke groaning from terrible cramps in her stomach. The goddesses disappeared at once. The disoriented woman struggled to sit up. The Druidess was nowhere in sight. She saw Reba's dead body next to her. Isadora screamed, "What have we done?" This sound distracted the boar. It returned to the oak grove to guard Orchid as she struggled to remain conscious.

Augusto climbed down from the tree to search for Senhora Bour da Bon. The lad was determined to rescue her from the evil witch disguised as a beautiful woman. He hustled over to help Isadora to her feet and pointed at the dead cat. "You can blame the wicked sorceress for everything. We must leave now!"

"What are you talking about?" Isadora bent her head back. She was distracted by the dazzling brightness in the sky. Dizziness overtook her and she sank down against the twin sycamores. Augusto grabbed her again. She slapped at him and tried to shove him away. The strong lad took Isadora by the arm and hauled her down the knoll against her will. She lost her balance, slid down the embankment, and bit a chunk of flesh from the inside of her cheek. Isadora spit out blood and asked him the whereabouts of Orchid MacCloud.

"I hope she is dead!" Augusto pushed her along the dirt road and hoisted her onto the carriage. He climbed up next to Isadora and made the sign of the cross. He whipped Crespo with the vigor of someone running from the devil. Isadora yelled for Orchid. Áine of Knockaine followed the orders given by the Druidess and pursued them.

Rampant wild imaginings displaced common sense as Augusto hallucinated that the dead Siamese cat—now the size of a Bengal tiger—chased them down the road. He sniffed the strong scents of wintergreen and sweet almonds before noticing the small creature flying overhead. Áine's tiny body was covered in turquoise leaves and red meadowsweet stalks. To him, she resembled a shark wrapped in kelp. The faerie goddess flew down toward Isadora and claimed that the Druidess had dispatched her. The paranoid Augusto decided that Senhora Bour da Bon had also participated in the night's satanic ritual. He scooted away from the woman slumped on the seat next to him. "You are a demon in female form!"

Augusto was preoccupied with his crazed thoughts. He failed

to steer his cart around a sharp curve. Crespo and the rickety volante veered off the road into the woods. The nag dodged a tree stump but the left wheel of the carriage smashed into it and tipped over. The two passengers fell out onto the ground. The wheel broke from its axle and rolled toward Isadora.

Áine of Knockaine landed in the treetops. She sighed with relief when Isadora tumbled out of the way. The pregnant woman pulled herself up with the help of a tree branch. Augusto ran after Crespo. The mare stopped after dragging the cart through the heavy brush. She lifted her injured front leg. Augusto shouted, "How can I get home now? This is your responsibility!"

"No, it is not! You should have spent the night in Guimarães as I requested."

Augusto unharnessed Crespo and confronted the devil worshiper. He recited part of a Catholic prayer. "Thrust into hell the evil spirits who prowl about the world seeking the ruin of souls." He led his limping mare back to the road. Over his shoulder he yelled, "You may follow me but keep your distance." He planned to take Senhora Bour da Bon to the nearest church and get rid of her. Áine followed them. She was careful to stay out of sight.

HOLD NO PREJUDICE

Orchid MacCloud had endured far worse injuries during her long lifetime. She sat up with caution and tore several strips of material from her gown. She folded one piece and placed it on the wound. It adhered to the clotting blood. She secured the makeshift bandage with a second strip of green cloth that she tied around her head. The magical boar continued to stand guard. "I offer my gratitude for your protection tonight. Please stay until I find out what happened."

Minutes earlier she had heard Isadora shouting her name and felt the vibration of horse hooves pounding the dirt road. Orchid struggled to her feet. She was anxious to discern the outcome of the night's disastrous events. She stumbled away from the grove of elder trees and discovered Reba's body beneath the twin sycamores. The boar followed her.

The Druidess sank down onto the cedar sprays and caressed her old friend. The Siamese cat's sandy-colored coat appeared dull and her sky-blue eyes stared into space. Her diamond-shaped pupils were dilated in death. Orchid closed them with gentle fingers as tears rolled down her cheeks. *It appears that our honorable intentions went amiss. Where does your soul dwell now, dear Reba?*

Orchid plucked a bit of fur as a keepsake and removed the gold gorget earrings from Reba's ears. She fastened them onto her own lobes. *I shall give them to Isadora's daughter Rebecca someday.* She lowered the cat's body into the blackened urn and tightened the lid. The Druidess knew that the portal to the otherworld had opened the moment Reba's brain shut down. She put the iron pig icon into her pocket and the wild boar disappeared. Orchid went to the oak grove to secure the urn in Reba's final resting place.

The purplish-blue dawn lightened the sky and church bells announced morning prayers. Augusto approached the outskirts of Guimarães. He followed the loud ringing to the Church of Saint Francis and propped Isadora against its outer wall. The adrenaline-fueled lad beat his fists on the wooden door until a parish priest cracked it open to glare at the disturber of his peace. A gust of wind blew the entry open. Áine of Knockaine shrank to the size of a hummingbird and flew inside to wait for Isadora in the shadow of the chancel.

The agitated Augusto pointed a shaky finger at the injured woman. "She is a demon in female form!" He took Isadora by the shoulders and shoved her into the arms of the priest. "Only God can save Senhora Bour da Bon's soul. The redheaded witch that I left behind at Citânia de Briteiros burns in hell!"

The confused priest shook his head. "No women work at the Iron Age settlement."

"I assure you that we meant no harm," blubbered Isadora. "We were curious tourists and not agents of the devil." They watched Augusto lead his lame horse down the cobblestone street and disappear around a corner.

The young priest introduced himself to Isadora. "I am Father Rodrigo." He wore a plain long-sleeved black cassock with a white clerical collar. He escorted the distressed woman through the portal and turned on a light in the narthex. The priest scanned her from head to toe and made a mental inventory for the report to his superior.

Father Rodrigo's eyebrows furrowed when he realized that Senhora Bour da Bon wore men's black trousers. He noted the mud clinging to her backside. Blood stained a cuff of her white shirt and red clots caked one corner of her mouth. The priest noticed a gold necklace dangling from one of her pockets. His eyes widened with surprise. *Perhaps she is a thief who hid out at Citânia de Briteiros.*

The priest took a cautious step backward. He spotted a gold cartouche attached to a leather band fastened on her wrist. A silver cross, a gold Star of David, and a pagan pendant hung around her neck. These unconventional mixes of religious symbolism gave credence to the lad's wild accusations. *Did she participate in a heathen ritual and dance with the devil under last night's comet?* He blurted, "The lad was right! You are a witch!"

Isadora winced from the pain inside her mouth. "I am a Jewish Gypsy. I have been called many names but never a witch! I demand to speak to the head of the parish!"

Father Rodrigo backed away unprepared for the woman's sudden aggression. "Wait here and please do not touch anything. The holy relics are priceless."

The injured woman stood alone in the expansive nave. She looked around at the Catholic trappings. The high golden altarpiece was illuminated by a series of arched windows. Isadora recognized Portugal's signature blue and white *azulejos* hand-painted tiles. The series depicted three scenes involving Saint Anthony of Padua. Isadora took a closer look. One set of enamel panels showed the saint at the seaside preaching to hundreds of fish that lifted their scaled heads above the water to hear his sermon. Another set pictured Saint Anthony holding a lily stalk in one hand and the Bible in the other. Inside the open pages of the holy book lay Baby Jesus. The last set portrayed the saint distributing bread to the poor.

She picked up a pamphlet lying on a wooden table and walked under a window. Isadora read about the saint who had filled those listening to him with a profound love of the Bible through his passionate preaching. The religious propaganda claimed that he even converted heretics and witches. She tiptoed closer to the imposing altarpiece with its gilded carvings. *Shame on them for such spiritual opulence.*

Isadora experienced a bout of nausea followed by a piercing pain. She sat on a wooden pew and cradled her belly. "I wonder if the incarnation took place? Does Reba's soul now inhabit my baby girl?"The pregnant woman bent over as another sharp cramp stabbed her. The pain subsided and she continued speculating. "What if I give birth to a cat?"

This annoyed Áine of Knockaine who hovered nearby. "That is quite enough!"

Isadora sensed a supernatural presence and straightened up. She saw a blurred movement in her peripheral vision and focused on the life-size bronze statue in front of her. She recognized Saint Anthony and he was not alone. A two-foot-tall woman with a mischievous smile and faerie wings cozied up to the sculpture.

Áine spoke with a tinkling Gaelic accent. "Your friend asked me to protect you."

"Where is she?"

"Do not worry about her. Believe in the magic and trust your choices, Isadora." Áine sprinkled glittering faerie dust over the head of the statue casting an enduring spell upon the pious saint. She sneered. "That is for the trouble caused by the Holy See during the Middle Ages. The Catholics persecuted the Druidess Orchid MacCloud."The faerie goddess disappeared.

Isadora called out, "Who are you?"

"He is our patron saint."The confident and booming voice of Monsignor Arzila echoed throughout the nave.

The pompous official in his early fifties entered the central part of the church. He was decked out in a floor-length gray cassock that stretched tight across his protruding belly. It was fastened from neck to ankles with gold buttons. His knee-length and loose-fitting violet mantel covered part of the cassock. An ostentatious jeweled cross bounced as he strode toward Isadora. A violet biretta topped with a little pompom perched on his fuzzy gray hair.

Prior to his entrance the church official had powdered his red-veined nose and puffy cheeks while chewing on a peppermint leaf to remove the odor of last night's port. He had crept into the confessional to spy on Isadora rather than attending to his morning prayers. "I extend an apology on behalf of Father Rodrigo. The lad that brought you to our door claimed that you are evil. What imaginations the young people display in these modern days." He waved a dismissive hand. "I am Monsignor Jorge Stefano da Costa Arzila."

"And I am who I am," countered the exhausted Isadora.

"Touché," laughed the clergyman. "Satan mocked God by saying, 'I am who I am not.' The devil is the greatest trickster on earth. Father Rodrigo reports that you demonstrate eccentric tastes in religious jewelry."

Isadora fondled the pieces around her neck and on her wrist. "I cherish these gifts from my family and friends. I hold no prejudice. I prefer to keep an open mind."

"Our Lord warned that every one of us must remain on guard to defeat the devil."

"I possess neither the energy nor the desire to debate whether evil exists as an inclination of the human heart or as an ever-present dark and wicked force. I must be reunited with my husband Luís as soon as possible. What means of transportation are available from Guimarães to Vale de Mendiz in the Upper Douro Valley? It is the closest town to Quinta Bour da Bon."

The monsignor bowed. "Allow me to offer the services of our carriage."

Isadora realized that she had left her money inside her knapsack back at the Iron Age settlement. She agreed with reluctance. Monsignor Arzila escorted her to his private office in the rectory. In spite of the early hour, he offered her a glass of port to settle her nerves. Isadora declined. The clergyman poured a glass for himself and sat down behind his desk. His bloodshot eyes focused on the pretty Senhora while he relished the golden-brown liquid. "Your husband's grandfather Julio provided generous financial support to the Diocese of Oporto before he married the Spanish Jewess Perl Alvares."

Isadora raised her eyebrows and took a deep breath. "For your information I am also a Jewess—and a Gypsy as well. Your point, sir?"

"The bishop convinced those in power to allow Julio to retain ownership of his business after he converted to Judaism for his wife. Bour da Bon Tawny Vintage Port has made your husband's family a very good living."

Isadora realized that the monsignor wanted compensation for his efforts. "I am certain that my husband will offer a generous measure of appreciation for your assistance to me."

Monsignor Arzila raised both hands in protest. "That is not necessary, Senhora." He paused for dramatic effect as a smug smile appeared on his face. "However, I accept with humble gratitude but only because you insist. I shall have Father Rodrigo send a telegram from Guimarães to Vale de Mendiz informing your husband that we are on our way."

SOLAR BARGE

Over on Estela Islet Maatkare rubbed away the kink in her neck from watching the comet. The pharaoh focused on her chief who was slumped in the throne. Her right leg had slipped out of the lotus position and her black boot dangled above the ground. Beneath the pliable leather the ring of eternity remained fastened around her ankle. Maatkare eyed the magical cartouche around the ancient woman's neck. The jasper stone hung below it on a leather band. *I shall try again to snatch one of her powerful pieces.*

Zendala snored and her eyelids twitched. She did not often venture into this stage of sleep and the dream she experienced aroused confusion. A woman with glowing skin and gold-streaked red hair stood in front of a massive oak tree with an urn in her hands. A bloodstained cloth bound her head and she wore gold gorget earrings that seemed familiar. She looked like a priestess at an altar presenting a sacred gift to the gods.

The ethereal woman chanted, "Esteemed guardian of our ancient Druid knowledge please accept my departed friend into your realm." The oak's sturdy trunk split open to allow space for the urn inside its central column. She stepped forward to lodge her treasure inside the niche. "Unite my friend with her beloved anam cara—her soul mate for eternity." The mighty oak sealed its fracture.

The woman turned and left the shadowy forest. In her dream Zendala recognized the silhouettes of Bastet and Sekhmet standing in the background. Their respective lime-green and amber cat eyes shone in the darkness. Zendala awoke when she felt a slight touch on her neck. She scolded Maatkare in a whisper. "What trouble do you make now, Pharaoh?"

A smooth lie slipped from Maatkare's mouth. "You looked distressed so I woke you." She withdrew her hand and stuck it in her pocket.

Zendala frowned. "I just experienced the most peculiar dream. My goddess sisters lurked in the woods watching a beautiful green-gowned priestess with hair the color of fire deposit an urn inside an oak tree."

Orchid MacCloud, thought Maatkare. The burden of guilt for ignoring Reba lay heavy on the pharaoh's heart and she sank to the ground. *This gives credence to Reba's call for help. The chief's dream must portray the Druidess entombing her body in a tree after Amunet killed her.*

Zendala asked with concern, "What is it?"

"I am tired from watching the comet all night. Do you have any thoughts about the meaning of your strange dream?"

"Perhaps this mysterious woman will join the Merciful Ones in the future."

"I presume that you already know about such things since you are a soothsayer, Chief. How many members do you envision?" *If Orchid MacCloud joins the coterie I shall find out what happened to Reba.*

"For ancient Egyptians seven is the ideal number. It symbolizes illumination, completion, knowledge, and spirituality."

The pharaoh returned her gaze to the sky. "We worship seven celestial bodies—the Sun, the Moon, Mercury, Venus, Mars, Jupiter, and Saturn." At that moment something unusual happened in the sky seen only by the two women. The icy center of the comet separated from its tail of gas and dust. Its nucleus grew bright red. The core moved up and over the comet's tail then settled beneath it. Maatkare gulped. "Did you see that?"

"I did." Zendala watched as the comet's tail grew in size and sculpted itself into the slender shape of a flat-bottomed vessel called the *Mesektet*—Re's nocturnal solar barge. They recognized its decorative prow that stretched higher than the stern. On both sides it was inlaid with the Eye of Horus. Huge snapping jackals with jute harnesses pulled the boat. Seth stood in the center of the hull personified as a muscular man with an aardvark's head, square-tipped ears, a forked tail, and hooves. He jabbed his spear at the elongated evil serpent Apep slithering back and forth beneath the vessel's flat bottom.

Heka armed himself with a bow and arrow behind Seth. His feet were spaced wide for balance. The god of magic's head darted right and left as he searched for Re's tricky enemy. The snake god Mehen wrapped his reptilian form around the sun god's body as a protective shield. Re stood ready to carve up the evil serpent Apep with his axe.

The vessel traveled in living color across the dark sky. Zendala moved off her throne. "Why does my father's solar barge appear to us tonight?"

Maatkare suspected that it was connected to Reba's distressed telepathic message calling for help. *I cannot tell her about that so I shall offer an alternative theory.* "Perhaps our deities grow envious of the attention paid to the comet. They wish to remind us of Re's power."

The women watched as the comet pushed the solar barge higher into the heavens. The black sky became muted with hues of the approaching dawn. Zendala headed toward the sleeping storks. "I shall wake the others so we can start our day with a morning catch."

Maatkare kept her eyes focused on the disappearing barge. She saw a vaporous Siamese cat peeking out from beneath a fold of Heka's magical cape. She jumped to her feet. *Reba rides through the underworld! This confirms her death. Zendala does not know that I have seen Reba riding on the solar barge. Her death may yet develop into my good fortune.* The scheming pharaoh sniffed away her tears as the sun rose in the east. She leapt off the steep cliff and transformed into her stork self to join the muster for breakfast.

***

Orchid waited at the Iron Age settlement on the hillside overlooking the expansive valley and meandering river. The sun rose between the twin sycamores where Reba and Isadora had spent the previous ill-fated evening. The Druidess expected a visitor. She stretched out her right arm that was covered by the long sleeves of her embroidered green gown. The magnificent barn owl swooped down from the sky to land with care on her extended arm.

"I bid you good morning, Blodeuwedd. Do you come to warn me of a brewing betrayal? Or perhaps your presence indicates a desire to assist in the nurturing of Rebecca."

The Celtic goddess possessed celestial awareness and hooted in Orchid's ear. "I come to tell you that danger lurks if you return to Quinta Bour da Bon. Isadora will betray you without intending to do so. I promise to provide aid during her child's birth in your absence."

"Thank you for your warning, Blodeuwedd. For my own peace of mind, I must attend Isadora at her daughter's birthing in case something went wrong with the incarnation."

"As you wish." The owl flew away.

Orchid returned to Reba's resting place within the mighty oak. She discovered scratch marks on the bark where the tree had taken custody of the blackened urn. "Who vandalized this sacred tree?" She examined it closer. The slashes occur too high for a lynx. The perplexed Druidess removed the iron pig icon from her pocket and asked the wild boar to stand guard once again. "Do not leave until I return." Orchid walked away and headed southeast toward the Quinta. She heard rustling sounds behind her followed by a hair-raising snarl. She quickened her step and did not look back.

Sekhmet restrained Bastet as she prepared to pounce on Orchid MacCloud. The cat-headed goddess argued, "Our sister's body is in that tree. Her remains belong to us."

"Do not blame the Druidess. Reba insisted on the incarnation."

Bastet countered, "We must perform ancient Egyptian funeral rites and make offerings to insure the reunification of Reba's ba with her ka."

Sekhmet stroked Bastet to calm her. "It is too late for that. Reba gave up her soul. Her ba now resides in the womb of Isadora Bour da Bon. Her ka has traveled alone to the underworld. There is nothing more we can do."

The cat goddess pulled away from her sister. "When Orchid MacCloud comes back I shall fight her to reclaim Reba's body for our family." The goddesses vanished.

***

The five wading birds fished in the tide pools for salty limpets and delicious blue mussels. After filling their stomachs, they flew up to the pinnacle. Iona landed next to Joan's grave and the others settled as women. The pharaoh leaned against the olive tree while Zendala and Mary lowered themselves onto flat boulders.

The youthful Blandina plopped down on the ground. She inquired, "Did we miss much last night?" Both of the ancient women regarded each other in silence.

"I saw the comet," blurted Iona. "It looked like a dirty snowball with a long skinny tail but the star shower reminded me of Seth's magical drops."

Mary sighed. "What a pity that we missed it."

Zendala offered, "It will not be as spectacular but the comet will pass through our skies again in thirteen years."

Maatkare asked, "What might we expect between now and then?"

Iona squealed before Zendala could respond. "The most important thing of all is that I shall become a Merciful One."

Blandina added, "We can visit Claude Monet at his home in Giverny."

Zendala brought the conversation back to the present. "Today I am flying to Quinta Bour da Bon. I want to be there when Reba returns from Minho. I hope that we can reconcile."

Maatkare's eyes widened but she held her tongue.

Iona shivered. "Please do not allow Reba to visit us here on Estela Islet. She scares me."

"Me too," mumbled Blandina. She recalled the frightening message Reba had conveyed with her mesmerizing sky-blue eyes. *Her diamond-shaped pupils pierced my soul.*

Mary stood and helped Zendala to her feet. The ancient woman walked away. She turned and smiled back at her coterie. "Wish me luck."

HER UNNERVING VISION

Perl Bour da Bon stood in the cluttered office at the Quinta holding a telegram that the postman had delivered. In spite of her cataracts, she managed to read the message announcing the arrival of Monsignor Jorge Stefano da Costa Arzila. *Why is he accompanying Isadora home? It sounds like my grandson's Gypsy wife has gotten into trouble.* The stiff old woman hobbled through a side door leading out to the courtyard.

She used two canes to support her weight and approached Luís. He was inspecting the invasive roots of the weeping willow tree. They caused such damage to the ceramic water pipes that at least once a year he threatened to chop down Afonso's favorite tree. Perl issued a stern warning as she brandished a cane at her grandson. "Your father planted this willow as a boy. Over my dead body will you cut it down!"

"You gave birth to twin sons. Why do you never speak of Diego?"

Perl waved away the sad memory as tears swelled in her milky eyes. "I forgot about that philanderer long ago."

Luís frowned and patted his grandmother's arm with affection. "I know that you still hold him in your heart. But what is the paper in your hands? Did Isadora send a message?"

A graceful glowing white stork flew into the courtyard. Zendala had spent the last few days scoping out the property in search of Reba. She counted on Perl to read the telegram aloud and the matron did not disappoint.

Luís was irritated that the Catholic clergyman found it necessary to escort his wife home. He expressed his frustration by attempting to shoo the big bird away. The stubborn stork stood its ground. Memories of interference in their family business by the Catholic Church several generations back still infuriated the vintner. "Keep Arzila away from me!"

Perl shuffled toward the wild bird. She squinted into its golden eyes and at the jewelry hanging from its neck. "Wait a minute! I saw identical trinkets on the old woman with similar eyes who purchased my Egyptian throne." Luís smirked at his eccentric grandmother and gave up hacking at the tree roots. The stork flew off and left Perl to ponder the coincidence.

The next day Zendala stepped out from beneath a shade tree as the carriage belonging to the Archdiocese of Braga approached the bend. The ancient woman let out a hearty laugh. "I suspect that Reba is warming Monsignor Arzila's lap."

She watched the neo-classical coach that was pulled by a stunning pair of Lusitano bay mares as it advanced. Its frame and windows were carved and gilded with intricate detail. Father Rodrigo sat on the elevated bench alongside the driver. Isadora and the monsignor sat inside the coach on velvet seats. The pregnant woman leaned out an open window seeking air.

The huge red wheels rolled to a stop in front of the pedestrian. A faint smile appeared on Isadora's flushed face. "Good day! Rest your weary feet and climb aboard!" She glared at the monsignor. He agreed that God's carriage provided room for another passenger. Father Rodrigo jumped down and bowed to the stranger with the golden eyes. He opened the side door and stepped back to help her onto the footplate of the carriage. Isadora leaned out the open door and offered her hand. "My name is Isadora Bour da Bon."

"I am called Zendala." She grasped Isadora's wrist for assistance and came into direct contact with the Noah's Ark cartouche. A series of images depicting her sister's entire life blazed through Zendala's mind. The seer had breached the cosmic barrier shielding her from Reba. The final picture froze and stamped an everlasting impression on her mind. The Siamese cat's shriveled body lay upon a bed of evergreen boughs. Her sky-blue eyes with their diamond-shaped pupils stared into space. Zendala let go of Isadora's arm and fell backwards off the carriage step. All of the breath left her lungs as if someone had punched her solar plexus. She regained her balance and held her stomach. "Reba is dead!"

Zendala escaped into the rows of grapevines planted along the dirt road. She ran as fast as her legs allowed. The heartbroken ancient woman transformed into a glowing white stork and flew away. In an ironic twist of fate, the Catholic delegation missed the extraordinary spectacle. Father Rodrigo had been fussing with Monsignor Arzila's biretta.

Isadora witnessed the remarkable transformation of the legendary White Stork of Mercy. The energy now flowing from the cartouche overwhelmed her and she fell into a troubled sleep inside the coach. Monsignor Arzila scooted closer to Isadora and attempted to understand her incoherent mumblings about the previous night at Citânia de Briteiros. The clever clergyman gleaned enough information to use in his favor. He sat back with a smug smile. The monsignor speculated about the positive results for his career if he delivered the Bour da Bon family back to Catholic Church. He imagined becoming the future Archbishop of Braga.

The sorrowful stork returned to Estela Islet. Zendala succumbed to anguish over Reba's death, but did not cry. Day after day the ancient woman slumped in the battered throne. She refused to eat or drink water. Blandina provided solace by reciting tender poems about love and loss. Mary tried to distract her leader with stories about her Maltese terrier. The pharaoh mourned alone and in silence. Regrets intensified her feelings of grief.

Iona busied herself with activity. She pecked a hole in the sandy loam adjacent to Joan's grave and placed a dead fish in the cavity. The storklet suggested that the others find offerings a cat might like. Blandina located a smooth blue aragonite stone that had washed onto the beach and tossed it in. The rock was polished by constant tumbling in the water and reminded her of Reba's frightening eyes. She felt guilty to be relieved about the cat's death.

Mary offered a ball of string that she had repurposed from a discarded fishing net. Iona used her wing to cover the cache with sand. Maatkare built a headstone in the shape of a pyramid using rocks that she found nearby. Mary arranged seashells around its base in the shape of a heart. The coterie invited their leader to visit Iona's humble monument to Reba.

Zendala appreciated their efforts but the pyramid brought back painful memories of Reba's hatred. "I should have enjoyed a loving sister rather than an enemy." The ancient woman sank down by the mock grave and wept for the first time. Re and Ba materialized next to their daughter. Her companions backed away and stood by the olive tree to give them privacy. Iona took a place between Blandina and Mary. They consoled the storklet knowing that it was difficult for her to see their stoic leader in such a vulnerable state.

Ba nuzzled her suffering child. "We felt the intensity of your pain and came at once."

The falcon-headed sun god lifted Zendala to her feet and wrapped his arms around her. "Hush now, the Siamese cat is no longer your foe. She now rides with me on the solar barge each night. I allowed Reba on board when she admitted that she loves you and regrets her behavior." That was not true but as a father he felt obliged to comfort his daughter.

Zendala's body sagged in relief. He pulled back and wiped the tears from her golden eyes that mirrored his own. She became confused. "Why did I not see her up there with you on the night of the comet?"

Re clarified, "You were meant to see Reba in the solar barge. You must have turned your gaze away from the sky too soon. Your sister was there snuggled under Heka's cloak. Maatkare recognized her. I am surprised that she did not tell you."

"She let me learn the hard way." Zendala cast a reproachful look at the pharaoh.

The sun god proclaimed, "It is time for you to lead the Merciful Ones again."

Iona hopped up and down. "The White Storks of Mercy need you." Zendala sniffled and smiled. She and her mother moved toward the storklet. Ba and Iona clattered their bills and threw their heads back in greeting. Maatkare ignored the Sacred Stork of the Bach. Blandina cast a shy smile at the intimidating sun god and welcomed Ba.

Mary approached Re. She demonstrated her respect with a curtsy. He took her hand and his predator's beak brushed its soft surface. The Scottish queen admitted, "I have interacted with ancient Egyptian deities many times over the centuries. However, I am still astonished by them." She thought of Heka, blushed, and inquired about the handsome god of magic.

Re threw his falcon head back and shrieked with laughter. "We spend far too much time together and grow tired of each other's company." He glanced at the fading light. "Soon I must return to prepare for our nighttime journey." Mary spotted Maatkare heading toward them so she rejoined the others by the olive tree.

The pharaoh strutted over to Re and bowed with formality. His focused attention down at her was unnerving. She broke the silence by complimenting the clever god's imagery with his solar barge on the night of the comet. "I saw your new traveling companion beneath Heka's cloak. Does this mean that Reba did not make it to the afterlife? Please tell me that she dwells in the Field of Reeds of eternal paradise."

Re's distrust of Maatkare intensified. He refused to reveal any details about the Siamese cat's dismal fate in the underworld. "Reba's situation is complicated. I shall tell you no more." He walked away. She was dissatisfied with his answer and followed him. The sun god ignored her and addressed his daughter. "Your mother and I feel deep pride that you discovered your destiny and recruited this unique group of peacemakers."

"Thank you, Father. Over the next few decades, we shall to grow to seven members and accomplish a great deal of good in the future."

Ba encouraged, "We hope that humankind learns to reject violence, embrace nature, and respect the diversity of all cultures."

Iona appealed, "If we fail can we stay with you forever on the Isle of Souls? I can look for Joan's bubble!"

"We welcome all of you at any time. That includes you, Maatkare." The pharaoh's demeanor toward Reba's mother did not soften. Re urged his mate to say her goodbyes. The Sacred Stork of the Bach and her sun god wished them well and vanished.

That night while her companions slept Zendala sat on her throne. She removed the cat figurine from her pocket and spoke to the pharaoh's gift. "It is easier to move on now that I know you love me, Sister." She closed her eyes and placed the tiny sculpture against her heart. A revelation appeared on the screen of her mind.

The ancient woman saw herself standing in the corner of a dark bedroom lit by a candle. She gazed at a newborn baby lying next to the mother who was covered by a thin sheet. The infant was swaddled in a blanket. Through an open balcony door

Zendala saw slender willow boughs swaying in the breeze. A single white Ghost Orchid was attached to one of the whip-like branches. The glowing blossom seemed to entice the waiting stranger to reveal herself.

Zendala stepped forward. She heard the whooshing sound of wings. A huge barn owl flew into the room and landed on the bed next to the baby. The ancient woman moved toward the child. She waved her arms to keep the nocturnal predator from carrying off the newborn with its strong talons. The surprised owl Blodeuwedd rotated her head and flew out the balcony door. Zendala approached the bed out of concern that the mother showed no signs of life. She bent down and touched the baby's perfect face. The infant's eyes opened and stared up at her in silence. Pupils shaped like black diamonds were centered in its sky-blue irises. Zendala inhaled with shock and a cry stuck in her throat.

The seer came back to her senses. She exhaled with a deep shudder and dropped the stone figurine. The ancient woman elbowed her way off the throne, which triggered the Eye of Horus on the relic's back support. The wooden seat flipped open and exposed its hidden compartment. The distraught elder paced back and forth. She was afraid to bend down and retrieve the figurine that seemed to be the source of her unnerving vision. "I shall not keep it in my pocket until I understand what is happening!" Zendala picked up the tiny sculpture and tossed it into the unusual hiding place. She snapped the seat shut and sat upon the throne once again to resume watching over her phalanx.

The image of a tiny baby with the eyes of a cat disturbed her soul and she yearned to find tranquility. The Great and Honorable Zendala whispered the mantra that had been an inspiration during her years in Tibet. "Peace… joy… love…"

ACKNOWLEDGEMENTS

How wonderful it would be if the White Storks of Mercy really existed—or perhaps they do! I have imagined many times that the Great and Honorable Zendala talked with me about her universal mission for peace. A Merciful One exists in all of us. Let us rediscover our respect and compassion for each other and for nature.

I am eternally indebted to my husband Thomas van Berkel whose patience endured over the past ten years while I wrote my trilogy. He often delivered espresso in the morning and chardonnay in the evening to keep me going. I am grateful to him for taking me to Egypt years ago where I experienced firsthand the incredible ancient culture that spawned my idea about how to begin the *White Storks of Mercy Trilogy*. Together we have visited all of the European locations referenced in the three books.

Words seem inadequate when thanking my incredible editor and sister Red Cedar. She remained my partner in this endeavor from the very first draft to publication. What a gift 'Bo' possesses. She fed my imagination with encouragement and offered her words of wisdom. My editor never gave up on her author. I am so grateful for our collaboration.

I hold deep love and gratitude for my departed mother Ada Mae and my grandmother Myrtle Anna who both live in my soul. I bow with adoration to my sister Judy for nurturing my writing muse, her daughter Ashana Chenoa. I cherish Judy's son

Brendon who is the ultimate lover of nature. To my wonderful niece Tocha Tiponi and her husband Paul—I wrote the *White Storks of Mercy Trilogy* for your girls Mia Izabel and Olive Mae when they are old enough to read it.

I express special thanks to my first readers and dear friends Carole Pearl and Catherine Colby. Their input was invaluable. My goddess of the desert Sioux Jones provided her unique guidance along the way with incredible Tarot card readings. Much appreciation goes to my proof editor Meghan Stoll. I am also extremely grateful to my publishing guru Larry Furlong at Alpha Graphics.

ABOUT THE AUTHOR

JONI ANDERSON VAN BERKEL is a Colorado-born writer and artist who divides her time between Scottsdale, Arizona and Zurich, Switzerland. She is happily married to her Dutchman from Amsterdam.

She was educated at the University of Colorado and holds both Bachelor of Science and Master of Architecture degrees.

Joni studied script writing in Europe and wrote her first screenplay, Bad Julia, with the late David Sherwin.

She has spent more than ten years writing her trilogy, White Storks of Mercy. The first book, Formation, is available on Amazon.

For more information, please contact her at
joni@whitestorksofmercy.com
or visit her website at
www.whitestorksofmercy.com

The second book of her trilogy, Reunion, will be out soon.

Photo by: Jeffrey Welcker